Celia Brayfield grew up in the London suburbs and was educated at St Paul's Girls' School and at university in France. She graduated from '*The Times*' typing pool to become first the *Evening Standard*'s TV critic and later a journalist who still writes for *The Times* and other media. Her first novel, *Pearls*, was an international bestseller; she followed with two more, *The Prince* and *White Ice*, before concentrating on modern social comedies: *Harvest, Getting Home, Sunset, Heartswap* and *Mister Fabulous and Friends*. Among her non-fiction titles is *Bestseller*, about writing popular fiction. A single parent with one daughter, she now lives mostly in West London.

Praise for Celia Brayfield

MISTER FABULOUS AND FRIENDS

'You can't help but care about the fate of this motley crew and their assorted families. Brayfield is a merciless and astute observer of middle-class mores' *Mail*

'Love, life and masculinity are all under threat in this funny, sad and moving take on the mid-life crisis' *Express*

'An easy and intelligent read . . . a sharp satire' *Irish Examiner*

'A witty, sharp novel that dissects the relationships of four male friends, all in the grip of their very different mid-life crises' *Woman and Home*

'A very amusing book . . . very moving, and the social observations ring true. A very enjoyable read, especially recommended to those who, like the main characters in the book, still have fond memories of the Bonzo Dog Doo Dah Band' *New Books Magazine*

'An unladdish insight into the weird world of mid-life crisis man . . . Funny, sad and moving' *Woman's Own*

'A delicious romp through middle-aged mores. Infidelities, redundancy and a sexual identity crisis are all on the horizon in this sharply comic novel' *Sainsbury's Magazine*

GETTING HOME

'Brayfield, with lightning flashes of wit and scalpel-sharp observations, pokes fun at a host of targets – rich mothers, community action groups, class prejudice, property tycoons, live TV audiences, precocious children and nouvelle cuisine. Gloriously vicious and compulsively readable' *Daily Mail*

'Her eye for the irritating minutiae of contemporary life is enjoyably sharp' *The Times*

'I couldn't be wrested away from it, though they tried' Fay Weldon

'Wonderfully funny' *Woman & Home*

'A juicy exercise in literary curtain-twitching. You wonder whether Brayfield achieved the madcap climax by dipping her pen in Viagra' *Evening Standard*

'A sparkling satire about the suburban dream' *Evening Herald*

'With sharp wit and snappy dialogue, Brayfield has produced a very funny, cleverly plotted novel that displays Fay Weldon's understanding of the pleasure to be derived from seeing the bad get their just deserts' *Daily Telegraph*

'A writer of enormous intelligence with the widest possible common touch' *Mail on Sunday*

'At once a biting social satire and a passionate denouncement of mindless environmental vandalism' *Good Housekeeping*

'A witty, dark tale of suburban lives going wrong . . . superbly readable' *Sunday Times*

'Brayfield's writing glitters: the humour is as sharp as a Sabatier knife, the satire immaculately honed, her observations precise down to the last shell-pink toenail. And under the wicked wit, some hard home truths' *Image*

HEARTSWAP

'Delicious – a laugh-out-loud book' *Evening Herald*

SUNSET

'Celia Brayfield's style is as exuberant as it is poetic' *Daily Express*

'Brayfield is a fine prose stylist' *Sunday Times*

HARVEST

'Heaven knows, a good read, but far from trivial. A brilliantly-textured "proper" novel about the women who surround and love, ever so painfully, a manipulative media man . . . a literary romance featuring the sophisticated English abroad in France' Fay Weldon, *Mail on Sunday*

'Cunningly plotted, extremely well-written and compulsively readable' Beryl Bainbridge

'The authentic tang of human emotion at every level' Claire Rayner

'A cleverly-plotted, witty black comedy, modern storytelling at its most enjoyable. The throwaway observations made me laugh out loud' *The Literary Review*

'Grand guignol in a gite – shockingly readable' *New Statesman*

PEARLS

'Absorbing, entertaining, its grammar impeccable, its theme the sufferings and eventual triumphs of a pair of beautiful sisters . . . Her Malaya is exactly rendered, her women sound and act like real women. Readers will devour it, as I did' Anthony Burgess, *Independent*

'A triumph – Celia Brayfield's first novel is a complex and delicious amalgamation of glamour and sensitivity, sensuality and betrayal, sweeping from war-torn Malaysia through the England of the Beatles. A rich, multi-faceted story, her plot is a masterpiece of construction, her prose literate, insightful and frequently witty' *Rave Reviews*

'A great adventure of our times' *Le Meridional*

Also by Celia Brayfield

FICTION

Mister Fabulous and Friends
Heartswap
Sunset
Getting Home
Harvest
White Ice
The Prince
Pearls

NON-FICTION

Deep France
Bestseller: Secrets of Successful Writing
Glitter: The Truth About Fame

Wild Weekend

CELIA BRAYFIELD

timewarner
books

A *Time Warner* Book

First published in Great Britain in 2004
by Time Warner Books

Copyright © Celia Brayfield 2004

The moral right of the author has been asserted.

A CIP catalogue record for this book
is available from the British Library.

HARDBACK   ISBN 0 316 72502 1
PAPERBACK   ISBN 0 7515 3528 1

Typeset in Garamond by M Rules
Printed and bound in Great Britain by
Clays Ltd, St Ives plc

Time Warner Book Group UK
Brettenham House
Lancaster Place
London WC2E 7EN

www.twbg.co.uk
www.celiabrayfield.com

For Fenella, in memory of many wild weekends.

Wild Weekend

*A story set in a village in England,
in the very near future*

CHAPTER 1

A Maiden Bid

The auctioneer said: 'Lot seventeen.'

Motes of dust drifted in the light from the mock-gothic windows. A few people were sitting on some of the hard chairs facing the auctioneer's podium, but none of them moved. A few more, maybe ten of them, stood around the margins of the floor as if they didn't want to get involved. None of them stirred. Towards the back, in the shadows under the room's empty gallery, there was a cough.

Oliver Hardcastle, a man used to outbreaks of mass frenzy on an hourly basis, was impressed. 'See,' he said to himself, 'you're in the country. People know what's what. They're down-to-earth. Grounded. Rooted. In balance with nature. People here don't wear themselves to frazzles running around chasing massive profits that are only virtual illusions existing in electronic space anyway. These people are real.'

'Lot seventeen is Saxwold New Farm. Farm buildings comprising a two-bedroom cottage of traditional brick and flint, with a recent pantile roof, set around a concrete yard with a barn of the same construction, plus a concrete-block general-purpose building.'

Farm. *Farm.* What a beautiful word it was. What a beautiful thing it would be. What a beautiful life he would have when the farm was his. Oliver's feet began to creep along the scarred floorboards, unconsciously taking him towards the front of the room, inspired by his eagerness to own the farm, and be real, and be one of this crowd who were listening to the auctioneer and knowing what they knew and saying nothing.

'One hundred and twenty-one acres, nine fields of handy sizes within a ring fence.' Acres! *Acres!* The true and ancient measure of England! He would have acres, rolling acres, and he would care for them and cultivate them and stride over them and be a proud, free man who owned his own land and supported his own being, instead of a slave in bondage in a cube farm, who toiled for global masters and lived off the labour of other slaves, a mass of humanity even more wretched than he, the people who produced his food, whose faces he would never know.

'With—' The auctioneer paused to check with the paper in his hand. 'Fifteen acres registered for Arable Aid.' And as if to gloss over this minor embarrassment, he picked up speed again and continued, 'All the main services are connected. Approached by a farm lane off the B237 through Yattenham St Mary, and the lot includes farmhouse itself partly demolished since the fire of 1997.'

Around the auction room, a few heads nodded. *Yes, we know.* Evidently, everyone in the room knew Saxwold New Farm, the lane to it, the concrete-block general-purpose building (useful size, that), the cottage and the ruined farmhouse. Everyone in the room remembered the fire of 1997 and knew how it had started, and why. Helluva blaze, they could have seen the smoke from Ipswich.

Everyone knew the score except the youngish bloke standing over at the side, the one in the waxed jacket that was practically luminous with newness and had never been scratched by a thorn or splattered by a tractor in its extremely short life. The youngish bloke clutching his bidding number with eyes lit up as if he had backed a horse in the Grand National and was watching it come in six lengths ahead. Another wallet from London looking for a weekend place for Lucy and the sprogs. His sort didn't want to know. That bloke was Oliver Hardcastle.

The auctioneer drew a deep breath. 'Who'll start me off?' he appealed. 'Who'll start me off at four hundred?'

Oliver looked around the room, at the faces which were far better than him at giving nothing away, faces reddened by the wind and pinched by the cold outside, chins drawn down into jacket collars as if to stop the mouths from speaking up, hands stuffed into jacket pockets to prevent them getting loose and giving way to expression.

'Four hundred,' the auctioneer pumped up his optimism. 'Four hundred, ladies and gentlemen.'

More dust settled on the carved mahogany garland over the main door. Somebody coughed again. Somebody else coughed. The auction was taking place in February, peak season for viruses. The first cougher got a couple more in.

'Four hundred now,' the auctioneer repeated.

'Stuff the bloody tax,' growled a voice at the back of the room.

Some murmurs of congratulation for this opinion. The

reason for the sale had been advertised, the list of lots proclaimed it. By order of the Inland Revenue, meaning their bailiffs had seized the property in lieu of unpaid taxes. That much Oliver had learned already.

Oliver felt his heart beating. He had bought a shirt, a soft shirt in lumberjack checks, mostly brown, to go under the waxed jacket, and his heart was thumping so hard that it felt as if it was going to pop off the shirt buttons. Not less than four hundred, surely? Here he was, a man whose daily grind involved unleashing tidal waves of wealth around the globe without a twinge of anxiety, and he was standing in a country auction room on the edge of cardiac arrest for less than half a mil sterling. Amazing.

'Three hundred, then,' the auctioneer conceded. 'Who'll start me off at three hundred?'

The coughing had stopped and a judgemental silence began to settle like a rain cloud spoiling a summer's day.

'Three hundred?' The auctioneer raised his eyes to the back of the room, then flourished his arm in triumph. 'Three hundred! At the back, there, thank you, sir.'

A few heads turned. A few people looked at Oliver, not that he noticed. A few chuckles resounded and above them a loud and cheerful voice accused, 'You took that off the wall, you bugger.'

The auctioneer blushed. He was a man of thirty-ish, pale-faced, with a thin neck standing loose in his shirt collar. The flush of shame spread in seconds.

The man standing next to Oliver smiled. It was a smile of boyish delight, such as was frequently seen in 1950s advertisements for chocolate bars.

Then, sensing bewilderment by his right elbow, he leaned

towards Oliver and whispered, 'He means the auctioneer made it up. Imaginary bidder. They do it to get things moving when the room's a bit cold.'

'That's a fantastic price,' argued the auctioneer.

'Too right, it is,' agreed the cheerful voice of his challenger. 'Your fantasy price, you mean.' Oliver saw that the voice belonged to a broad man who had spread out over several seats in the front row, turning round now to spar with the rest of the audience.

'It's worth a whole lot more,' the auctioneer said, his courage fading as his embarrassment bloomed.

'But where's the money going, eh? That's the question, isn't it? Bastards put old Frank out of business, didn't they? Damned if they're getting my money for that.'

Some growls of approval greeted this explanation, and the broad man turned around on his seats to see the extent of his support.

'There's a reserve set,' the auctioneer explained. 'Below three hundred I cannot go. They'll be selling in London if it don't fetch the right price here.'

At the word 'London', distaste rippled through the room like a seismic disturbance. 'Of course,' Oliver explained to himself, 'they want to keep the land in local ownership. But when I'm the owner, I'll be local, so that'll be OK. What they're afraid of is some pension fund snapping it up.'

The broad man turned around again, agitated.

'Don't look at me,' he pleaded to the nearest rows of onlookers. 'Don't you go looking at me.'

'Go on, Colin, you know you want to.' This was from the boyish smiler beside Oliver, who spoke in a pleasant light tenor and an accent as hopelessly posh as a Wimbledon announcer.

'Yeah, go on,' agreed a few other voices.

'More trouble than it's worth, it's got to be,' the broad man said at once. 'Frank was a good enough farmer. If he couldn't keep going, nobody could.'

'So, gentlemen.' The auctioneer regained his fragile authority. 'Do I have an opening bid? At three hundred thousand pounds, Saxwold New Farm?'

Oliver's heart threatened to crack open his ribcage. He took a grip on the white laminated card bearing his bidder number, and twitched it.

'Three hundred? Anybody?' The auctioneer was looking everywhere but at him. Oliver raised his card blatantly, then felt panic and waved the card above his head at arm's length.

'Over here,' called the posh speaker, distinctly surprised.

'Ladies and gentlemen, for the last time of asking . . .' The auctioneer had his gavel hand in the air and was scanning the far horizon.

'Over *here*,' called the posh voice again, waving to catch the auctioneer's eye.

'Oi!' The broad man heaved himself to his feet to get the auctioneer's attention and pointed in Oliver's direction. 'Over there. You've got a live one.'

'Oh gosh, so sorry,' the auctioneer mumbled, dropping his programme as he apologised. 'Are you bidding, sir?'

'Yes,' said Oliver, hearing his own voice hoarse with relief. 'I am bidding.'

'Three hundred thousand pounds, then?'

Oliver nodded and flashed his card definitively at shoulder height.

'Thank you, sir. I have an opening bid of three hundred, can I hear three-fifty?'

'Get over yourself,' the posh speaker suggested.

The auctioneer persisted. 'Any more? Any advance on three hundred thousand pounds? Are we all done?'

'Course we're all done,' said the broad man over his shoulder, for now he had turned around again and was leaning over his chair-back, eyeballing Oliver with bullock-like curiosity.

'To you, sir, gentleman at the front here, let me just get a note of your number, gentleman at the front, on a maiden bid, Saxwold New Farm at three hundred thousand pounds . . . *sold*!'

For an instant, a heart attack seemed like a real possibility. Something in Oliver's chest leaped like a salmon, his ears buzzed, the room went misty and he felt dizzy. A farm. He had bought a farm. He was, technically at least, a farmer. His dreams were about to come true.

A hand as subtle as a spade slapped him on the shoulder, and its partner, he realised, was advancing to be shaken. They belonged to the broad man, who had heaved over in his direction through the startled crowd.

'You'll be just down the road of me,' he said, curiosity radiating uncontrollably from a red face embellished with a craggy nose.

'Don't tell him that,' the posh one advised. 'He hasn't signed the cheque yet.' He was a willowy individual who seemed to sway as he spoke.

'Pleased to meet you,' Oliver said, shaking the spade-like hand as firmly as he could.

'Not half as pleased as I am to meet you,' said the broad

man, only partly joking. 'They were all on at me to buy old Frank's place, but I've got enough to get on with of my own. So you're welcome and good luck.'

Oliver wanted to ask what had happened to old Frank, but the moment did not seem right.

'This is Colin Burton,' said the willowy one. Even in the gloom of the auction room, you could still see that his pale face was thickly freckled and his hair was worn in a ponytail. More like a romantic poet than a son of the soil. 'His land is next to yours. And I'm Florian Addleworth. You'll find me up the road, other side of the village.'

'Oliver Hardcastle,' he introduced himself.

'So, welcome to Saxwold.'

'Thank you.' So much, thought Oliver, for all that stereotypical rubbish about country people keeping to themselves and resenting strangers and having bad manners. I'm getting downright social grace here.

'You'll be weekending?'

'Er, no. I hope not. I'll be living on the farm.'

'Don't mind us,' said Florian, the willowy one. 'We're just nosey.'

'That's us, all right.' The broad one was watching carefully, to see how much prying was acceptable among the middle classes.

'So you'll be living on the farm,' Florian prompted. 'And . . .'

'Yes and . . . well, and farming. I hope.'

'Farming?'

'Farming, eh?'

'You can come over and laugh at me any time,' Oliver proposed.

'We'll do that, don't you worry,' said Colin.

'You've farmed before?' enquired Florian, as if this would be the only possible excuse.

'No. Never. Not yet. So it'll be a bit of a learning curve.'

'Learning curve,' Colin repeated, as if delighted to have discovered such an apt and tactful expression. 'Well, we all gotta go through them sometime, don't we?'

'Lot eighteen,' called the auctioneer, with a stern glance in their direction. 'Lot eighteen, arable land at Bungay, with planning permission . . .'

'You'll come and have a drink?' Colin suggested, rolling back a step like a wary steer in case the suggestion was badly received. 'You've done that before, I hope.'

'Oh yes. Great,' said Oliver. 'Er, yes. Great.' He shut up, suddenly fearful that whatever he said was going to brand him as everything he himself despised, and allowed his new neighbours to conduct him out of the auction room and off to a pub, with a short courtesy stop at the office for the signing of the cheque.

'I am a farmer,' he told himself, his hand trembling with ecstasy as he signed his name. 'I'm a farmer. I've cracked it.' And he felt good, as if for the first time in his thirty-four years his planets were lining up for the great cosmic conjunction that would propel him inevitably towards a real life.

'You're going to do what?' asked the Managing Director of his bank when news of his leaving flashed up to board level.

'Farm,' said Oliver, smiling because he still couldn't stop, even though the cheque had cleared and the deeds to Saxwold New Farm were on his desk at home. 'I've bought a farm and I'm going to be a farmer.'

11

'You're mad,' said the MD, not smiling.

'I can afford to be,' Oliver pointed out.

'Nobody can afford to be that crazy.' The MD still wasn't smiling. 'Don't come back here when it all goes pear-shaped. You were a very promising analyst, we fast-tracked you from the day you joined.'

'Yes,' Oliver agreed. 'And I am grateful.'

'You've had the highest bonuses in our UK office. You were going to be promoted to the board in six months. And this is all you can think to do.'

'It was all I ever wanted to do,' Oliver told him.

'Pity you didn't share your thoughts with us a bit earlier.' Now the MD was looking downright sour. 'We wouldn't have wasted our resources if we'd known there was going to be a loyalty issue.'

'Which is why I didn't tell you,' Oliver said. 'And anyway, you never asked. Nobody has ever asked me what I really wanted to do. Nobody here can imagine anybody wanting to do anything other than work for this bank and get big bonuses.'

'So what's your problem?' asked the MD, moving from sour to thunderous.

'It's your problem,' Oliver informed him. 'I haven't a problem in the world, right now.'

'You're mad,' said the MD again. Oliver decided it was time to clear his desk and leave. His colleagues watched him in silence.

'You want to do *what*?' said the woman who called herself the woman in his life. She was, in Oliver's opinion, a nice-ish person apart from the chronic hearing problem. He found that he met an extraordinary number of women who had hearing problems.

He was a pleasant-looking man, in a brown-haired, brown-eyed kind of way, added to which there was something about him that gave people a feeling of confidence and security. Whenever he explained his life's mission to a woman, giving due emphasis to its incompatibility with any kind of pairing off or settling down, she assumed the kind of vague, non-specific smile that deaf people who can't hear often use to cover up the fact that they aren't following the conversation.

It could not be alleged that the women with whom he had this conversation were in any way predatory or manipulative, but when Oliver said, 'I don't want a relationship' or 'I don't want a girlfriend' or even 'Look, I'm sorry but I don't actually want *you*,' he never said it loudly enough for them to hear him, in the larger sense. It seemed as if their aural nerves only transmitted the key words, 'relationship', 'girlfriend' and 'you'.

Oliver didn't hold the women wholly responsible for this problem. In his heart, he knew that he wasn't getting through because the bits of his soul were still lying around, unconnected, waiting to be bolted together. His identity was a work in progress. Doing what he had to do, to become what he wanted to be, left him with his real self still a blueprint. He looked good, but he was nothing but a heap of unresolved paradoxes and unexplored desires.

The results of this communication failure were often distressing, and sometimes quite ugly. Often, women immediately invested their confidence in him and looked forward to a lifetime of shared security.

The woman now standing in his flat had managed to get further than all the rest. She had moved a lot of her clothes into his wardrobe and was on to the final phase of assimilation, contriving for him to meet her friends and making noises about her family. He was getting out at the right time.

'I'm going to be a farmer,' he repeated.

'You can't. You can't be a farmer, you live in London.'

'I'm not going to live in London any more.'

'Don't be ridiculous. Where else would you live?'

'I told you. I've bought a farm. In the country. In Suffolk. I'm going to be a farmer.'

'And what am I supposed to do?'

'Well, whatever you like. Come down at weekends, maybe.'

She was standing with her back to the wall of glass that was considered the most desirable feature of his flat, which was, properly speaking and without exaggeration, a penthouse. Through the wall of glass, he had panoramic views of the Thames. All the way from Westminster to the flood barriers. A mass of dirty water, known to be largely recycled human waste, fringed with high-rise workplaces and more glass-walled living spaces, and beyond them the less-than-premium development sites still forested with cranes, all bound together with coiling snakes of traffic and overcast with a haze of rubber particles, vehicle emissions and mass human exhalation including particles of mucus, phlegm and water vapour bearing over three million different viruses. Oliver sincerely hated this view and couldn't wait to sell it. Nor, he realised, could he wait to get away from the woman standing in front of it. From all women, in fact. As far away as possible. They were just too damn difficult.

'I'd rather throw myself off your bloody balcony,' she announced.

Oliver sighed. Near his solar plexus, an express elevator hurtled earthwards. The day had already been too long, and the night would be even longer if he didn't handle things right.

'Look,' he said, in what he thought was a kind, placatory and decent manner. 'Why don't you take a couple of hours, get your things all packed, and then I'll call you a taxi?'

She burst into tears. They always did that. It made him feel dreadful.

Miranda Marlow also felt dreadful, in a flat, insignificant, lowly and wet kind of way. In fact, she felt like a worm. Never, as long as she'd been a conscious adult, had Miranda been able to get off the phone after a call from her mother without getting that old invertebrate feeling. The instant she heard the maternal 'hello' it was as if her arms and legs disappeared, her worldview readjusted to a height of one millimetre and a mantle of slime covered her entire body.

'How are you?' Clare Marlow had asked.

The best answer was something short and unlikely to attract attention. 'Fine,' Miranda had replied.

'Good. I thought we should have lunch.'

'Ah . . .' Miranda knew well that her diary was as windowless as a prison cell. 'Could we make it dinner? Only . . .'

'You know it's bad for your metabolism to eat after seven,' Clare had replied.

'It's just I've got a lot on at the moment . . .'

'People won't respect you for having bad time-management skills.'

'We're doing the big presentation today and . . .'

'You can delegate. Women never want to delegate, why is that?'

'I can't delegate my own project.'

'I've got something important I need to discuss with you. Don't sigh like that. We need to be in touch with each other.'

'Yup, we do that,' Miranda had answered, making sure it came out too bland to rile her mother but sarcastic enough to satisfy herself. 'How's next week for you?'

'Useless. It'll have to be the beginning of next month.'

'Really urgent, then.'

'Everything's really urgent, isn't it? You just have to learn to prioritise.'

And so they made a date and Miranda felt like a worm.

'She said we needed to be in touch with each other,' she told her best friend, Dido Hastings, as they reclined, side by side, on her sofa, waiting to get the energy to get up and go out. Again.

'Maybe she just wants to see you.'

'Maybe there is life on Mars.'

'She *is* your mother.'

'You don't have to make excuses for her. You wouldn't swap, would you?'

'Your mum's your mum, isn't she? Anyway, you wouldn't swap either.' Dido's mother manifested herself in their lives in one of two ways. Either it was calls to say she was going shopping in Barcelona and did Dido want to come, or it was calls from the exclusive detox-clinic-of-the-month saying she'd just admitted herself and did Dido want to visit.

'I know her, you see,' Miranda went on. 'My mother wants to have lunch urgently, which means that she wants to get me on side for something that she's already planned.'

'She must want you to help with something. I think that's nice. Isn't it nice?'

'Well, yes, and whatever it is I do want to help her if I can but . . .'

'It's the being planned that you don't like.'

'It's the knowing I'm just another item on her To Do list. That's what I don't like.'

'Well, my mum doesn't do To Do lists. I think you're lucky.'

'My mum made me do my first To Do list when I was five. I think *you're* lucky. Shall we go to the Thai or the bar? I've got that presentation thing tomorrow, I need an early night. Oh, God, why can't I stop organising all the time?'

'Because you can't,' said Dido. 'Because I never organise anything and you get antsy. Because you wouldn't be you if you didn't try so hard. God, I wish I had your problems.'

Miranda strove for perfection. Dido did not strive at all. Miranda had built a career, Dido had been washed through fifteen jobs in seven years as if being borne along like a leaf by the force of life itself. Miranda had a flat, and Dido was often to be found staying there because she had moved in with a man, rented out her own flat, and then changed her mind about the man.

They looked like an odd couple. Miranda had her hips so well controlled that hipsters just slipped off them and Dido had a backside that made people think of the urban myth about being able to rest a pint of beer on a well-shaped bum. Miranda had organised hair; it was short and did what it was told. Dido had such long and tangled hair that everyone believed it was extensions.

Miranda's place was a large room within walking distance of her office. 'I like living in a handbag,' she told people. 'The design is just perfect. What else could I want?' She had three white walls. A wood floor. A great painting. A witty statement lamp. There was also a day bed, in red velvet, where Dido slept. And a bathroom. Actually, a wet room, grouted impeccably because Miranda had taken an afternoon off work to supervise the process. The main room was six metres square, which they considered very decent.

'Some people have a picture in the attic,' Dido had once said to Miranda. 'But you've got me.' She was an optimist to the last lymphocyte in the marrow of her bones. Dido would give money to a homeless man who was begging on the street and be absolutely sure he was Brad Pitt doing research for his next movie. Miranda would give money to a homeless man who was begging on the street and be absolutely sure he was a crack-head and she was only helping him to die.

When the effort of striving got too much, Miranda would give herself a spa weekend or a holiday, determined to master the art of creative vegetation that came so naturally to Dido. Lately she had felt the perfection thing taking over. She had caught herself wishing she could make sushi. All those little grains of rice, so utterly controlled. Her fingers itched to slice and roll and wrap things in seaweed. She knew that this was mad, but she didn't know how to stop.

Of course, the striving could be tough on the people who loved her, although, as Miranda saw it, they didn't really love *her*, just her illusion of perfection. Except for Dido. Dido had known her from years back, before the perfection sickness set in.

It made things worse that Miranda was in the brave-new-world business. Her job was to explain to people why they should want to live in the places that her bosses had designed for them. Her employers were an international planning group and her early night was needed so she would be able to present their latest triumph, an award-winning scheme to build a new corporate headquarters, with associated fitness centre, retail facilities, crèche, brasserie and car park, in the centre of London.

It went well. The audience, press and planners both, seemed impressed. Afterwards they stood around in huddles, murmuring respectfully. Even the media took note. She was interviewed for a TV news programme.

'And now here's the spokeswoman for the new Clerkenwell Sweep, Miranda Marlow. They're calling it "The Bedpan", Miranda. Local residents have complained about the building, they say it's ugly, they say it's not in keeping with the rest of Clerkenwell, the Wren squares, the Hawksmoor churches. How do you feel about that?'

Hurt, thought Miranda. Wounded to the quick, stabbed in the soft white underbelly. But I'm good with pain. I expected this criticism and I know what to do. She smiled at the interviewer, a clear-eyed, open-hearted smile of pure agony, and spoke to the green fur sausage that covered the microphone. 'The local people we have spoken to are as excited about the Sweep as we are, and they're proud that Clerkenwell will have one of the most beautiful modern buildings in Europe.'

It sounded so right. Even as she heard herself, she believed it. One useful thing she had inherited from her mother was the extraordinary gift of sounding right. Not bossy, domineering, dictatorial right. Just simple, obvious, law-of-the-universe right.

She sounded right but she knew, in the deep space of her consciousness, that she was wrong. It was true that she herself adored the Clerkenwell Sweep. So did its architect, and their boss in Denver, and most of the rest of the architectural profession. '*A waking dream of vernacular cosmopolitanism,*' that was the consensus.

It was also true, however, that nobody had actually asked the people of Clerkenwell for their views. The ruling from Denver was that people were always defensive when presented with change and in the mass they had no imagination. Therefore there was no reason to seek their views.

As a building, the Sweep was a star. As a place to work or live in or go for lunch or fall in love or play with children or die with dignity — well, Miranda could not bear to think about that sort of thing. She was as sensitive as a spring flower. The only way she could get through life was to wrap herself up in beauty.

Every morning she battled through the crowds at her station, and had to insulate herself in a book from the compressed humanity in her train. She struggled to the office on teeming pavements, feeling that people around her were angry, savage and in despair, and their pain hurt her so much she had to concentrate on the pictures of the beautiful buildings all around her office to blot it out. And it was only a few more degrees of agony to move from these Londoners, who hadn't enough air to breathe or ground to stand upon or reasons for living, to AIDS orphans in Africa or street children in Manila or people dying by the roadside in Calcutta.

There was nothing to be done about any of this, and if she thought about it for more than a second she was buried in an avalanche of suffering. So she chose her thoughts carefully, and got by on giving all her attention to the Clerkenwell Sweep, and anything else that claimed to be beautiful and came with the promise of hope.

Miranda knew a lot about art and architecture and design. She craved things that looked good because looking was more comfortable than feeling. In her ideal day, she got through without feeling anything at all. Her perfect 24 hours was filled with images. Images were low-risk, low-maintenance, low-stress. Images could not make you feel like a worm. Find the right image and life could be bearable.

She had the picture of the Sweep firmly in her mind, silver-scaled, gleaming in the sunlight, a huge round-sided edifice surrounded by the puny figures of its human admirers. She herself had put these tiny plastic people on the model, to indicate that people were going to love it. They were little ant-like creatures gawping in awe. Local residents. Good decoration. Like trees, one of those accessories that clients always expected an architectural model to have, but nothing to which you actually committed the firm, or put in the specification. Easy to put people on a model; impossible to think about how people had to live.

'But surely,' the interviewer pressed on. 'But surely . . .'

Her grey eyes regarded him. He groped for words. Her eyes widened, her fine eyebrows raised themselves. 'The most beautiful modern building in Europe,' she almost

21

repeated. 'We believe London deserves the Sweep. With the Guggenheim in Bilbao, the Louvre in Paris, the Pearl Tower in Shanghai, it will be a symbol of the vibrant life of the city.'

'Attracting thousands of tourists,' the interviewer found himself saying. 'A world-class monumental must-see.'

'Exactly.' Now Miranda felt relieved and wanted to smile. She had to frown to stop it happening. Smiling on television, her mother had taught her, would make her look lightweight. It was bad enough that she wasn't particularly tall. And her hair was so fair there was no real choice except to be blonde. And her face did sort of line up with current aesthetic norms of prettiness, even if her nose could look a bit of a courgette in full profile.

'Thank you, Miranda Marlow, spokesman for the proposed Clerkenwell Sweep. The planning enquiry opens today . . .' As he burbled his conclusion at the green sausage, the interviewer realised that he'd been de-railed. Just how he couldn't exactly say, but the damn woman had subverted his argument. He was sure he hadn't meant to back the Sweep. But the way she said it, it had felt so *right*. And now she was standing there all calm and normal, making him feel silly for being worried.

'Thank you so much for that,' said Miranda. 'You must have done a lot of research.'

'Uh . . .' Now the interviewer was absolutely sure he was being heisted but there was nothing going on you could actually identify. You just set out for one place and mysteriously ended up in another.

'Do call if you'd like to do a follow-up.' She gave him her card. Miranda Marlow, Group Communications, Urban

Phoenix Group UK. A little red phoenix logo. Acclaimed international town-planners just ripe for a good documentary. The idea spontaneously manifested itself in the interviewer's mind, just as the Sweep was undoubtedly destined to manifest itself in the middle of Clerkenwell . . . but when? 'We're anticipating the enquiry will last about six months,' she said, before he asked.

'Ah . . .' The interviewer found himself talking to empty air. Miranda had escaped. She walked quickly down a curving alley, saw a café and plunged into it. A few minutes later she emerged, carrying a ham and cheese croissant in a paper bag. Croissants were good for anxiety. She hailed a taxi and cruised back to her office, eating quickly to finish the evil thing and get rid of the evidence before anyone could guess what she had been doing.

Once, when her mother had been trying to cheer her up, she had said, 'It's easy to be successful, Miranda. Just look at all the idiots who manage it.' The words sank into the soft depths of Miranda's young mind and stayed there, inhibiting all her gentle instincts. For Miranda was not at all her mother's daughter. Her heart was sweet, caring and tender. If Clare had a real lust for power, her daughter had a true craving for peace and harmony. So Miranda lived in a painful state of tension, trying to over-ride her true self and follow her parental programming. Croissant attacks were the main symptom.

'What's the matter with me?' she asked Dido, that evening, flopping onto her sofa with exhaustion after hounding herself through another day of perfectionism. 'Why can't I just slow down, chill out, let go?'

'Because you're not like that,' said Dido, reasonably. 'You're high-energy, high-creativity, high-achieving . . .'

'No I'm not. I just flog myself through stuff because I'm afraid of screwing up.'

'But that's *fine*,' said Dido, whose attention was wandering towards her own ambition of renewing her manicure before going out for the evening.

'No it isn't,' said Miranda. 'I'm turning into the sort of person who totally creeps me out. Did I tell you what I said to Will?'

Will, until recently, had been her boyfriend-since-college. They had made what Miranda had thought was a mutual decision to break up, move on, and stay friends. A few months of careful, content-free chats on the phone and then, out of nowhere, Will had had a real anger-management failure and snarled 'Oh, get a life!' at her. She had found herself saying, 'I don't have to – I have a lifestyle.'

'I mean, how could I have said that? It's just . . . creepy. I mean, isn't it?'

Dido was raking though an old wash bag full of nail varnishes. 'No it isn't,' she said in an absent tone. 'He was just being nasty because he'd found out you were seeing somebody younger.'

'It wasn't serious,' she protested.

'None of them are serious, are they?' said Dido. 'But it's none of Will's business, is it?'

'You're sure it doesn't say that I can't be serious myself? If I'm hanging with some non-serious boyfriend?' Boyfriend? Ouch. Miranda was beginning to find that word a bit juvenile.

'Nah,' Dido reassured her. 'It just means that you're not all banged-up in a Big Thing. You are free to accept a better offer. But not from Will. Nothing wrong with that.'

'My mother,' said Miranda, 'doesn't buy it. That'll be why

24

she wants lunch. The best thing about Will was she couldn't be on my case about not having anyone. I bet that's what this is about. She doesn't buy non-serious.'

'Your mother doesn't buy anything. Except those pointy shoes, I suppose. I can't believe she actually sends out a gofer for them. Just tell her you'll get serious in your own good time.' Dido began to paint her nails. Choosing one colour had been too much for her that evening. She was doing every finger in a different shade.

Miranda had a hideously familiar and usually absolutely accurate feeling that her mother was about to weigh in for another round of troubleshooting her life for her.

A little later, she and Dido found themselves in a reasonably sophisticated place in Soho, where Miranda waved to attract the attention of the Tequila Boy. He was olive-skinned and mean-looking, in a prettyish, Johnny-Depp's-secret-lovechild kind of way, and he wore his shot glasses on bandoliers over his shoulders and the bottles attached to his belt, in the area where hips are found on meatier men.

'Will you sort us out a couple of blacks?' she said sweetly.

'Two blacks for the ladies,' said Tequila Boy, popping the glasses out of his harnessings with a flourish.

'Where are you from?' she asked.

'How do you know I'm from somewhere?' he countered, juggling the bottle out of its holster.

'Just a wild guess.'

'A wild guess, eh?' He poured two shots, with a lot more style than precision.

'I kind of like wild stuff.' She mopped up a few drops of spillage with a fingertip, and licked it. 'What time do you finish?'

'Late.'

'Too late?' They exchanged a friendly quota of eye contact.

'Maybe not too late. Some of us go over the road to . . .' And he named the nearby club that went on all night.

'I might see you there,' Miranda said, thinking what-the-hell, the Urban Phoenix owed her a late night or ten.

'You *might* see me there,' Tequila Boy pouted, capping off the bottle.

'OK,' she sighed, 'so tell me a time.'

Dido watched with wide eyes as her friend's new date sauntered off to his next customer.

'I bet he's a great dancer,' she said. 'I can't believe you just did that *again*. That's just . . . wicked.'

'Wicked is good, I'm OK with wicked. It's serious I don't like.' Miranda shrugged. Waiters, barmen, Tequila Boys — they made her feel like Samantha in *Sex And the City* — sexy, grown-up and . . . in control.

CHAPTER 2

Beyond the Cocktail Apron

A couple of years after Oliver Hardcastle sold his view of the
Thames and moved to Saxwold New Farm, Clare Marlow sat
in a restaurant on the river's south bank, conveniently close
to Westminster, and waited for the arrival of the Adviser to
the Special Adviser to the Prime Minister.

She had taken up ambition late in her life, in the same
spirit that some women dedicate themselves to playing
bridge, or gardening, or doomed and humiliating love
affairs. Having been universally acclaimed as a nice woman,
such a nice woman even, and having raised a lovely daughter
in Miranda and a son who at least had the decency to leave
home as soon as he could, she realised that it was time to
move on.

At the first whiff of fortune, not to mention fame, Clare
Marlow had given up her aspirations to be nice and became
driven, obsessive and bored by the friends who tried to put
her in touch with how she was changing.

After a few years, the friends had washed their hands.

Her husband retreated to Cambridge and burrowed into his old college, where he could study trade in pre-Roman Britain in peace. Her son got religion and her daughter got a long-hours job. Clare never even noticed. She had become a hopeless power junkie. Nothing, but nothing, had ever given her such a buzz.

The sweetest part of it all was that she had never been meant to do anything, let alone anything important. Her whole life suddenly became a subversive statement. No woman of Clare's vintage had been intended to be summoned to a power lunch with an Adviser to the Special Adviser to the Prime Minister. She twisted her glass of still mineral water against the light and waited for destiny to make its next offer. She could have waited for ever, so delicious was the defeat of the dreary blueprint that had originally been drawn up for her.

The Adviser felt a twinge of nerves as he approached the figure at the table. She was perfect. She had all the attributes of a great statesman: a face for television, a way of speaking in short sentences that were virtually meaning-free and the ability to remain a size twelve without the aid of cigarettes. She was not encumbered by any significant flaws, such as a conscience or a good memory for promises. She had a family, a husband and two children, the majority of whom were available for photographs, non-criminal and not noticeably insane.

She had had flaws, but he truly admired the way she had identified and remedied them as soon as it had become appropriate. Take the voice thing. Way back whenever, Clare Marlow's mother and father had managed the Scotch Wool Shop in Neasden, the least wealthy part of the North London conurbation, a region whose dialect sounded like two steel cables scraping together in a howling wind. By listening to the radio, Clare had acquired a BBC accent by the time she had been summoned to Cambridge for her university interview. Just as efficiently, she had later ditched these rounded tones in favour of a South London whine.

At the same time, she had realised by instinct that her presentation was too competent, too elegant, too much like some Eighties superwoman, and she had seized the opportunity of hiring a holistic publicist with whom to go shopping and buy the kind of clothes that, in a visually aware world, would proclaim vulnerability, foolishness, maybe even spirituality, rather than her natural and frequently indulged love of Gucci.

By all the laws of nature, such as nature was understood in London at the dawn of the twenty-first century, it was inevitable that one day Clare Marlow would be lunched by an Adviser and invited to consider a public office. And (the Adviser straightened his tie with pride as he thought of this) the honour was his.

Clare never mentioned the fact, because she had learned that it was career suicide to suggest that there had ever been such a thing as the past, but a woman of her class and vintage was intended by her fellow men to be a homemaker. The destiny her own mother had pictured for her was of greeting her husband at the door every evening with soothing words, a pitcher of chilled martinis in her manicured hand and a frilly red, white and black cocktail apron tied with a pretty bow around her wasp waist.

Her own mother's aspirations for her had also included a Goblin Teasmade among the wedding presents and a home with a vinyl-tiled floor that Clare would be able to clean with a sponge mop and a product advertised on the television. Miracle detergents! Labour-saving devices! In addition, she had had visions of her daughter living in a half-timbered house with lawns front and back, instead of a terraced dwelling with a coal hole and a concrete yard. She had seen her daughter as a mother herself, enjoying the supreme happiness of having the leisure to walk to and from school twice a day with her fine, floppy-haired son and sweet, curly-haired daughter, all neat in their spotless ankle socks and snugly buttoned coats with velvet collars.

No one had ever planned for Clare Marlow to be the CEO of the vast insurance and finance group known as Mutual Probity, as well as a homemaker and a mother, but she had pulled off the hat trick. Her parents had pretty well died of anxiety as they watched her soar into a social stratosphere beyond their understanding, but she had never looked back to notice them.

At Cambridge, where her mother had dreaded that she would become a frump and a spinster, Clare had acquired a husband with the greatest of ease. Male students outnumbered female by nine to one the year she went up to one of the women's colleges, equipped with an exhibition, a bicycle and a prescription for the Pill. Following marriage, the children had been no problem – not really, anyway. First the boy, then the girl. She dressed them both in miniature denim dungarees rather than velvet-collared coats, and this led her naturally to go into business with another mother, selling designer baby clothes by mail order. Once she was dealing with balance sheets, Clare began to feel the intoxication of power.

Her little business had been bought by a bigger business, and she had found herself a director. An even bigger business had bought that business, and she had become a managing director. Power became more than an optional perk, it was a personal obsession. The first half of her life suddenly seemed like a cosmic waste of her time. The years she'd frittered away trying to be a flower child or a foxy lady or a yummy mummy, when she could have been mastering the universe!

Power over what, or who, was irrelevant; any power would do. Halfway through her life, Clare Marlow had woken up from her nightmare of socially sanctioned pointlessness and looked around wildly for new worlds to conquer. Her strategy was simple. 1) money, 2) politics and 3) television. Why not? And here she was, making the transition from 1 to 2, and being lunched by the Adviser.

'The thing is, Clare,' the Adviser said, cutting to the chase as soon as they could dispense with the waiter, 'we want to give you something big. Foreign, Home, that big. I mean, we're not in the business of wasting anyone's time, are we? We know that if you're ready to move on from the commercial sector, the offer needs to be right.'

'Of course.' She preened, with reservations. So he wasn't going to offer her Foreign or Home. Well, too much to hope for first off, perhaps. Her future was still unrolling exactly according to plan. Just a few weeks ago, at an industry dinner, the Prime Minister personally had sounded her out about going into politics. Perfect timing. As the CEO of Mutual Probity, now the country's leading financial services provider, her present position was getting ever so slightly uncomfortable.

Shortly after she put her family photo on her desk at Mutual Probity, she discovered that she was sitting on a time bomb. The group had no more dirty linen in its accounting history than any other global enterprise, but that was to say that it had almost a million imaginary customers on its books and had mis-reported last year's loss as a profit.

Her job, she had deduced, was not to act like a girl and make a fuss, but to act like a man and keep this quiet as long as possible. She'd done brilliantly to hold the lid on the mess for the past six years, but sometime something had to give. Come this April and the end of the financial year, things were going to get sticky. With Enron and Worldcom still sensitive memories, a failure of investor understanding on such matters was imminent. She had, in fact, been lumbered with the whole nightmare. More than anything in the world, Clare Marlow really hated to be embarrassed in public. She had been looking to make the move. Urgently.

The Adviser was in his early thirties. He certainly watched *The West Wing*. He probably owned the boxed set of DVDs. His shirt was crisp and his eyes as sharp as kebab skewers. His hair knew it was supposed to bounce with discipline, like Rob Lowe's hair, even if his nose was twice as large and his complexion a distressing shade of greyish-beige, and pitted with old acne scars. There was a trace of Rob Lowe around the middle of his face, which was significantly blank. Botox? Cocaine? Social anxiety? All of the above? Did it really matter?

Clare saw that the Adviser had perfected the art of checking the restaurant doorway for the arrival of useful contacts while seemingly focusing only on her. It was the merest flicker, a lizard's blink. If she hadn't been so good at that manoeuvre herself, she'd never have noticed.

He had ordered boyishly, something to do with sausages, and he was eating it boyishly, which meant in large mouthfuls, hastily swallowed. Odd that such a high-flyer should never have learned that the more important you were, the less notice you should take of your food. Clare understood this instinctively. She herself had a small disc of fish, a farmed fish whose flabby flesh she did not exactly eat, but occasionally touched with her fork, as if she could have cared that it was leaking a mild solution of poisons and antibiotics on to the plate.

'So, what have you in mind?'

'We've been asking ourselves how we could make the best use of your skills. And what would be the best way of introducing you to the public at large. We did some work with focus groups which suggests that awareness among the general audience could maybe be a bit higher. Your profile in the business sector couldn't be better, of course.'

'Thank you.' Profile! Awareness! He was talking her language. Still, she felt a zephyr of doubt. Flattering that they'd researched her image, but this approach was just too itsy to be the hors d'oeuvre to a plum job. It wasn't the preamble to a poisoned chalice either, but they'd have been mad to try that. All the same, he was trying to soften her up for something.

'And no presentation problems. That's a nice bonus for me.' The Adviser meant that he'd been going crazy with the Minister she was to replace. The *Sun* headlined him as The Incredible Pink-Faced Blob and he had a tragic tendency to look like an obese paedophile dressed by Oxfam. Clare Marlow was an elegant woman. Famously elegant, even. She had authoritative height, honest eyes, those small camera-friendly features, the right sort of blonde hair and a nice taste in snazzy little suits. She understood the iconography of the power necklace: metal, heavy, a classic unchanged since Boudicca was Queen of the Iceni. She was also given to discreetly erotic footwear: pointed, black, agonising, a style which had endured since Sacher-Masoch's Venus was wrapped in her furs. An Adviser's dream, really.

'But we need to get you noticed,' he went on.

'What are you softening me up for?' she asked him, with her useful, faux-decent smile which sent the meta-message that she knew the game and was not offended.

He paused. He swallowed. He made eye contact. He stopped himself taking a deep breath and made himself sound natural. 'The PM wants to start you off at the Fieldcare Agency.'

She paused. She swallowed. She held the eye contact. Fieldcare? Fieldcare? She pasted on a look of grave concentration while groping for the translation. Nothing made you look more past it than not keeping up with new official bodies. No, wait, Fieldcare was a department – wasn't it? Christ, it was Agriculture! All this bullshit, and all they were offering was Agriculture.

She frowned and stopped herself saying, 'Agriculture? Forget it!' Instead, she countered him swiftly, 'What about Northern Ireland?'

Her lunch partner dived in with the hard sell. 'The PM really wants you at the cutting edge, Clare. He's thinking about a three-term career for you, minimum. We can't risk losing you in Ireland, anything could happen there. We admit that the Fieldcare sector has been underperforming but we're confident that with the right person at the top . . .'

'Underperforming? Why am I not surprised?' Clare played for time while her mind struggled for data. She knew nothing, absolutely nothing, about agriculture except that no Minister of Agriculture had ever made it to Downing Street. You might as well get lost in Culture or Sport.

Agriculture. Farming. The country. No, the *countryside*. A jumble of images from TV commercials came into her mind, women with old-fashioned hair running in slow motion through golden wheatfields, men with smelly dogs trudging up hills for no viable purpose.

Next, she remembered a TV programme showing an angry crowd walking beside tractors. A demonstration! *Yokels*, for heaven's sake, in those terrible tatty green anorak things. And *toffs*, God help them, in those mouldy tweed jackets that never fitted anywhere. She had needed to check the TV listings to make sure she wasn't watching *The Fast Show*.

She found she had no data on what the issue under protest might have been, but a clear memory of a pink blob of a man being ineffectual on television. Hah! So there was at least some media potential in the job. 1) money, 2) politics, 3) television. Fieldcare could serve her purpose. Perhaps that was what the PM had sensed when they talked.

She remembered that April was imminent. This year, April was going to be the cruellest month. There was a real danger of a Bank of England investigation at Mutual

Probity. Almost more worrying – she seemed to be the only one who could see the big black clouds piling up, ready for a massive blame-storm.

'The Fieldcare Agency,' she said again. 'The name's not good enough. It doesn't say "Government". No sense of national leadership. Sounds more like an NGO.'

A look of relief washed over the Adviser's face. 'If you wanted to go for a new corporate image . . .'

'Essential,' she told him. 'We need to communicate our vision. Agriculture that's competitive, safe, *modern*, for Christ's sake. I'd want to reframe the whole sector, distance ourselves from yesterday's headlines, transcend the historical issues of class conflict, tell people we're about ethical production, managed to the highest standards, viable in the global marketplace.'

'Fantastic!' the Adviser encouraged her, already seeing his triumphant return to the office with the new minister's head. 'And responsible land use, that's the buzzword at the Treasury.'

'We must talk about the package,' she segued, nifty as a tango diva.

'Of course, of course.' She had thrown him. Clare Marlow also had a fine instinct for the use of silence. She paused, mouth half open, as if ready to deliver the key word, waiting for his offer.

There are no silences in *The West Wing*. The Adviser panicked. Words piled up against his teeth, scorched his tongue, broke free of his lips and spouted over the table. He gabbled. He garbled. He actually uttered the upper limit of the figures he had been authorised to indicate.

Clare Marlow shut her mouth. She allowed the light of

inspiration to burn down behind her eyes. Slowly and blatantly, she checked the restaurant door for the arrival of a more interesting contact. She flashed recognition at a couple of people she might have known at nearby tables. She sighed a gentle sigh, the sigh a mother allows herself when she picks up her baby and finds it needs changing, again. Poor thing, can't help it.

'That's just ballpark, of course,' he twittered helplessly. 'There is some flexibility, a bonus tariff, performance-related, of course.'

She put him through another thirty seconds of silence, then uttered the figures she required.

The blank area in the middle of the Adviser's face seemed to spread until he looked as if paralysis stretched from ear to ear.

She shrugged. Her right hand twitched slightly towards her cold cup of camomile tea.

'Ah . . .' He was gasping like a doomed goldfish. 'Ah . . . of course. Of course. Ah . . . I'll put that to them. Report back. Shouldn't be a problem. May need to put in a few tweaks . . .'

'It shouldn't be a problem,' she repeated back to him.

'Ah . . . no. No problem at all. That I can foresee. So . . .'

'You can report back,' she encouraged him, a hint of warmth appearing in her face.

'Certainly. Will do.'

'Good.'

'Ah . . .'

Was there something else? She let her left eyebrow ask the question with a light, ironic twitch.

'A constituency.'

'Meaning . . .'

'We need to get you elected.'

'Well, yes. Naturally.' *Of course I did not forget that.*

'There's a by-election coming up in North London. Safe as houses. Absolute heartland. Shouldn't be a problem.'

'Good. Now. About the brand.'

Clare racked up the tension for another couple of minutes, then allowed her eyes to roll up and to the right, body language for 'I'm having the Big Idea now.'

'Responsible land use. Ethical production. Global viability,' she intoned the new mantra. 'We need a name that says all that. How about . . .'

The Adviser was quivering like a racing greyhound waiting for the hare.

'Agraria,' said Clare Marlow. Just a shade of a drawl on the middle 'a', just a hint of projection on the final diphthong.

'Genius,' the Adviser breathed. 'Agraria. They'll love it.'

In the taxi on her way back to Mutual Probity, Clare had a moment of proper pride. 'You've come a long way, baby,' she said to herself, 'and now the sky's the limit.' Westminster. The Cabinet, I should hope. My crowning achievements start here. No cocktail apron for me.

She looked out on the grey winter streets of London. Where had it all gone right? Clare had no memory of an epiphany. Memories of any kind just took up space in the mental hard drive. Nostalgia was death. To have a past at all was to deny yourself a future. She was not in the habit of looking back over her life, but just then she was curious to see if there had been some great defining moment when she had rejected the cocktail apron and set out on the road to glory.

All that came to mind was a conversation she had had at school with a girl with fluffy fair hair, a lazy, irritating girl who had been memorable mostly for the idiotic excuses she made for forgetting her homework, a girl who had never got more than a C for anything, whose greatest gifts were for mucking about and fooling around, and who was prime suspect when the swimming pool was emptied, or a fire alarm set off, or on the never-to-be-forgotten morning when the marble bust of the school's founder was discovered wearing a pair of red lace knickers on its head.

The whole school community, down to the first years and the cleaners, understood that the Clares of this world were not expected to mix with creatures like the fluffy girl. The whole community except the despised one herself. Somehow they had ended up on the same sofa in the sixth-form common room, on a day towards the end of the great summer cycle of exams. Even in their fast-track London girls' school, where the inmates were lashed ruthlessly in intellectual blinkers towards scholarships to Oxford and Cambridge, there is a whiff of Saturnalia in the air on a day like that.

The fluffy girl, obviously too stupid to understand the taboo she was breaking, said to Clare, 'What are you going to do when you're grown up?'

Clare returned the accepted response. 'Oh, I don't know.'

'You'll go to university, won't you?' the fluffy girl pushed her luck.

'My mother says it's silly to look too clever,' Clare said.

'So does mine. Boys don't like it, do they?' And the fluffy girl had smiled, half to herself, as if she had extracted the answer she had wanted, and Clare, at the age of sixteen, had

had a lightbulb moment and decided that she was not fluffy, and never would be fluffy, and would never make excuses, or get a C, or listen to her mother, or do anything else that the fluffy girls of this world did. Being too clever, and looking too clever, were going to be her life's work.

'But that's bollocks, isn't it?' she said confidently. And the word 'bollocks', which passed for an obscenity in their world, made the fluffy girl giggle.

Clare never giggled. Giggling was frowned upon at that school. Giggling was frowned upon at Cambridge. Giggling was for the fluffy girls. That small noise, echoing unexpectedly down the years, gave her a warm sense of superiority. Her favourite feeling.

Naturally, Oliver's first move was to buy a tractor. A shiny blue and yellow tractor, the boy's toy to end all boy's toys. *Oh wow, oh wow, oh wow – I'm a farmer and I can get on my tractor and ride it down to the pub.* Every morning, it twinkled at him joyfully from the dim interior of the concrete general-purpose building He had never considered money so well spent.

'You could have got a grant for that,' pointed out Florian Addleworth in The Pigeon & Pipkin one evening.

'You should've come to see me,' said Colin Burton. 'I was looking to get a buyer for my mine. She's a bit light for what I want, now I'm sticking with the pigs. I could've moved up to a bigger one and you could have had mine cheap.'

'Mm,' said Oliver. 'I've heard yours, of course.'

Nothing was said for a minute or so. Oliver looked at his two new neighbours and they looked at him. Florian took a diplomatic sip of his pint.

'You've heard it, have you?' said Jimmy, another farmer whose land bordered Oliver's, a wiry man with bowed legs in worn jeans and a gap between his two front teeth that made his smile look more humorous than he intended. Nobody was sure how he got his nickname, Jimmy the String; maybe because he was so thin and so sinewy, or maybe because he preferred baling twine to any other material for leading his dog, closing his gates, lacing his trainers and keeping on the doors of his Land Rover.

'Yup,' said Oliver.

They all three raised their glasses. Oliver reflected that the tractor he heard growling around the edges of his farm in the early morning sounded as sick as it was possible for an engine to be when it was still capable of running. Florian, Colin and Jimmy reflected that this new wallet wasn't half the fool he looked. The landlord, who was doing what he always did and listening to the conversation while fiddling about with his glass-washing machine at the far end of the bar, decided that the wallet was going to give Colin Burton a run for his money, and about time too.

The sixth person in the pub was the local vet, Lucy Vinny. Being a woman, and unaware of the rules of conversation between men, she said to Colin, 'Half the county must be able to hear that heap of old iron. What is it with you, Colin? Every piece of machinery you've got on that farm of yours seems to start with problems the day you buy it.'

This was considered by all the four men to be quite unnecessarily candid a remark.

'Anyone know what the score is?' Oliver asked immediately.

'Nil-nil,' said Florian. 'Five minutes of the first half to go.'

'Still time, then,' added Colin.

'Yup, early days.' Oliver agreed.

Jimmy said, 'Best get one in soon, eh?'

Oliver and Florian, not wishing to appear elitist, had been talking about the soccer match between Norwich City and Ipswich Town, while Colin and Jimmy, who regarded soccer as having being ruined by celebrity pussies while rugby remained the sport of unsullied low-profile manliness, were interested in the France v Wales international at Cardiff. All four suspected that they were at cross purposes but chose not to go there. Especially not with a woman listening.

After this bonding moment, it was determined in the pub that Oliver was better than the average wallet, and in fact probably a good bloke, and certainly worthy of being helped out when he needed it. Which he obviously would, sooner or later and almost certainly sooner.

Oliver knew a lot about farming. His goal was to run the best organic farm in England and, with his heart set on this destiny, he had learned all he could from books and from the Internet.

'Isn't there a college for people like you?' his mother had asked, when she had reluctantly accepted that her son was not going to be a glorious banker for ever. 'Agricultural college, or something. Where young farmers go to learn the latest techniques.'

'The latest techniques are ruining the land and producing food that makes people ill,' he informed her. 'It's the ancient farming methods I'm interested in.'

'Well, I'm sure they teach those too,' his mother had argued, her voice tailing off because she knew that she had bred the stubbornest creature on earth and there was really no point trying to talk to him once he'd made up his mind.

Oliver had no desire to learn in the company of others. It seemed an uncomfortably intimate idea and a pointless waste of time. Instead, like a Victorian philanthropist obsessed with reforming streetwalkers, Oliver fantasised of the tawdry fields, cruelly exploited by agribusiness, which would grow green and innocent again under his benevolent care.

Now he had found the fallen woman of his dreams. Saxwold New Farm, at the end of Saxwold Farm Lane, near the village of Great Saxwold in the county of Suffolk, was, he assumed, a prosperous homestead once. Now it had been reduced almost to dust by the demands of the frozen pea industry.

The hedges had been grubbed out and only a few rusting wire fences marked the borders of the fields. Docks and ragwort, the ugliest and most invasive of weeds, plants more at home on urban wasteland, were taking over the grass. Here and there a few trees had survived, those too gnarled to be worth felling.

Where the land should have sloped prettily down to the bend of a small stream that meandered through it, the copses and thickets had been cleared and the naked shoulders of the earth were eroding down to a marsh.

Over all this desolation stood the ruin of the old farmhouse, some canting walls bodged together from old cobbles and new bricks, half a roof, a pile of masonry and two fallen beams poking out like fractured bones. At the opposite end of the spread was the farmyard, the tractor's concrete palace and the barn, roofed in rusting corrugated iron. It had been used to store pesticides.

43

Finally, on the lane, standing upright as if traumatised by witnessing the rape of the land around it, was a small cottage built of red brick and flint, its walls bowing visibly under the weight of a lurid new tile roof. At the back was a neglected garden garnished with the rusty carcass of a car.

Around the edge of his land curved the lane, leading to the ruin. Up the lane and a few minutes down the B237 road in the direction of Yattenham St Mary lay the rest of the village of Great Saxwold, a handful of dwellings in the same brick-and-flint. One housed a dead shop, with sun-bleached, flyblown advertisements for Vimto and the *Daily Telegraph* still curling at the windows. Another was a former school, now three luxury apartments for week-enders. No one had got around to taking down the blistered red sign for the post office, long since rationalised and its letter boxes gagged with steel plates. The village huddled protectively around its last remaining amenity, The Pigeon & Pipkin.

The present management of this pub had installed slip-pery, fake-mahogany armchairs and gaudy brass chandeliers, hoping to emulate a traditional urban wine bar trying to emulate a traditional country inn. Oliver decided that, since his days as a serious drinker were now behind him, the vulgarity of The Pigeon & Pipkin was not a material issue.

His crusade of redemption began immediately. Money was no object when he at last indulged his fantasies. Colin, Florian and Jimmy watched with open mouths as the heli-copter which Oliver had hired circled their land for a morning, while the co-pilot took photographs from the air that revealed the ancient field boundaries.

After some pleasant hours on the Internet, Oliver found a dowser who was recruited to search for stopped-up springs; then he hired a digger to excavate a pond. He had the recent pantiles ripped off the cottage roof and called in a thatcher to restore the cottage and the barn to their traditional splendour.

The master plan for Saxwold New Farm had been elaborated over years. The sad fields of weeds would be ploughed in and mulch crops planted to transform the soil from a sour, black crust to a rich, light loam. He had long yearned to sow comfrey and now he could ride out on his tractor to scatter the seeds.

He passed glorious wind-scoured days marking out the mediaeval hedge banks, on which he reinstated hundreds of hawthorn and hazel bushes. On the stream banks he installed copses of alder and young oaks. Finally, he bought a ton of wildflower seeds to mix with fine grasses and scattered them rapturously on the meadows-to-be. Nothing in his whole life had made him happier than watching that first mist of green appear over the dark earth.

The first phase, the redemption of the land, he then considered complete. Next he planned to have sheep, a traditional lowland Suffolk breed, broad-backed, black-faced, dainty-footed, all set to nibble his new-grown grass and grow fat just as their ancestors had done since before the Romans whacked down the A12 from Londinium to Camulodumum.

In this frenzy of biological redemption, Oliver lost his taste for numbers. He spent money like a drunken sailor. Or, indeed, a drunken banker, which was exactly what he almost became. Unopened bank statements found their way into the kindling basket and were used to light his roaring log fires. The radio woke him at 6.20 with *Farming Today*, when his spine was still as stiff as a concrete post from dragging sacks of seeds aboard the tractor the day before, and he collapsed into bed at nine every evening, intoxicated with environmental righteousness and several pints of Foulsham's India Pale Ale. Finance seemed a far-off unreality, part of the hellish life he had left behind. Visits to his on-line investment sites were made less and less frequently; the need to check any of the balances of his affairs seemed quite unreal. So when his holdings underperformed, Oliver never noticed.

His lavish style of farming, however, was much commented upon at The Pigeon & Pipkin and, since it had been accepted by all who drank there that that Oliver Hardcastle was a good bloke, the community decided to step in to save him from himself.

'You want to have a word with Florian,' Colin advised him. 'He sounds like a right pussy, of course, but I've never known anyone get more out of the Ministry bog-roll.'

'Bog-roll?' Oliver muttered, feeling the sweet refreshment of his first gulp of Foulsham's radiating through his weary body.

'The paper comes out of the Ministry,' Colin expanded. 'About grants and stuff. If there's a grant for it, Florian'll find it.'

Oliver looked to Jimmy for confirmation. Colin's methods, he had discovered, were not his. Jimmy's methods were not his either, but Jimmy, and his father and his great-uncle before him, had farmed the same land at Saxwold for more than seventy years.

Jimmy did not waste energy in conversation. When the silence became unbearable, he finally squeezed out a sentence. 'Florian's a good man for the paperwork.'

Colin decided it was time for unpalatable truths. Next to him, he pointed out in what he considered to be a confidential tone, Florian was the richest farmer in the area, having obtained a huge government grant to plant a vineyard according to biodynamic principles. His business plan counted on the fact that he and his key workers, who were in fact his brother and his brother's wife, and their five children between the ages of eleven and one, would qualify for an impressive range of benefits. His new dark green Range Rover gleamed in the car park.

'Look at that place of his,' Colin continued, forking in the last of his Salmon and Tuna Cobbler. 'Says it all. Painted up to the tits, top-of-the-range equipment, no expense spared.'

'I thought he'd . . . well, you know. I thought his family helped him out.'

'I thought you said you were supposed to be a banker?' said Colin. 'People like the Addleworths never take a punt with their own money. But you bankers don't like us farmers very much. So the Addleworths send their sons to these universities to learn how to get money out of the government. And whatever they paid for young Florian's education, it's worth every penny. I mean, British wine? Who's going to drink the stuff? But you can get a hell of a lot of money for making it.'

Florian was a wine-maker. His vineyards, stretching to the edge of the village of Great Saxwold itself, reeked of over-investment. At the entrance to the *domaine* was a new thatched lych gate and a huge painted hoarding which proclaimed

CHATEAU SAXWOLD in squirly eighteenth-century script. Underneath, in smaller squirls, was the mission statement: *the finest English wines from grapes grown on biodynamic principles.*

A stack of barrels rose beside it, their brass fitments glinting in the sun, when there was sun. A newly gravelled drive lined with topiary hedges led to the barn where Florian held invitation-only wine tastings for the local gentry, most of whom were his relatives, for the Addleworths also had been in East Anglia for generations and were impressive proof that, for the aristocracy, there is nothing to do in the country except breed.

Oliver discovered that Colin hired men from a labour contractor to harvest his potatoes and asked no questions about where these men had come from, what language they spoke and whether they had work permits. Jimmy went out himself on his ancient tractor far into the night and ploughed by searchlight. Florian employed his relatives, and in the autumn a small army of the posh poor arrived in battered Range Rovers to pick grapes for him. All Chateau activities were governed by the phases of the moon and the vine terraces echoed with cries of, 'Do look out, Tristan!' and 'Is it time for lunch yet?'

The vines themselves were trained in immaculate rows and bordered with banks of lavender. A rose bush ended each row, complementary planting, Florian explained, to keep vine fungi at bay. So much, most people had granted him, but when he announced his plans to dig energised cows' horns into the soil to refocus its energy, most of the clientele of The Pigeon & Pipkin experienced a deficit of tolerance.

Florian's wine, Oliver was soon assured, tasted like cat's piss, for all he talked about blending and grape varieties and the weather. The Pigeon stocked the stuff, and a few restaurants owned in the diaspora of Florian's family around the country, but nowhere else did. Sales were not impressive, so Florian was diversifying into mead. For this, he needed honey, so his first move had been to find a new grant to apply for, set up twenty-three beehives, and paint them all in the vineyard's colours of navy blue and gold.

'I was wondering,' Oliver began when Florian appeared in the bar, 'if I could ask your advice.'

'Delighted. I didn't know you were interested in biodynamic farming.'

'Er – well, before I get started, I was thinking I should look into grants and things.'

'Too right. I'm sure the Government had its pound of flesh when you were in the City. Time to collect! That's the brilliant thing about this game. You can actually get some-thing back for all that bloody tax. Come to dinner and I'll explain how it's done.'

Assuming that, since the vines were young, Florian would not be drinking his own wine just yet, Oliver took along a halfway decent bottle of burgundy. Florian's sister-in-law, very thin, very blonde, very twitchy and another member of the posh poor, took charge of it in a spasm of embarrassment and vanished to the kitchen. She emerged in a few minutes with a small glass of murky purple syrup.

'This is our Pinot,' Florian explained. 'A lot of growers can't get Pinot grapes to ripen at all in England, but we've got a south slope that they really seem to like. We're not selling it yet, but I'm quite pleased with it.' Oliver swigged with goodwill and a gout of acid liquid exfoliated his tongue, leaving a fair amount of grit behind. The top note was mouldy carpet and the aftertaste was indeed cat's pee. His own bottle remained unopened and he was to find it, some months later, among the tombola prizes at the village fete.

On the paperwork, however, Florian was as good as his billing.

'What you want to do,' he advised, hunting out leaflets from the filing system in his surprisingly well-ordered office, 'is to make applications under this new Stewardship Scheme. Hedges, landscaping, set-aside – you can get the whole lot financed as long as you say you're doing it all for tourists and/or conferences. We even do weddings now.'

'But I don't want to get into tourists,' Oliver protested. 'If I did, I'd have gone into leisure and catering. I want to produce food.'

'Just say you're going to do shearing demonstrations or something.' Florian gave an airy flick of his wrist. 'Or harvest mini-breaks or something. We do it. Converted the stables for grape-picking weekends and a few blending seminars. The Government doesn't actually want you to grow food, that's the thing. It's cheaper to buy it all from Israel or Guatemala or somewhere.'

'But surely . . .'

'It's democracy, Ollie. We've got to do what the majority of the population wants us to do.'

'You mean that because most people insist on buying tasteless food produced at a fatal environmental price by virtual slave labour in the Third World, because they don't think and can't think and want to spend all their money getting wasted in Ibiza so they'll never be able to think again, we have to give up growing anything at all?'

'A bit harsh, but yeah, that's about the size of it.' Florian said this in a calm, sad voice that pulled at Oliver's heartstrings. He saw that, behind the exquisite courtesy and Hugh Grant mannerisms, Florian was just as angry as he was.

'You're a terrorist, aren't you?' he said suddenly. 'You sit in your office here scamming the system because you're forced to by the regime.'

'Look, just get the forms,' said Florian, 'and I'll help you fill them out.'

As a banker, Oliver had been brilliantly slick at analysing political initiatives. As a farmer, however, he was pathetically inept at making those initiatives work for him. He never quite understood that the whole intention of official policy was to stop farmers growing food. When a man is about to realise his life's ambition, he doesn't want to know that it has been officially declared wrong. When a man has proudly volunteered to adopt the human race's primary profession, the very activity that separated humans from animals all those millions of years ago, he isn't about to admit that it is now a terrible mistake. However patiently Florian talked him through it, the concept was too ugly to get into his brain.

About ten thousand other farmers were in the queue ahead of him when the Agricultural Conversion Grant Part IV became available, so he missed the boat. His form applying for a Heritage Stewardship Award was a few checked boxes short of the bureaucrats' ideal. He soon lost heart; the application pack for the European Hedgerow Regeneration

Subsidy was so huge that he left it unopened in the log basket, next to the pile of unread bank statements.

Occasionally, when The Fieldcare Agency managed to attract the media's attention, Oliver, Colin, Florian and Jimmy watched their doom as it was sealed, speech by speech and scandal by scandal, on the TV in The Pigeon & Pipkin. The four of them spontaneously congregated there because they were the only unmarried farmers in the area and sitting at home alone to watch their profession die was just too hard.

Come August, when the skylarks sang from dawn to dusk in the cloudless skies and Colin Burton lost his profit on three fields of cauliflowers because they were not white enough to please the man from Marks & Spencer, when the ripening corn was turning bronze and Oliver's reserves had dwindled to a four-figure sum, he judged that his fields had become meadows and were ready to rock. His grass was a triumph. As dense as velvet, as fine as baby's hair, frothing with silver husks, springy to walk over, every new blade glistening with dew every morning. He planted a couple of fields of potatoes, and the sight of the young plants, waving their leaves like little green flags, gave him confidence. It was time for the sheep. He bought two hundred and they thundered down the ramp of the lorry that brought them like the firstcomers at a football match running for their seats.

Over the next few months about half of his ewes died lingering and distressing deaths. Lucy Vinny, the vet, a woman he would come to know much better in the months that followed, diagnosed poisoning from the toxins still present in the ground, a cocktail of pesticides and growth-promoters used when the farm had grown peas for a multinational frozen food company. 'It takes about three years to wash out of the soil to the extent you can actually raise livestock,' she said with an irritated sigh.

'I should have talked to you first,' said Oliver.

'Yes,' she agreed crisply, 'and I'm afraid you'll be seeing me again soon.'

'I hope so, I was planning on lambs,' he told her.

'I wouldn't advise it,' she said, patting his arm sympathetically. 'Not for a while.'

He went to the pub.

'Bloody useless sheep,' Colin said, through mouthfuls of Chicken and Broccoli Bake, 'always getting the bloody vet down for 'em. Get into ducks, that's where the money is.' He waved his fork expressively.

'What do you think, Jimmy?' Oliver asked him.

'About ducks? We've been fine with ducks this year. Price is holding up.'

'I meant about sheep,' said Oliver.

'Oh, sheep. Best do what vet says,' Jimmy said. 'We always done that.'

It could not be said that Oliver Hardcastle was a chauvinist. It was just that women didn't talk quite loudly enough for him to hear them, in the larger sense. Or maybe Lucy Vinny made a mistake by patting his arm, or by speaking so crisply and looking so certain, with her striped shirts and navy sweaters and neat little pearl earrings. Or by obviously preferring four-legged animals.

Lucy's life was her horses; nobody in the pub knew much about horses, but hers were certainly elegant animals and every now and then someone in a great flash car would come

53

from miles away to buy one, and make admiring remarks about her eye for good bloodlines. On Sunday mornings, Lucy took one of them out for a hack then sometimes came trotting down to The Pigeon & Pipkin for lunch and hitched the horse in the car park like a cowboy. It was the sort of rural eccentricity Oliver would have fancied indulging himself, but he was afraid of looking like a prat.

In this little morass of wistful denial and fantasy rejection that surrounded Lucy in his imagination, her message, telling him to forget about lambs, sank gently, and disappeared. And Jimmy's advice – well, Lucy and Jimmy had some funny understanding. Odd, since she was definitely on the posh tottie side and he was an old-style son of the soil, but they always did agree and she rented a couple of his fields to graze her horses. So Jimmy's opinion, Oliver considered, couldn't be relied on if Lucy was involved.

The ram glared at him from its web page, its creamy fleece almost touching the ground, its magnificent horns curling confidently down to its dusky cheeks. Oliver reached for his mouse and made the booking.

For a short time, all went well. The ewes seemed to like the ram as much as he did, and when, with the proper etiquette, they were introduced, most of them succeeded in getting pregnant. Then about half of them miscarried. Of the remainder, most managed to give birth, but every one of the lambs was dead within a fortnight. To bury the sad pile of fleecy carcasses, he hired a small JCB. When the bill for the burial took him into overdraft, he barely noticed. At first.

The bounced cheques finally gave him the clue, and Oliver sat down for a day of reckoning, at the end of which he concluded that he had no money. He found himself in the traditional position of an English farmer, in debt and up the creek. Full of righteous anger, he drove to London and marched into the offices of The Fieldcare Agency itself and demanded restitution.

A visit from an expert was promised, and some weeks later a woman with a cast-iron assumption of superiority and a briefcase full of leaflets arrived at Saxwold New Farm.

'I'm sure we can help you,' she began in the tinkling-cymbal voice of a person who's simply brilliant with theory and thinks practice is something that is only relevant to professional golfers. 'Our Protected Landscape Management Scheme is designed specifically for people like you.'

'Great,' Oliver responded, wondering why he felt so uneasy.

'Tourism is a definite possibility.'

'You mean, you want me to go on holiday until my soil isn't poisoned any more?'

'Ah, no.' She had been trained to expect some degree of intellectual challenge with a farmer interview. 'I mean diver sifying into farm holidays. A small hotel, that's something you could do.'

'No it isn't,' said Oliver.

'Of course it is,' she said, in the sort of voice people use when encouraging a three-year-old to get started with the finger-paint. She rifled through her briefcase for leaflets, saying, 'Farmyard experience weekends are definitely going to be the next big thing.'

'When I was a banker,' Oliver said, 'and people told me something was *definitely* going to be the next big thing, I knew I was looking at a no-hoper.'

'People with your skills are exactly who The Fieldcare

Agency hopes to attract into the countryside,' she assured him. 'I've got a very positive feeling about this.'

'That was the other thing that was the kiss of death, people saying they had a very positive feeling.'

'I can't see how we can move forward here without a positive attitude, at least.' She blinked.

'It's difficult to be positive after you've found out that your land is so sick that anything that eats anything that grows on it lies down and dies.'

'That's only a short-term issue.'

'So is my overdraft. I need to make some money.'

'Tourism can be extremely profitable.'

'I don't want to be part of the tourist industry. I want to be a farmer. Have you come here to tell me I've been wasting my life?'

The woman from The Fieldcare Agency seemed used to this line of argument. 'Nobody is saying that, Mr Hardcastle,' she replied, quick on cue. 'You *can* farm and have crops and animals and everything – er – traditional. Tourism just means sharing it with people.'

'But I can't have crops and animals, can I? My land is toxic, whatever grows on it comes up poisonous. That's why you're here. Hello?'

At last, a shadow of doubt appeared on her face. 'The Fieldcare Agency does recognise that people want the countryside to be cared-for, even if only for aesthetic reasons. There are some husbandry options which we can recommend as alternatives.' She rummaged in her briefcase. 'Leeches. For medicinal purposes. There is a demand for them from alternative practitioners.'

Oliver winced. She winced in turn. 'Well, if you don't like

56

that, we could look at other ways of achieving profitability. People in your position can escape the commodity trap by selling something for which customers will pay a premium price. Turf. Have you considered turf at all? Grass for people's gardens, you know.'

'Yes, I've seen a garden.'

She ignored his sarcasm. 'Or energy crops. I've just put a farm in Somerset over to a new strain of wheat that gives us a cereal starch from which compostable plastic bottles can be produced.'

'A new strain of wheat? How's that, exactly?'

'Oh well, if you have ideas about GM.'

Oliver suddenly felt very tired. He rubbed his eyes hard. 'Of course I have ideas about GM. I'm an organic farmer. We're not the first people you'd see planting genetically modified crops, are we?'

'Our job is to help people to reinvent themselves,' the woman said, sorting her leaflets into a neat pile and putting it firmly in his hands. 'I'll leave you to read through these and maybe follow up with you in a few weeks.' When, she implied, you've come to your senses and given up all this stupid nonsense about growing food.

Oliver threw the leaflets on his compost heap No 2 and went down to The Pigeon & Pipkin.

'Bloody women,' said Colin Burton, through mouthfuls of Thai Tuna Surprise. 'Think they can bloody tell you what to do.'

'Tough job but somebody's got to do it,' said Lucy Vinny, raising a mild laugh.

'She kept saying they wanted to attract more people like me into farming.' Oliver shook his head.

'I suppose she meant people with money to lose,' Lucy suggested.

'It was never going to happen. The moon was in Capricorn,' announced Florian.

'We know how it's going to bloody go, don't we?' Colin continued as if no one else had spoken. 'We've seen it with the electric, then the telephones, then the trains and then the bloody post office. Some government department gets itself a new logo and a fancy letterhead, gives itself some poncey name, the fat cats get fatter, price of everything goes through the bloody roof, nothing bloody works any more and a couple of years later the whole thing goes down the bloody tubes.'

The regulars around them bleated their agreement. Oliver felt comforted and bought another round.

'What you want to do,' said Florian, 'is get hold of some cow horns and bury them at each corner of each field on the first day of the waxing moon. They'll act like energy sponges, soaking up the earth's vibrations and cleansing the ground. I've got a few horns I'd be happy to pass on.'

'Thanks, Florian, 'preciate that,' Oliver mumbled. He never knew what to say when Florian started on with the New Age stuff.

The landlord of The Pigeon & Pipkin, skilled at making a profit from farmers' problems, decided to observe the ancient country custom of a lock-in, and it was 2am before Oliver got back to Saxwold New Farm. Halfway up his glowing oak staircase on the way to bed, the journey suddenly didn't seem worth making any more, and he fell asleep on the half landing, sitting with his back propped comfortably against the wall.

At 4am, he woke up. He was cold. His head ached, his throat was lined with sandpaper and his eyeballs had gone rusty in their sockets. He got stiffly to his feet and looked out of a window. Outside, in the icy March night, his poisoned meadows lay quietly under a blanket of white mist.

Not as quietly as they should have done. Here and there, the mist was churning. Now and again, the sound of a grunt reached him. In the surreal half-light he could see the field where his potato plants, which had been declared too deadly to be harvested, had been bolting away while he wondered what to do about them; now their tops were waving, they were agitated.

Oliver felt drunk, and cold, and stiff, and unhappy, and tired, but in this soup of misery he could also identify anxiety. He staggered out with a flashlight and found that he had company. A pale but cheerful face appeared, with a snout and floppy ears, and a mouth full of young potatoes. Another face loomed into his beam, then another, then many more. In his toxic potato field, there were pigs. Colin Burton's pigs. Hundreds of them, rooting around in the earth and snarfing down every potato they found.

'Stop!' Oliver bellowed into the misty gloom. 'Stop! Stop, you stupid animals! You can't eat that. You'll all be poisoned. Stop it! Get back!' He ran forward, waving his arms, tripped and fell face first in a patch of mud. The pigs, startled, lumbered around, flashing their ample pink buttocks, then trotted rapidly away, all in different directions.

Oliver got up and ran around after them for a while, then realised that his task was hopeless. Colin was too deeply and drunkenly asleep to hear the telephone, so Oliver felt he had done all he could, and decided to deal with his neighbour in the light of day.

Strangely, the pigs did not die. It was two days before they were all rounded up, in which time they ate almost all the vegetation remaining on Oliver's spread, and none of them suffered any ill effects at all. In fact, they had fattened very nicely.

'Pigs'll eat anything,' Colin Burton affirmed with pride, speaking through a mouthful of Salmon and Cauliflower Gratinee. 'There's nothing'll harm a pig. Why d'you think I raise 'em?'

'The pig is a natural detoxification plant,' Lucy Vinny informed him. 'Unbelievable digestive enzymes. At college we did experiments dissolving all sorts of things. Even safety pins.'

'The pig's cleansing capacity was well known to our ancestors,' Florian lectured him. 'The legend is that Ireland was infested with poisonous snakes until St Patrick introduced pigs, which ate them all.'

'What do you think, Jimmy?' Oliver asked his neighbour.

'About Ireland?'

'About pigs.'

'My dad always said you couldn't go wrong with pigs.'

This time, Oliver heard him, in the larger sense.

'You could consider high-welfare pork,' admitted the woman from The Fieldcare Agency when he telephoned to run past her the idea of raising pigs. 'Free-range, antibiotic free. That is the kind of premium-price product for which there is still a market.'

'Good,' said Oliver. 'That's it then. Problem solved. Why didn't you say so in the first place?'

'Our remit is to help the agricultural industry diversify.'

'I'm not an industry, I'm a farmer.'

And so Florian filled out a new sheaf of forms and seven Beccles Black Backs, six sows and a boar, arrived at Saxwold New Farm to save their owner's bacon. Over the winter, he got particularly fond of the smallest of them. She had two spots around her eyes, like a panda in negative, and as she chomped her way through his stunted crops she seemed to have a smile on her snout. When he came out with the feed bucket, she almost danced over to greet him. He had to call her Miss Piggy.

Six sows, of course, would not take him very far on the road back to solvency, but the tragedy of the lambs was the saddest experience of Oliver's life to date, and it had taught him caution. He steeled himself to make a budget and then, to get him through his first winter, he measured out a half-acre plot around the ruined farmhouse, and put it up for auction.

Sweeney, as the tabloids would later name him, was born in a very good area. His family home was a disused drain hole under a mound of brambles on a vacant lot at the back of a rotting old corner shop in the poshest part of Fulham, where the human inhabitants were utterly puritanical about sell-by dates. Every household put out a banquet in bin bags every week. Some of the residents actually put out food for the foxes as well. Sweeney's father, a third generation urban fox, had laid claim to the drain hole for the past two years. Sweeney's mother was his second mate.

The living was superb. Beside the domestic bin bags, there was refuse put out by the French restaurant and the gastro-pub, numerous well-fattened cats and puppies, occasional hamsters, gerbils and rabbits, hundreds of very slow pigeons and the sandwiches thrown away by schoolchildren. If they braved the traffic on the nearby high street, Sweeney's family could also count on kebabs, dropped on the street by people who were too drunk to eat them, and curries, regurgitated by the people who were too drunk to know they were too drunk to keep them down. Until he got the mange, Sweeney's father was relatively sleek. So, until she started feeding her cubs, was his mother.

Sweeney was one of seven. Todd, his brother, was first. Then brother number two. Then a sister. Then Sweeney himself, two more sisters, and a final brother who didn't look too clever. Their mother licked them, nestled her brush around them against the damp and cold and lay still to let them feed. Their father brought in a portion of Kashmiri Chicken, on the bone. This was in the spring.

In summer, the foxes taught their cubs how to hunt, taking them with them on their nightly patrol along the bin bags. Live food, of course, was more fun to hunt and could be the best eating, but it was hard to find a good kill. Pigeons in the park roosted out of reach during prime hunting time at night. Rats were plentiful by the railway line, but their taste was vile and they carried disease. Cats were good, especially young ones. Every telegraph pole on their street carried a home-made appeal poster for a missing kitten.

One night in the park they found a dying human, a huge carcass, lying on its back, limbs jerking in the final moments of life. The entire family gorged themselves all night. The cubs never forgot that feast, the taste of the soft, warm flesh and the sweet red blood.

As the temperature fell in autumn, the adult foxes began to scrap with their offspring and finally drove them out of their own territory and out into the world to find their own living. Sweeney and his siblings ran along the grey streets and the gloomy gardens, disputing the hunting with cats and the carrion with magpies as they searched for their own territory.

The youngest brother, still the smallest, froze to death in the first frost of winter. Brother number two was run over by a car. One of the sisters got gastroenteritis and died. Come January, the remaining sisters got to the open space by a railway line, where they found themselves mates.

Sweeney, being an animal fatally lacking in independent drive, followed his brother westwards. For a few nights they tried to move in on the yard of a factory where airline meals were prepared, but five foxes already based there fought them off. They tried the grounds of a tennis club, but the security guards had dogs.

When Sweeney and his brother made their big mistake, they were not particularly hungry. They too had succumbed to the mange, which itched like hell and made them tear out their own fur in lumps, but they were getting regular meals. They had found themselves reasonable homes in a public park, Todd in the prime site under the roots of a sizeable tree, Sweeney in a space under a shed.

In the daytime, a few humans came in and out of the shed and a lot of young ones played around it. In the evening, the shed was abandoned but soon plates of food appeared outside, put down by the humans. Pappy stuff, no fun to chew, but it kept the ribs lined. So the brothers were pampered. In fact, they got gung-ho, and started to come

out in the twilight, certain of finding the food and determined to get it before any cats did. Let alone the pitiful
hedgehogs whom the play-space workers actually intended
to feed.

The foxes were not hungry at all, just attuned, with their
black-and-white vision, to a certain kind of movement, the
spasms of a life in danger, the struggles of prey that was
already wounded, of which they had an instinctive memory,
enhanced by their experience of the dying man in the park.
Twitching limbs promised a feast. Slinking from under the
tree roots at the end of a day, Todd's eye was caught by just
such a movement. The leg of a juvenile human, sticking out
of some covering, flailing irresistibly.

It was so small, so young, so tender! It was going to be so
delicious! Todd seized the prey in an instant and pulled it
safely out of sight under the shed. The noise of his attack at
once woke Sweeney in his lair, and they managed a few good
mouthfuls before screaming humans found them and beat
them back. They fled to Todd's hole under the tree, lay low
for a couple of hours, then emerged again, hoping to find
that at least something remained of their great kill.

The park at night was normally dark and undisturbed,
except for a few male humans who would try to mate with
each other under cover of the shrubs. That night, to the
foxes' alarm, a large number of humans arrived, bringing
vehicles and strong lights with them. Suddenly there seemed
to be a pack of them in the park, howling and barking and
brandishing weapons.

Panicked by the noises and lights, Sweeney and Todd
streaked for cover. Their earths, they found, had been
blocked with rubbish. Todd was netted by the public

lavatories. Sweeney, making for the railway line, dared a clean run across the bowling green and was cornered in the subway, where he went down to a tranquilliser dart.

The fox brothers found themselves in cages, in a container that stank of dogs and cats, which, from the shuddering, swaying and roaring, seemed to be moving.

CHAPTER 3

The Smell of Real Money

'I never thought you'd go in for pigs,' said Bel Hardcastle, Oliver's mother. She gave a sad sigh and put an apple crumble in front of him. It was a Sunday and he was visiting her in her pretty little house in the south London suburb of Putney. 'Such rude-looking animals, I always think. And the smell. And the flies. Garrick! Don't do that. You'll get your nose burnt.'

Garrick, a golden Labrador who was still far below the age of discretion, had thrust his muzzle under her arm and was yearning in the direction of the crumble.

'Like them or not, pigs are the only thing I can farm until my soil recovers,' said Oliver firmly. 'Get down, Garrick. Bad dog.'

'He's not a bad dog, he's just hungry,' said Bel.

'He's not hungry, he's begging,' said Oliver.

'I suppose you could say you've made a right pig's ear of your farm,' cackled Oliver's stepsister Toni, who was, at that point, sixteen, with a bullet on a chain around her neck.

'Shut up, Toni,' said Oliver, picking up a spoon and getting stuck into the crumble. 'Anyway, the smell won't bother you here in London. Get *down*, Garrick.'

Bel Hardcastle passed her son the cream. 'Oh well, I suppose needs must when the devil drives,' she said, letting her voice tail helplessly away to dissolve the threatened sibling confrontation.

Bel Hardcastle liked old sayings. She liked everything old: old buildings, old furniture, old paint colours, old films on the TV on Sunday afternoons, old values and old photographs. She liked classic cars and vintage champagne, if somebody else was buying it, and old shoes that didn't pinch her toes.

At one point, with time on her hands between husbands, she had embroidered an old poem on an old piece of linen:

Grow lovely growing old
So many fine things do
Laces and ivory and gold
And silk need not be new
There is healing in old trees
Old streets a glamour hold
If all of these, then why not we
Grow lovely growing old?

When he was a boy, this embroidery had worried her son Oliver. He found something creepy about the butterflies and roses which his mother had scattered around the blue cross-stitch lettering. The wobbly line of the final question mark irritated him. The whole damn artefact symbolised everything about her that annoyed him.

Oliver had grown up with his mother and her various husbands in various flats in London. She liked old husbands, too, and they tended to prefer convenient mansion flats which were a short taxi ride from their offices. Nevertheless, Bel Hardcastle had always considered that her heart was in the country, because everything good and right and traditional about English life had its roots there. She believed this more passionately because her own roots were in Warsaw, where her Christian-born father and her Jewish-born mother had married in 1938, to the outrage of both their families. They fled to London only a few days before Hitler's army crossed the border.

Her parents brought Bel up to blend in, at which she had excelled. Urban as her homes were, with their narrow windows, fitted carpets and clanking radiators, she decorated them with historic English chintzes. Her furniture looked as if it had been inherited from a family who could trace their ancestry back to the Wars of the Roses, although she had bought it all at an auction in Chelsea. She got so good at it that it decorating in the English style became her profession.

Bel considered herself a countrywoman by proxy. She had lived in London all her life, but she read *Country Life* in the bath and *Country Living* at the hairdresser. She always kept a Labrador and had walked them in Kensington Gardens, Parson's Green and Putney Common, wearing green Wellington boots. While planting her summer window boxes, she fantasised about a country garden with hundred-year-old topiary and herbaceous borders. She listened to *The Archers* on the radio every evening, and again to the Sunday omnibus edition, and every time the announcer said, 'An everyday story of country folk,' she felt a glow of pleasure in her hard-won security.

Bel had been slightly startled when her son announced that he wanted to be a farmer, but since his planned career path promised to solve the essential difficulty with farming, which was the problem of poverty, she approved of it. Oliver really should have seen the next move coming.

'I'm not looking forward to pigs at the bottom of my garden,' she said.

Oliver generously ignored his mother's remark. She was getting a bit dotty, after all.

'It takes at least three years to get approved organic status for land that's been used for commercial farming,' he lectured his stepsister.

'You didn't know that before you took off, did you?' Toni said, watching with disdain as he ate.

'Of course I did,' he lied with a dismissive frown.

'Pigs will just root up my roses,' Bel persisted. Nobody took any notice.

'Anyway, I've sold the ruin,' Oliver continued. 'Went to auction on Wednesday. Telephone bid from London, cash on the nail. So that and the pigs should see me through until I get my organic certificate.'

'I know you've sold your ruin,' his mother informed them.

'You can't know,' said Oliver, with annoyance. 'How can you know. I only knew myself yesterday.'

'I know because I've bought it,' she said.

'You've what?' Oliver's fork stopped halfway to his mouth.

'I've bought the ruin. The farmhouse.' Content now that the conversation was going along the lines she had imagined, Bel gave herself a second helping of crumble.

'You have?'

'Yes. I have.'

'What do you want to do a stupid thing like that for?' demanded Toni, voicing her stepbrother's thoughts to perfection.

'Because it's time we moved out of London,' said Bel. 'My heart has always been in the country.'

'Yeah, well mine hasn't,' Toni said, her voice rising in panic. 'You can move wherever you want. I'm staying here.'

'You can't stay here because I've sold this house too.' Bel sounded dangerously reasonable. 'And earlier than I planned to, because of you, Toni. I've just got to get you out of London before it's too late.'

'Well, it's too late already and thanks for asking me,' Toni sneered, rising from the table in blind rage and treading on the dog, who yelped histrionically and ran into the hall. 'You can forget this stupid idea right now. I'm not going anywhere.'

And she followed the dog, and slammed the door.

'Have you thought about this?' Oliver asked, trying not to sound as dismayed as he felt. He could get out of the situation. It wasn't a done deal, it was his mother. He could just make her take the money back. Keep it in the family.

'Of course I've thought about it,' Bel said calmly, pouring more cream than she wanted to give herself strength. 'I knew you needed the money, and I knew you were having trouble selling the house. Well, it isn't a house, is it? It's just a heap of stones. I don't want to crowd you or anything, but I just can't take the risk with your sister any more.'

'Stepsister,' he said.

His mother ignored him. She lowered her voice and

70

widened her eyes to hint at the unimaginable evils that might befall a girl in the metropolis. 'She's had a ring put in her tummy button, Oliver.'

'Oh, keep up, Mum.' He was almost unkind. 'They all do that. It doesn't mean anything. She'd be a freak if she wasn't running along with her peer group at her age.'

'I can't keep vodka in the house,' Bel continued. 'She and her friends, they drink the most appalling amount. It's every weekend. They get ill. You know.'

'They're just asserting their right to behaviour formerly considered masculine,' her son informed her. 'It's only a phase. I'm sure all this binge-drinking and violence will be completely passé in a generation or two.'

Bel Hardcastle shuddered. She was a gentle woman and the mere word 'violence' made her feel anxious. 'A generation or two! That'll be much too late. She needs a man's influence in her life, even if it's only yours.'

'Cheers, Mum,' said Oliver.

'I've found things in her room,' she went on.

'What things?'

His mother got up and fetched her handbag. From it she produced a small plastic envelope containing a piece of card printed with symbols. 'It's drugs, isn't it?' she asked him.

'Er . . .' It was a while since Oliver had actually done any drugs himself, and fashions changed. Still, small sparkling chips of crystal, rather like downmarket diamonds, didn't seem to be making the right fashion statement for an intoxicant. 'I think they're some kind of makeup,' he guessed. 'They stick them on their eyebrows when they go clubbing.'

'Oh don't be ridiculous. What kind of fool do you think I am? Really, Oliver!'

'But you won't get her away from the drugs thing if you take her off to Suffolk,' he reasoned. 'Moving her to the country won't help. They're all doing stuff there.'

'Not so easily and probably not in the college car park,' Bel said. He recognised a resolute manner that his mother very rarely displayed. Hope of damage limitation began to drain away. 'And don't forget, Oliver,' she dropped her voice almost to a whisper, 'in a couple of years, when she's eighteen, she'll get her own money and I won't be able to do anything about it. Do you want her to be giving all her inheritance to the drug dealers?'

Toni was an heiress, something Bel never talked about because the thought made her so anxious she felt faint. Mr Lumpkin's brother, a gay man with a gift for property investment, had died before him and left his niece a small block of flats in Brighton and the accruing rents therefrom. Since his experience of life had led him to believe that all mothers were evil and that personal wisdom is perfectly formed well before the age of eighteen, he placed this little fortune in trust for Toni and made sure she would get all as soon as she was old enough to vote.

'Don't you see,' Bel pleaded with her son, 'this is my last chance to save her and get her into a good environment. If I wait any longer she'll be legally an adult, she'll have her own money and I won't be able to do anything, will I?'

'But you don't have to panic,' he tried to assure her. 'It's probably just a phase. Don't worry. I'll give you the money back, I'll find another buyer . . .'

'I do have to panic, Oliver. It's now or never. What's the matter with you, all of a sudden? It's as if you're annoyed that I want some of the nice quiet country life that you've been enjoying yourself the last few years. Let's face it, I won't be getting married again, will I?' Now Bel shifted to her personal warp-speed overdrive, emotional blackmail. 'You are my only son, after all. Why shouldn't I live somewhere we can see each other every now and then without having to plan it like a military operation?'

Oliver sighed. Part of what he loved about living in the country was living his own life, with all the freedom he could desire to exist on the slimy cuisine of The Pigeon & Pipkin, to leave his sweatshirts unwashed and talk bollocks to Colin and Florian and any other companions who were less than his intellectual equals.

A mother, at this time of life, just cramped a man's style. And his mother, unfortunately, was an absolute prize cramper. He could visualise the future too well.

Bel was capable of thinking up a dozen things a son could do for her every day. He could see his future with crystal clarity. Investigate the septic tank. Prune some savage rose. Change really fiddly light bulbs. Help her with shopping whose volume rivalled an international aid shipment. Talk to the tattooed thug at the garage about her car. Dig a vegetable garden. Get rid of the wasps' nest. Would you just, another little job, and while you've got the ladder out. Fix this. Pick up that. Have a little word, dear. A man's work was never done with a woman like Bel Hardcastle in the neighbourhood.

Nor would he ever hear the end of his filial obligations.

'Wouldn't you be happier somewhere like Cheltenham?' was his final throw. 'Suffolk's quite flat, you know. And cold.'

'And cheap,' Bel had said in a decisive voice. 'You need the money and I need a bargain. And a pension. Have you ever thought about what I'm going to live on in my old age?'

'You had a pension.'

'It's with Mutual Probity and it'll be worthless in a year, the way they're going.'

'You're making a good living.'

'It's very up-and-down, doing people's houses. And you have to have insurance, nowadays, and heaven knows what else. London's become a nightmare. The last job I did the parking charges cost more than the plumbing. And I've got debts to pay.'

'I'm not blaming you,' he insisted. 'Of course I understand. I just don't see why you have to come and ruin my nice quiet country existence.'

'Darling, you'll hardly know I'm there. We'll probably see each other less after I move in than we do now. Anyway, I've already bought it.'

'But I can give you the money back,' he said again, his heart once more sinking like an out-of-control elevator hurtling earthwards in a Hollywood thriller.

'My mind's made up,' she said. 'I don't want to talk about it any more. I shall have enough to do making the place habitable. Really, Oliver, you should be grateful that somebody's bought it at all. It's nothing but a heap of rubble.'

Saxwold Old Farmhouse was, at that time, slightly more than a ruin but still nothing resembling a house. It lay at the far end of the twenty-acre home field, just some old walls, a pile of blackened stones with a couple of charred beams sticking out of it, and a lot of ivy trying to cover the farmhouse's shame. Oliver had soon heard that the fire of 1997 had been started by the owner himself, faking an accident in his first attempt to solve his financial problems.

An old sepia photograph, or rather, a copy of an old sepia

photograph in the bar at The Pigeon & Pipkin showed that it had once been a fine small manor house. Oliver had no inclination to restore it himself. Homemaking, he felt, was a woman's job. Real men knew nothing of curtain headings and pargeting. 'The cottage'll do me,' he had said.

Twenty acres seemed quite a large field until his mother moved to the other side of it. From the front door of his cottage he had a direct view of the collapsing corrugated iron lean-to that was to become his mother's new kitchen. He had done very little to make his cottage comfortable, and Toni needed to complete her final term of school, so for a few trying months Bel supervised the rebuilding work from Putney by making constant telephone calls to her son.

Once the roof was on and the lavatory was installed, he saw her determined figure in new green Wellingtons, standing in the daily rain on the pile of rubble from which her kitchen would rise. He could hear her voice, a plaintive but persistent coo like that of a dove in lust, as she directed the builders.

Oliver heard another noise, even less sweet to his ears, the savage drone of a moped on which Toni raced up and down the lane. At heart, Oliver did love his mother, even if she cramped him. Toni, however, he detested. From the day she had arrived in his life, a sulking dead weight hanging from her father's veiny hand, he had felt a loathing so passionate he was almost ashamed of it.

Bel liked old husbands. She had married two of them quite easily, having a muzzy smile, creamy skin, Slavic high spirits and a way of flirting as if she really, truly, honestly didn't know what she was doing, all of which fitted exactly

75

the ideals cherished by many men over the age of sixty. Given that her stepdaughter felt no responsibility to treat her decently, her son was the only young thing that Bel Hardcastle really liked. Even though he was throwing his money away on his farm, driving her crazy by turning up his nose at every girl he met and showing no interest whatever in giving her grandchildren.

Her first husband, Oliver's father, an accomplished bon viveur, had fallen asleep at the wheel of his Jaguar on the road to a vineyard somewhere near Bordeaux, run into a tree and died when he was sixty-three, his wife thirty-seven and his son only eight. Her second husband, a bewildered but energetic widower in his sixties, had seemed like the perfect solution to all her difficulties, except that the surname he had to offer her was Lumpkin. He even came with a daughter, Antonia, then two years old and produced by her nanny with bows in her hair, who promised to complete the perfect boy-plus-girl family for which Bel had yearned.

They had ten happy years together before Mr Lumpkin, a clumsy man at the best of times, tripped over on a golf course in Majorca, knocked himself out and drowned in an artificial lake, making Bel a widow again, and not a rich one. Trustingly, she had spent her own money on Aubusson-style carpets and hand-painted murals at her husband's London flat, not realising that he did not exactly own it. He proved to be a life tenant only, and had died leaving her homeless and considerably poorer than when they married. Not to mention the problem of little Antonia.

The child was the only flaw in what had otherwise been a marriage of perfection. Bel had imagined that bringing up her stepdaughter would be a simple matter of handing over jam sandwiches three times a day and letting her play with the shifting population of adoring dogs and ungrateful cats that snoozed on various surfaces around their home.

She imagined that all children wanted what she had wanted, and indeed enjoyed, a childhood like a long sun-kissed dream devised by E. Nesbit. The parents' role was to provide visits to the zoo, Beatrix Potter books to read together and, for a little girl, adorable puff-sleeved cotton frocks with smocking and sashes.

That regime, without, of course, the frocks, had raised Oliver successfully, but did not work on his new sister. In the year before Bel Hardcastle came into her life, Toni's mother had left her, and her father, and disappeared. Bereaved, confused and two years old, Toni focused her feelings on the most blameable object in her universe, which was Bel.

From a very early age, Toni had seen herself as a ghetto child and taken a pugilistic attitude to her stepfamily. The terrible twos turned into the frightful fours, the screaming sevens and the traumatic twelves. By fifteen, she had developed hair like an electrocuted lavatory brush and mauve-lidded eyes, which glared menacingly at everyone who approached her.

Even in kindergarten, the things Toni could do to an adorable smocked frock were painful to behold. She said that zoos were cruel, and Beatrix Potter was one sick fuck. She was first suspended from school when she was five. Her main interests were vodka and black eyeliner, both of which she used to excess. When Bel moved her to Suffolk, rural life did not slow her down at all. Now her moped buzzed around

Great Saxwold until the small hours of the morning, sounding like the attack of a mutant hornet.

'Responsible land use,' Clare Marlow said to the Adviser. He was now her own Adviser, on loan to Agraria from the Special Adviser's department. 'Talk me through the PM's thinking on that.'

He coughed. 'To be honest, it's more the Chancellor. He's thinking about making land reform a plank in his housing strategy. The main plank, actually.'

'It was in the pre-pre-budget leaks,' she said. 'Anything new since then?'

He shrugged. 'Population set to grow at about two hundred thousand a year. Or a million every five years, two million per decade. Housing costs in the South East up another 17% in the first quarter of this year. Bottom line – the price of a small family house within commuting distance of London is now enough to buy a Saudi prince a palace. Only answer, as the Chancellor sees it, is to build more houses. Only problem, no land to build on.'

'Well, there is land, obviously.' Clare Marlow went out of London when she had to drive to an airport to go on holiday. Even around the airports, she had noticed loads of land just lying around idle, with nothing but a few trees on it or some sheep that looked rather grey. So much better if all that waste ground was turned into hotels or a fourth runway or something.

She also had memories, from her childhood, of vast boring spaces out somewhere beyond the airports. Her parents had occasionally made duty visits to relatives in these regions, piling into their Standard Vanguard and toiling down a road signed to Basingstoke. These trips were not holidays. They were the duty an English soul pays resentfully to its blood ties. A holiday, to her mother and father, involved a charter flight to Spain. All England had to offer was tedious grass, pointless hedges, messy old trees, acres and acres of mud, and, of course, the rain. Why, the whole country was just rotting away out there.

'Oh yes,' he agreed, 'there's plenty of land. It's the right sort of land that's the problem.'

'The right sort of land?' Clare frowned, her brain-wheels spinning. 'Shall we say: appropriate residential resource?'

'Absolutely.' God, the woman was worth her weight in gold. She was almost worth what they'd agreed to pay her. 'Appropriate residential resource. Absolutely.'

'Which is what?'

'It's not what people think it is.'

'Well, things never are what people think they are. In what way?'

'People think that . . . appropriate residential land is a brownfield site.' Did she know what that was? She gave nothing away, it was hard to tell. 'A place that's been built on before.'

'Old Army base, old airfield, old graveyard, old factory, old bus garage . . .'

'You've got it.' He thought about mentioning the Millennium Dome but decided against. OK, that had been a brownfield site, but people didn't talk about the Dome now. The word had left the language. A chain of pseudo-French restaurants had renamed itself. At New Millbank, if it was necessary to mention a semi-spherical structure, people were going for 'cupola'. 'The King's Cross cupola,' he'd heard people say. Cupola was kinda cute, kinda European, kinda post-Tate-Modern. So . . . don't mention the Dome.

'But a brownfield site isn't appropriate,' Clare prompted him, wondering why he'd suddenly gone blank on her. She'd allowed forty minutes for this meeting. Ten seconds of silence was just a ghastly waste.

'It's the development cost,' he explained. 'Your people are working on a paper for you. Basically, greenfield sites are up to two-thirds cheaper to build on. No old drains to dig up, no old power lines to rip out, no existing structures to raze, no problems with chemical residues or anything like that. Just turn up on Day Zero and start building.'

'I get that,' she told him, trying not to sound impatient. 'And this is Agraria's problem why?'

'Because . . .' Here it was, the pitch, the big one, the real reason she'd been hired, the justification for the salary bigger than the national debt of a small country. 'Most of the greenfield sites we've identified are actually agricul- tural land. There's literally thousands of acres of redundant farmland out there, and we've got to find a way of getting hold of it.'

'So? Can't you buy it? Farmers aren't averse to making money, are they?'

'Well, actually yes, there is a faction you could actually say that about, according to the groups we've done in the rural communities. Bizarre attitudes, some of them. And there's protective legislation, of course. Ghastly cat's cradle of laws that go right back to World War Two. Labyrinth of planning regulations too. But the Chancellor's office have done a brilliant job rationalising the whole nightmare, just sweeping away the old mess and putting in place a simple system of checks and balances administered directly from Whitehall, cutting out all that potential for provincial corruption and speeding up the whole process. That'll be in the next pre-budget leak.'

'So it's a problem of perception, then?'

Yes! She *was* good, damn good! 'Exactamente. It's all down to information management, working with people's expectations of the countryside, that kind of thing. People need to realise that our cities are living organisms and should not be contained by crude and insensitive planning legislation.'

She was making notes. The great thing about women ministers, he'd noticed, they made notes, rather than getting their assistants to ring up your assistants the next day and ask for your notes.

'And what's the problem with these people?' Clare asked.

'We've found that there's a lot of clinging on to the old-style romantic ideas about the rural environment. Even after everything, the swine fever, the salmonella, the foot and mouth, the dioxin run-off, the tornadoes, the two-headed lambs, the radioactive sugar beet — after all of that, there's this hard core that want to believe all that Victorian non-sense about a green and pleasant land. And there's a lot of arrogance too. People think they've got a right to enjoy green space which they haven't paid for.'

'Well,' she said, in a dangerously reasonable tone, 'my predecessor didn't help you there.'

'I know,' he sighed, careful to keep the sigh regretful, not apologetic. 'All those TV commercials for farm experience holidays and rural tourism.'

'All that guff about landscape stewardship. Landscape stewardship! Nobody can pronounce that, what were they thinking?'

'It seemed an appropriate response in that time frame. Back then, people didn't appreciate that agriculture had a part to play in the bigger picture. That's what the PM meant when he decided to look outside the political sector for a CEO.'

'So what you're telling me is − nix to all the Fieldcare policies, slam on the brakes, screaming wheels, whole new direction, why waste land growing grass when it could be your new patio? '

'Basically, yes.'

'Right,' she said, rising to her feet in her eagerness to meet the new challenge. 'Why isn't that paper ready yet?'

She was holding out her hand to shake goodbye. He experienced something between an arm wrestle and martial arts throw, and found himself in the outer office, walking past her assistants on his way to the lifts. Oh, the joy of a corporate-sector appointee! The new Minister's time-management skills were truly awesome. And she was so tall.

The new Minister sat down and called in her civil servants. They had been a disappointment to her. The Blob, as she was calling her predecessor for short, had at least hired in some younger faces, but they had not been the hottest graduates of their years. Some of them had degrees from the University of Exeter rather than from Oxbridge.

Exeter, Devon, indeed all the territory west of Basingstoke, Clare now regarded as her own personal Afghanistan, a godforsaken mountain fortress where the last of the fanatical terrorists were probably holed up in caves, wearing the Barbour instead of the burqa.

'Responsible land use,' she said to her staff. 'That's my strategic focus. Our priority targets will be in the South East. I want maps. Land-use maps. Kent, Sussex, Surrey, Hampshire, Wiltshire, Warwickshire, Avon, Nottinghamshire, Cambridge, Essex, Suffolk, Norfolk . . . basically, everything south of The Wash, excluding Wales. And Cornwall, you needn't bother with that.'

'Ah . . .' There was always one. The one with the spiked hair and the white skin.

'Yes?'

'Sorry, you've lost me, Minister. The wash?'

'It's a geographical feature of the east coast of England,' she filled him in. 'Approximately the same latitude as the North Wales coast.'

'Er . . .'

'OK, make it everything south of Birmingham then. Am I clear?

'Oh, yes, Minister. I've got it now.'

'I want viability figures, cost per acre per product, that kind of thing. How many square miles it takes to produce one cow, one ton of wheat, a million eggs. As much as you can get. With global comparisons. As disadvantageous as possible to the UK. The land cost of the same product in Canada, Brazil, South Africa, France. We've got to get home to people what the real price of the food on their plate actually is.'

'Ah . . .'

'Leave the metaphors to me. Your job is to get me the figures. I need data to work with here.'

'Ah, when . . .'

'Tonight.'

Such colour as their faces had drained away.

'If you need technical support, call it in. I need this data.'

'Ah . . .'

'That's all. I'll see you again this evening.'

Evening! The staff twitched with shock. This was not, traditionally, a long-hours workplace. Except during the crises, of course. In the normal run of things, Agriculture was the one ministry that could get you home in time for *EastEnders*. After a moment of stunned immobility, they slunk away, hoping feebly that this regime was just a new broom showing off, and that next week the Minister would settle into their old routine.

Clare Marlow thought of the planned lunch with her daughter again. Very important to keep Miranda on side. A successful politician might be allowed one embarrassing offspring – George Bush, Margaret Thatcher, Ronald Reagan, Winston Churchill, none of them damaged by the antics of their less-than-perfect children. But two . . . well, two was different. Especially if two meant both. Therefore, all.

If all your children were failures, well, what did that say about you? Even the Queen had managed to get one of her kids right, more or less. Besides, being seen with a presentable daughter showed that you were in touch with the young.

She wasted a minute of thought on her son. Simon had been born the way he had intended to go on, skinny and inconsolable. Now he was somewhere in the Midwest of America teaching youth with even less intelligence than himself all about the reptile people of Atlantis and their intergalactic conspiracy to take over the earth. The tabloids hadn't picked up on Simon yet, but it was only a matter of time.

There was nothing to be done about her son, which made it all the more imperative to secure Miranda as an asset. Clare was thinking a spread in *Hello!* magazine, a fashion feature in *Vogue*, maybe something in *Vanity Fair* even, or a lifestyle interview in the *Sunday Times* at least. Much co-operation would be required of Miranda. And it was about time the girl got herself a partner, too. She must be pushing the envelope of the median age range for a woman to be single.

Perhaps it would take a carrot, a bonus, a bribe, a sweet-ener of some kind. What sort of thing did her daughter like? Clare found she had no data. She had noticed Miranda's regrettable taste for young, cute and brainless men, but she had simply deleted the information, as she did with any-thing that conflicted with her vision of how things ought to be.

In her car on the way to the restaurant, the solution came to her. In business, when a team needed to bond, you sent them off to a country house hotel somewhere to get drunk and go paintballing, in between blasts of new management mantras and brainwashing with the corporate strategy. Why not do the same thing with her daughter?

What they needed was a weekend at a country house hotel, some place with chintz bedrooms and log fires, per-haps a cut above the usual venues for corporate bonding, a place with a good gym, nice food, fine wine. Perhaps they would be able to stroll through some landscape on Sunday morning. Dress it up as a low-stress detox rebalancing weekend. No paintballing, of course. Nothing messy, good heavens, no. The thought of anything drippy or squidgy or sticky or squelchy made both Clare and Miranda feel positively nauseous.

Two miles to the east of Suffolk, on the icy waters of the North Sea, a trawler rocked on the swell, its engine idling. The night was cloudy, and the only illumination came from the searchlight mounted on the wheelhouse. The shaft of light picked out the black shape of a rubber boat on the deck, and the form of one of the crew, moving around the craft, releasing the ropes that held it to the deck.

Two younger men came forward to help him, their inexpert fingers slipping around the knots. The older man waved them aside. Tolvo stood back and folded his arms in his heavy jacket. He looked up into the darkness. No stars. No Rigel, no Aldebaran, not even one of the Seven Sisters. Ever since he had been a small boy, craning against the glass of his bedroom window on the eleventh floor of an apartment block on the outskirts of Vilnius, Tolvo had felt that the stars were looking after him. When they were not visible, he felt superstitious.

He looked out over what he knew was the sea. An occasional pale smudge where a black wave broke out a cap of foam was all his eyes could register. 'No moon, no stars, not much wind,' he said, hoping to convince himself as well as his friend Juri, who was standing beside him swigging the last of their vodka. 'No trouble. Perfect.'

'Perfect,' Juri repeated. 'How far is it?'

'Not far,' Tolvo said.

'Not far,' repeated the fisherman, trying to give encouragement. 'Ten minutes, for strong young guys like you. Just get in and paddle. Don't stop or you'll freeze. Keep the boat behind you. You'll see our lights, at least. Keep them at your back, you'll be OK.' He raised his arm out into the blackness, indicating the right direction. 'Ten minutes. No problem. Just keep paddling.'

He'll say anything to get rid of us, Tolvo thought.

From the wheelhouse, the captain shouted, 'Get them away, what are you hanging about for?'

'Right,' said the fisherman. 'Take the other end.' Tolvo grabbed the thin nylon rope that ran around the edge of the rubber craft. The three of them dragged the dinghy to the side of the trawler and heaved it up on the iron gunwale.

The fisherman said, 'You're lucky there's no wind. Give her a good shove and there's a decent chance she'll stay the right way up. I've got the rope, don't worry. One, two . . .'

On 'three' they pushed the craft over the side and heard it fall on the water. The fisherman made fast his rope and fetched a flashlight. 'Your lucky night,' he told them. 'It's the right way up. OK, over you go. Big one first.'

In truth, neither of them could fairly be called big. Both nineteen, never well fed in their lives, they were skinny and small. Juri, two inches taller, red-haired and round-faced, had the honour of being considered big when compared to Tolvo, who was fair-haired, and hollow-cheeked, and even in babyhood had dark circles around his eyes. Juri gave the fisherman his bag, climbed over the side of the boat and down the metal ladder. From the last rung he jumped, landing squarely in the beam of the flashlight, helpfully held in the centre of the dinghy.

'Your friend's not an idiot,' the fisherman said, throwing Juri's bag down after him. 'What more can a man ask for, eh? He could get a job doing that.'

'Not where we're from,' Tolvo said at once. 'Would we be here if we could get a job doing anything back home? There are no jobs in Vilnius. Not unless your mother's fucking the foreman.'

'Yeah, well,' growled the seaman. 'Get moving, your turn.'

Tolvo threw his bag down and then, clumsy in gloves and boots, struggled over the side to the slippery rungs of the ladder. When he had stood on the deck the ship's rise and fall on the swell had seemed as peaceful as the breathing of an animal asleep. Now it seemed to toss viciously as if trying to shake him loose and hurl him into the water. Death in thirty seconds, that was what they said about falling in the sea in winter. He wanted to be an astrophysicist, not a gymnast. Below him was nothing. The rubber boat was a lump of black on the black waves.

'For fuck's sake, get those brats off the boat!' He heard the captain's roaring voice above the crash of the swell.

'Jump, Tolvo!' Juri encouraged him. He could make out the pale circle of his friend's face.

'Don't make such a fucking racket!' the captain yelled. 'Let 'em go to hell, I can't risk this any longer.'

Tolvo released his hold on the ladder and leaped in the general direction of Juri's face. He landed in the nose of the boat, shipping an icy splash of water as he fell, and the free rope tumbled on top of him.

'OK, well done, that's it, don't panic.' Juri was gabbling rubbish, dragging him up to a sitting position by the shoulder of his jacket. 'It's OK. We're cast off. We're free. Here – take your paddle. Get this thing moving. Only ten minutes. Keep the lights behind us.'

Resolutely – to be anything less than resolute was to let

fear wash over them like the freezing water, in which case it would have been simpler to just lie down and die right there – they settled side by side, stuck their paddles into the inky sea and propelled the boat forward. The air froze their faces. Behind them, the trawler engine clanked into action.

'Fucking bastards,' Juri growled between his teeth. 'They're going to turn. We won't be able to see them. We'll be rowing round in circles.'

'It'll get light soon,' Tolvo assured him. 'In the east. So if we keep going west, we're bound to hit land.'

'If we don't get caught.'

'Well, if we get caught we'll get a warm bed and a decent meal before they ship us back to Vilnius. How bad can it be, eh?'

'Don't talk crap,' said Juri.

'It's not crap, I heard it from this guy at school. Somebody in his family was sent back by the British police and they'd been kept in a hotel, with food vouchers and everything. This is a really rich country, Juri. You've no idea.'

'You'll believe anything. However rich they are, they didn't get that way by being stupid, did they? Let's just shut up and paddle.' But Juri dug into the water more cheerfully.

In an hour, the sea around them began to lighten. Their mood lightened with it. The waves were breaking in caps of white foam and the sky behind them showed a couple of sickly stars. Ahead was darkness. A stubborn line of darkness. As the skyline paled, the land showed up, as black as a slice of hell.

'Is that it?' Juri asked.

'Got to be,' said Tolvo. 'Unless we've paddled so far

around England that it's France or Holland or some other fucking place. It's land, whatever it is.' The dinghy, he realised, was heaving beneath them. The sea was rising. 'We're getting a wind to carry us in, too. You see, God's on our side. I told you.'

'You don't believe in God.' Juri stopped moving, paralysed by the final arrival of success in his life.

'Keep paddling, mate,' Tolvo implored him. 'Or we really will go round in circles.'

In another hour, they were staggering through a thin crust of ice over shallow water, dragging up their boots from the muddy bottom at every step. There was enough light for them to see their dinghy, which they had abandoned behind them, floating up the creek on the tide. The wind in the reeds made a ghostly whine and every now and then, where the rising water broke the thicker ice, a crack like a shot echoed over the shore.

Tolvo found a bank ahead of him, climbed on it, and stamped his feet to get the blood flowing again, then jumped for joy. 'It's England,' he said, still not daring to raise his voice. 'We've made it.'

'Well if this is England,' Juri gasped as he floundered from the mud to join his friend on solid ground, 'it's a fucking puddle of mud and it really stinks.'

Tolvo sniffed the icy air. Cold as it was, there was a distinct pungency about it. 'Who cares?' he said. 'Whatever it is, that's the smell of real money. I can get used to it.'

'Have you ever been to a Farmers' Market?' Miranda asked Dido, on the phone from her office.

'Of course not, angel. Why would I do that?'

'Well exactly,' said Miranda. 'But we've got this job in from Birmingham for a new shopping centre and they want a space for a farmers' market.'

'Don't they know they're a city? I mean, how many farmers' markets are there in Manhattan?'

'I know, I know.'

'What do people do there?'

'Buy food, I suppose. They must be people who cook, mustn't they?'

Buying food. Miranda didn't like the idea. Food meant fat, and fat meant failure and failure meant hatred and hatred meant death. She lived in terror of food. The fear of eatables ran in her mind all the time, like the stock market prices running along the bottom of the screen on the TV news. Living proudly on the edge of what she assumed to be hunger, everything she might eat had a moral weight to which she was sensitised. Bread: bad. Cookie: horrific. Chocolate: obscene. Apple: unnecessary.

No junkie was more powerfully conscious of how long it had been since the last hit and how long it would be before the next one. Nor more attuned to where the next hit would come from. Miranda had a mental map of her life on which all the food outlets she had to pass flashed food alert warnings: the coffee shop on the corner – beware the muffins! the kiosk at the station – danger! chocolate!! the kebab shop on the way home – toxic hazard!! chips!!!

What she thought was hunger was something else, a corrosive mixture of guilt and anxiety which ached in her stomach. Miranda had never been honestly hungry in her life. Instead, she had learned from birth that food was her enemy. Her childhood had been fenced about with food prohibitions: no milk, it gave you allergies; no squash, it rotted your teeth; no butter, it stopped your heart; no sweets, they sent you mad; no tuna, it would poison you.

She was winning the war against food, but the battles were another matter. Get up, eat nothing. Go to work, eat nothing. Get through another morning with the Urban Phoenix Group, eat nothing. Get a report written, eat nothing. Go to a meeting, eat nothing. Come back from the meeting – surrender to the coffee shop, eat a cream cheese Danish with a mocha grande. And pass the rest of the day in sugar shock, and drink a bottle of wine, and get a chocolate bar from a vending machine and be eating naked toast at 2am. Go to bed. Get up, eat nothing.

Sometimes she was thin. Sometimes she was very thin. Sometimes she was not really thin. All the time, Miranda had food in her thoughts. It was different for Dido. She could smoke. Miranda could not smoke because smoking also killed you and her mother would disapprove.

Cooking was worse than food. Cooking was as scary as free-fall parachuting. Being alone with all that food! Being intimate, vulnerable, out of control in the presence of the enemy! Cooking was something Miranda was afraid to try.

They both knew people who cooked, of course. Miranda's Will had been proud of his green curry, and Dido's mother had been able to roast a chicken when the occasion demanded it. They saw that cooking appealed to some people, but they were sure it would never be part of their lives.

Her general intention was to eat only in restaurants, where food was controlled by somebody else, and could easily be rejected and conquered. You had to order something, but there were always ways of not eating. Miranda tended to play safe and ask for chilli sauce to pour over anything that might tempt her.

When they had to be at home with food, the answer was to buy something ready-cooked, tamed and enslaved, less threatening to them. And pretty. Pretty food, somehow, was not so frightening. Dido sometimes bought luxury ready-meals from a late-night supermarket. Miranda sometimes bought sushi boxes from Pret A Manger. The colours were so delicious, especially those little green chips of cucumber. Cucumber: harmless.

'The thing is,' Miranda said carefully, aware that her friend was hard to motivate and could be volatile, 'that people who go to these farmers' things must be sort of the target market. But I don't know about them. I'm not sure how to approach them.'

'You mean you want to go to a farmers' market and find out what kind of people use them?'

'Yes. I think I should, don't you?'

'Angel, don't ask me, what do I know about your job? They're probably just people with nothing to do on Sunday. I mean, I've got nothing to do on Sunday either. So if you want to do it, let's go. When are these things anyway? They do have them in London, I suppose.'

In the end, they fixed on what was billed as a Spring Food Fair in Covent Garden, which offered the compensations of going shopping for shoes at the same time then, perhaps, if they had the energy, being able to check out the Tate Modern in the afternoon. Sunday in London could be a real problem.

'The shopping is important,' Miranda insisted, making a note on her Palm. 'Good retail outlets. Part of the destination concept.'

On reaching the Fair, they strolled curiously between stalls stacked with cheeses and jams that had been set up, incredibly, in front of the boutique windows, obscuring the displays of tiny sweaters and skinny frocks. The air was full of the smell of freshly baked bread, which they tried not to inhale in case it made them hungry. Miranda believed that if she felt hungry all the time, she would eventually get used to it and not feel hungry at all. The plan wasn't working very well. Her mother was having a career change, there would be fall-out. Three times in the past week she had found herself diving into the corner café for a culpable muffin. On that Sunday morning, she lasted seventeen minutes before suggesting they hit the coffee stall.

'They look s-o-o-o-o-o ordinary,' said Dido and she wriggled on her chair, flicking her curls from one shoulder to another as she inspected the passing crowd. 'Is there supposed to be something special about market customers? I mean, they're just all sorts of people, aren't they?'

'Mmm,' Miranda mumbled over her coffee. 'Keep it down. I don't want to be obvious.'

'Oh gosh, yes, sorry.'

Out came Miranda's Palm again, and into it went notes. Smoked salmon. Apples. Game pies. Women, C2?, 25–34. Men, AB, 45–54. Tourists. All sorts, just like she says. Browsing. Tasting. Carrying purchases. Parking?

'Oh. My. God,' said Dido.

'Mmm?'

'Oh. My. God. Look over there.'

'What? Where?' Miranda could see nothing but food: hams, huge glowing masses of meat, dangling indecently from the nearest stall. Beyond them she could see biscuits, simpering wickedly, half-veiled in transparent plastic. Opposite was the goddamned bread that had got them into this mess, great billowing floury crusty loaves flagrantly lolling about in baskets. If Dido was going to fall for food, Miranda felt she would be in real trouble.

'Next to the bread,' Dido said. 'Isn't he gorgeous?'

She knew that languishing tone. It was a man. Panic over. Where was he? Next to the bread. Next to the bread was a really hideous stall, done up with curly fake ironwork and a painted sign in faux-copperplate reading *Château Saxwold*. For heaven's sake.

Behind the stall was a man who, she saw with foreboding, was exactly Dido's type. Pretty. Messy. Probably mad. Long bronze hair in a ponytail. Freckles, the poor sod. Great big Bambi eyes. Wrapped in a navy blue apron on which was printed a facsimile wine label that also read: *Château Saxwold.*

In the blink of an eye, Dido was at the stall, not even trying to look interested in the pyramids of wooden boxes and their gleaming glass contents.

'Hello,' said the man.

'Hello yourself,' said Dido.

Miranda hurried after her friend. It was her role in these episodes to give Dido as little as possible to feel embarrassed about afterwards. The two of them were standing in helpless silence, trying to think of something to say.

'So . . .' Miranda scrambled for a good conversation starter. 'You make your wine in England.'

'I have a *domaine* in Suffolk.'

That word – *domaine* – was so exotic it made Dido hiccup. Fortunately only once. It was an immensely appealing event, making her curls waft around her face as if stirred by the same zephyrs that are forever blowing flowers on Botticelli's new-born Venus.

'My vines are grafted on Pinot roots from Italy. Some of them, anyway.' He was speaking as if suddenly short of breath, his eyes a little large and a little fixed, well and truly held in that trance which all Dido's passions fell into more or less the moment they met her.

'Do they like living in Suffolk?' prompted Miranda. He wouldn't snap out of it. They never snapped out of it until Dido moved into their homes. Then snapping took place within hours, although the parting usually took a bit longer. At least, Miranda predicted, she would have her place to herself for a couple of weeks.

'Oh yes. Our slopes face south and are sheltered from the east, so it's ideal. We work according to biodynamic principles, which means managing natural forces to maximise the health of the plant. It was the Romans who brought vines to Britain originally.'

'What,' murmured Dido, 'have the Romans ever done for us?'

'Exactly,' he said.

An angel passed. A couple more angels passed. A damn squadron of angels flew by in formation, trailing pink love smoke in their slipstreams.

Miranda, desperate, said, 'Do you do tastings?'

'Oh, heavens, yes.' The man almost snapped out of his enchantment. He flourished a corkscrew, selected a bottle from a half-barrel of ice water beside him, and opened it. The wine was the flaring yellow of high-visibility jackets. He poured three splashes into short-stemmed glasses.

'Pinot grapes have red skin but clear juice, so you can

make red or white wine with them. This is something I'm trying at the moment, quite a complex blend.' He picked up his glass, held it by the foot, swirled the liquid and sipped.

Miranda copied him. A jot of liquid shrivelled her tongue. This must be how oysters felt when lemon juice was squeezed on them. Oysters: harmless. Lemon juice: good. In the wine, the dominant note seemed to be screen-wash, with a strong aftertaste of cat's pee.

Dido picked up her glass by the foot, giggled, raised the glass, stumbled on a perfectly flat pavement and splashed most of the wine over herself, in the region of her right nipple.

'Oh dear!' the man cried, as if she had crumpled before him in a dead faint. 'How awful of me! Your sweater! And it's so cold! Here, let me help you!' And in another blink of an eye he was standing in front of his stall, in front of Dido, dabbing the spill tenderly with a perfectly clean tea towel emblazoned with the legend: *Château Saxwold*. She held her hair aside for him. And his free hand and her free hand were drifting irresistibly together, they were touching, they were nestling, and entwining, and drawing closer . . .

'Here he is,' said someone outside the magic boy-girl bubble. Miranda turned to see a dark woman with a to-die-for shearling jacket, bearing down on them with — no, it couldn't be. Yes, it could. Yes, it was. The ears. The nose. The apologetic stoop, the hands behind the back. Prince Charles was beside her. 'This is our famous new wine-maker,' the dark woman said, her voice as rich as espresso truffles. And the man disengaged from Dido, stepped forward and bowed as if he'd been taught how to do it at school. Which, in fact, he had.

Confusion broke out, and the boy-girl bubble burst, and Dido was actually rubbing her eyes in surprise while the proprietor of Château Saxwold bustled about answering royal questions, finding glasses, flicking his cloth about and pouring more wine.

'Come on,' said Miranda, pulling gently at her friend's damp sleeve. 'We've got to go.'

'But . . .' Dido was still looking around in bewilderment, as if the spell had only moved away a few yards, and if she could find it and step into it the bubble would enclose her again.

'Let me give you this,' said the man, suddenly snatching a few seconds' break from his well-drilled fawning while the royal one sniffed earnestly at his glass. He pressed his tea towel into Dido's hands, which were clasped at bosom height in the pose of a pre-Raphaelite princess. 'You might need it. And if you aren't totally put off . . .'

Dido squeaked in distress.

'Perhaps I could invite you to one of our tastings?' A card was plucked from the back of the stall and pressed on her after the tea towel. 'They're quite informal. I'd love you to come. Do come. Won't you? Look, there's a map on the back . . .'

The royal one had swallowed his wine and appeared to be in some distress.

'The Angevine just adds that lovely fresh finish that people expect of an English wine,' the man said, turning back without missing a beat. 'In this year particularly, when we had a late spring, the Pinot grapes were a little on the pale side . . .'

'Come on,' urged Miranda, and Dido agreed to be led away in the direction of a taxi.

After two hours of sleepwalking around the art gallery, answering in dreamy monosyllables if Miranda tried to hold a conversation, she suddenly came back to earth, grabbed Miranda's hands, and said, 'What did you think? Isn't he divine?'

'Yes.'

'What do you mean, yes? Just yes?'

'I mean yes. What do you want from me? Yes, he is divine.'

'You don't really think so. You're just saying that.'

'Yes.'

'What does that yes mean?'

'It means yes, you're right, and no I don't really think so, and yes I am just saying yes.'

'But how can you not think he's divine? Did you see his eyelashes?'

'Yes.' Miranda was wary. 'I saw his eyelashes. Look, does it matter what I think? He obviously thinks you're divine. That's what matters, isn't it? He invited you to taste some more of that filthy wine.'

'God, it was filthy, wasn't it?'

Miranda whistled with a relief. 'So you're not completely out of your mind.'

'Oh, but I am,' Dido assured her, shutting her eyes in bliss.

CHAPTER 4

Hi. Goth. Ick.

Sleepily, the warden of the Kensal Rise Urban Farm snapped on the lights in her office, then hurried through to the reception area and turned on the lights there. The clock on the wall showed that it was nearly 2am. Her hand was almost shaking with sympathetic anxiety. How long had the poor animals been kept in fear?

Carole pushed up the sleeves of her over-large sweater. In the examination room, she wiped down the table with anti-bacterial cleanser and turned up the heating. Then she went back to her desk to wait, leafing through the Farm's record book to pass the time and comfort herself with her past achievements. Injured pigeons sent to the Blue Cross, orphaned hedgehogs homed, the donkey saved from a funfair.

Occasionally, she had pasted in a press cutting and occasionally a photograph showed her. At these pictures, she turned the page quickly, covering up her lined face and her spidery limbs. Her mission was to protect animals now. What she looked like didn't matter any more.

Once, Carole had been photographed for a living. Crazy days. A top model, living on Marlboro Lights and cocaine. Her name was still well-enough known to get her a newspaper headline when she needed one. Her face, deeply lined and never made-up, was a ruined travesty of the face that had fronted million-dollar cosmetics campaigns.

She kept one of her old photos in a frame on the wall; it served to get her respect from strangers. Since those days, year by year, everything except the animals had disappeared from her life. Friends didn't understand that the animals came first. Men just took advantage. People she worked for wanted their pound of flesh.

Her hair was still long and blonde, but there was no life in it, and her eyes were still big and blue, but they saw the world through thick spectacles because who could be bothered fiddling with contact lenses when there were animals suffering? Vanity was such a terrible waste of time. Her voice could still be soft and low, but she got so angry with the world that it was often strident.

Blue lights flashed outside the office window. The buzzer at the door sounded and she got up to let the police in. The sight of the foxes, cowering in their cage, was almost too much for her. 'Oh, aren't they just beeyoootiful! Hello! Hello, there! Oo-so-cute! Oo-so-sweet! What gorgeous brown eyes you've got! What a great big fluffy-wuffy tail you've got! And who's this? Is it your great big fluffy-wuffy sleepy-weepy bruvver?'

Frantically, Todd scratched at the bars of his cage, in his terror treading on Sweeney, who lay beside him, still groggy from the effects of the tranquilliser dart.

'Bring them through here,' she said, opening the door to

the examination room. 'They'll be fine here until the vet arrives.' Two policemen, wearing thick leather gloves, carried the cage through the door and put it on the table.

'Careful now. Take it easy,' she wasted a few words on the constables before turning back to the foxes. 'There, there,' she soothed them. 'There, there. All over now. All safe. We'll give you a nice dinner and then . . .'

'No food until the vet's seen them,' one of the police ordered. 'This is a forensic. We'll be wanting them . . .' He found he couldn't use the word 'destroyed' to this babbling ninny. 'Put to sleep,' he finished, in a confidential tone.

'Why?' she demanded, angry in an instant.

'They attacked a baby, that's why,' said the second policeman, defensive in the thickening atmosphere of sentimentality. 'Little mite'll be scarred for life. The doctors said she might lose a leg, even. We're going to need rabies, stomach contents, everything. Our vet's on his way now.'

'They didn't mean to,' Carole argued. 'Foxes in their natural habitat never approach humans. They've been driven mad by urban living, that's all.'

'Whatever,' the second policeman said. 'Tell that to the kid's parents.'

Carole turned her back on him and gave the fox her full attention. 'Poor foxy-baby,' she crooned. 'Poor little thing. Don't be scared, little one. Don't be frightened. Who's a handsome boy, then, with his lovely white whiskers? Who's a bit gorgeous, with his sexy black socks? Oozy-woozy-snoozy-cutie-whiskerchops!'

The policemen looked at each other and turned to leave. Then the second constable had a thought. 'I'll need a receipt,' he told her. 'And watch out they don't escape. Crafty, foxes are.'

'Highly intelligent animals.' She rummaged reluctantly for a suitable piece of paper. 'That's why they adapt so well to urban living.'

'Yeah, well,' the second policeman responded. She created the document in round, childish handwriting with four-petalled flowers instead of dots on the 'i's. The police took it and made for the door and the fresh air of the street.

'Don't you worry, snootie-cutie-soxy-woxy-whiskerchops,' Carole said to it, wiggling her fingers at him through the bars of the cage. 'We'll have the Urban Wildlife Protection Act on 'em in the morning.'

At a less stressful time, the fox might have found her fingers, bony as they were, quite appetising.

When Toni Lumpkin arrived in Suffolk, and found that she was hundreds of miles away from her friends, who immediately deleted her from their speed-dials and never bothered calling again, she ran away and took the first coach back to London.

Back in Putney, her friends grudgingly offered her the use of their bedroom floors, but she had to keep moving on before their parents tumbled. She had no address, and nobody would give her a job without one, and she was afraid of going to the dole office because they would find out that she was under eighteen, and send her home, and anyway she had no address for the benefits, so she had no money. Very quickly, her friends got twitchy, then frosty, then impossible to find. Eventually, she called the Old Farmhouse and suffered the humiliation of being collected by Oliver and driven home.

She spent the first few weeks crying, sleeping and putting on a lot of weight. Came the autumn, and she was forced by her cruel stepmother to walk half an hour down a muddy lane to the bus stop, then take a one-hour bus ride to college in a poxy little turnip-head town every day. Life was bleak for Toni. But then she found Goth.

Goth was there on the Internet. An idle browse at 3am, when the goddamn owls (or whatever they were, probably they were rats but her stepmother was too stupid to realise) were flopping about in the attic above her head driving her crazy and Goth just popped into her thoughts, so she looked for it, and found sites all over set up by Goths who had kindly posted reports of all their activities, and pictures of themselves in their wonderful gear, just to give a kick to somebody like her.

Goth saved her life. There was music to download, fabulous stuff that howled in her headphones as if the people who played it knew all about not having any proper parents left and being stuck in the muddy freezing backside of Suffolk and having to get a bus and go to college. She dyed her hair black, shoplifted fishnet tights and found some wicked crochet gloves and a couple of lary old crucifixes in a junk shop. Going into college in her first outfit was an excellent experience. The rest came naturally.

'She needs a father figure,' wailed Bel to Oliver, feeling that it was somehow judgement on her lifestyle that Toni had sprayed 'Goth 4 Ever' on the wall of the Sports Hall in the neighbouring village of Yattenham St Mary. 'Someone to set boundaries for her.'

'Don't look at me,' Oliver protested. 'I'm not about to be anyone's father.'

'She's in that pub every night — could you at least have a word?' his mother implored him. 'They must know you in there.'

'I can't ban her,' protested the landlord of The Pigeon & Pipkin, when Oliver made the request. 'That sister of yours is literally my profit margin for the month. I haven't done so well since foot and mouth when we had all them slaughter-men and Army types come in. Your sister's keeping me in business. Her and her friends.' Oliver's follow-up argument, that Toni was underage, withered on his lips.

Heaven knew where the friends had come from. No sooner had Bel congratulated herself on saving Toni from the bad influences of London than the bad influences of Suffolk had flocked to her side, drawn to the glamour of Goth like moths to a flame. The tawdry calm of The Pigeon & Pipkin was shattered by stocky girls whose calves bulged above the tops of their fetish boots and etiolated youths with bolts through their eyebrows and black nail varnish.

The landlord put down a floor in a lean-to at the back of the bar, installed a Western-style saloon door and imported a pool table. Half the bored youth of the county was soon to be found in there of an evening, striking menacing poses and glowering at the other customers, who thought they added a nice bohemian touch to the ambience. Especially that girl with the skintight lace shirt that showed her bra. And most of what was inside it. And the one with the black leather skirt, she wasn't bad either.

Toni had a gift for leadership. The Saxwold Sukkubi, as she decided they should be, soon spawned imitators, and her moped became a style icon, so swarms of black-clad rural youth soon buzzed around the lanes on weekend nights, visiting each other about their Gothly business, which was mostly finding delight in each other's company and hoping to discomfort anyone without a visible piercing. This was a tough assignment, for tolerance had taken root in those parts, and was doing better than the potatoes.

Toni's first graffiti on the Sports Hall was soon joined by other messages: Batz From Hell, Goth Will Never Die, Kabbalah Kannibals, decorated with pentagrams and obscene sentiments written in runic. Delighted, a new lecturer at the nearby art college obtained funding for a module in graffiti art, and sent his students out to copy this manifestation of street culture.

The days lengthened, the holidays began, her stepmother was always on her case about getting a job and the summer evenings went on for ever. 'We'll have a graveyard party,' she announced to the Sukkubi. 'Get candles and some bottles and stuff.'

The Goths sat around in the churchyard of St Oswin's, Great Saxwold, in the balmy August nights slugging back cider and arguing, by the light of red candles filched from Bel's dinner party drawer, over the proper form for a satanic ritual. The vicar welcomed them warmly, proposed a joint service at Harvest Festival and reported to his bishop a real breakthrough in the diocesan inter-faith mission.

'Right, we're getting out of here,' Toni told her followers in disgust. 'We're not having some poxy vicar playing his poxy guitar at us. We want a rally on the beach. Show our strength. Flex our muscle. Have a bit of a rumble with the pikeys from outside, maybe. That'll make them take notice.'

On the first day of the August Bank Holiday weekend, the Saxwold Sukkubi planned to get together on the sand dunes at a nearby seaside resort to hold a mass rally. Word of the event spread, as Toni intended it should, and inspired other bands of young in time for them to organise. To the south, they styled themselves the Colchester Hellcatz and in the north they became the Bungay Vampires. When all three clans met in front of the candy-coloured beach huts, they fell into pleasant conversation, admired each other's jewellery and swapped cigarettes. No pikeys appeared to taunt them.

The *East Anglian Times*, desperate for a real news event at any time and doubly so in the dog days of summer, sent down a photographer. Anglia Television, already committed to a documentary series titled *Tribal Britain* and hard up for undiscovered clans, sent a researcher. What had been planned as an enjoyable day of outrage on the beach degenerated, in Toni's opinion, into a media circus.

Passionately, she harangued her associates from the roof of a boarded-up ice-cream kiosk. 'Don't buy into their conspiracy! Goths refuse to be media victims. We despise the hypocritical values of those who seek to stifle the voices of protest! Fuck off back to Norwich, media scum!'

The wind whipped her words away. Puzzled, the black-draped crowd dragged on their cigarettes and stood about amiably, kicking up the sand. Only the TV reporter, who was angling her camera about eighteen inches under Toni's chin, heard what she had said.

'Brilliant!' the reporter encouraged Toni, batting her Betty Boop eyelashes. 'Could you give us a bit more that we can actually beep?'

'Tosser!' Toni yelled, exasperated. 'Get out of my face or I'll do yer!'

'Fantastic!' the reporter said, and went to organise the crowd into a menacing squad who chanted 'Goth forever!' and followed up with some well-choreographed stone-throwing.

By then the Old Farmhouse was in its final stages of restoration. Toni's bedroom, in which she spent as little time as possible, had carpet, a white-painted four-post bed with muslin curtains, and flower-sprigged wallpaper. She said it made her feel sick and dragged a mattress up into the attic.

The house was coasting through the final phases of its redemption. A nice girl from Norwich had come and marbled the skirting boards. The kitchen garden was planted and running to a glut of beans and tomatoes. The drawing room had sofas, huge billowing items covered in Bel's favourite chintz, and on one of these, on that Sunday, Bel was dozing gently to the distant hum of the dishwasher, planning to wake at cocktail time and catch up with the week's news review on the television which twittered comfortingly in the corner.

'Scenes of violence on the beach at Southwick yesterday when gangs of local youths clashed . . .' she heard. Bel half-opened her eyes. Oh no. Gangs. Violence. This was what she'd left London to escape.

'Get out of my face or I'll do yer!' she heard, and recognised the voice.

'Good God. Toni!' She sat upright and watched the rest of the bulletin, which featured Toni and her companions at length.

'Toni! Have you seen this! Whatever did you mean, you'll do her?' Bel asked in a disingenuous squeal so piercing that Garrick startled in the gnawing of his Sunday bone. 'Toni! Come here at once. Go and find her, Ollie darling.'

Oliver pretended to hear nothing and continued with the preparation of his mother's first vodka and tonic of the evening. When she felt offended, Bel had a way of launching these faux-innocent enquiries which both her children found maddening.

'What?' Toni demanded, scowling at the doorway.

'You're on television,' said Oliver.

'Oh, for Christ's sake,' said Toni, flinging herself horizontally along the chintz sofa, so she looked like a giant black slug in a rose garden. 'So what?'

'No, but I don't understand!' Bel protested, pleased with this response. 'What were you all doing there? What did you mean, do her?'

'Can you call another woman a tosser?' Oliver enquired, walking carefully around Garrick to hand his mother her tinkling glass.

'I can call you a tosser,' Toni retorted.

'And what's that, as well, a toaster? A towser. Whatever you said.' Satisfied with the line the dispute was taking, Bel sipped her cocktail. 'Lovely, dear. Just how I like it.'

'Well, of course you can call me a tosser,' Oliver argued, 'but I don't think you can apply that term to a woman.'

'Pathetic,' growled Toni. 'I'll do you and all, if you don't get off my case.'

'Will somebody just tell me what she's talking about?' Bel appealed. 'I'm not up with all these crims, whatever they are, or this gangsta rap or whatever they call it. What is all this doing-you business?'

'You know what she means,' snapped her son. 'You're just putting on this stupid act.'

'I am not!' Bel protested happily. 'I just want somebody to

tell me what Toni was talking about. After all, if my daughter goes on the television I'd like to know what she's saying.'

'Stepdaughter,' said Toni to her mother. To Oliver, pointing at the glass, she said, 'Do I get one of them?'

'I don't know,' he answered. 'Do you? I mean, have you got legs, are there hands inside those spiderweb mitten things and are you actually quadriplegic and do you want a drink enough to get your arse into gear?'

'Dar-ling!' his mother reproved him. In Bel's worldview, the primary function of a man was to keep women happy. When she herself was the woman in question, that function assumed paramount importance. When all that was involved was the pouring of a drink, that function was a sacred duty. When, as in this case, the simple application of old-fashioned good manners would stop an argument turning ugly, there was no higher duty a man could perform.

Reluctantly, Oliver returned to the recently distressed oak side table on which his mother kept alcoholic supplies for her drawing room and reached for the vodka. 'Ice?' he hissed at Toni from between clenched teeth.

'Ice'n'slice, cheers,' she answered.

'Toni!' Now Bel was really offended. 'I don't mind you being Gothic, or whatever it is, but I can't stand you being vulgar!'

Oliver skirted the dog a second time and placed a second tinkling glass on the polished silver coaster by his stepsister's ear. Toni sank more deeply into the sofa, kicking her booted legs. An outraged yelp was heard and the dog scrambled to its feet and ran for the door.

'And don't be beastly to Garrick,' Bel added. 'He's only a dog.'

*

Carole sat at the least conspicuous corner of a table, in a room above a video store on one of the massive traffic interchanges for which central south London is notable, and doodled on her agenda. The meeting was still on item three, Letter-Writing Campaign, and it was 9.30pm. Around the table sat nineteen people, who were all younger than her, drooping, scratching their beards, massaging their temples and coming to the end of a wrangling debate.

'Are we all agreed now?' the Chair asked them. 'Are we all agreed that every local group will recruit a minimum of five volunteers to do letter-writing and delivery for the Death Threat Sub-Committee? Letters to be delivered by the end of April this year?'

Among members of GLAAC (Greater London Animal Activism Caucus) there was some murmuring.

'No, I'm sorry,' declared the Chair, a non-assertive man who resented his role for requiring him to assume authority. 'We've been through this, there's no other way the Death Threat Sub-Committee will meet its targets. It's essential that the threats go out in time to get to the MPs before the Fish Farm Bill, so when our guys introduce our amendment on psychological stress in oysters, the key people understand just how serious this is. We've taken a vote, it's a clear decision by the majority of the Caucus sitting in official session.'

'Death threats don't work,' complained the delegate from Highbury.

'We don't know that, there's never been any research,' countered the delegate from Brentford.

'Typical scientist, going on about research,' parried Highbury.

'Well, pardon me for wanting a few facts,' Brentford sneered.

'WE ARE AGREED,' declared the Chairman in a firm voice. 'ITEM FOUR. URBAN FOX CONSERVATION.'

Involuntarily, Carole shrank into the neck of her sweater. This was her moment. Her paper was among the bundle before them. In this company, she knew she was permanently guilty of the crime of glamour, and therefore needed to tread carefully.

The Chair turned to her without smiling. 'Move to congratulate you, Carole, on the fantastic media coverage this week.'

'Congratulate the animals,' she suggested at once. 'Weren't they adorable? Those photographers were just going ga-ga all over them.' Invoking the new Urban Wildlife Protection Act, she had succeeded in getting the two foxes protected by a court order while an inquiry into the alleged attack on the baby took place. They had been named in the process.

'What are they called?' the photographer asked.

'We haven't chosen names yet,' Carole told him.

'Well, we'd better think of something. They'll want to know their names. What do you call a fox, anyway? Mrs Tiggywinkle?'

'That's a hedgehog. What was the fox called? Mr Tod. That was it.'

'Todd, then.' The photographer wrote the name on a piece of scrap paper. 'That one with the black feet. And this one can be Sweeney.'

Before Carole could protest, the accused foxes were named after a nineteenth-century cannibal mass murderer. She

112

looked apprehensively around the table, and was relieved to see nothing but jealousy on her colleagues' faces. The pictures taken at the photocall at the Farm appeared on the national news throughout the evening and the next day the front page of both the *Sun* and the *Daily Mirror*. The *Sun*'s headline read 'CONDEMNED'. Seven hundred and forty-three readers had called the paper offering to adopt the foxes.

'We second the motion to congratulate,' said the delegate from Brondesbury. There was a chorus of yessing around the table, with much nodding of heads.

'Absolutely,' the Chair agreed. 'Minute that, OK?'

'But we need to focus on the bigger picture,' she ventured. 'While we've used the legislation successfully, this does highlight the growing problems we are experiencing with urban foxes.' There was more nodding around the table; from Brixton to Richmond, everyone, it seemed, was aware of the fox situation.

'What we should be asking ourselves is, are these animals happy? I mean, this incident – alleged incident, I should say – only happened, if it did happen, of course, because of the stress the foxes were suffering in an urban environment.'

Again, a chorus of approval. So far, thought Carole, so good.

'If my colleague from Brentford will allow it, there is research on fox behaviour, quite a lot of it that was done prior to the Hunting With Dogs Act. I found no mention of attacks on people. What is alleged to have happened is clearly not in their nature. It's we humans who have turned these animals into killers. Potential killers. Possibly.'

'We get it,' the Chair reassured her.

'So I'd like to propose a strategic sub-committee on urban foxes,' she said, hearing her voice fade with nerves. 'We should be giving these poor animals a decent chance to live in their natural habitat. We should set up a repatriation programme. Reintroduce them into the wild.'

'Good thinking,' murmured Highbury. Brentford sniffed. Brixton and Richmond leaned forward and spoke together.

'Are you putting yourself forward to head this up?'

'I would say,' the Chair put in swiftly, 'that given her achievements this week and the profile Carole has acquired thereby, that she would be the natural chair of such a committee, if we were to convene it.'

Richmond thought of his track record with the wetland voles and the meagre coverage that had been worth. Brixton thought of his achievements with the Coldharbour Cockatoo Project, which had led to his first TV appearance. No, Carole was not going to ride off with their glory on the back of a couple of foxes. Just because she had once been a model. 'Point of order,' Brixton began, with a graceful grin to indicate that his protest was being made in ironic spirit, 'point of order, Chair. If I might remind you . . .'

The Chair groaned to himself and, under the table, started to compose a text to his partner waiting at home. After this, there was going to be a guest presentation from AASS, the Anti Apian Slavery Society, proposing an action plan to liberate oppressed bees from their hives. And four more items on the agenda after that. It was 10pm already. No chance of breaking before the pubs shut.

'Isn't it nice to get a bit of time just for us?' Clare Marlow said to her daughter.

'Lovely,' Miranda agreed. Her mother was looking glossy, the way she did when she was very pleased with herself. In a few seconds the mystery would be solved. 'I was thinking – have you got something to tell me?'

'Well, yes, actually, I have.'

'Oh God. No, sorry, I didn't mean to say that.'

'Of course you didn't. And it's not "oh, God",' her mother told her. 'It's "oh, good". At least, I think so.'

'You mean, good news?'

'Yes, darling, of course that's what I mean.'

Miranda quailed, as usual. If a phone call from her mother made her feel like a worm, lunch usually made her feel as if she was role-playing Slobodan Milosevic on trial for war crimes. Whatever she said, she'd be condemned anyway. All the hours and the effort that Miranda put into being excellent, ace and generally perfect would suddenly seem about as useful as Slobodan's passionate lifetime commitment to Serbian nationalism. And to make it worse, you knew that the whole world would be watching.

She had done all the perfect stuff, all the same. She had bought a new outfit, because her mother had seen all her snazzy little presentation combos already and would be bound to tell her so. She had had her hair cut, her colour refreshed, her nails painted. The night before she had done an extra hour of yoga, to make sure her whole being was as calm as it could be, and during the morning she had had a yoghurt with her coffee so she wouldn't feel hungry and lay herself open to criticism of eating too much. Lunch with mother was obviously salad, and heaven help you if you ate it all. They had before them two piles of gutless green stuff grown in Dutch polytunnels and reeking of balsamic vinegar, of which only a few leaves would actually be eaten. Lettuce, thought Miranda: harmless. But oil: death.

Miranda had memories of her mother being different. There had once been a Mummy who had long hair and went about in dresses and played silly games at bathtime. That Mummy had once got slightly cross when her brother, Simon, climbed out of the bedroom window and played Spiderman over the flat roof at the back of their house. That Mummy had occasionally bought cakes and had actually fried things like fish fingers for her children to eat. Miranda had a clear but astonishing memory of that. Fish fingers. Most of the time, as far as Miranda remembered, that early Mummy had smiled and been nice to her.

Everything seemed to change at the same time. Mummy started her business, Miranda started her periods, Daddy started living at his university and Simon started to get weird. Then Mummy turned into Clare, and wasn't at home so much. When she was around, she was hard to please and very rarely smiled.

The new Mummy had short hair and her lovely soft tummy disappeared. She stopped wearing dresses and started to wear suits. She was always very worried about wasting time. Miranda assumed that all these changes were natural things that happened to people as time passed. After all, she had changed herself, from a silly little girl into a fully fledged high-achieving almost-perfect woman.

Just occasionally, Miranda caught sight of herself in a mirror or a shop window and noticed a look in her eye that was — well, you could say, defensive. Wary. Almost hunted. But it was just the way the light fell on her face.

'So what do you think of my new job,' Clare asked her daughter.

'Congratulations,' hazarded Miranda.

'It's really exciting, being in politics. Well, in government, anyway.'

'Goodness.' Miranda found this a useful all-purpose response with her mother. 'I never thought my mother would be an MP.'

'A minister.'

'How did they do that?'

'Safe seat. By-election. They can do that when someone's got the skills they need.'

'That's great,' said Miranda, wondering what this new job for her mother was going to mean for her. She knew Clare. She'd known her all her life, after all. Clare would not be wasting time with her. There was an agenda.

'Don't you want to know why they chose me?'

'To be a minister? Yes, of course. Sorry, I'm feeling a bit blank this morning. Minister of what?'

'Technically, it's Agriculture. But we're doing something about the name.'

'But you don't know anything about farming.'

'That's not the skill-set. They, meaning the Government, need someone good at managing change.'

'Great,' said Miranda. It seemed to be an acceptable response. 'Will you have to be photographed at agricultural shows and things?' The idea of her mother in green wellies, pinning a rosette on a cow, seemed completely unfeasible.

'Well, I'll have to be photographed,' Clare said, trying to sound as if it was going to be a cross she had to bear. 'Probably with you, at some point, if that's OK.'

Aha. So that was it. Miranda breathed a little easier and said, 'No problem. Whatever I can do to help. And Daddy?'

'I suppose so.'

'Shall I ask him when I see him? It won't be for a few weeks.'

'Darling, would you mind?' said Clare. 'I'm going to be so busy. It would be a real help. When the time comes.'

Mr Marlow could seldom be tempted out of his college at Cambridge. He had made ground-breaking discoveries about the metal trade in pre-Roman Britain. Once or twice a term, he invited Miranda to a college function, an evening that would act on her nervous system like some deadly drug used by Amazon Indians to paralyse piranha fish. Although she liked her father. He'd always been your stereotypical nutty professor, sweet and vague and good at losing things, and amazingly impressed when she found them for him. He seemed to like her, as well. If she asked him, he'd probably turn out for a photograph with her mother. Then scuttle back to his college on the next train.

Now that her role in this new drama was on the table, Miranda relaxed a little. She ate half a cherry tomato. It looked as if it had oil on it, so she left the other half.

For a while, she let herself believe that she just might have got away with it. Her mother was – bloody hell, she was positively hyper. Becoming a politician seemed to have induced a state of instant euphoria. Now Clare was glowing, excitable, up, up, UP. Her eyes sparkled. She was smiling constantly. Being nevertheless a tall and elegant woman, she came over rather like some crazed warrior queen. She even said something nice about her daughter's new sweater.

For a silly moment, Miranda had wondered if the good

news was going to be that her mother had found a new man and was going to propose divorcing her father. Which, in Miranda's opinion, and the opinion of everyone else who knew them, would be the honest thing to do, since Mr and Mrs Marlow were living lives so far apart that they only met for Christmas and, as now seemed likely, the occasional photocall when Clare needed to look normal for the media.

'How's the Clerkenwell Swoosh?' Clare asked her daughter.

'We called it the Sweep,' Miranda corrected her. 'Swoosh had connotations of globalisation and capitalism.'

'Very wise,' Clare approved. 'The Clerkenwell Sweep. Anyway, how's it going?'

'The planning inquiry began last week, we think it'll take at least six months.'

'That long?'

'That's par for the course, Mum. Planning is a long process. Just hearing the Church submissions about the graveyards will take a week. Six months is quite quick, really.'

'Graveyards. Oh yes. Well, you'll let me know if there's anything I can do, won't you?'

'Oh, sure.'

'Seriously, darling. I've met some bishops lately.'

Rats. The wonderful thing about urban renewal, when Miranda had drifted into the profession, was that her mother had almost no reason to be interested in it. Apart from the occasional argument about the right ingredients for the perfect shopping mall, there had been no grounds for maternal meddling in her career. Now she could see that Clare was set to become a control freak on a scale that would make

Napoleon look laissez-faire, and, God help everyone, she would soon have the power.

'So, how's it going to be, being in politics?' Miranda enquired, hoping to start a diversion.

'Early days, of course,' her mother mused. 'I think I'll have to wake them up a bit, of course.'

'Pretty laid-back, are they?'

'Yes, darling, you're right, the old regime were so laid-back they were practically horizontal. They're in for a few surprises. I made it a condition of taking the post that they had a complete corporate makeover, new logo, new name, everything.' She made it sound as if her department was due for compulsory hair-and-makeup. 'Tell me,' she dropped her voice confidentially, 'what do you think of "Agraria"?'

'Agraria?'

'As a name.'

'Name for the department? Oh – ah – great. Really great.'

'Not too sort-of classical?'

'More neutral. But modern. And efficient. I do like it.'

'Excellent. There's going to be such a lot to do, Miranda. Which is why I thought we should make some plans.'

Now what?

'You've been working so hard, darling.'

'Not more than usual,' Miranda said, feeling doubts rising like floodwater.

'Well, yes, you do really drive yourself, don't you?'

'Wonder where I got that from?'

'I know, I know. I'm just as bad. A terrible role model for you.' *This was not looking good.* Her mother never admitted anything. Nor did she ever play for sympathy. Unless something cosmic was coming down. 'And it's going to get worse. I'm preparing a very important announcement for the next round of pre-budget leaks and our people are going to be number-crunching night and day. I'll have to be with them.'

'Of course. Ordering in the curry at midnight, all that stuff.'

'Is that what people do in your office?'

'Oh yes. When we've got a big job on, we just get dinner for everybody from The Light of Kashmir. That way saves people sloping off early and leaving me to pull the whole thing together at 3am.' Curry: total disaster. 'I just have the raita, of course,' she reassured her mother quickly.

'Darling, I'm right, you know I am. You never used to eat curry. It's got more calories than any other restaurant food, you know that. You must be stressed, if you're turning to that kind of junk. You're doing too much.'

Damn. She'd walked into that one, all right.

'Do I look tired, then?'

In the normal way, Clare would have been the first to tell her daughter she looked as beaten-up as a marathon-runner's socks. For some reason, that didn't seem the right response now. What was needed here was not the motivational stun gun but something else. Concern! That was in the right area. A special kind of concern, a sort of soft, warm duvet-like, wrapping-up kind of impulse. Motherly concern! That was it. How the hell did the motherly stuff go? She had, she realised, suffered some loss of parenting skills.

'You look fine,' she told Miranda, groping for more words. 'Terrific. But . . .'

'But what?' Here it comes. It'll be the haircut. Or the streaks. Or the shoes. Fine? Terrific? What would have been the problem with pretty? Other people thought she was pretty. Tequila Boy thought she was pretty. Actually, what he'd said was, 'Still pretty.'

'I'd just like to spend some time with you,' her mother was saying. Lamely, for God's sake. 'You know. A one-on-one or something. When all this is over. Over for a while anyway.'

'Meaning?'

Motherly concern, motherly concern. 'We could get away to relax a bit. Share a bit of downtime. I was thinking about a holiday, darling. Just a little one.'

'A holiday?' Holidays were not Miranda's favourite. They gave you time to think. She was afraid to stop working for fear of finding out what her life added up to without work. Who needed the time to get bored? Or to be exposed to all that foreign food. Olive oil: fatal. And a holiday always put stress on a relationship, and her relationship with her mother . . . well, Miranda just didn't want to go there.

She hadn't had a holiday for at least five years. Her mother had a peculiar expression on her face, almost anxious, almost concerned, almost . . . maternal. Maybe this new job was going to change her. Miranda was not used to registering her mother's interest, at least, not in this clichéd sort of way. 'Where were you thinking of?' she ventured.

'I can't do anything long-haul. And Europe would be a bit sensitive, given we're going to have to take a stand on the New Common Agricultural Policy. But I thought, maybe a little holiday together. I don't know where the time goes. I never seem to see you. I thought . . . a weekend some-where . . . a long weekend, of course.'

Miranda's heart was touched, a sensation she usually tried

to avoid. Her mother actually missed her. Actually wanted to be with her. Was actually proposing a weekend together. A weekend away. Well, how worm-like could you bear to feel, for just a weekend?

'Somewhere really nice,' Clare was saying. 'Like a country house hotel or somewhere. We could just flop out and be pampered for a few days. Go for some walks, or something. Have a cream tea.'

A cream tea? My mother has just censured me for being in the presence of curry and ordered steamed fish, a glass of water and a salad with dressing on the side. She knows perfectly well there are enough calories in a cream tea to feed an African village for a week. Why am I not more suspicious, Miranda asked herself. Why do I think this is quite a decent idea? Why have I suddenly gone all silly and gullible?

Miranda felt a most definite yearning for things she wasn't sure she'd ever experienced but still associated with comfort – things like old oak trees, satin eiderdowns and home-made jam. Subliminal visions of leafy lanes leading to half-timbered houses flashed across her mind. A Proustian blast of scents wafted past – new-mown grass, wet earth, roast lamb. All of which was bizarre, considering she'd been brought up on duvets, yoghurt and concrete.

There was no denying this multivalent craving. To her own surprise, she heard herself say, 'What a great idea. A weekend in the country! That'd be just heaven, Mum.'

'Really?' Clare was blinking. She had been fully prepared for her daughter to pull that disparaging face she knew so well, to slump as if fatigued by the mere effort of communicating across the years that separated them, to let out that half-stifled noise between a sigh and a sneer, and to say she was really much too busy to take a weekend out and what was Clare thinking to have such a stupid idea?

'Of course, really,' Miranda followed up, downing the last of her peppermint tea and preparing to wrap up the encounter. 'Would you like me to find a hotel? I could book for us. Just give me some dates. Get your assistant to give me some dates.'

Ten minutes later Clare's car dropped Miranda at her office. After they parted, the new CEO of Agraria sank back in her seat in a strange reverie, the documents she'd brought for the drive untouched beside her. Her mind ran on with sunlight dappled through a canopy of leaves. Apple crumble. The noise a Wellington boot makes when the wearer knocks her foot against the doorstep to loosen its grip on her heel. A dog wagging its tail, a Labrador, of course.

Clare Marlow shook herself. Labradors, Wellingtons, apple crumble? Everything she hated about the bad old England. The whole concept was putrid with history, rotten with elitism. And dogs just smelled, even small ones.

Bamboo shoots, J P Tod's, balsamic vinegar – that was the kind of world where she belonged. Low-maintenance, accessible, multicultural – the kind of world she would be allowing the rest of the country to share once responsible land use became a reality.

She had a seizure of doubt. A country house hotel! Was that really an appropriate choice for the head of Agraria? Suppose the press got hold of it? What could a *Daily Mail* columnist make of the CEO of Agraria telling farmers to give up on stewardship and sell their land for building, when she was all the time planning to nip off for a weekend of luxury rural tourism herself?

Clare considered her options. Could she turn the thing around to look like a fact-finding tour? *Fact-finding?* Had someone just given her a brain transplant? Fact-finding was so passé, so desperately Seventies. Now that facts were irrelevant, who the hell did fact-finding? Low-profile, that was the way to go. A low-profile family break. Play the privacy card.

And yet, the mere words 'country house' had this strange magic. Even in the high-speed glass-walled lift back to her office in Agraria's new headquarters the most hideous clichés crowded into her thoughts: curtains billowing in a summer breeze, swallows twittering under eaves, bees about their business in a herbaceous border, a country pub, for God's sake.

'Will you call my daughter,' she asked her assistant, 'and give her a weekend date some time around Easter? We're planning a bit of a family break. She wants to book the hotel, which is fine, but perhaps you could suggest that assumed names would be appropriate? I'm not one of these people who just treats their family as a photo-opportunity. Privacy is the priority on this one.'

'Yes, Minister,' her assistant said. Clare felt a frisson of delight. Wonderful to hear for real something she'd only ever heard from actors on the television before. Like the first time you went to America and heard the phone ring just once, the way it did in Hollywood movies.

'Have you got any cigarettes?' Juri asked Tolvo as they stood wearily outside a barn at the end of their working day.

'No.'

'Have we got any paraffin?'

'No.'

'What are we eating tonight?'

'Nothing, until we get some paraffin. Then we can have potatoes.'

'Where are we?'

'We're in a place called Saxwold somewhere in England.'

'You sure? Sounds like we're in hell.' And Juri punched his friend's arm and laughed, his breath hanging in the cold air in clouds of steam.

Potatoes, pounds sterling, paraffin and cigarettes were now the four corners of the known world to them. During the hours of daylight, from 7am to 5pm, they stood beside a belt that carried a rumbling river of potatoes from a cold store and graded them, picking out the biggest and dropping them into blue plastic crates and letting the smaller ones flow on to the yellow crates at the end of the belt.

The work could be varied by carrying full crates to the lorries and fetching in more empty crates from the yard. The potatoes were as cold as lumps of ice, but sorting them was softer work than washing off the mud. The new kids did that. When they had been new, it had been their job. They also ate the potatoes, and one of the older men had worked out a way to distil something comfortingly close to vodka from the potato peel.

'We need something to drink,' Juri insisted when they got to their caravan. 'It'll thin our blood and stop it freezing. Why the fuck is it so cold here? Aren't we thousands of miles south of Vilnius?'

'Can't be. They must have lied to us at school. Anyway, it's not just the cold,' Tolvo said. 'It's the wind and the wet. This temperature is above normal for Vilnius in winter, but

126

with high humidity and a wind-chill factor, it feels colder. That's all.'

'Too fucking right it feels colder,' said Juri.

They worked and slept in all their clothes, with two pairs of mittens on their hands, and if they took off anything to light a cigarette or take a piss, their exposed flesh still burned like fire.

The pounds sterling they collected at the end of each week from the labour contractor, who went first to the bungalow of awe-striking luxury at the far side of the farm, where his customer, Colin Burton, paid him in cash.

The boys got £1.80 an hour, ten hours a day, seven days a week, making £126 a week. In addition, they had a caravan to live in, with sleeping bags and a few utensils, and water from a standpipe and all the potatoes they could eat. They spent £5 a week on paraffin for the stove in the caravan, and bought the fuel and their cigarettes off the gang boss, who bought them off the contractor, who had had them sent up on his own minibus, which rattled up from London every week or so, when Colin called in more labour or some other guys gave up and went home. They got through a packet of cigarettes a day, each.

The money they kept in cash in their money belts, well hidden under layers of clothes. This was the only possibility. The other workers were from God knew where. Albanians, some of them. Arabs. Bulgarians, Romanians. Thieves, all of them. They'd come into your caravan in the night when you were asleep and steal your money from under your pillow. And stick a knife in you if you made any noise. So Tolvo and Juri had their own knives.

All this lore had come to them from a man who was the

son of someone who worked in a hospital with Tolvo's mother, the same man who had sent them a map, a phone number, a card for the telephone and some British coins, so that once they'd got off the salt marshes on the coast, and found a signpost, and a telephone, they'd been able to call their contact, who had them picked up the next day, and taken straight to the farm, and introduced to the gang boss and the contractor, on his next visit. So they were protected, even if they were illegal.

The same man spoke enough English to talk to Colin about what he wanted done. Tolvo had some English as well, but it wasn't the same, learning at school and talking to people. He had to try every word three or four times before he pronounced it well enough for the farmer to understand. Still, the man was always laughing, and when Tolvo tried to talk to him he laughed even more, so there was no harm done.

They were there for the money, and their reasons for the money were different. The men only talked about their reasons to themselves, each running an internal monologue from the moment they stepped out into the freezing mist that lay over the land in the morning. 'If I can stick this for six months, I can go to university,' Tolvo said silently in his thoughts. 'If I can stick this for six months, I can go to university. If I go to university, I can be an astrophysicist. If I go to university, I can be an astrophysicist. I don't have to work at the bus garage. I don't have to work at the bus garage.'

'This is for you, nephew or niece,' said Juri to himself as his arms fell into the routine of tossing potatoes into the crates. 'This is for you, nephew or niece. And you'd better be a good baby, after I've gone through all this for you. This is for you, big sister. This is for you, big sister. Even if you had to marry a useless idiot. Useless idiot.' Juri's sister was a teacher, and so was her husband. She had lost her first baby that summer. It died in the seventh month of her pregnancy, because, the doctor said, she had not had enough proper food. When she got pregnant again, his mother and his brother-in-law had sat him down for a talk.

CHAPTER 5

A Bailiff Calls

The house was finished. Even Bel admitted it. Most people would have considered it finished some time earlier, but when it came to her own home and her own future, Bel was on a mission and so it was not until she had placed the ultimate and final embroidered pillow for the second guest bedroom that she was mentally prepared to sign off the enterprise.

And then there had been the garden. She who had been confined to window boxes all her life broke free and bought clipped box bushes by the lorry-load. Followed by mature roses, full-grown trees and an instant herbaceous border. 'Shouldn't you wait for it all to grow?' Oliver had asked.

'Don't be ridiculous,' she had answered. 'You sound like that silly little man on the television who thinks he's a sex symbol. Nobody waits when they're restoring a house. You can't tell a buyer that it'll be a great garden in ten years' time. They want it now and if you can give it to them – boom! Up goes the price.'

As if to make her point, she made him drive her to a specialist poultry breeder many miles away, and came back with six speckled hens whose empty little heads were ornamented with idiotic pom-poms of white feathers, as if their useless brains had been extruded into cocktail hats. The birds lived, not in a chicken coop, but a Wendy house painted pale blue outside and inside decorated with the wallpaper offcuts from the Rose Bedroom. Oliver feared the day that Colin and Jimmy would discover this feature. All the same, he liked the chickens. They made him laugh.

As the final gesture, Bel changed the house's name, and had it carved in a discreet stone plaque by the door: The Manor House. 'Manor', she thought, was worth a good ten grand more than 'Farm'.

The building which Oliver had first known as a heap of rubble was now a small mansion of rose-red brick that loomed majestically at the end of a gravel drive. Inside, its walls were painted a rich cream, ample curtains flounced around the windows and a full complement of newly acquired heirloom furniture stood about, glowing from the energetic application of pure beeswax polish.

Outside, the former dairy, henhouse and piggery had been reborn as a series of walled gardens, where flowers could riot in safety, protected from the vicious North Sea winds. The big trees had been skilfully lopped and a new avenue of pleached limes led away across the sweeping lawn to the site of the proposed swimming pool.

Bel set out to create this magnificence with a massive mortgage and the firm idea that the house would provide her pension, something which neither of her husbands had given thought to, despite their shared illusion that being masculine and older than she was had conferred great wisdom upon them. When Bel realised that she was unmarried, likely to remain so, with no marketable skill other than that of creating beautiful homes, and that, furthermore, she was hurtling towards the age of sixty at frightening speed, she spent a year in a state of panic before putting her faith, and her money, and her borrowing power into The Manor House.

'I'll turn it around and sell it on in a year,' she announced to Oliver. 'Then I can do something clever with the capital and be a merry widow.'

'Good plan,' he told her, while guilt like a samurai sword virtually disembowelled him because he was now in no state to take care of his mother. And at that point in economic history, even Oliver could think of nothing clever that anyone could do with their capital.

No sooner was the new damp course being drilled in the house's dank walls than Bel forgot whose money she was spending. Her husbands had both enjoyed being the big man who paid the bills, and she had adored the illusion that they had been taking care of her. A chequebook of her own was an awesome weapon; she would have felt more confident picking up a loaded Kalashnikov. Credit cards she saw as magical mischief-makers, as nasty little imps who would hop out of your wallet and cause havoc if you weren't careful.

A budget, she knew, could keep everything under control, but budgets were what you did for a client. When Bel sat down to write out a budget for herself, she felt hideously lonely, her confidence drained away and her pen faltered on the paper.

I have nobody to take care of me now, she thought. I'm on my own. Oliver's in worse trouble than I am. Toni's running wild. It's all hopeless. I can't think.

She went outside, and stood in her new garden and felt the weight of the sky pressing down on her head. Tears started in her eyes. No, she told herself, you can't give in. This isn't happening. You're just lonely because you're in a new place. It will all be all right. It will.

Bel had acquired the habit of being spoiled, and at the back of her mind there was still a man born to indulge her, pottering quietly offstage somewhere, ready to emerge and make everything sunny. She felt the company of a conceptual husband, who admired her creations and financed them from his ever-open chequebook, almost as warmly as a real one. No matter that she had searched for this ideal all her life and never found him. It will all be all right, she assured herself, drying her tears and going inside. Bel still had faith, and in that faith, she spent money like – well, just like her son.

Soon the bills came in, from architect, builder, decorators, auction houses, department stores, garden centres and a marvellous little woman in Lower Saxwold who made curtains. Never, in Bel's imagination, let alone in reality, were these bills totalled, let alone paid. Her mind was entirely occupied with swatches, colour charts, room schemes and bidding, at an auction in Norwich, for a carved walnut pediment that would fit perfectly over the front door, and an eighteenth-century chiffonier that really was the finest piece of its period and style she had ever seen.

Once these finds had been delivered in triumph, Bel cajoled Oliver into fixing the pediment over the front door, which he did with bad grace and a barely adequate complement of nails. She installed the chiffonier in the drawing room and put the bills into one of its drawers, where they disappeared from her consciousness completely.

Over several months, the bills were joined by reminders, statements, threatening letters and a note, in writing so tiny that Bel could not read it without spectacles, from the marvellous little woman in Lower Saxwold, deploring the attitude of a rich bitch who felt able to exploit a poor artisan so shamefully. Bel hated her spectacles; they made her feel unnecessarily competent. She used them only to read the menu if she was lunching with a woman friend.

It was the little woman of Lower Saxwold who first went to court to claim her debt, and on her behalf, one drizzly afternoon just before Easter, a muscular man in denim rang the doorbell. Hoping for an opportunity to outrage a stranger, Toni answered the door.

'Mrs Annabel Hardcastle?' the large man asked.

'Nah. That's my stepmother. She's out,' Toni growled. The man had a certain look about him. He had a sheaf of cheaply printed forms in his hand and the weary air of one who was lied to day in and day out. Toni scented officialdom. She smelled wrongdoing. She changed her approach, switched her threatening slouch for an appealing simper, and asked, 'Is it anything I can help you with?'

The large man was taking in the lion's head knocker of polished brass, the discreet sign reading 'The Manor House', the classical black-and-white tiles in the hall, the mingled aroma of lavender and beeswax and the impressive half-moon Empire-style console that Bel had been unable to resist at her last auction. 'I think your stepmother may have just overlooked a little bill,' he hazarded, his thick lips framing the dainty words with a struggle. 'If I give you this,' he handed over one of his forms, 'you could just give it to her and tell her someone from the court came round.'

'Someone from the court – are you a real bailiff?' lisped Toni.

'The unreal kind don't collect much money, unfortunately,' said the large man.

'You *are* a real bailiff!'

'It'll be a week or so before I have to come back,' he told her, adding a weighty wink. 'But I will have to come back, mind. So don't forget to tell her.'

'I'll give her the message,' Toni promised.

'THE BAILIFFS CAME ROUND!!' she trumpeted at Bel, the minute her stepmother returned. Oliver trudged in behind her, weighed down with bags of shopping.

'Are you sure, dear?' Bel brazened with a daffy toss of the head.

'HE'S COMING BACK IN A WEEK SO YOU'D BETTER PAY UP,' Toni broadcast to the nation.

'Don't be so dramatic,' Bel dismissed her.

'IF YOU DON'T BELIEVE ME YOU CAN READ THIS!' Toni waved the smudgy document under her stepmother's nose. Oliver, who had put the shopping in the kitchen, emerged with aching arms and grabbed the paper.

'Let me look at that.' His tone was lofty and disbelieving. He adjusted it at once. 'Ah . . . oh. Sorry, Mum. It is from a debt collection firm. It is – well, it's a notice to pay.'

'It says that at the top,' scoffed Toni.

'I must have forgotten somebody's bill,' Bel twittered, trying to disguise a guilty blush.

'Two thousand, eight hundred and something, and their costs, making three thousand and twelve, fifty.'

'That much,' Bel marvelled.

'Is it going to be a problem?' Oliver asked gently, his mind's eye quite dazzled by metaphorical flashing lights. And drenched with guilt in his turn because if his mother had overspent, as she usually did in doing up her own homes, he was in no position now to help her out, as he'd always done before.

Bel's blue eyes filled with tears. She tried to say 'yes' but found that her mouth wouldn't co-operate.

'You've done it again, haven't you?' Oliver asked. She nodded.

'And are there any more of these that you're expecting?'

Bel was about to shake her head when Toni intervened. 'There's hundreds of them, I should think. Every time the phone rings it's somebody else about a bill. She keeps them in that thing.' And she pointed a scornful, black-webbed finger at the chiffonier.

Oliver pulled at drawers until one resisted him. He pulled it firmly and a fountain of papers sprayed out. 'Oh Christ,' he said.

'I have paid some of them,' protested his mother. 'I'm sure I have.'

When Oliver had finished examining the bills, and marrying them up with his mother's chequebook and credit cards, he found that she had, indeed, paid the £325 for passementerie, which represented the five red silk tassels on the keys to the drawers of the chiffonier. Everything else that could be unpaid, the builder, the plumber, the electrician, the mural painter, the landscapers, the garden centre, the gas, the electricity and the telephone, was unpaid and had been so for several months. In the case of the utilities, he discovered the ultimate final red-bordered bills, lying urgently on top of the pile.

'Angel, I am on the cadge,' Dido declared, appearing in the kitchen area in the middle of a Saturday morning. In Miranda's flat, that meant that her friend had made the supreme effort of flopping off the day bed, attaining verticality, and skating, in her baby-blue angora socks, across over three metres of floor to within conversation distance of the kettle.

'Oh yes? So what else is new?' Miranda dunked her tea bag. Fennel, this morning. Fennel tea was what she chose when she had that nasty feeling that someone was tying knots in her lower oesophagus. A feeling of being choked and then some.

'You know you're going off with your mother next week-end?'

'Could I forget?'

'And you know you took me to that market thing and I met this lovely man who was just s-o-o-o-o-o fit?'

'The man who made the filthy wine.'

'Well, yes. The wine was a problem. But he was lovely, wasn't he? You thought so, you said so?'

Miranda sighed. Dido fell in love quite often. About once a week, fifty-two weeks a year. Miranda knew this because she had a memory. Dido had a memory too, but so many things happened to her that her memory got stuffed up and didn't work properly. She darted through life like a shubunkin in a fish bowl, fluttering her gorgeous outgrowths and never wanting to know if she had swum this way before.

'He makes wine, angel. Isn't that perfect?'

'No, it tasted like screenwash. You know it did.'

'You're so critical! Who cares if it's good? He looks like that actor.'

'What actor?'

'You know. The gorgeous one.'

'Martin Kemp.'

'No, not mean. Just gorgeous. In films and things.'

'George Clooney.'

'Sweetheart, can't you be serious?'

'Well, anyway. I remember him. You met him.'

'Did I ever meet him.'

'And you need a favour.'

'Don't rush me. Yes, I need a favour. You see, I need a lift. You're going to Suffolk next weekend. Did I get that right?'

'Yes.'

'To some lovely hotel.'

'I hope it's lovely. It was in all the guides.'

'And the man I met – he lives in Suffolk. Don't you remember?'

Miranda remembered the appallingly designed sign, and the labels, and the tea towel, all reading *Château Saxwold*. 'I suppose.'

'And he invited me to visit,' Dido went on, now trying to hop around the end of the bed like an excited child and slipping in her socks.

'He gave you that card.'

'And I called him up, you know.'

'Oh God.'

'Well, we can't all be in control all the time. You know I'm weak. I just had to call him. There was a number, he must have meant it. We were on the phone for just hours. But he doesn't know.'

'What doesn't he know?'

'That I'm going to surprise him.'

Surprises upset Miranda. In her own life, she planned to avoid being surprised as much as possible. On the other hand, if Dido had to go a week without a surprise, she wilted like a dying flower. Dido wasted days plotting to induce extra serendipity into her life, and the lives of everyone she knew, whether they liked surprises or not. What was a birthday without a surprise party? How could anyone resist April Fools' Day? Why bother to get out of bed or go out of the door, unless you were absolutely sure you'd bump into someone you weren't expecting to see?

'Suppose he doesn't like surprises,' she suggested, knowing how Dido would respond.

'I lo-o-o-o-o-ve surprises,' she said. 'I can't wait to see his face when I walk into his wine-tasting. And – here's the thing – it's next weekend. Easter. Look.' She held out the invitation card, and Miranda saw that it was true. 'And what's even more amazing . . . it's got to be near where you're going. That place, what did you say its name was?'

'The Saxwold Manor Hotel,' Miranda said. Beside Dido's bed was the *Country House Weekend Guide to Britain*, open, face down, with a mug on it. Her friend had been browsing.

'Yes, I looked it up. I'm not completely idiotic, am I? It's actually in . . . ta-daaa, somewhere called Lower Saxwold. And his *domaine* – is that what they call them? His place, anyway, where they do the wine, it's in somewhere called Great Saxwold. Look!' She flourished the card. 'It's got to be almost the same place, hasn't it?'

139

'I suppose,' said Miranda. Coincidence wasn't as bad as surprise, it wasn't as deeply upsetting, or so horribly worrying, or quite such absolute proof that the nature of life was fundamentally mischievous and unpredictable, but she didn't much like it, all the same.

'Well they can't be far away. Angel, isn't it brilliant? If I can get a ride with you, and book a room, and . . . well, I was passing, I thought I'd drop in. He'll be so totally surprised.'

'You were just passing his vineyard in Suffolk. He does know you live in London.'

'He won't think of it that way. He did invite me, angel. I could say I was staying with friends. It'll be sort of true, won't it? So I was thinking you could maybe give me a ride to Suffolk. Next weekend. You are going to drive, aren't you?'

'We were going to drive down together. Ye-es.'

'Together – oh God, your mum! This isn't going to work, is it?' And Dido suddenly crumpled up like an incinerated moth because, as she had been aware for twenty years, Clare Marlow disapproved of her. Maybe it was the icy voice on the phone that had given her the clue when she rang Miranda up at home, or that tomb-effigy grimace that passed for a smile of greeting on the very rare occasions in which she had actually met Mrs Marlow.

Miranda remembered the directive her mother had issued on the last day of school. 'There's no need to keep up with everyone you knew here. Nobody expects it. Stick with the first team, of course. Your real friends. You can keep up with the others with Christmas cards and things. Everyone will understand.'

So Miranda had edited references to the friend who had

been so emphatically damned as excess baggage on the flight to achievement, and allowed her mother to believe that they had gone their separate ways. If she knew that Dido was practically a permanent fixture in her flat, things might turn ugly.

On the other hand, Miranda knew, from lifetime experience, that as soon as Dido found that man again, she would be gone and you wouldn't be able to find her even if you wanted to.

Dido was drooping, visibly. Her nature was as sweet as banoffee pie and manipulation came hard to her. But this was an emergency. The man of her dreams was in Suffolk. Simply going there did not occur to her. Getting on a train, taking a taxi? Unthinkable. Where would she find a train, how would she buy a ticket, what would she have to say to a strange taxi driver? She had no experience of independent movement. If you wanted to go, you went with a friend. Or lots of friends. Then all the love around you just bubbled you all along to where you were going. A friend with a car was best, of course.

'I don't have to check into your hotel,' she said to Miranda humbly. 'I wasn't thinking of that. There'll be a pub, there's bound to be.'

Miranda sighed. The other thing, of course, was that she had never fallen in love.

Whatever Dido had felt, whatever had drawn her across the Covent Garden pavement like an invisible string, whatever spell had taken hold of the two of them and wrapped them in its magic bubble and kept them safe from the crushing great ugly world outside, Miranda had never felt it. If it hadn't been for Dido, she would never have believed that there was such a phenomenon. Things like that just didn't happen. To her.

But since they happened to Dido, and since her friend was now sitting on the floor looking up at her, transfigured like a martyred saint in a painting, Miranda felt the force. And the force made her say, 'Well. OK. I can't say no, can I? We can work something out. But it's got to be the pub – definitely. Mother will just go postal if it's more than the car. You know what she's like.'

And Dido squeaked with joy, and leaped up and ran on the spot, her feet thumping the floor softly in her flopping angora bedsocks, and flung her arms round Miranda's neck, getting curls in her fennel tea.

'Oh hooray! Oh, thank you so-o-o-o-o-o much! Oh, it's going to be so-o-o-o-o much fun. Oh, you really really are an angel!'

'Don't worry,' she said a little later. 'About your mum. I've got very good with mums now. I shall charm her. You'll see.'

'You'd better.'

'What are you going to do, anyway? On this weekend. You and your mum. What do you usually do when you have a holiday?'

'We never have holidays. She's too busy. Or I'm too busy. This is a first. First on an adult-to-adult basis, anyway.'

A nostalgic sequence started emerging from Miranda's memory. Holidays before her mother changed. Gîtes in France, apartments in Spain, visiting friends in England. There hadn't been much money, she realised from a mature perspective, but the old Mum had been pretty clever. Especially in her pony period. Miranda winced slightly. To think, she'd once had a pony period.

'Didn't you used to go on those pony camps?' said Dido. 'I used to be so jealous. And your mum. She used to be a real Marbella cowgirl.'

'That was then,' Miranda said firmly. 'That was the old Mum.'

In accordance with the rota at the parish church of St Oswin in Great Saxwold, Bel Hardcastle was doing the flowers for the Easter weekend. The occupation raised her close to her own personal nirvana. To Bel, no work of human hands anywhere in the world surpassed the glory of an English country church decorated for Easter. The soaring swathes of blossom, the golden blaze of daffodils, the ivy trails, the moss nests, the scarlet early tulips, the occasional glory of a precocious crown imperial, the little pots of violets and primroses done by the children. It was all absolute bliss. This year, it would be bliss as art-directed by her.

Her pleasure did not have much to do with God. Bel didn't dare believe in God. Her parents had both renounced their religions for love of each other. Both her husbands had been vaguely negative about the idea and her son was a robust atheist. All the men in her life agreed that religion had been the cause of all the wars in history and all the cruelty, barbarism and genocide that went with them.

And the actual facts about Easter were really quite distasteful. Crucifixion seemed like a ghastly thing to celebrate and it quite put her off churches that they all contained statues of a man being tortured like that. And resurrection? Well, that was just silly. And the hymns weren't nice either, not even the old ones. The green hill couldn't be far enough away for her.

Nevertheless, the process of bedecking the church with the

traditional tributes from her garden made her rapturous with joy. It meant that she was part of the village, an admirable and gracious and traditional part. Maybe it was widowhood, and all the anxieties that came with it; maybe it was racial memory, from generations of ancestors who had never been part of their own community, only part of its ghetto, and had kept their wealth portable and their expectations low and their heads down for centuries, but Bel wanted passionately to belong. The fact that this weekend, Easter weekend no less, had fallen to her in the rota, seemed like God's official blessing on her new status as the châtelaine of The Manor House.

Naturally, she had conscripted Oliver to help. He was leaning off a ladder trying to get a grip on a branch of frothy yellow forsythia and steadying himself with his free hand, which was wrapped around a carved griffin's head. From this vantage point, he noticed a muscular man dressed in denim standing at the South Door.

People normally came through the South Door rather flustered, having had to prise open the wire mesh gates that stopped swallows nesting in the vaulted roof of the porch in unsanitary numbers. They would stand there hesitantly, getting ready to drink in ancient peace and looking about them for the famous twelfth-century font carved with a bas-relief of John the Baptist.

This man was showing no readiness to quaff deep draughts of ancient peace, nor any curiosity about the font. He walked into the apse with a menacing lack of hesitation.

'Can I help you?' Oliver asked in a sturdy voice indicating that he would stand no nonsense, even if his mother had bullied him up a ladder with a bunch of flowers.

'Not you, sir,' the man replied, in a familiar voice

indicating that any man who had allowed himself to be bullied up a ladder was beneath his consideration. 'The lady. If this is Mrs Annabel Lumpkin.'

'Oh dear,' Bel squeaked. 'However did you find me?'

'Young lady at the house told me you might be down here,' the man continued. 'I'm from the court. I left some papers with her when I came by a few weeks ago. Did you by any chance have time to look at them?'

'Ah . . .' Bel flapped her hands. All her life, when things had failed to work as they should, she had flapped her hands as if she believed that stirring up the air would somehow whip up a solution to her dilemma. She had flapped her hands over flooded carburettors, burnt toast and the deaths of both her husbands. It hadn't worked then and, she realised with a ghastly freezing sensation in her stomach, it wasn't going to work now.

If there was one mannerism which Oliver observed in his mother that drove him absolutely crazy it was the flapping of her hands. He took them personally. Every frantic phalange felt like a disaster appeal aimed straight at his soft filial underbelly. His usual response to a maternal hand-flap was to stomp away in a morose silence and come back only when he was quite, quite sure that the danger of emotional blackmail had receded.

This time, however, he was up a ladder, with a branch of blossom in one hand and a leering gargoyle in the other. It was not an ideal position for a dignified exit. In fact, since the West Door and the Vestry were both locked, the only way out of the church was past the large man in denim. He was one hundred per cent trapped in a hand-flap situation. There was nothing to do but take charge.

Oliver speared the flower arrangement with the forsythia branch, more or less in the position that his mother had been trying to describe to him, then let go of the griffin and came down the ladder.

'Oliver Hardcastle,' he said, shaking the bailiff's hand firmly. 'This is my mother. It seems that her affairs have got into a bit of a mess lately.'

'Yes, it does,' the bailiff replied, smooth as custard. 'I've got another of these notices here. And another one came into the office just as I was leaving. I'll have to be back with that next week now.'

Manly and capable, Oliver took charge of the papers. His eye briefly grazed the sum owing. It was in five figures. Smaller than his own overdraft, but bigger, much bigger, than all the spare cash he could lay his hands on just at that moment.

'What's the form in a situation like this?' he continued, trying to exude man-to-man confidence.

'Well, the debtor pays the sum owing,' the bailiff answered, with more than a hint of sarcasm. 'Unless the debtor hasn't got the money, in which case the court will consider a request for time to pay.'

'Ah,' said Oliver, sensing that his mother's hands had ceased to flap. 'Time to pay. How does that work?'

'You fill out this form.' The bailiff, like a magician, flourished more paper from its hiding place. 'Giving a statement of your financial affairs. You make a proposal to pay and the court accepts what it considers is reasonable.'

'By instalments,' Oliver suggested with a hopeful nod.

'By instalments, certainly, but in this case, in view of the sum involved and since there has been a notice outstanding quite a few weeks already, it would be best to send the first payment with the application.'

'What sort of money would they be . . .'

'Five hundred should do it. Cash or banker's draft.'

From behind him, Oliver heard his mother squeak again. 'No problem,' he said firmly. 'Thank you so much for explaining all that. We'll get something to you by Monday. No, it's Easter, isn't it?'

'Looks like it,' said the bailiff dryly, indicating the rioting daffodils all around him.

'Monday's the bank holiday. Tuesday. Is the court open on Tuesday?'

'Tuesday as ever is,' the bailiff said, furling the rest of his documents into his briefcase with a jovial flourish. 'I'll say good afternoon, sir. Madam.'

Once they had heard the tinny slam of the swallow-prevention door, Bel let out a wail, the sort of noise a kitten might make when it felt in need of a saucer of real milk and had been offered a saucer of soya-based kitten formula instead. 'Awful man! How could he? The Vicar might have come in,' she protested.

'He's only doing his job,' Oliver said. Bel wailed again. There was no hope for it, he was going to have to put his arm round her. 'Surely someone can lend you five hundred pounds?'

'No, they can't.' She sniffed and sniffed again. 'I've borrowed every penny I can, Oliver. I must be on some list of naughty people, now. The last time I went to the hole in the wall the machine ate my card. I hate those things. Why can't we all go back to chequebooks? Much nicer.'

'Because everyone always wrote cheques when they hadn't

got any money,' Oliver sighed. That very morning, his bank's computer had sent him a letter to tell him that if he put any of his cards in their holes in the wall, they too would be consumed by the machines. He could feel his mother's breathing getting irregular. Any minute now she was going to cry. The one thing he hated more than the hand-flapping was crying.

'Let's go to the pub,' he said, giving her a hug. 'I can buy us a drink, at least.'

'I haven't finished the flowers,' she protested, indicating the ancient flagstone floor still littered with foliage. 'And I promised the Vicar you'd help me with the bell ropes.'

'What bell ropes?' he asked, feeling suddenly weary. Much too weary to be leaping around St Oswin's Norman bell tower like Quasimodo. Which was no doubt what his mother had pledged him to do.

CHAPTER 6

Finding the Right Occasion

It had been very difficult to find the right occasion.

'I need to be the headline speaker at an event that's appropriate to the message,' Clare instructed her staff. They looked uneasy.

'There's always the invitation to the Royal Agricultural Show,' one of them ventured.

'I don't want to be photographed with any cows. Not now, not ever.'

The group winced.

'National Farmers' Union conference? Always gets a lot of coverage.'

'Farmers are not the target audience,' she said, trying hard not to snarl. 'We anticipate resistance from the farming lobby. That's why it's important to plant our flag in the moral high ground from the beginning.'

The staff promised to look into the question and trailed back to their desks. In the normal run of life, the Minister for Agriculture never made headline speeches. He turned a blind eye to the state of his realm and a deaf ear to the needs of his petitioners and kept his head down. This need to speak on an issue of national importance was totally out of line.

In the end, Clare herself had to spend a midnight hour on the Internet to find the right event. The Royal Conservation Society conference struck her as ideal. Staged at the right time and the right place – just before Easter, in some cavernous public hall handy for the Westminster TV studios. She had the Adviser phone and offer her presence.

'Are you sure?' he said, bearish all of a sudden. 'Conservationists can be a bit blinkered. Maybe you could open an agricultural college or . . .'

'And stand up and tell all the young who're studying to be farmers that they're wasting their time and getting into debt for nothing?'

'Oh, yes, well. There is that. But you could just not make a big announcement. Low-profile it. Just publish the report, draft a bill and let it take its course through Parliament without anyone wanting to start a public debate or anything.'

Low-profile? No. No. No. This is about profile. Profile is all. With profile I have power, without it I am powerless. I need television and I need it now.

'I know I'm new to this,' she said, without a smile, 'but it looks to me as if the one way to start a debate is to give the impression that you're trying to avoid having one. There will be a public debate about this, whether we seek it or not, and that being so, I want to control it from the start. Our agenda, not theirs.'

'Dangerous,' the Adviser muttered.

'Danger is my business,' she told him, as if neither of

them were aware that Mutual Probity had collapsed into insolvency, her successor had been arrested at his mock-Tudor mansion in Surrey and a Bank of England investigation was about to start. 'I think, rather than take questions after the speech, we can set up a separate press conference. Not so intrusive. We don't want to look as if we're hijacking the whole event. There are rooms in that building, aren't there?'

And so Clare Marlow, CEO of Agraria, addressed the conference of the Royal Conservation Society on the theme of 'Unlocking Our Land'. Two thousand delegates filled the auditorium. It was hard to see much through the lights, but they seemed docile enough. A lot of youngish, deconstructed types in V-neck fleeces, a few grey heads. As she had guessed, not much diversity, not even many women. So much the worse for them. Time to wake up their ideas.

When she had given the Adviser the first draft of the speech, he had admitted that it was the most scintillating moral tap dance he had ever read.

There was applause when she was introduced. Polite. Mystified, understandably. Perhaps even wary. Probably the first time a senior politician had taken notice of them without being forced into it by a demonstration.

'Our land is the most precious resource that we in Britain have,' came somewhere near the beginning. The audience was silent. No argument there.

'In past generations, we thought of our land as our essence, what Britain was all about.' The past! That great evil, the resort of war, depression, slavery, famine and barbarism! Who could want to continue what had gone on in the past?

'But what is a nation? Its land or its people? And who does the land really belong to? And what is the price that we are paying for their ownership?' Paying a price. Us and them. Always pushed the right buttons, those ideas.

Time to introduce the report. *Country Life: A Cost-Benefit Analysis*. Infrastructure. Subsidies. The real cost of a rural road, per mile. The real cost of a school bus, per pupil. The price of a British lettuce compared to a Spanish one. To sum up: high-quality open spaces in minority ownership, given over to producing food nobody wanted at prices nobody could afford.

She moved on rapidly to the implications. Food quality. Health and safety issues. Bad management. Global inequality. There was still silence among the audience. Being experienced in corporate apathy, it didn't worry her. It was exhilarating, putting over the argument that had been devised so carefully by the light of so much midnight oil. She was rolling out the facts like troops into battle, sending them out on the offensive with victory in sight.

'We must ask ourselves, is it right that ownership of the land with highest amenity value should remain sterile in the hands of a few individuals who are paid by the many simply to keep that resource for themselves?'

Something like a soft growl sounded from the hall. The space had a hideous echo. Difficult to tell if it was one person talking, or several muttering, or a consensus gathering strength.

'Let us look at this issue from the other side,' she said. 'While millions of acres of redundant land are being preserved as if they were holy relics . . .'

The growl grew loud and harsh. Did somebody shout? At

the side of the stage she saw a white face. The Adviser. If he was going to funk at the first speech, he should make himself invisible.

Don't get shrill. Do a Maggie, drop the pitch. She started with the numbers, aiming for a good strong contralto. 'The need for land is growing. Our cities are becoming more densely populated, with all the social evils of overcrowding that that implies . . .'

Good, the audience were silent again. She was on firm ground. Crime. Violence. Drug and alcohol abuse. Mental health. Imploding social services. Hospitals, schools, transport, blah-blah-blah, blah-blah-blah. Totally attack-proof. No grounds for disagreement whatsoever.

Then on to house prices. Tricky, but she'd identified the right approach. Rattle the cage. Risky, but it was the only way. Boom and bust. Affordable housing, key workers. Crashing prices. Nation of debtors set to become a nation of bankrupts.

Meaning was a wonderful thing. Put two facts together – but what were facts? A fact was just the information you needed at the time. Put two of them together, any two, and any fool would feel proud of himself for finding the link. Meaning was pixie dust, meaning was moonshine, meaning was the leprechaun's pot of gold at the end of the rainbow. Meaning only existed because people wanted to find it.

Between any two facts, most fools would find the same link. Add a third and the whole thing turned into DNA, the self-perpetuating spiral, the secret of life, pulling in facts by itself, making bonds at random, on and on for ever, spinning out meaning to infinity, letting everybody believe they were wise and omnipotent and in charge of the process. When really, they were just children playing a computer game, pressing buttons to make things happen in the world of unreality they'd bought at a store all the time.

'So if the few, the selfish few, who seek to hold on to our land when it is so desperately needed . . .'

Again, like the distant roar of the sea, they were muttering out there.

'. . . and future generations . . .'

She saw the Adviser wince. Almost felt his pain over the empty spot-lit space between them. Damn, how could she have forgotten? Never, ever, talk about future generations. Nothing set the old bullshitometer off like that expression. You might as well light up a neon sign saying DANGER!! BLACKMAIL IN PROGRESS!!

Future, yes, the future was good. Generations were the problem. The idea always landed like a sack of shit. Especially with business people who, if they had children, cut them out of the family photograph along with the first wife and consigned them to the dustbin of their personal history.

She took her eyes off her notes and went for the look of evangelical conviction that she'd practised. 'If we are to have a land worth living in, we must agree that it's time to shake off sentimentality, to let go of the past, to acknowledge the economic realities of the society in which we live . . .'

A clap. Clapping! Yes! There it was, the noise that made her right. Clare looked at the Adviser. He wasn't there. Where was he? Checking the room for the press conference? 'The new Rural Development Council . . .' she began, starting down the home straight. Another clap. Another. Another. Clapping. Hell and damnation. They were slow-clapping.

The bastards, they were giving her the slow hand-clap. The bastards.

Only another ten lines. The Rural Development Council. Recommendations. Tangle of planning laws. Cumbersome procedures. Reclaiming our land. Unlocking our potential. Building the future. Thank you very much. Good afternoon. Goodbye. They were shouting now. She couldn't hear what. All bigotry and ignorance, anyway. We knew there would be resistance. We anticipated this. Just not so vicious. My God, there was that stab of fear, the blue-white blade of terror flickering down her throat, not felt since she was an under-sized six-year-old getting shoved around the school playground. Walk quickly. Quickly. You are not going to pee your pants. Just get off the stage.

The Adviser was there, in the shadows where the cameras couldn't find him. 'Don't say it,' she muttered as she passed on her way to the press conference. 'I know. I wanted the public debate.' Damn, the press conference. Now it was going to look like a heist. And all the media would talk about was the row in the hall, forget the issue, forget the strategy, focus on the row.

The last lorry of the morning, loaded with crates of potatoes, lurched out of the yard into the lane, and the potato pickers allowed themselves a fifteen-minute break. Juri and Tolvo selected a broken crate to save their trousers from the mud, sat down back to back and lit up cigarettes.

'Let's talk about food,' Tolvo suggested over his shoulder. 'Anything as long as it's not potatoes. Or cauliflowers.'

'Oh, God. Those cauliflowers.' Colin had turned his loss-making crop over to his pigs and his workers. The pigs were equipped to digest vast quantities of cellulose, the men were not. Juri especially had suffered. 'You passed more stinking gas than a cow when we got those cauliflowers.'

'I didn't pass as much as you – you could have fuelled a power station, you were farting so much.' Tolvo reached around and poked his friend in what was once his stomach. 'You could have run the national grid off that little methane factory. Or sent a space probe to Saturn for twenty years.'

'I thought my guts were going to split,' Juri recalled. 'Or maybe some alien had raped me and I was having its babies or something. God, the pain. I'll never look at a cauliflower again. Not even pickled. Forget it.'

'It was a change from the potatoes,' Tolvo pointed out. 'Potatoes with onions. Potatoes with greens. Potatoes with greens and onions. Potatoes with onions and greens.'

There were sixteen men working on the farm, and one or two among them could brew up something like a meal from what the gang could scavenge – the potatoes that were still lying in the fields because they were too small to be picked up by the gathering machine, some onions found in a rotting heap in a corner of one of the barns, and what they could find that was edible in the field margins and the roadsides.

The gang possessed a pan and a piece of pork fat that wasn't too bad but nobody knew where it had come from. The British were apparently too lazy to pick up firewood, so they had plenty of free fuel. Spring was starting, the days were longer. In the half-hour of twilight after they finished work, Tolvo and Juri had dared to venture down the lane, looking for nettle tops, rose shoots and anything else that wasn't actually poisonous.

'I've been dreaming about food,' Juri went on, taking the

very last drag on the very last millimetre of his cigarette. 'Forget women. I can't think about women. If I got a stiffie in this state, I'd probably think it was a sausage and cut it off and fry it or something.'

'I can't believe you're giving up on women,' Tolvo said.

'It's true. If Britney Spears walked into this yard right now, stark naked, and said, "Come on Juri, come here and fuck me, fuck me till my tits drop off," all I'd be able to think about is what she'd taste like roasted with cream and mushroom sauce. All I ever dream about now is food. Last night, I was dreaming about cucumbers.'

'I heard that about you,' Tolvo said. 'They said on the handball team you had a thing for cucumbers.'

'I tell you,' Juri assured him with a sober face. 'The way I feel right now, your ridiculous handball team could have their way with me all night with all the vegetables of their choice if I got a cucumber of my own to take home at the end. I'd slice it very thin and do it with dill and vinegar, Hungarian-style. And cream. Loads of cream. Cream as thick as axle grease. Lovely.'

'My grandmother,' Tolvo began, 'used to make these little pastries with cream cheese. They were all buttery and crisp on the bottom, and the tops stood up like little pig's ears and they were so thin you could see the light right through them, and when you took a bite they just melted in your mouth. She made them for birthdays and saints' days and stuff. When she could get the butter. And she mixed the cheese with spice and raisins, when she got some raisins.'

His stomach rumbled at the memory and they both laughed. 'Britney Spears would taste like pork chops,' Juri

157

declared, stretching out his legs. 'All sweet and pink and juicy.'

'And J-Lo would taste like steak. Oh God. Imagine that bum in lovely slices, just fried a little, with maybe a tomato sauce.'

'Oh God, tomato sauce! Tomatoes, even. I think I'll die of joy when I see a tomato again. What about Christina Aguilera?'

'Chicken,' Tolvo suggested. 'Actually, not such a good chicken, I don't think. She looks a bit stringy. Not much fat under the skin. You can have Christina Aguilera and Britney, if I can have J-Lo.'

'OK,' Juri agreed. 'I just love chicken fat. Just by itself, Polish-style. With just a little sprinkle of salt. There are chickens somewhere round here, I've heard them.'

'Yeah, but if we steal one everyone'll know who did it, won't they? People don't steal food in England because everybody's too rich, so they'd know it was us. And then their cops would be on to us and that'd be it, game over, everybody goes to jail and we'll lose all our money. Same with the pigs. They've all got tags in their ears, they'd know if they lost a little porker and we'd all be stuffed.'

'We could buy a chicken, maybe.' Juri's voice was wistful. 'Just once. If we went into that village.'

'We're not allowed off the farm. We're illegals, remember?'

'Yeah, but everybody knows we're here. You know, when someone comes by on the road, like that woman on a horse the other day, who waved to us? They're all quite friendly. They know who we are, and what we're doing here and they don't care. Come on, Tolvo. Be a man for once. Let's go into that village and buy a chicken. Buy anything. I'm going to die here in this disgusting freezing English mud if I don't eat something like real food.'

Tolvo frowned. He had moral obligations. Juri spoke no English, so he would have to do the talking. Juri's contact had got him the job. And when people passed them on the road in the evening, it was true, they smiled and waved. Or at least they just looked. They weren't hostile, anyway. And chicken was his favourite thing to eat in all the world, next to the cheese pastries.

'OK,' he said. 'You're on. Saturday. Maybe they'll let us off early if we say we'll do an extra half-hour tonight.'

'My best mate,' said Juri, weighing down on him from behind with a hug that was more like a garrotte. 'I knew you'd be up for it. Cock-a-doodle-doo! Chicken dinner here we come. I want the parson's nose.'

'You two!' yelled the foreman from the doorway to the barn. 'Stop arsing around. Get over here, get back to work.'

They scrambled up and ran to the shed so eagerly that he turned to watch them with a suspicious frown. They looked too cheerful to be innocent. OK, they were good lads who worked well, but nobody actually liked this job.

'You know what,' said Tolvo, taking his place by the belt as the machinery started and the first kilos of spuds rumbled down the ramp.

'What?' Juri worked opposite him. They had found out the hard way that if they bent for the same potato at the same time, they cracked their heads together.

'When we get back home, we could set up a website for people with fantasies about eating pop stars. We could get some clever animations guy to maybe doctor a few pictures, and people could just post their fantasies and share them.

Call it "Eating Pussy". We'd get thousands of hits just from people looking for porno who'd made a mistake.'

Juri wasn't really listening. He never really listened to anything about computers or anything about business. Tolvo loved Juri but if he didn't wake up he'd probably still be picking potatoes in ten years' time.

'Yeah,' he said, grabbing at the passing spuds with both hands and clawing them into the crate in front of him. 'You know what? I think I'll pass on Christina Aguilera. She would be too stringy. I'll take Buffy instead. There's a lot more meat on her.'

'OK,' Tolvo agreed. 'I think she'd be kinda tough, with all that kicking and martial arts and stuff. You can have Buffy.'

'With mushrooms, don't you think? Do they have mushrooms in England? How come we never see any?'

'Come on, Juri, stop daydreaming, look a bit keen, can't you? We won't get half an hour off if we've spent the whole afternoon loafing.'

'God, I love bread. Fresh white bread when it's still warm and the crust cracks when you break it . . .'

A little earlier that day, Oliver and his mother entered The Pigeon & Pipkin, where Bel's courage was further challenged by the discovery of Toni and some black-clad friends at the bar.

'Oh, Gawd.' Toni swivelled her mascara-crusted eyes ceilingwards to indicate her despair. 'Can't I get any peace around here?'

For the benefit of the friends – a girl in slashed PVC and two boys in Lycra dishcloths – she let the question come out as: carneyegerranypissrahnere?

'You can't be drunk already,' said Bel, crisp and accurate for once.

'Nunahyerbisnesswoteyeam,' drawled Toni.

'Well, it is my business, actually,' Bel said, raising her voice to bell-like clarity. 'Since you *are* . . .'

'Oworlride, erewego!' Toni raised her own voice in turn, managing to drown out the words '*only seventeen*'. 'Come on, come on. Eyenossstandinferanymoreothiz. Lessgerroutavere.' She lurched away from the bar towards the pool room, her friends following with much jingling of chains.

Oliver and his mother installed themselves by the fire with two plates of the dish of the day, which was Turkey Mediterrané, a sort of orange porridge with congealed lumps that were quite convincingly like meat. Since it was an emergency, Oliver also decided on a bottle of wine. The top of the cellar was a Chilean Chardonnay. In an earlier life, it might have been adequate for cleaning a bicycle chain, but in their present state of distress it was better than nothing.

Their pleasure, such as it was, did not last long. The television in the corner, normally only switched on for football matches, suddenly flickered into life.

'Huh?' Oliver demanded of the landlord, with an expressive wave of his fork.

'Colin wants it,' the landlord explained. 'New minister, or something.'

'Agriculture minister,' Colin explained, halting his consumption of the Turkey Mediterrané.

'Got another new one,' said Jimmy.

'Woman, isn't it?' said somebody else.

On the screen, a presenter, a man in a suit with an artistic silk tie, was outlining the situation. 'Clare Marlow, the

CEO of Agraria, formerly known as the Ministry of Agriculture, had a hostile reception today when she addressed the Royal Conservation Society conference in London. Clare Marlow is with us in our Westminster studio . . .'

A standard interval of nodding and thanking ensued. Oliver noted that the new Minister appeared to have put on a pink jacket to disguise the fact that she was one hard-eyed heartless harpy. Something about her definitely gave him the chills.

'So,' the interviewer began. 'You've come from the commercial sector, Clare, the former managing director of Mutual Probity, the troubled multinational financial group. What makes you think you can do this job?'

'Good question,' Colin growled, his fork frozen in mid-air with contempt.

'Not Mutual Probity,' said Oliver. 'Not that bunch of crooks.'

'She looks like the Queen Mother,' Bel announced. 'Wearing a brooch on her shoulder like that. And that dreadful haircut. Why do women make themselves ugly as soon as they go into politics?'

'British agriculture needs strong leadership,' Clare was heard to reply. 'I believe in responsible land use, ethical production and global viability.'

'Well don't we all?' growled Colin, slurping down the first third of a new pint.

'And Father Christmas,' said Oliver.

The interviewer tried again. 'Surely twenty years of profit-imperative thinking . . .'

The CEO of Agraria cut him off immediately. 'Land is a

162

vital national resource and we must make sure that it is managed appropriately. Britain's transition from a rural economy based on food production to a mixed land development situation . . .'

'Will somebody tell me what the fuck she's talking about?' This was from Colin.

'Selling farmland for building?' hazarded Oliver.

'. . . must achieve our democratic objectives. The people of Britain have got to get what they need from their land. And their greatest need is undeniably housing . . .'

'Well I never,' said Jimmy.

'. . . housing that is affordable and accessible, the right home in the right place at the right price . . .'

'What's that got to do with farming?' demanded Colin.

'Or conservation,' said Lucy, newly arrived with pink cheeks from fetching her horses from Jimmy's paddock.

'And the new Rural Development Council? Isn't this just a smokescreen to hide the process of selling our farmland off to developers?'

The new Minister knew the old trick of ignoring the question. 'We need to address the question of how best to manage this change . . .'

'Oh come on,' the interviewer struggled against the rising flood of jargon. 'Surely we need first to examine whether this change should be made at all?'

'Ensuring a fair distribution of resources to all . . .' Clare carried on as if he hadn't spoken.

'It's bollocks,' said Colin. 'We knew it was going to be bollocks when she changed the name. It's a done deal, they're going to sell us off to the fat cats and the golf clubs and there'll be damn all we can do about it. Turn her off before we all get ill.' This was to the landlord, and seconded by angry noises from the bar. The TV was duly extinguished.

Oliver reached for the wine. For the first time in his life, he didn't want to think about the future. Especially when the present was demanding some urgent troubleshooting. He thought he had twenty pounds in his pocket, and some small change.

His mother had been stirring her food listlessly. Oliver lowered his voice and began tiptoeing towards the topic of the bailiff, the debts and the availability of ready cash. 'So you really are absolutely maxed out?' he asked.

'What do you mean, maxed out?' Scenting some entertainment, Bel revived a little.

'You know what I mean,' her son said sternly. 'I mean, are your credit cards all up to the limit?'

'Oh dear, they're all over their limits, I should think. I tried asking for a new one, but they won't send it.'

'Once a court issues a judgement against you, it goes on the credit control computers,' he explained.

'I do hate computers,' she sighed. The Turkey Mediterrané tasted revolting, but it was warm and it had made her feel better. In Bel's case, 'better' meant that she was falling back on her default programming, which told her that the nearest available man would soon lick the world into shape for her.

'Well, I'm no saint either,' he told her, resolutely topping up her glass with the last of the bottle. 'I've borrowed every cent I can, too. It won't help us if we're both on credit blacklists. Just at this point in history, I can't put my hands on five hundred pounds. I wish I could, but it can't be done. You do understand that, don't you?'

164

'Well, yes, dear. I suppose I do . . .' His mother, still clinging to the vision of the hero with the mighty cheque-book who was waiting in the wings to leap to her rescue, twinkled her eyes at him. Oliver found this highly annoying, particularly since, despite her faults, he adored his mother and would have gladly given her his last five hundred pounds, if he hadn't long ago blown it on the black-faced ram.

He made a tent out of his fingers, frowned in what he hoped was a caring manner and was about to reassume all the bankerly gravitas he had discarded so readily when he left the City when the fake-mahogany door of The Pigeon & Pipkin was flung open by an outraged hand.

'Colin! Ollie! Have you had one of these?' Florian Addleworth stood in the doorway, flipping his hair out of his eyes and trembling more than his lurcher who was shuddering at his heels. Florian held up a piece of paper.

'What is it?' Colin demanded from his lair in the fireside corner that was not already occupied by Oliver and Bel. 'Yesterday's lottery ticket? New directive from Agri-wotsit? Or some other kind of bog-roll?'

'No, this is serious,' Florian protested. 'It's a warning. From some animal rights nutters. They're going to attack the vineyard. Look!' He waved the paper at arm's length, so indignantly that his scarf unwound itself from his neck and fell to the floor and frightened the dog.

'I got one of them,' observed Jimmy. 'They stuck it on my gate with some old nail.'

'That's right,' Florian agreed. 'They pinned mine to the vineyard sign.'

'Ridiculous, Florian, dear. You haven't got any animals,

have you? They must have got the wrong farm,' Bel soothed him. She liked Florian. He had good looks and nice manners. She was of a vintage that diagnosed any young man with long hair and no girlfriend as gay and therefore thought it was rather sweet of him to be still in the closet. Florian was not gay, but not worried to be considered as such by well-meaning women like Bel. After all, it stopped them trying to fix him up with their daughters.

'Of course I haven't got any animals. Well, except the dog, obviously.' Florian waved his arms, knocking to the ground the murky print of Constable's *Haywain* in a fake-mahogany frame that adorned the pub wall. 'They mean the *bees*. They're off their trolleys. Look at this!'

He held out the paper again and Colin grabbed it. 'Bloody ridiculous,' he declared, sweeping the indictment towards his nose with one vast red hand; the other continued to scrape up the last of his Turkey Mediterrané. 'That's the absolute bloody end. Bloody idiots! They want shooting, the lot of them.'

'It's the equinox,' said Florian with a fatalistic shrug. 'Wild chaotic weather, an equinoctial gale forecast tonight, and stress and tension general. All the elements of life are coming into a new psychic balance as night and day approach equal length. So I suppose we should expect some sort of disruption. But really . . .'

'How can your bees be off their trolleys?' said Bel.

'Honestly, Colin,' Lucy Vinny sighed, perching on the nearest bar-stool.

'I'd string 'em up if they came on my land,' he assured her.

'You can't do that,' Jimmy warned him, 'you get prison

for that nowadays.' There was a momentary chill in the bar as the company noted, from the calm and serious tone of his voice, that Jimmy's ancestors had almost certainly strung up intruders in bygone ages.

Oliver reached over and took the leaflet. 'Honey Equals Slavery,' he read. 'Boycott Honey and Honey Products. Every Beehive is a Concentration Camp. Millions of bees work until they die of exhaustion every year. Bees make honey to feed themselves and their young; when man interferes with this natural process by stealing honey, he condemns bees to a lifetime of slavery as they work to produce more. We think of honey as a natural, wholesome product but it is in fact created by an artificial process which causes cruelty and suffering. Commercial beekeepers force-feed their insects on sugar syrup . . . do you do that, Florian?'

'Oh, please,' Florian sniffed. 'How would you go about force-feeding a bee? Will somebody tell me that?'

'But is the rest of it true?' demanded Bel. She was always responsive to the idea of something small suffering but the possibility of life without beeswax polish and royal jelly moisturiser felt distinctly bleak. 'Do millions of them die every year? It's all some silly joke, isn't it?'

'Well, the *drones* die,' Florian admitted, assuming his best pedagogic manner. 'Drone bees are the small sort-of mutants whose sole purpose is to work for the benefit of the hive. They die when they're no longer needed. Except the drone who mates with the queen. He dies at once, of course.'

'Good heavens,' said Bel, now concerned to distance herself from any connection with any species of black widow.

'But the queen lives on for years. The rest of the drones die off in the autumn because the workers just shove them out of the hive. I mean, they're pretty tough on their own, bees. Then the workers kind of chill out over the winter, living off the honey. So I suppose that bit is right. But they always make masses more than they need. I mean, bees are like that. They just . . . buzz about being busy. That's what they do. Nobody forces them. If they weren't happy they'd just fly off, wouldn't they?' He appealed to Lucy.

'I can't believe I'm hearing this,' Lucy said. 'Of course they would. Don't take any notice, Florian. Idiots.'

'I suppose they are right in one way. I mean, it isn't natural, is it? Not completely natural, it can't be.' Bel patted her hair by way of apology for these harsh words.

'Not, it's not natural and from the bees' point of view it's a damn sight better than natural.' Lucy Vinny thumped down her glass in exasperation. 'The natural way would be for the natural predators to steal the honey and smash up the bees' nests in the process. Birds and bears and things. Much worse than man.'

'Terrible mess,' agreed Colin. 'Seen it on the telly.'

'I thought I was quite nice to my bees,' said Florian. 'They've got the best hives money can buy, all fitted with wood inside, no plastic or anything. And plenty of flowers, planted specially. What more can you do for a bee, anyway?'

'We haven't got any bears in Suffolk,' added Bel, who had decided she was happy to promote any conversation that was not about how much money she owed people and what she was going to do about paying it.

'AASS,' Oliver read from the back of the leaflet. 'Anti Apian Slavery Society. Active in this area now. Bee Oppressors Beware. The Slaves will Fly Free. Don't they fly free now?'

'They got to fly free,' Jimmy pointed out, concerned that

these newcomers might have missed the point. 'Otherwise they don't find any flowers to get any pollen to make any honey.'

'Of course they fly wherever they want,' said Florian. 'I'm not exactly keeping them in the hives with razor wire and attack dogs, am I?'

'AASS. Arse,' Colin chuckled. 'Sounds about right, doesn't it?'

'Oh, for God's sake. Give that to me,' Lucy reached out for the leaflet. 'I'll take it to the police after I've finished this afternoon. Whoever these people are, they can't go about the countryside threatening damage.'

'Fat lot of good that'll do.' Colin had finished his food and was polishing his plate with a piece of bread. 'Nearest police must be in Ipswich now. Too busy with shoplifters and parking tickets to come out here. If I was you, Florian, I'd go for the dogs. Keep the loonies at bay. Real dogs, I mean. That lurcher of yours wouldn't scare a kitten.'

Oliver noticed that his mother was showing signs of distress. Her forehead was wrinkled and she seemed to be shrinking down in her seat. The momentary sparkle she had managed when Lucy spoke of bears had fizzled at the mention of attack dogs. The idea of violence on top of bankruptcy was sending her into panic mode.

'Time we headed home,' he said, getting up to settle the bill. Toni, from the pool room, favoured him with a malevolent stare before turning her back as they left. Even the attendant Goths winced a little at such rudeness.

'It's all a bit much, isn't it?' said Oliver as they drove back to The Manor House. 'Never mind. They're just a bunch of nutters.'

'I do mind.' Bel was looking sadly out of the window, uncheered by the cascading primroses in her son's hedge-banks. 'Sometimes I think the world's just gone mad. Slave bees. And,' she drew a shuddering breath and tried to catch Oliver's eye, never having entirely understood that a person driving a car needs to watch the road, 'what are we going to do about the money, Ollie, dear?'

'I don't know.' Oliver found he had neither the energy nor the hardness of heart to give his mother's debts any more thought at that moment. 'Never mind. Something will turn up.'

In his years as a banker, he had found that this observation, for all it had origins in the deeply flawed personal philosophy of Wilkins Micawber Esq, was usually close to the truth. For some people, things had an extraordinary propensity for turning up. Look at the farm, that had turned up. And the pigs. And . . . well, things went in threes, too. *I can't believe I'm trying to believe this,* said what remained of Oliver's capacity for rational thought. Outside, it began to rain.

'If something's going to turn up, it'd better hurry,' his mother said. 'We need it by Tuesday.'

'Then something will turn up by Tuesday.' *I must be out of my tiny fucking mind.*

Brueghel, Dante, Brian de Palma – no artist who has ever lived has conceived a scene as hellish as Junction 4 of the M25, the orbital highway that lies around the neck of London like a noose, on any given afternoon, from about four o'clock onwards. At three on the afternoon before a bank holiday weekend, it looked like the ninth circle of hell.

Dido, Clare and Miranda, cocooned in Miranda's car, were approaching the busiest intersection of the busiest road in Europe at the busiest time of the year.

For miles around in all directions, chains of cars inched ever-so-slowly onwards towards the ultimate standstill at Junction 4. Outside the vehicles a sadistic drizzle fell through the exhaust fumes, dissolving enough chemicals to create acid rain. In the sky, the sun seemed to be paling at the sight of this atrocity and began to withdraw its light. Inside the cars, children grizzled, couples fought and solitary drivers picked their noses and thought about suicide.

They drove, if it could be called driving, through desolate half-streets, the fresh new suburbs of seventy years ago now dying a lingering death as the road sucked out their life. The once-neat houses were crusted with the black grime of vulcanised rubber.

The windows that once had opened to let in fresh air from nearby green fields were now sealed against the ceaseless roar of engines and the toxic blast from the exhaust pipes. People still lived here, Clare noticed with surprise, and some still had daffodils blooming in their gardens, though the petals, seen through a miasma of vehicle filth, were not yellow but a dingy green.

Clare looked out on pebble-dash and stone cladding, peeling paint and cracking plaster, rusting cars in weed-choked drives, pale faces at dirty windows. She had time to waste, a new sensation. Her thoughts, seeking any focus except the disaster of her speech, were drifting. Who could possibly live here? People who couldn't live anywhere else. The poor. The marginalised. The desperate. Those with no purchasing power. The people she had never considered before.

The people she did not need to consider now. Politics, she reminded herself, was about having the power to do what the electorate wanted you to do. Not trying to find solutions to questions like why it was necessary for some people to live in the ninth circle of hell. Nor placating a bunch of tree-hugging hippies. Her mistake. Never again.

Dido did not look out of the windows. She knew she couldn't bear the view. All those dirty grey houses with their gallantly neat gardens and the gloomy hulks of cara-vans and conservatories around them. It would only make her cry. She had a book, *Gucci-Gucci-Goo*, with a pink and blue cover sprinkled with butterflies and babies, and she read it as if her life depended on it. Imagine, pretty pink books with people having babies in them, instead of just moaning about their boyfriends. Maybe a baby would be rather sweet. Babies were getting really must-have, really to-die-for. Suppose she had a baby with Florian – yes, a good thought. It would have her legs, obviously, and her hair, but maybe his adorable nose, with all those freckles. They could get married, have a wedding in a country church with little bridesmaids in flowery frocks and posies tied on the chair backs . . .

The humiliating memories of yesterday refused to fade, so Clare decided to read some of her documents. She issued something close to a smile in Dido's direction as she twisted in her seat and reached into the back of the car for the case of papers she had brought with her to fill up those fearful long afternoons of a holiday. So annoying, that Miranda was still friends with this Dido creature. But not as bad as it could have been. Clare admitted to herself that she was feeling a little bruised. Too bruised to start in on the bonding process straight away. With Dido along, Miranda seemed a bit more relaxed, anyway.

Clare began reading the first document, a set of proposals for incentives and penalties which would induce farmers to give up their land for building. A wave of nausea hit her at once. Damn! Her official car never gave her motion sickness, but this stupid thing her daughter had was obviously not so well designed. She sighed and put down the report.

Millimetre by millimetre, the car gained the ramp of the slip road leading to the M25 north. The sky was black, the drizzle relentless.

'Are you sure this is the right way?' Clare asked Miranda.

'Yes, this is the right way,' Miranda replied, gritting her teeth.

'Aren't we going heading for the west side of London? I thought we were meant to be going east?'

'To go east, you go west first. Otherwise you have to go through, which you can't do any more since the Central Pedestrian Zone was created. Going through would take twice as long.'

'Surely . . .'

'Miranda's brilliant at directions,' Dido put in. 'I'd be completely lost around London without her.'

'But if we've got to go east . . .'

'If you don't believe me, why don't you ring up one of your drivers and ask him?' Miranda snapped. 'You haven't driven yourself anywhere for fifteen years, Mum. What would you know about it?'

Clare reminded herself that the purpose of this weekend was to bond with her daughter. 'Of course, you're absolutely right,' she said, making it sound as warm as she could. 'I do apologise, Miranda. Sincerely, I do. I made a mistake and I'm really . . .'

While Miranda's attention wavered, a van cut in ahead of her and immediately braked hard. 'You're not making some corporate damage-limitation statement,' Miranda snapped, stamping on her own brakes just in time. 'Just . . . let me drive, OK?'

'OK. Actually, you're driving very well.'

'Gee, thanks.'

'You're an ace,' Dido told her, her eyes never leaving the page. 'I'd drive through Africa with someone like you.'

Outside, the drizzle graduated to rain, of the sort that England often experiences on the eve of a major public holiday, the persistent, monotonous, interminable downpour from a uniformly dark grey sky, the rain that is an eternal continuum of precipitation, the rain whose beginning nobody remembers and whose end nobody can imagine, the rain which English people describe, with doom in their hearts, as having settled in for the night, which is a traditional national understatement, because they mean that it will probably keep on raining like this for ever and if, by some fluke, it ever stopped raining, they would all be too depressed to notice anyway.

In front of Miranda, a white rental van barged into the lane as if its driver couldn't live unless he advanced that exact ten feet at that precise second. Three people were squeezed into the front seat, the passengers apparently semiconscious with boredom, their heads lolling and eyes half-closed.

And it was only 3.17pm on Thursday afternoon and they were only just at the foot of the slip road leading up to the

M25 northbound. Still to come was the M11, which would lead to some other motorway whose number Miranda, as Little Miss Perfect, had written down on her route notes which were held to the dashboard by a little magnet with a built-in light. Little Miss Perfect could never, ever, afford to get lost. Especially not with her mother on board.

The van carried thirty-eight urban foxes, all sedated for the journey by Carole. Some were sitting and swaying groggily. Most were lying, muzzles on paws, only their eyes rolling in panic. Several had vomited. One or two were trying to stand and falling against the sides of their cages of heavy-duty plastic. There was some whining, some growling and every now and then an outbreak of howling. The smell was intense.

Carole, who was driving the van, felt distinctly sick but said nothing. It was natural for animals to smell and a few hours of discomfort was nothing when they were going to be released into the wild to live a good, honest, natural life at last. And she was going to make her name as a result of a new initiative in animal activism. That was important, too.

In fact, she was taking part in two exciting new initiatives. The Transport Officer had pointed out that if the fox repatriation programme picked the right spot, the AASS team could mount a combined operation and the van wouldn't have to come back to London empty.

'Are you sure this is the right way?' one of the AASS team asked as Carole made the imperceptibly slow turn on the northbound slip road. 'Aren't we supposed to be going east?'

'You have to go west to go east from this side of London,'

she explained patiently. He wasn't to know, he was the vegan from Los Angeles who was a member of the original Anti Apian Slavery Society of America. His name was Ashok and he was impressively healthy and absolutely hardline about the veganism. People naturally looked up to him for these qualities. Carole was ashamed of herself for disliking him.

The other one was the Video Guy – the cameraman who was to record the historic events of the weekend. He was squeezed up against the passenger door; his eyes were closed and he hadn't said anything. Maybe he was asleep. Carole was aware of the camera in a case at his feet, in the same way that she might have been aware of a rattlesnake. She could never lose the gut feeling that a camera was something deadly.

'But the sign back there said north,' Ashok persisted, in that brainlessly gentle way that went so well with his ideology.

'We've been west, we're turning north, then we'll be going east in about another hour, if the traffic keeps moving,' Carole assured him.

'Why?' he asked, blue eyes vacant.

'The mayor pedestrianised the centre of London. You can't go Through any more. You have to go Round. And if you go In to go Round, everything's solid anyway. So you have to go Out, then Round.'

'Wow,' he said. 'I can't imagine that.'

'We can't imagine it and we live here,' Carole said. She had resisted the suggestion of teaming up with the AASS squad from the beginning. The last thing she needed now was to get lost in this crush of selfish, gas-guzzling cars.

Bees were not real animals. She was quite sure of this in

her own mind, but not about to say so because ugly things happened to people who spoke out on that kind of issue at Caucus meetings. But bees were definitely insects, and it was only a loophole in the drafting of the ruling articles of the Caucus that allowed them to get involved with them.

Personally, she thought it was time to clarify the Mandate with a few clauses. Personally, Carole felt the Chair's interpretation of the Mandate was too broad. People thought she was stupid because she had once been a model, but she had learned a great deal and she would show them all soon. They needed to focus more. Stop frittering energy away on insects when there were real animals suffering, thousands of them, every day.

Carole felt tears prickle her eyelids at the mere thought of animals in pain, going hungry or getting cold. All her winsome childhood and her beautiful youth, she had felt like a victim and no one had listened to her. Now she empathised so strongly with any creature that was suffering and could not speak that she sometimes spent all day on the verge of tears. Hunted eyes, bedraggled coats, fur matted with blood — no, no, stop it now. Things without eyes didn't touch her feelings the same way. Oysters, bees, anything invertebrate — she just couldn't respond. Besides, bees stung you. Several of them had stung her once during a school sports day, and her foot had swollen up so much she'd had to scratch from the hundred metres hurdles, which everyone had known she was going to win.

'In LA, if we have to go east, we can just go east,' Ashok was saying. 'I mean, we can't go west anyway, because we'd get to the ocean. Do you have ocean here?'

'We have sea, mostly.'

'I suppose that's kind of like ocean. But why would anybody do that? Stop cars going through the city. I mean, that's what a city's for, isn't it, for people to go around in cars. It was the mayor who did that?'

'He couldn't do anything else, I guess. Nobody could get through the centre in a car anyway, unless they took all day. Especially after the last Tube disaster. And the old London authority didn't have any power or any money or anything. All they could do was fart around with the traffic regulations.'

'Didn't people complain?'

'Oh yes. And one borough, Kensington and Chelsea, tried to secede from the city and become independent.'

'Oh wow.'

'They should have let them. They're all toffs and Arabs down there anyway. So that was when the new Federal London Authority was set up. But taking down all the barriers and resurfacing the streets and everything is so expensive, and they have to spend all their money rebuilding the Underground after the Oxford Circus disaster. So nobody's doing anything about the pedestrian zone.'

'Oh my. I didn't know you still had circuses in England.'

'It's not a real circus,' Carole began, drawing a deep breath for another long explanation. Amazing that people could speak the same language and still not understand each other at all. 'I mean, I suppose it must have been a circus at some point otherwise why the name, but we banned them years ago.'

'You should get the name changed,' Ashok advised generously. 'Who would want to commemorate something like a circus? It seems so thoughtless.'

'Yes it does,' Carole agreed. She could see the possibilities. A renaming campaign. She could go on television. 'That's an excellent idea.'

'Except it's bollocks,' said Video Guy, dragged into wakefulness by the idiocy of the conversation next to him. 'Circus is just Latin for "round". Oxford Circus was a round street, like two crescents. No implications for animal welfare.'

'Well,' Ashok said tartly, 'how nice of you to wake up and rain on our parade.'

'It's raining anyway,' Video Guy riposted, opening his eyes briefly.

The car ahead had not moved for some while. Somewhere beyond it, through the sheets of rain, a yellow light began to flash. Then another. Then a blue one. Several blue ones. They heard sirens.

'Do you have drive-by shooting here?' asked Ashok.

'Your mother, eh?' said the girl among Toni's companions in the pool room of The Pigeon & Pipkin, a chunky lass with a square face on top of a cuboid body, who went by the Goth name of Frenzi Fee. She was racking up the balls for a new game. One of the boys had gone to the bog and not come back. The other was sitting in a chair in the corner, not moving. It was coming up to five, and they'd been drinking steadily since lunchtime. 'I mean, what is she like? Eh?'

'Yeah, what is she like?' Toni agreed. 'Coming in here.'

'My mum would never,' Frenzi Fee asserted, rolling herself off the table and leaving the balls perfectly aligned. 'She knows I'd kill 'er. She wouldn't dare.'

'Uh,' Toni grunted, agreeing that a mother should be

properly intimidated but at the same time feeling criticised. And angry. Flaming cheek, really. Six months ago this bunch of tossers hadn't had the first idea about being a Goth. She'd taught them everything she knew, from sourcing early Sisters of Mercy cuts to finding the Halls of Cthulu website and playing the strange games that lay therein. And now they were trying to give her lessons and tell her what it was all supposed to be about.

'Anyway,' Fee challenged her, lining up her first shot. She was winning, just. Toni needed to get this game. 'What you gonna do about it? You gonna let 'er get away wiv that?'

'Well, I can't hardly do that now, can I?' Toni replied on auto-speak, encouraged to see her opponent's ball connect at a bad angle and leave the rest of them lying around on the green baize, as useless as a bunch of sheep.

'Well, wot are you gonna do then?' This question came exactly as Toni was about to make her shot. At the eleventh nanosecond, Toni changed her mind, stood up and walked thoughtfully around the table. Hah! Pitiful, really, trying to put her off her game like that.

It had been a long, cold, wet winter. The graveyard parties and the beach picnics were long gone, nothing but guttering memories. Hard to believe they had ever happened. Toni had tried to persuade some of her London friends to come up and sample the scene. A couple of them had turned up, done a weekend and gone home mumbling about how it was a long way and the petrol was expensive.

She had spent the last of her money on a new tattoo, a flaming heart with 'Jesus' written on it, up on her right thigh. She had designed herself a web page, black with purple text, in the name of Scary Minx. She had just about worn holes in her Cruxshadows CD. She had decided to collect gargoyles, after finding, in a skip, a cement cast of a little demon with one wing slightly chipped. Trouble was, the only other gargoyles she spotted were still attached to churches. And all through the long dreary winter, Toni had been playing pool. She'd got good at it. Much too good to enjoy playing with pond life like Frenzi Fee.

Toni was more bored than she'd ever imagined it was possible to be. Goth had been great when it started, but it had all been too easy. And the winter in the country! It seemed likely that she would shortly go mad. And it was all Bel's fault. Bel had dragged her to this dump, Bel had stopped giving her money, Bel was blackmailing her about going to college, getting exams, all that crap. Yup, payback time was on its way. Definitely. She'd do something. Bel would be sorry. Who knew what or how, but she'd do it.

'I dunno wot I'm gonna do,' she explained. 'I gotta think about it. It's gotta be something that she knows it was me but don't know it was me, innit?'

Whack! The first ball went down. Yes, Jesus loved her. Toni strutted around the table corner and looked for her next shot.

'How's that?' Fee asked. When she was puzzled she really did look cross-eyed. If you put someone like that on a TV programme playing some yokel in a country pub, they'd say you were making her up.

'Think about it,' Toni advised. She whacked down another ball and felt more energetic. 'Stormin',' she said, to nobody in particular.

'Stormin',' Fee repeated, glad that natural authority was asserting itself. Toni was one cool bitch. It was a real honour to get beaten by her.

For three women who did not normally have to give the elements any consideration, it was a bad time.

The rain. Rain so heavy, so wet, so despair-inducing that the global-warming lobby could have ordered it specially.

The wind. Wind in huge howling gusts that heaved at the side of the car like a drunk rugby team trying to tip it over.

The dark. Darkness that was deeper, blacker and infinite, darkness without stars or moon or streetlights, darkness made worse by the reflections of the car headlights on the wet road, a treacherous kaleidoscope that strained Clare's eyes as she drove.

The noise. And, when they stopped for petrol, the cold. Cold that ripped through their flimsy urban garments and stabbed at their arms and legs. Cold like knives. Cold that actually made Miranda wish she wasn't so thin.

They were frightened, and vaguely outraged. They had done everything to deserve comfort and being at the mercy of nature like this was all wrong. There was supposed to be warmth, and light, and stability, and dryness, not cold, dark, danger and wet. This was not the way things were supposed to be at all. Dido was pouting. Clare was getting angry. Miranda felt guilty; she should have checked the weather forecast or the traffic reports or something. It was her fault. This was all happening because Little Miss Perfect had fallen down on the planning.

Somewhere past Newmarket, somewhere bare and alien and rain-lashed, Clare had taken over at the wheel. We'll share the driving. That had been the deal. Why was the country so goddamn far away?

Driving meant gripping the wheel, trying to stop the car aquaplaning every time they passed another vehicle, peering out through the windscreen to where the beam of the headlights vanished into a curtain of water. Feeling waves of spray surging away from the car tyres, aware that every swipe of the wipers threw a festoon of water into the air. Her eyes were tired, her neck was stiff, her back ached. The foot on the accelerator had cramp.

Crash! Something hit the windscreen.

'Bloody hell!' shouted Clare, wrestling with the steering wheel. 'What was that?'

'It was only a tree branch,' Miranda said, shocked into daring to think that her mother needed reassurance.

'Why the hell was it falling into the road? It's dangerous!'

'There's a storm,' Dido pointed out. 'The wind must have broken it off. It must have just blown off a tree.'

'Well it shouldn't have blown off a tree. We could have had an accident. Things like that shouldn't happen.' Especially, thought Clare, not to me, the CEO of Agraria. Nor to me, the City golden girl of the past decade. And definitely not to me when I'm trying to keep my only viable offspring on side. 'Where are we?' She tried, and failed, not to sound accusing. 'We must be in Suffolk by now, surely?'

'Absolutely, I'm sure we're in Suffolk by now,' Miranda said, telling them both that she had no idea where they were. 'Sorry,' she said.

'I wish I could read maps,' said Dido. 'If I could read a map, I'd know where we were, I'm sure I would. But I always get maps upside down, they just don't work for me.'

Clare stifled a sigh. If Miranda was starting with the apologies, things were not looking good. And why had she brought Dido along? She hadn't seen the girl in six or seven years, and she was even more irritating now than she had been. Ditzy, disempowered and dysfunctional; amazing that there still were women like that.

'Sorry, I should know where we are,' Miranda said again.

The car was going up again. Up on some bridge thing. A long way up. There was light, orange light, from streetlights. Huge overpass of some kind. Nasty feeling of a whole lot of nothing underneath it. Wind howling louder, rain lashing faster. Twenty miles an hour, that was all you could do. Clare had not imagined that the country would have colossal outcrops of concrete such as this.

'Darling, is this right?' Clare asked, her voice as harsh as tearing Velcro. 'Are we meant to be going over this bridge or whatever?'

'Sorry, yes, I'm sure it's right,' Miranda said, reading her directions again for the hundredth time from the little light in the dashboard magnet that had seemed so neat two hours ago and now seemed like some childish toy. Her directions said nothing about a bridge. Which seemed to be what they were on. 'We must be on the M14 still. It can't be far now.'

'Shall we give the hotel a call?' Clare suggested, trying not to clench her teeth.

'Ooh, yes. Good thinking, Mrs Marlow. If we call them, maybe they can talk us in. Or tell us where we are, anyway.' Dido was scrabbling in her bag for her phone. Her bag was almost an independent life form, made of some multi-coloured patchwork of stuff held together with crochet and felt flowers and sequins and buttons, containing an ample

184

space in which her survival pack of possessions could lose themselves.

Miranda's bag was neat, leather, lots of zips and handy pockets. It was by her feet, and the phone was easy to extract.

'It's like we're a jumbo jet having to make a forced landing,' Dido was saying as she dumped out her bag on the back seat.

'No it isn't. We're lost, that's all,' Clare stated, then realised she'd come on too harsh. 'I mean, we might be lost. Mightn't we, darling?' It was no good, her voice was still coming up from the permafrost. Keep on with the 'we'. Do not say 'you'. Do not make your daughter feel that this is her stupid fault, even though it is her stupid fault and she obviously hasn't a clue where we are. I must not be critical, I must not be critical, I must not be critical.

'I suppose we should tell the hotel we're going to be late,' Miranda conceded. Little Miss Perfect had put the number of the Saxwold Manor Hotel in the speed-dial. She hit the button and said, 'Hello?'

A man's voice answered, a wonderfully calm voice, a voice redolent of log fires, stiff drinks, comforting suppers. It made her feel a few degrees less worm-like. 'Saxwold Manor Hotel – can I help you?'

'I'm terribly sorry,' she began. Get yourself together, girl, get this sorted. 'Um – we have a reservation—' False name, they were using a false name. Something about privacy, her mother had said, and who did she think she was kidding? False name because she was a politician now and keen to protect her back. The booking was in the false name, but what was it? The traumas of the journey had erased it from her memory. Oh God, she'd have to ask. Clare would just nuke her for forgetting. And it was ten to one Clare wouldn't know the name either, because the bloody assistant had talked to Miranda about it. 'Ah – a reservation for the weekend, for a twin room – ah . . .'

'Yes, I have it here,' said the blissfully stress-free voice. 'You're going to be late, is that it?'

'Yes,' Miranda said gratefully.

'Any idea when you might be arriving?'

Wonderful man! He was just totally up there with people who didn't know where they were or what they were doing. 'Ah . . . I'm sorry, I don't really know . . .'

'Having a bit of trouble finding the way?'

'Ah . . . yes.' Heavenly, heavenly person. How did he know?

'Simplest thing, go around Ipswich on the bypass. That's all you can do, you just follow the road. Over the Orwell Bridge, huge thing, can't miss it.'

'Oh! I think we just went over it.'

'You'll be about twenty minutes away then. Take the next turning off the bypass, signed Woodbridge, second on the left off that, pass the pub, left again, can't miss it.'

'Turning for Woodbridge, second on the left, pass the pub, left again, can't miss it.'

'Don't worry, take your time. Look forward to seeing you.'

Can't wait, Miranda thought. Oh, to be warm and safe and *there*, wherever it was, just as long as it wasn't on this endless road. And with that heavenly, heavenly person. Don't worry, take your time! Nobody, ever, in Miranda's entire life as she remembered it, had ever told her not to worry and to take her time.

'Oh good,' said Clare. 'If there's a pub we can leave you there, Dido.'

'Couldn't be more perfect,' Dido said, shovelling her myriad possessions back in her bag.

In the Saxwold Manor Hotel the concierge, a fifty-eight-year-old man, a man recently retired from his first career as a cruise line purser, a gay man who'd at last felt safe to come out now that his three children were married with children of their own, in short, a man who'd seen it all and done most of it, made a note that the guests who'd booked The Aldeburgh Suite would be arriving late.

In the car, Miranda found herself focused on the bright spot in all this misery, the definite idea that whoever the man in the hotel was, and whatever she might do in his presence, he would look after her. Miranda had always been sure she didn't want anyone to look after her. If you'd asked her then, she'd have said so. And she would have been wrong.

Clare drove on. The rain hammered on the roof of the car. Dido decided that it would not be rude to put on her headphones now and chill with her new iPod.

They took a turning for Woodbridge. It looked convincingly like the right turning to take. Eventually, there was a second road on the left, after a few things that couldn't possibly have been actual roads because they were small or awkward or messy or shut off with a gate or a chain, or in some other way not really road-like.

After a considerable while, a long, wet, cold, wind-blown while, Clare spoke again from her permafrost and said, 'This can't be right.'

'It must be right,' Miranda tried not to plead. 'We took the turnings, we did what he said.'

'But we're in the middle of nowhere. Surely we should have passed the pub by now . . .'

As she spoke, some garish lights blurred past the window.

'There it is,' cried Miranda, with relief. 'There's the pub! Left past the pub, that was it.'

They drove on. No left turning appeared. No right turning appeared. They were in a long tunnel-like twisting lane overhung with thrashing trees, with no exits. After ten more minutes, Clare said, 'Let's go back to the pub and ask directions.'

She slowed, stopped, and tried to turn the car around in what seemed to be a woodland picnic area. Being strictly an urban motorist, Clare did not appreciate the essential idiocy of leaving the safety of the Tarmac for a patch of muddy ground well covered with wet leaves. When the front wheels were six inches from regaining the road, the back wheels started to spin.

'What on earth . . . ?' Clare demanded.

'Sorry, sorry. I'll get out and push,' said Miranda, flinging her door open into the downpour.

'Wass happerhapperhappernin'?' asked Dido, slurred and dissonant because she still had her headphones on.

'Don't get out . . .' Clare began. It was not part of the plan for Miranda to get wet and cold and even more tired than she was already. But the door slammed and she saw her daughter's black form floundering to the rear of the car. Then she felt a flurry of clothes behind her, and a blast of cold wind on the back of her neck as Dido scrambled out to join her friend.

It took time, and a hard struggle, and much swearing, and a bit of luck, and some fallen branches pushed under the back wheels plus a twisted ankle, three broken nails, a definitively ruined pair of Manolo Blahnik boots, a rip around the shoulder seam of Miranda's coat and the complete destruction of both their hairstyles, but in a quarter of an hour or so Miranda and Dido made it possible for Clare to drive their car back to the roadway. The rain, of course, did not let up in the least during this difficult operation. And when they got back into the car, wet, muddy and gasping, Miranda's mother instinctively flinched away from them.

When they reached the cheerful glare of the pub car park, Miranda flung herself out into the rain again without saying a word, followed in a few minutes by Dido, struggling with her bag.

Miranda dragged open the pub door and advanced purposefully towards the bar, vaguely aware, in the smoky depths of the room, of a few rural types raising their noses from their glasses.

'We're looking for the Saxwold Manor Hotel,' she began, registering the landlord's unpromisingly blank face as she spoke.

'Round here, is it?' he answered, even less promisingly.

'I think so,' Miranda said, scanning the blackboard on which the wines of the month were offered and beginning to think that a nice glass of something red and velvety would do wonders for her karma.

Dido floundered to her side and dropped her bag, from which several wayward items immediately escaped. 'Do they know it?' she asked, as if the indigenous people did not speak English.

'The Saxwold Manor Hotel. It's in Suffolk. Somewhere called Lower Saxwold,' Miranda said.

The landlord sucked his teeth. 'I dunno . . . I can ask,' he offered.

'Maybe a quick glass of Rioja,' Dido suggested. 'If we've got to wait a bit.'

'Oh, all right,' Miranda conceded at once.

The landlord, hearing 'rio-ha' instead of the accustomed 'rio-jar,' decided that perhaps these two rather scruffy young women might in fact be the messengers of destiny finally bringing to his door the sophisticated clientele of which he had almost despaired. He poured the glasses with a will.

'Saxwold Manor Hotel, anybody?' he demanded of the room at large.

'Round here, is it?' asked Colin Burton, wondering if one of these bedraggled women might in fact be destined to become Mrs Burton Number 4. The one with the long hair, perhaps. She might clean up rather well.

'It must be round here,' said Lucy Vinny, 'if it's got Saxwold in the name. Unless you mean Saxwold St Swithin, that's in north Norfolk.'

'This is Suffolk, isn't it?' Dido asked, experiencing a wrench of panic.

'Oh yes,' Colin reassured her. 'This is Suffolk, all right. No worries there. And you are in Great Saxwold. Lower Saxwold's a couple of miles down the road. Can't be far away.'

'And these are the only Saxwold places in Suffolk?' Miranda pressed on, determined to force these yokels to get their brains in gear.

'Unfortunately,' said a voice behind her. Shades of irony, undertones of humour. A London voice, for heaven's sake. Miranda turned around with an encouraging smile.

Before her stood a blessedly urban sight, a painfully thin, pitifully white-skinned, reassuringly spike-haired figure dressed in black and clanking with crucifixes, its fingers webbed in black lace and its feet squeezed into shiny black boots. It was clutching an empty glass, which seemed a reasonable basis for negotiation. Fellow metropolitan, thought Miranda, fellow traveller in this strange land, I salute you. Actually, I trust you.

'So if this is the only Saxwold in Suffolk,' she pressed on with hope in her heart, 'and we're looking for the Saxwold Manor Hotel . . .'

'No point asking her,' Colin insisted. 'She's not local, she won't know. And the rest of them Gothicks or whatever, they'll be three sheets in the wind by know, hardly know their own way home.'

'Oh, I won't know, won't I?' Toni replied, giving Colin a near subliminal wink just before Miranda turned back to her. 'Don't take any notice of him, he's bin rat-arsed himself all evening. 'Scuse my French. What was it, Saxwold Manor Hotel?'

'Yes,' Miranda confirmed. 'Could I, er . . .' She indicated the glass.

'Cheers, large vodka,' Toni replied smartly, failing to stop an ungothly smile from warming her lips. If she could get this yuppie tart to buy her a drink, surely she could also figure out a way to piss off her stepmother. An idea was taking shape. Maybe she could actually have a bit of fun, if such a thing was actually possible in Saxwold when it was raining. Which Toni doubted severely.

'Saxwold Manor Hotel,' she said again. 'It's dead simple. You just go on through the village, take the first left, go on down that road about ten minutes and where the road forks, take the left, and it'll be straight ahead of you. Big white house with a couple of them stupid-looking stone dogs out-side.'

'Left, left, big white house with stone dogs outside,' Miranda repeated. Yes! They were nearly there.

'No sign,' Toni warned her, in an earnest voice which, had Miranda not been wet, cold, exhausted and deeply inter-ested in the second half of her Rioja, would have immediately signalled a porky pie of ample proportions. 'Very discreet sort of a place, no publicity or anything.'

Miranda and Dido missed the suppressed chuckle raised among Colin, the landlord and Lucy Vinny. All they retained was the impression that this was a nice pub, a jolly pub, a bit naff, maybe, but still a pub which even Clare might enjoy visiting for a drink or two before dinner. As for discreet – why, wasn't the whole weekend supposed to be discreet, from the new Minister's point of view?

'Got you,' Miranda assured her. Discreet, eh? Her mother was going to love that. And chill, and smile, and stop criti-cising her. Everything was going to be OK. She could hardly wait.

'So – I'm not staying with them, you see,' Dido explained to the landlord, her wet hair like straps of seaweed as she pulled it aside from her face. 'So I've got to find somewhere else to stay tonight. I don't suppose you've got any rooms here, have you?'

The unpromising look returned. Please God, Miranda prayed, let him have a room for Dido. My mother will just kill me if . . .

'Funny enough, we did have some bookings this week-end,' he was saying, searching behind the bar for something. When he found it, it was a large desk diary, already dog-eared, containing a shopping list, a flyer from the Anti Apian Slavery Society, and the room booking details. 'But I do have one left. There's no en-suite, that's the thing . . .'

'No problem,' Dido told him with relief. 'It'll be fine. So that's me sorted, angel. Don't worry about anything. You've got my number, haven't you? We can talk tomorrow.'

They kissed, Miranda paid, and parted. Back on the road, now full of hope for the weekend, Miranda directed Clare down the first left, then down the left fork, and then to a halt on the gravel drive of The Manor House in front of the stupid-looking stone dogs.

Clare turned off the engine and flopped back in the seat, saying, 'I hope to God this is it.'

'Of course this is it,' Miranda assured her. 'I'll go in and get someone to get the bags.'

Dido, with the eyes of all the bar upon her, flicked back her hair decisively and wavered in the general direction of her luggage.

'Let me help you,' said the landlord.

'You're so-o-o-o-o kind but I can manage,' said Dido gallantly.

'Let *me* help you,' said Colin Burton, striding forward from his corner.

'It's no trouble,' said the landlord, nipping around the corner of the bar with previously unseen speed.

The two collided in front of Dido, whose hands flew to her lips to hide a smile.

'Oh for God's sake,' said Lucy Vinny.

Jimmy sat on his usual stool and smiled. The landlord, who got to the handles first, tried to pick up Dido's bag, misjudged its weight, and staggered. In the end, she and he took a handle each and they struggled out of the room towards the back of the building.

'Toni,' said Colin Burton, turning to her as soon as the coast was clear in the bar of The Pigeon & Pipkin, 'what have you done? If I'm not mistaken you just sent that woman off to your mother's house and told her it were a hotel. You naughty, naughty girl.'

'Yeah, well don't sweat it, Colin,' Toni replied, returning to the pool room to tell the story.

CHAPTER 7

Checking In and Checking Out

Outside The Manor House Miranda slicked back her wet hair out of her eyes, dabbed on some lip gloss and got out of the car. Large white house, stone dogs, no sign. Yes, yes, yes. This was it. At last.

Through the teeming rain and biting cold, her traumatised boots found their way up the exquisitely lichenous stone steps. With the one finger whose nail was still intact she pressed the brass doorbell.

No reply. She pressed again, hearing the bell peal somewhere in the guts of the building. For a while that was all she heard. Then a dog somewhere cranked out a bark. Just as she was about to ring again, heavy steps sounded from behind the door, accompanied by heavy paws. A light came on, a beautiful, welcoming golden light. There came the sounds of fumbling, unlocking, dechaining.

The door swung open, and the golden light flooded out into the night, followed by some large brainless dog thing that pushed past her legs and disappeared into the darkness, barking madly. Miranda staggered forward through the heavy door, out of the cold and wet and into the gold and warmth. It felt like passing through a time warp into a parallel universe.

And there, holding open the door, was the man. The man who, in the obscure lower depths of her subconsciousness, she already believed would take care of her whatever she did. The heavenly man. Well, he was just as she would have imagined, if she had allowed herself to imagine him. Big, solid, calm, with an adorable, slightly fuzzy look of bewilderment on his face. His fine face. In fact, he was very fine, fine all over. Class-A, from his gorgeous messy hair to his gorgeous feet. Feet which were in socks only. But who cared? Suddenly, this weekend was looking up.

'Hi,' she fluttered happily. 'I'm so sorry we're late. But we did phone.'

'Er, yes,' said Oliver, holding the door a good bit wider. A large WOW had filled his head. A very large WOW. Who was this appealing creature and why had nobody warned him about her?

'The bags are in the car,' she said.

'Of course,' he said. 'But do come in. It's a filthy night, you must have had a terrible time getting here. Come in and sit down and let me pour you something.'

'Oh yes,' she said. 'My mother's just coming.'

Mother? Ah! Obviously this mother was some friend of his mother, and this appealing creature was her daughter. Obviously, faced with the sudden likelihood of being made bankrupt, his mother had forgotten to tell him that she had invited these people for the weekend. So far, so excellent. Oliver could do a damn fine job of impressing a mother, when he had to. Impressing the prospect before him, however, was the overriding imperative.

'Come through into the drawing room. I've got a fire going,' he urged her.

'Lovely,' she replied. Drawing room! Such a sweet, old-fashioned expression.

And it was lovely. Annabel had done the drawing room in cream, her favourite, most luscious shade of cream, with quite a lot of raspberry reds and old-rose pinks. It was warm, and calm, and pretty. There were pictures of contented cows in sunny meadows in gold frames. Oliver's fire was blazing enthusiastically and the reflections glimmered from the polished sides of some big chest thing with drawers. The scent of a huge bowl of hyacinths mingled with the tang of wood smoke. It was exactly as Miranda had pictured the lounge of the Saxwold Manor Hotel.

She flung herself, with just a touch of provocation, on a handy chintz sofa. 'A glass of red wine would hit the spot,' she told him. 'Or just send the waiter. Better get the bags before my mother gets irritated. Maybe I should order something for her. Make that two red wines. I'm sure your house red will be fine.'

'Right,' he agreed. 'I'll just let *my* mother know you're here.'

A family business, thought Miranda. How quaint. I suppose people still have family businesses in the country.

He left her patting the cushions and blinking at the fire, and went to the kitchen for his boots and a word with Bel, whom he discovered chopping onions disconsolately.

'Well, they're here,' he said, looking hurriedly around for his boots. One was clearly visible under the kitchen table.

197

'Who's here?' she asked.

'The people who've come for the weekend,' he answered, dragging out the first boot and thrusting a leg into it.

Boys! Bel Hardcastle exclaimed to herself for the thousandth time since she had brought a son into the world. They just rush in where angels fear to tread and assume everything's going to be OK. 'Oliver! You might have told me.'

'I'm telling you now,' he said, bending to search all levels for the second boot. There it was, in Garrick's basket. With the top chewed off. But the foot still OK. Well, maybe a couple of holes. What the fuck.

Why is my son looking so insanely cheerful? Bel asked herself, noticing a bounce in Oliver's deportment that had been lacking for some time. In fact, he hadn't looked so happy since the day he bought the farm. It was on the tip of her tongue to say something pained about being taken for granted, but it seemed a shame to spoil his new mood.

'So, these people,' Bel said carefully.

'This girl and her mother,' Oliver was fighting his way into his second boot and trying to open the back door at the same time.

This girl and her mother! Girl! And her mother! At last! At last! Wedding bells! Grandchildren! Yes! Yes!

'I've got to get their bags from the car,' he told her, stamping his heel down the last reluctant inch. 'They must have had one hell of a journey, all the way from London on a night like this. I promised them a couple of glasses of red. The bottle's open already.'

And he dived out of the door into the cold black night, eyes bright and a smile on his lips. One of those boy-meets-girl smiles! At last!

198

Bel dropped her knife, washed her hands, took off her apron, fluffed up her hair, rooted out a lipstick, took the shine off her nose, smoothed her skirt, changed her shoes and set off for the sitting room. Yes! There was a girl on the sofa. About the right age. Maybe a little old but maybe she was still tired from the journey. Old could be good. Keen to get on with the children.

Not too clean. Actually, she had mud on her shoes and it was getting on that eyewateringly expensive tapestry rug. But she didn't mind. She. Did. Not. Mind. The shoes were good. You could always tell a person by their shoes. Good shoes, nice clothes generally. Probably she had a job, a good job even. Maybe quite tall. Quite pretty, except for the nose. Oliver had a very nice nose. Could be blonde but the poor thing was so wet from the rain it was hard to tell.

'Hello?' Miranda heard a presence near the door.

'Oh, hello.' Bel advanced into the room, holding out her hand. 'I'm Oliver's mother. Bel. Do call me Bel.'

The poor thing was shy. She was looking at the hand with a little worried frown as if she didn't know what was expected of her.

That's a bit quaint, Miranda decided. Introducing herself like that. Maybe they're going for a family atmosphere or something. Quite sweet really. Making people feel at home. 'I'm – ah – Miranda,' she said, realising that she still didn't know what name had been used to make their booking.

They shook hands. Firm, thought Bel. She knows her own mind, this one. Soft, thought Miranda. A bit ingratiating, but then that's her business, I suppose.

'Did you have a ghastly drive from London?' Bel asked.

'Complete nightmare,' said Miranda. 'Is it always like this on holiday weekends?'

'Yes, I'm afraid it is. But you're here now, that's the important thing. Oliver's getting your bags, isn't he?' Helpful, that's my son. And strong. And reliable. Any girl would be lucky . . .

'I'd love a glass of wine,' said Miranda. 'And I'm sure my mother will too. She's probably just locking the car.'

'Of course,' Bel agreed. 'Red, wasn't it? Oliver likes red.' Made for each other, that's what you are. You like red wine and Oliver likes red wine. It's a perfect match. 'Stay by the fire, get warmed up. I'll bring the glasses in here.'

Perhaps, Bel thought as she dashed back to the kitchen, I'd better not call her dear, or anything else like that. Young girls can be a bit funny, always worried that they're being patronised. Now, where's that bottle?

Heavens! Where are they going to sleep? I've got the ironing all over the bed in the Rose Room. What about sheets? And towels? And the bathrooms – nobody's cleaned one of those baths since I washed Garrick in it last week. Oliver will have to hold the fort while I get the rooms ready.

She threw together a tray with salted nuts, cocktail napkins and three impeccably filled wine glasses, and carried it to the drawing room as fast as she could manage. Then nearly dropped it. There was the mother. Oh dear.

'Isn't this lovely?' said Clare Marlow, standing in front of the fire and feeling the glorious warmth on the backs of her legs. 'So well thought out. With all these marvellous things. Antiques, obviously.' People always called old furniture antique.

'I'm Bel Hardcastle,' Bel said again, putting down the tray and turning around to offer her hand.

'Pleased to meet you,' Clare said. 'And you're the owner?'

'Yes indeed.' Beyond firm, that shake. A vice-like grip, quite honestly. A classic bone-crusher. Obviously she'd spent all her career dealing with men and absorbed those awful boardroom manners. Crunch, crunch, my dick is bigger than your dick.

'Well, congratulations. You must be very successful.'

'Not really.' Bel felt herself blush, just a little. 'Maybe it just looks like that.'

'It certainly does.' Clare reached for her glass. So did Miranda.

Bel reached for her glass in turn, and raised it. 'Well, good health, everybody,' she said. Good healthy babies. At least two of them. Soon. As soon as possible. If the other mother was a boardroom type, she wouldn't be interfering, at least.

'Er – yes,' Clare agreed, sipping graciously. Miranda gulped. This woman was pretty good at the old family atmosphere stuff. It was even working on her mother.

Crashing and stamping resounded from the hall, followed by the patter of dog feet. Garrick appeared in the doorway, caught a beam of disapproval from Bel and lumbered around to head for the kitchen. Outside the door, luggage thumped on the floor.

'Oliver!' Bel called. 'Won't you come and entertain our guests? I need to – ah – check on things.'

In another minute, Oliver reappeared, more tousled than before but now wearing shoes.

'We've all introduced ourselves,' she told him as she made

for the door in her turn. 'I've got to sort the bedrooms. And see what I can do about dinner.'

Much was accomplished in the next twenty minutes.

Oliver discovered that the appealing creature was called Miranda.

Bel aired two bedrooms, made two beds, cleaned two bathrooms and battled out into her garden to pick posies of spring flowers to put in Ironstone cream jugs on the dressing tables. Then she chopped a second onion, dragged out the larger saucepan and rummaged in the deep freeze for some pheasant breasts.

Clare learned an enormous amount about Saxwold. Inhabited since the Bronze Age at least, and close to the site of a notable ship burial whose sumptuous grave goods, including the important Saxwold Cauldron, were now in the British Museum. A busy port in Roman times, since when, of course, the sea had retreated. Captured by Oswin, king of Dacia, in his wars against the Mercians in the sixth century. Hence the dedication of the parish church. Oswin didn't deserve to be a saint really, probably wouldn't have been canonised nowadays, never martyred or anything like that, probably not even a Christian, but was made a saint for 'doing Christian deeds'. Obviously they were pretty desperate for British saints in the sixth century. The village was mentioned in the Domesday Book, of course, as quite a substantial settlement although obviously in decline even then because the port was long gone. Welcomed Wat Tyler in 1459, as well as the Pilgrimage of Grace in 1536, and managed to escape the notice of the Roundheads in 1647. Enclosure of Saxwold Common achieved in 1703, with only minimal rioting. Lord Nelson slept in Saxwold Manor on his way home from sinking the Danish fleet in the North Sea in 1801.

Oliver listened to himself in horror, unable to stop drivelling through this history stuff he didn't even know he knew even though he was sounding like a complete prat. Helplessly, he heard the unstoppable gush of tedium continue at full force but couldn't find a way to end it. A deep pit of silence, full of invisible horrors and unavoidable doom, was yawning in front of him and it seemed the only way to avoid it was to keep talking. Oliver had never considered himself anywhere near suave, and a couple of years in the country hadn't given his conversation skills much of an outing. Now he was like one of those mythological characters cursed to spew out toads and snakes whenever he opened his mouth.

All the time he was talking on autopilot, part of his brain was trying to identify the face of this scary woman with laser eyes who was shredding his nerves a little worse every time they made contact with his. But he knew her face was familiar. Maybe she was an actress in a soap opera, but somehow he didn't think so.

And at the same time, he was watching the appealing creature wilt in front of him, sinking into the cushions and curling up as if she was going to burst into flames and spontaneously combust with boredom. Oh God, oh God. How to get out of this before he completely stuffed his chances?

I have to get him on his own, Miranda thought, watching the log fire burn down while she drifted pleasurably into a trance of warmth, comfort, relief and red wine. And preferably a thousand miles away from my mother. She's making him feel like a worm. We'll have that in common, anyway.

My mother would be so mad if she knew I was eyeing up the waiter, or whatever he is. Can I really pull this off? Can I really grab this gorgeous boy and stop this weekend being a complete waste of time?

'I wonder,' she said, when Oliver at last paused for breath, 'if we could have another log on the fire or something?'

'Goodness. Yes. Of course. Right away. ' Oh, the relief. A way out of this mad labyrinth. Oliver came down from his cloud of panic and noticed empty glasses. 'And let me get you another drink.'

He poured more wine, piled the last logs in the basket on to the glowing embers and was heading for the door to fetch in some more from the woodpile when Bel reappeared, saying, 'There, everything's all ready. Would you like to take up the bags, Oliver, and show our guests to their rooms? I've put Clare in the Rose Room and Miranda at the end of the corridor.'

It seemed advisable to get old Laser Lids settled first, so Oliver grabbed what he guessed was Clare's bag and said, 'Would you like to follow me?'

'We'd better decide what to do about dinner,' Clare said to her daughter.

'I'm absolutely knackered,' Miranda said firmly, adding, 'How late is it?' in case her mother hadn't got the message.

Just for once, the communication was perfect. 'Yes, it is late, isn't it? Don't let us put you to too much trouble. Maybe we could just have something in our rooms?' Clare said to the hotel owner. 'You could send up some sandwiches. Could we see a menu?'

A menu! Send up some sandwiches! What a nerve the woman had! How right she had been to get out of London and leave these awful rude people behind. A menu, for heaven's sake! Bel struggled not to sink to the same level. 'I'm so sorry,' she said, smiling her sweetest to shame the demanding bitch, 'there's not much choice tonight. Some cold chicken, or ham, or we've got a rather nice local cheese . . .'

'Oh no,' said Clare quickly. People occasionally had local cheeses in the Agraria offices. They seemed to be greasy, stinking substances that probably worked out at a thousand calories an ounce. No, no, no. 'Just chicken's quite all right.'

'And for me,' Miranda added. Chicken: OK in small portions without the skin.

'Well,' said Bel. 'That should be easy enough.' And she suppressed a flounce as she made for the kitchen, where she poured her sense of offence into two of the most lavish club sandwiches she had ever devised, featuring home-made mayonnaise and generous amounts of crisp bacon. These were prettied up with salad and installed on trays with napkins, just in time for Oliver to take them up to the bedrooms.

Bel thought of saying something about the other mother, but restrained herself. Plenty of time to be critical after they were married. Just let them get married. Please.

When she was alone in her room, Miranda whipped out her phone and called Dido.

'You'll never guess,' she began.

'Oh no. Not you too. Who is it?'

'The waiter. He's gorgeous. Do you think I can?'

'What about your mother?'

'She won't know. Not tonight, anyway. We're having an "early night". We're tired. Supper on room service.'

Dido's giggle, a contralto skylark, echoed in her ear.

'Sounds good to me. Go for it. Get him to go out with you somewhere.'

'I've got to, haven't I? It's now or never. Right, gotta run. Needa shower.'

In another ten minutes, Oliver was knocking at her door. 'Room service,' he said, jokingly.

The door was opened, and there she was, all amazingly wet and in a bathrobe, rubbing her hair with a towel. 'Oh, it's you again,' she said.

'Yes, it's me,' he confirmed. It seemed like a safe thing to say. 'Where would you like your supper?'

'Just put it on the table over there,' said Miranda, watching him as he walked across the room. Absolutely gorgeous. Now or never.

'So, what are the pubs like round here?' she said.

'Well, there's only one in the village,' he answered, inhaling the scent of woman plus bath gel. An aroma so wonderful that his brain fogged up like a shower-room door. 'The Pigeon & Pipkin. It's your basic country pub really.'

'I think we stopped there on the way – to ask directions. I suppose it's a pub in the sense that they sell alcohol.'

'Yes. Otherwise nobody would go there.' Her hair was all smooth, even when it was wet. How extraordinary. How lovely. How beautiful, the way it grew just like that . . .

'Isn't there anywhere a bit more funky? Or whatever you do for funky round here?'

Was she leading up to something? Nah. Was that bathrobe wrapped as well as it could have been? Well . . . 'There's The Yattenham Arms on the road to Yattenham St Mary. That's the whole nine yards – log fires, oak beams, inglenooks or whatever.'

'You go there?'

'Sometimes.'

Not the sharpest tool in the box, this one. Standing there like a pudding, missing all the tricks. Definitely more balls than brains. Miranda toyed with a piece of lettuce then crunched it with meaning. 'Is it easy to find, this Yatterwhatever Arms place . . .'

'Yattenham Arms. No, you can't miss it, just turn right at the end of the lane, go through the village, stay on that road till you get the sign for Yattenham St Mary and it'll be bang in front of you in about five minutes.' OK, this looks good, Oliver thought. Can I run with this? 'I could show you tomorrow, if you like.'

'Why not show me tonight? You'll be free before they close.'

'Um — yes. Yes I will. Yes, that's a good idea.'

'What time and where?'

Would his mother be charmed if she knew he was making a move on her friend's daughter? Probably not. Unless this was, in fact, some plot of his mother's to get him hitched. He wouldn't put it past her. But since he had no plans to get hitched, it would be best if his mother knew nothing. Either way, proceed with caution. Where the hell could they meet without his mother knowing? 'Why don't we say ten? I'll wait for you out by the car.'

'Great,' she said. 'I'll be there.'

Bloody hell. I've been pulled. Oliver found himself walking along the landing, in fact, trying not to skip along the landing, or even, metaphorically, to run along the landing with his jersey over his head being hugged by his teammates and waving in triumph to the roaring crowd.

*

207

'This is it,' said Video Guy in the hired van full of foxes. He was no longer sleeping but making himself useful reading the map. 'This is the B237 and that was the place called Something St Mary and if we take the next turning off it we should go through Great Somewhere and that's where we're staying.'

'Thank God for that,' mumbled Ashok. The two men had changed seats. Ashok had been unable to read the map. 'You have such bizarre names for places in England,' he had said, and, clearly mystified, he had opened out the map and turned it around and around, intermittently blocking Carole's view of the road, and getting them thoroughly lost somewhere north of Cambridge, where they shouldn't have been at all. The first episode of disharmony had taken place at that point.

'Yes,' said Carole. Her arms ached from the steering wheel and her feet ached from the pedals and her back ached from the length of time she had been driving. 'So how far are we from the drop zone?'

On the map, she had marked the location selected for the release of the foxes into the wild with a large red cross in a circle. Video Guy could hardly miss it. 'It's only about half a mile from Great Somewhere,' he said. 'We can just drive on a bit later. Or maybe in the morning.'

'We're going there first,' she insisted. 'Poor little loves, they'll be miserable after all this time in the van. I don't want them to have to wait one more minute before we set them free.'

'Do we have to do it in the rain? Does it ever stop raining in England?' asked Ashok.

'No,' said Carole and Video Guy together. 'Except for

global warming,' Video Guy added. Carole nodded, agreeing that it was their duty to let every American know exactly how disastrous their country's energy policies were for the rest of the world. They would both have been content to release Ashok into the wild as well.

In another hour the first part of their mission was accomplished. Sweeney, and thirty-seven more formerly urban foxes, had been turned out of their cages and let loose at the edge of a ploughed field, where most had streaked for cover on shaking legs, and hidden themselves in the hedges.

Carole, wearing leather gloves, had had to pull the most terrified animals out of their cages. Sweeney was the last. He sank down to the earth as if he could disappear into it. 'Don't you worry, Tickletums,' she said to him. 'All over now. No more cages. No more city. You're free.'

'You're free. Better get used to it,' Ashok agreed, looking at the cowering animal with mild fascination. 'Is he all right? Are they meant to do that?'

'He'll be fine when we've left him,' said Carole, a lump in her throat. 'He's just scared, that's all.' Sweeney had become her favourite. Even though there had been traces of human flesh in his stomach contents.

Out in the darkness they could just make out another fox, hopelessly disoriented, slowly running around in small circles. Sweeney was trembling on his belly, tongue lolling and eyes wide.

'Time to say goodbye,' said Ashok, waving a languid hand.

'Bye bye, Gorgeous,' called Carole softly into the darkness. Her eyes prickled with tears.

'If we don't get moving the pub'll be shut,' called Video Guy from the van, where he had retreated for a cigarette.

'Oh my,' said Ashok. 'I can't believe we're going to be staying in a real English pub.'

In another hour, Sweeney dared to move. He slunk to the edge of the field and crept along beside the hedge. The territory, as far as he discovered, was harsh. Cold, wet, no cover, no hint of food. And a disgusting smell. A smell that made you want to puke. A smell that called a shapeless red rage out of the depths of his being. It was the smell of badger, but Sweeney knew nothing of badgers. All he knew was that he had to get away from the stink.

Best not, Oliver thought, let on too much to my mother. Don't want her getting on my case about girlfriends again. Just talk about other things.

Best not, Bel thought, ask too many questions just now. Don't want him getting all stroppy because he thinks I'm interfering. Just make light conversation.

'Terrible rain . . .' they began together, as soon as Bel had poured her soup. So they laughed, only a little jittery, and Oliver allowed his mother to finish on the subject of the weather.

'Supposed to brighten up tomorrow . . .' they said again in unison, and laughed again, and this time Bel allowed Oliver to finish on the subject of the forecast for Friday and rest of the weekend.

'She's a bit . . .' he began again, at the same time as Bel ventured, 'I'm quite glad that . . .' By then they were on to the bread and cheese, and bold enough to explore the subject of their older guest's courtesy-free presentation.

'She is a bit . . . grand, isn't she?' said Oliver.

'I'm quite glad that they're having an early night,' was as far as Bel was prepared to go, but then, to show understanding, she added, 'I suppose they do get like that, women who've had to make their own way in a man's world.'

'I'm sure I know her face from somewhere,' said Oliver.

'She's got one of those faces,' his mother agreed. 'Is it because she looks like somebody in one of those soap operas? I never know who's supposed to be famous nowadays.'

'Oh, well,' said Oliver, thinking it best to get out of this sensitive area as fast as possible. 'I'd better be getting back. Shall I lock up the chickies for you?'

'Darling, that would be marvellous.'

No worries there. So far, thought Oliver, striding off in the direction of the henhouse, so good.

No problem here, thought Bel. So far, so good.

The Yattenham Arms was more than a pub. It was a work of art, lovingly assembled over centuries, handed on from one artist to the next, always evolving as an expression of rural conviviality.

First the massive walls had risen, as lumpy as the thighs of Rembrandt's Venus. Layers of limewash, the colour of clotted cream, held the ancient plaster in place over the unspeakable heaps of stone, cob, horsehair and downright rubbish of which the walls were built.

Above the walls rose the roof, a mound of thatch, dishevelled, barely contained by rusted chicken wire, drooping in places almost to the ground, which gave the building the air of a semi-comatose shaggy mammoth crouching by the roadside. The thatch was burrowed by mice and nested by a colony of stonechats; as long as there was daylight, scores of these inexhaustible tiny birds flew in and out of the roof, twittering a non-stop symphony of avian triviality.

Inside, there were beams. Beams as wide as cows, each one the whole bole of an ancient oak, blackened by the fire smoke of centuries, pitted with peg holes, studded with two-hundred-year-old nails and cunningly rebated for the cable bringing television programmes from the satellite dish that nestled in the ivy which blanketed the quavering brick chimney stack outside.

The main fireplace, where huge logs smouldered in a sleep of ages, was as big as a small room by itself, tucked behind the carved stone lintel. This bore, in bas-relief, some attractively primitive devices whose significance nobody knew except Florian Addleworth, and he knew better than to let on that they were his ancestral coat of arms. It was unwise to have ancestors when you were a claimant of government subsidies by trade.

The bars were so small, so low in ceiling and eccentric in shape that they hugged their customers in intimate embraces and drew them to sit down on various dark, heavy and lopsided items of furniture that awaited them. The stools had worn legs that lurched and wobbled on the rough-cast floors. Oak settles, elm benches and massive carver chairs with barley-twist bars and lion's-claw feet, their slippery seats softened with lumpy cushions of ragged chenille, stood in anticipation around tables spotted with candle wax and ring-marked with ales.

The walls were hung with old tools, pitchforks, ploughs and harrows, and leather straps displaying horse brasses, polished until their stars and sunbursts shone pale as silver.

212

Over the main bar, the landlady, for the pub was now in a woman's hands and in everyone's view all the better for it, fixed a fresh swag of dried hops every summer, where their flowers faded to the colour of antique lace and their scent blended with the smells of the fire, the beers and the great, tottering ploughman's lunches that came up from the kitchen in an endless procession all day during the tourist season. The Yattenham Arms depended on tourists, because the perfect dream of timeless rural hospitality was way too expensive for anyone living near it, except when they had a hot date to impress.

Oliver had a hot date to impress. He had known her two hours already and never seen her with her hair dry before. The way it stood up so fine and cheeky, like the new feathers of a baby bird. She was wearing some little black top thing with a lot of holes in it. Women went for things like that, he remembered. London women, anyway. Little holey garments, little baby-bird haircuts you wanted to reach over and ruffle. Maybe London women had their points. Truth to tell, he had not met many Suffolk women with whom to make a comparison. Lucy Vinny seemed to be the only free female under forty in the whole county, and she was in love with her horses.

It started out as one of those sweet-as-a-nut evenings. Everything just went as right as it could possibly have gone. The perfect seat was free for them, the very high settle right by the fire, the one that was probably hand-carved with courting couples in mind by some lust-promoting artisan of the randy Restoration era.

Maybe it was the mother thing, that little extra childlike thrill of putting one over on their custodial parents, but they just clicked. Whatever he said, she thought it was witty. Whatever she said, he sounded as if he was listening, even though 80 per cent of his available neurones were mesmerised by the holes in the top. Click-click. Click-click. Sweet as a nut.

And then there was the beer. The Yattenham Arms kept a classic cellar. Nothing short of sex can give a man like Oliver such simple joy as discovering a really gorgeous ale that he had never sampled before. They stumbled on it quite by accident, both looking to drink something that wouldn't render them too drunk to enjoy any greater and more physiologically complex pleasure that might be on the cards for later. A pint of Foulsham's Old Pheasantplucker seemed to fit the bill.

Paying for the pints broke Oliver's last tenner. Damn! Cash-flow crisis! Amazing that this woman could make him forget.

'So how long have you been in the hotel business?' Miranda asked, when her pint was approaching half-full.

'I'm a farmer,' he replied, 80 per cent of neurones still decoding the thrilling communiqués from his optic nerves.

'Oh, you're a farmer,' she assented. Was this going to be a problem? A waiter was so gloriously uncomplicated. A farmer might have a bit more baggage. Baggage always messed things up. And he probably didn't live at the hotel, either. Not quite so convenient. Still . . . 'What do you farm, then?'

'Not a lot,' he said. 'I'm turning my land over to organic production. Takes a few years. I've got some rather fine pigs, just a few of them. The rest is set-aside, for now.'

'So the hotel keeps you busy in the meantime?'

'The Saxwold Manor Hotel, you mean? Well, they've said

they'll consider a Christmas order when the time comes. Nice, but not what I'd call busy, really.'

Click-clunk. Clunk. Clunk. And clunk. Something about this patch of conversation seemed a mite choppy. Hard to say what it was, since they were now in the eye area. She had the most wonderful clear grey eyes. Nearly blue, really, but just that important shade more sincere. With the finest starriest eyelashes. Possibly the most beautiful eyes he had ever seen. And he had fine dark brown eyes, the sort of deep, soft brown that makes you think of brown sugar or silk velvet or a Burmese cat, with the eyebrows that were just nothing but downright damn imperious. Possibly the most gorgeous eyes she had ever seen.

The television, which lived in the old bread oven on the opposite side of the chimney breast, stopped showing football and began with the evening news. About 2 per cent of Oliver's neurones registered the change.

'And what do you do in London?' he asked, as if it was important.

'Communications in a town-planning group,' she said. She might as well have spoken in Finnish, for all he grasped the implications.

'Enjoy it?' he asked.

'It's challenging,' she answered.

She doesn't really like this job, Oliver's personal Babelfish translated for him. *She'd probably be up for taking a few days off.* Not that you want to get into that. Bit too cosy, bit of a commitment.

The TV news moved on to a fresh item. A hall full of people. Some woman making a speech. Angry people. People on their feet with ugly faces. Close-up of the woman.

About 5 per cent of Oliver's neurones registered this.

But the glasses were empty. And the landlady was reaching for the set of old brass harness bells, which had once tinkled above the mighty shoulders of a Suffolk Punch as it plodded honestly over the meadows, on which she pealed a warning to her customers that closing time was only half an hour away and that they should, therefore, approach the bar with their last orders.

'Another pint?' Oliver said, on autopilot.

'Maybe a shot,' Miranda suggested, thinking that a little shiver of something more powerful might just hit the spot. 'Do they have tequila?'

Silly me, she thought. This is a classic English country pub. Therefore they keep the fermented juice of some Mexican cactus. Yeah, right. Is this event going pear-shaped?

'I'll find out. Be right back,' he promised. The trouble with having to go to the bar was that he had to lose sight of her for at least a minute. The way she was sitting there. Just perfect.

As he was ordering and paying with almost the last penny he had in the world, Oliver became aware that whatever was passing on the TV over there in the old bread oven was holding the attention of the people around him, who were gazing at the screen with glassy eyes and open mouths. Following a simple herd instinct, he looked in the same direction. And with nothing better for most of his brain to do, he finally received the information that had been trying to get through from his peripheral vision for several minutes.

The woman making the speech, and seen in close-up, and now sitting in some studio talking to the camera, was a woman he knew. It was the woman whose bags he had carried up to the Rose Room at his mother's house. The woman he had lectured neurotically on the early history of Great Saxwold. The woman who was the mother of the woman sitting so perfectly on the high-backed settle, waiting for the very tequila that was at that instant cold in his hand.

'Who is that?' he blurted to the company in general.

'Well,' somebody advised him, 'it would be the Minister for Agriculture if there was still a Ministry of Agriculture, but now they're calling it some poncey new name, I don't rightly know what you'd call her.'

A significant episode of grunting indicated that many of the listeners could have advised the speaker on appropriate vernacular terms for the new Minister.

''Cept another bloody Islington farmer, getting ready to sell off the land to her fat-cat cronies,' said somebody else. 'I thought the Blob was bad enough. Least he was just stupid. This one's another one out to sell the family silver. Looks like we didn't know when we were lucky.'

Recognition hit Oliver like a badly managed hammer descending on an unwary thumb. Owww! That woman was the boss of Agraria. That woman had been on the TV earlier in the day, trying to put another filthy scam over on the Royal Conservation Society, for fuck's sake. That woman was evil *and* stupid with it. And here he was, getting ready to make a move on her daughter.

When he got back to the table, the conversation suddenly curdled. Ninety per cent of his neurones were deployed in telling him he was the biggest moron east of Birmingham. His hormones simply crashed. Over in the limbic system, joy was running out like bath water. A long, scratchy silence took place. She got one of those ironic little smiles on, more of a twitch than an actual expression of pleasure, the sort of smile only London women did. He remembered more things he didn't like about London women, and about women in general.

'So,' he said, realising that his reasons might be demanded if he didn't say something, 'what made you think of Suffolk for your weekend?'

'Oh, I don't know,' she said, trying to remember. 'I think we just wanted a really nice country house hotel and somebody recommended yours.'

Yours. Meaning mine. Meaning my really nice country house hotel. His memory centre scrambled into action. Hotel. She'd used that word before. Were they both making big mistakes here?

'Somebody recommended mine?' he said, finessing. He'd been a master of finessing, just a couple of years ago.

'Yes. And it was in all the guidebooks. Saxwold Manor Hotel. My mother wanted somewhere small. For privacy. She's got very keen on privacy since she got her new job.'

'New job?' Yes, it was all coming back.

She'd gone. Not physically, of course. All the physical being was still present, the haircut, the eyes, the clothes, the stuff inside the clothes. But the person had left the building. So the eyes were flat, and the haircut silly, and the sitting on the settle nothing remarkable. The spirit had fled. It had been, his memory centre offered, a nice spirit. But maybe just one of those hormonal illusions. Maybe she really was just a flat-eyed London woman after all.

What was left was a perfectly painted façade, saying, 'You've just twigged it, haven't you? You've just seen her on TV.'

'I thought she looked familiar.' No, he refused to feel guilty. It's not my fault there's a hologram sitting here, obviously about to start giving me the lines it's used a thousand times before with other people. I didn't do this. It just happened. And anyway, she was trying to con me, right? She was the one who knew who she was and didn't let on. This is her fault.

'Well, if you are a farmer,' Miranda went on, 'you probably would have figured it out. She is sort of in your area.'

'You must think I'm pretty slow. Not realising straight away.'

'It's nothing to do with me,' she said, knocking back the liquor in a what-the-hell way and then folding her arms. 'I mean, she is my mother. But I'm not a Mummy's girl, if you see what I mean. She's always much more interested in her job than whatever we're up to. When she was in business, that took all her time. Now I suppose it'll be worse, with being a politician. So that's probably why she wanted to come away this weekend.'

They think they're in a hotel. The deduction just wouldn't go away. It was jumping about in the foreground of his consciousness, trying to get his attention. That woman is the Minister of Agraria, or whatever it is, and they think they're in a hotel. Yes! And we need some money by Tuesday. Aha!

Something could be done here. Several things could be done here. Money could be extracted. Scores could be settled. Justice could be administered. The new Minister, or whatever she called herself, could be given a truly memorable mini-break, and be obliged to pay at least five hundred pounds for it.

Politeness. The last refuge of a scoundrel. 'Well, I suppose we're honoured that you picked our place. Good to know we're recommended.'

'Oh you are. Lots of stars.'

'Good. That's good to know. Well,' he downed his shot, 'must be getting back, eh?'

Are there sadder words in the whole spectrum of human communication than 'Must be getting back'? Is there anywhere in modern English a sentence that drags along a more melancholy subtext? It's over. It's finished. It's fucked. It's not worth another breath. And I'm not even going to waste the energy it would take to say so. Just let it lie here and finish dying, I'm on to the next thing.

Miranda blamed her mother. She'd done that before and it always went down well. If my mother wasn't a power-freak, if my mother wasn't on television, if my mother wasn't here in this godforsaken place with me, it would all have been fine. Good. Great, most likely. Brilliant, there had been a good chance of brilliant, even. Until my mother was in the picture and everything took on that old familiar pear shape.

Oliver drove her back to the hotel. When she was safely in her room, he tiptoed up the stairs and went to wake up Bel. After a short and thrilling conversation, he left and went back to the farm, where he sat up far into the night with his computer.

Toni buzzed home on her moped some time around 2am. Fortunately, she was extremely drunk. Had she been less drunk, she would have felt extremely annoyed. Some woman had turned up at The Pigeon & Pipkin. Some woman with tangled long hair that wasn't even extensions, and an arse you could rest a pint on. Some woman who looked fucking useless, and who hung around the pool room looking fucking useless, until the other Goths pissed off home, because they were just babies and had to be home when their parents said.

Then Useless had kind of lurked around the edge of the pool table, and rolled a ball over the green baize in a useless kind of way, and suggested that Toni give her a game. And Toni — she was extremely annoyed at this recollection when it surfaced through the pool of vodka in her head — had not only agreed to do so but also suggested putting a tenner on the outcome.

Well, Useless won the toss. Then she had heaved around the table, and flounced and fluffed and tossed her hair and fiddled around with her bra straps and walked around the table again and tossed her hair again, and pulled up her long drippy skirt to tie knots in her bootlaces, and taken her jacket off, and snapped her knickers, and tossed her hair again, and walked round the table again, and bent over to line up the first shot, and wiggled her bottom, and decided against the shot she'd set up, and stepped back, and stretched her arms, and tossed her hair, and snapped the other side of her knickers, and leaned down again, and lined up a shot again, and almost touched her cue to the ball, and pulled it back, and almost touched it again, and tossed her hair again, and at last made an extremely average break.

So Toni had put down a few balls and then missed an easy one, because what did it matter? This useless tart didn't know what she was doing.

And old Useless had stepped up and gone through the whole performance again, and then suddenly there weren't any balls left on the table. She had upped and sunk the lot. A fluke, obviously. So that was a tenner to Useless, but she'd bought another round with it, so Toni hadn't minded another match. She really had intended to get her game sorted the next time.

So now it was late, and she seemed to be down at least fifty quid. Worst of all, the useless female had been so fucking sweet about the whole thing. Such a lot of, 'Oh, you must think I'm so awful, coming in here and winning all this money,' which was exactly what Toni did think, but of course it was all made worse by letting the whole bloody pub know what was happening. Which occurred because, every time she won, Useless went tripping up to the bar, flicking her hair for England, and bought another round. Toni liked a drink as much as anybody, but not at the expense of her social standing.

It was a good thing the bike knew its own way home because at that time Toni's impression of Saxwold Farm Lane was not very precise. The landscape in general was a blend of grey smears, dark to either side of her and pale in the direction she was going. Above, in the upwards direction, there was a very large moon. She spent most of the journey looking at the moon. It was her own moon, shining specially for her Gothly soul, radiating wisdom and understanding and . . .

Some fucking animal ran across the road. Some deer or badger or fox or some other fucking stupid animal they had in the country. Toni swerved to avoid it and fell over. No harm done, but nobody really likes to fall in a hedge full of horrible prickly tree things. Still, it could be quite comfortable, if you didn't move. Toni decided not to move for a while, since the moon was being so nice and making her feel better.

While she lay there, another animal thing ran out in the lane. It was a fox. In the half a second it took to cross the track, she saw it quite clearly. Just like the foxes in London, really. A bit more fly, maybe. Running ever so fast, legs a blur of motion, body strangely still, its tail trailing in that slinky way.

Another fox ran across the road. Then another one. Then two together. Toni realised that she must be extremely drunk.

After a while she realised that she was also really cold, and that it was a really cold night, and that the fields and everything were breathing out this horrible white mist stuff, so she defied the thorns and pulled herself out of the hedge to get back on her bike and finish the journey to this fucking stupid place that was supposed to be her home.

The door of The Manor House crashed open because her stepmother had fixed it so it did that, probably to keep tabs on her, and the stairs were really slippery and dangerous, which was obviously another thing her stepmother had fixed on purpose to get at her. Toni fell down the stairs twice, but since God looks after fools and drunks and Gothly girls who've lost fifty quid playing pool, and since she was wearing her biker's boots, no real harm was done. After she'd had a shower, and sat and listened to the Sisters of Mercy for a bit, she felt restored enough to rip the boots off and roll onto her mattress in the attic.

The noise of the door woke Clare, just in time, because things were not going well in her dream world, where she was about to be dragged off to a blood-spattered torture chamber to discuss her involvement with Mutual Probity. She decided to sit up for a while and read the appendices to the new report. Winston Churchill, Margaret Thatcher . . . none of the great politicians had ever needed more than four hours of sleep a night.

The nightmare had been hyper-real. Masked men with machine guns, who said they were the Fraud Squad, had dragged her out of bed at her home. She had been put in a holding cell full of ostriches that tried to peck her to death, then dragged through a howling mob into a courthouse where this mean judge, who looked exactly like the PE teacher who used to scream at her on the lacrosse pitch more than thirty years ago, told her she was a cancer on society. The prosecuting counsel, in a wig of snakes, demanded the maximum penalty of death by paper-shredder. She was being marched back to Holloway when she woke up. The gateway to the prison was looming over her and they were getting ready to pull out her fingernails.

Since Toni had been way too drunk to find her headphones, the Sisters of Mercy howled inconsolably from the attic to add to Clare's distress. I will forget Mutual Probity, she told herself. I will think about responsible land use and the new plan. But her thoughts refused to fall in with the strategy.

I will find a name for this deal, she vowed. Strategic Land Development Plan – no, too blatant. Fields for the Future? Even worse. Planning the New Jerusalem? Good God, no. No, no, no. I'm too tired, I can't think. There is nothing to be done about Mutual Probity now anyway. It wasn't my fault, I did the best I could, I got out at the right time. Nothing is going to come my way from that one.

The thought of Miranda came into her mind. Hesitantly. Her daughter was always so hesitant. Never said what she thought, never knew what she wanted. Not knowing what you want, of course, is the best way to make sure you never get it.

In her own way, Clare loved her daughter. She wanted for Miranda the same things she had wanted for herself, a life of proud achievement. Why would any woman want anything else? Proud achievement gave you everything you could possibly want; it filled your time, healed your wounds, paid you plenty and gave you, on a daily basis, that electric tingle in the blood which came from beating the system.

Clare could not imagine that Miranda might want something else for herself, something more complex, something she herself could hardly define. She could not imagine because she had declined to develop her imagination beyond the vision of her own fulfilment. Imagining things for other people was really quite dangerous. You could end up feeling for them, and then you were stuffed. So Clare's imagination lived in a cage, and only broke out in her dreams.

She was beginning to be afraid that Miranda was going to fail. The girl was so fragile. Her father's influence. He'd spoiled her with sympathy. Now Miranda was a bravely maintained façade covering . . . what? Clare had never known. The only clue was that secret not-quite-smile that appeared sometimes, to tell you that the inner Miranda was working on something.

Come to think of it, that not-quite-smile had appeared only a few hours ago. While the dreary young man who seemed attached to this place was going on about the history of Suffolk. Miranda obviously hadn't realised that her mother was watching her, but it had been impossible to miss the way she had revived while he was talking. And he wasn't a bad specimen. Not the sort of inbred three-nipple cousin-fucker you expected in the country.

Romantic love was a concept that Clare despised. In fact, she despised emotion generally: chaotic, destructive stuff, the enemy of personal progress. Not that she hadn't given romance her best shot. For a few years it had seemed to Clare that she really was in love with the man who became her husband. It was shortly after their marriage that she realised she'd been suckered by society. The man beside her had no interest in her. He was as terrified of her, and of the little bundle that was their son, as he was of the rest of the world. Even now, Miranda seemed to be the only part of his life of which he was not stammeringly afraid.

What Clare had assumed was courtship on his part was only a desperate dash in the general direction of full human-ity, in which he had almost immediately lost heart. The man she had loved, with his gentle eccentricity, dry wit and kind heart, had vanished and been replaced by a twitching, scurfy, subterranean creature forever scuttling under a book to avoid human contact.

Romance, Clare concluded, was only a nineteenth-century device for the subjugation of women. A modern woman had no need to buy into her own oppression, only touch base with the externals for pragmatic reasons. After all, the world was not completely free of nineteenth-century attitudes, so a woman needed to go along with the pretence of love for the sake of a marriage, which was still a necessary evil.

A tick in the marriage box was only something you had to have in order to protect yourself from the bad opinions of

226

others. But who was to say that her daughter might not think differently? She'd always been on the soft side. In a playful sense, Miranda might actually enjoy a relationship with a man. Possibly even a man in the hotel business, although she ought to be able to do better.

Still, since Miranda had to marry, it was good to know that she could respond in that way. If a life of achievement wasn't going to be for her, perhaps she could still reflect some honour on her mother by landing a trophy husband.

This thought was immensely comforting. The caterwauling music in the roof had stopped. Something was shrilling outside, probably a bird. It was quite a racket, but not really unpleasant. Clare decided to go back to bed. An extremely comfortable bed. Very attractive, with its flower-patterned quilt and lace-edged pillows. That old elitist look could work, in the right setting.

All round, it was an extremely comfortable hotel. A good idea of hers. All her ideas were good. It was going to be OK.

CHAPTER 8

Sting City

Bel woke early and ricocheted out from under her quilt, propelled by the excitement of the charade she was about to stage. She was running on a full tank of irrational indignation. Imagine! That silly woman thought she was in a hotel! Outrageous! And trailing her daughter along with her as if she was some girlfriend of Oliver's! Why, it was practically fraud! Who did these people think they were? Thank goodness Oliver had worked out what was going on.

So now, the only honourable option was the sting. The sting would redress this ridiculous insult. The sting would take care of that nasty bailiff man. The sting the two of them richly deserved. Hah! Did they think they were so clever, just because they were from London and went around in silly shoes and ugly jewellery? Well, they'd find out that country people weren't so stupid.

While the sun was rising through the veils of mist, Bel dressed and padded downstairs. A mess of muddy boot-prints tracked up the hall and up the staircase. Toni, of course. Poor lost child. What to do about her? Swiftly, Bel fetched the mop and restored the entrance to hotel-like perfection, washing away her pangs of stepmotherly guilt as she did so.

Next, the transformation of the dining room. Since she had spent the last few months set-dressing the house for the buyers she hoped would reward her as soon as she sold it on, all the accessories were to hand. The beautiful oak refectory table, meant to suggest elegant dinner parties, slithered readily across to the wall to become a serving surface. She bustled ingeniously around the ground floor collecting smaller tables. The dining chairs, high-backed, their broad seats upholstered in fresh checked linen so they begged the sitter to stay put, pour another glass and have a third helping, clustered around them with a will.

Bel had always loved to entertain and the saddest part of being a widow was that you were expected to have nothing but twee little lunches with your girlfriends, instead of filling your house with party guests and spending a day loading crostini for them, or urging friends and family to come over for Sunday lunch and pulling a mighty roast out of the oven to reward their compliance.

Years of hospitable marriage had endowed her house with everything it needed to meet the present challenge. She took the tablecloths and napkins out of her linen cupboard. The best silver, the silver she had inherited from her first husband, she picked out of the mahogany canteen that had only seen the light of day for Oliver's christening and her second wedding.

Flowers! Vases! She grabbed a coat and some boots, and went out into the garden with her secateurs to cut her newly planted daffodils, forage for primroses and bring down branches of blossom from the gnarled old tree at the far end of her land that had survived the builders. There were some cut-crystal tumblers which could hold posies for the tables.

Then it was back to the kitchen. Bel had enjoyed being a full-on mother. It was more than ten years since Oliver had filled her house with hulking, monosyllabic and ever-hungry friends who would be transformed into appreciative young men by the simple offer of a cooked breakfast. Wistful for those days, she still filled her freezer with the supplies she needed to produce that transformation, and so quantities of sausages, bacon, black pudding, croissants, bread and orange juice were ready to be defrosted and deployed in the sting.

Eggs, butter, tomatoes and mushrooms were there in the kitchen already, and as for jam — what woman who goes the whole nine yards with country living fails to fill a shelf or ten with jam? Damson, plum, rhubarb and ginger, apple and bramble . . . and the jam dishes, and the spoons, and the plates and the cups . . . It was a new pleasure to be able to produce this illusion of lavish hospitality from the things she had assembled in the course of doing what came naturally to a woman with a warm heart, pert taste buds and a liking for lovely possessions.

'Fantastic!' whispered Oliver as he arrived, a little bleary, when the sun was just above the hedges. 'Mum, you're a genius. It's totally convincing. I'd book in here myself. And you've done all this in no time at all.'

He brought the products of his time on the computer, seven printed cards. Inside a charming border of wild flowers, black and white with cross-hatching in lino-cut style, were two messages. Six cards read simply: *Breakfast: £17, Full English Breakfast: £25.* These he placed next to the daffodils on the small tables. The last card was smaller, and he placed it on the console table in the hall. It read: *We regret we are unable to accept credit cards.*

'We're being so naughty,' said Bel, looking extremely pleased with herself.

'Naughty?' her son hissed, checking with the ormolu Empire mirror to see if he looked sufficiently like a waiter to pass in the full light of day. 'Not as naughty as what that woman wants to do to my farm. To the whole bloody country. Are they awake yet?'

From the innards of the house, the plumbing hissed into action. 'Sounds like it,' Bel suggested.

'OK,' said Oliver. 'Let's get ready to rumble.'

At The Pigeon & Pipkin the day began grudgingly, with limp toast and tepid tea served in a corner of the bar where the smoke from last night's cigarettes still fusted in the air. From the kitchen, the curses of the landlord's wife, as she ripped open packs of frozen crabsticks to mix with soya mince for the special dish of the day, Soft-Shell Ocean Pie, could be distinguished over the dragging tape of The Carpenters' Greatest Hits.

Carole, Ashok and Video Guy were the only visible guests. They made bold to discuss their plans over the meal.

'How exactly do you liberate bees?' Carole asked.

'Well, generally,' said Ashok, 'I just put on my freedom suit and, you know, turn over the hives so the tops kind of fall off and all the bees can get out.'

'Can't they get out anyway?' asked Video Guy.

'I suppose so,' Ashok said. 'I guess it is more kind of a symbolic gesture than an act of actual liberation.'

'Where do they go when they're liberated?'

'Oh, they go off and swarm somewhere in the forest.'

'What forest?' the Video Guy asked.

'I'm sure you have forests in England,' said Ashok, smiling forgiveness.

'There was a sign on the road,' said Carole. 'Some forest or other. We'd better be sure. I don't want to find we've liberated thousands of bees to have them die of pesticides in the fields. Excuse me,' this was to the landlord, who was cringing in their direction with a new pot of tea, 'isn't there some kind of forest round here?'

'They call it Yattenham Forest,' he said. 'Out beyond the village, that way.' He put down the teapot and gestured vaguely. 'But there aren't any trees. Well, there are some trees, some pines and sort of mixed woodland, I suppose, but not like you'd think in a forest.'

'Not Hansel and Gretel,' the Video Guy suggested.

'They've talked about planting trees.' Momentarily mystified by the folkloric allusion, the landlord hesitated, then decided to plough on. 'Getting it back to be a proper woodland like it used to be, but nothing gets done, you see.'

'But there are some trees?' Ashok said.

'Oh yes. There are some of them.'

'That should be OK,' Ashok reassured his companions. 'As long as there are trees. The queen just finds a place and the rest of them just, like, gather around her. Then they build a real nest, up high, away from the bears, in the hollow trunk of the tree or something. That's not decaff, is it?' He turned to interrogate the landlord's retreating back. 'Can I get some decaff over here?'

'You do know we don't have bears?' asked Video Guy.

'Of course I know that.' Ashok spoke with honeyed sincerity. 'Bees are kind of instinctive, you know. They do what they've always done. So they're always wanting to nest up in the trees, even when their natural predators have been hunted to extinction.'

Hunted to extinction. He let the words lie there on the table, with the toast crumbs and the smeared residues of last night's beer, accusing them. You *Old Europeans.* You've trashed your heritage already, and you're so bad you're taking issues with me now when I've come over here from a much better place to help you out. This is Baghdad all over again. Kosovo all over again. Normandy all over again.

'So this freedom suit,' Video Guy began.

'I'm afraid I only have the one,' said Ashok, wondering what to do about his piece of toast. 'Is that actual butter?'

'Sorry, yes,' Carole told him. 'You can have the marmalade. That doesn't have animal products.'

'Are you sure? Not even gelatine?'

'What's a freedom suit?' asked Video Guy.

'Well, it's kind of an old biological warfare suit that somebody got from some army place, but some of the guys painted it up, so it does make the point about what we're doing. And of course it is pretty well sting-proof.' Ashok peered closely at the label on a plastic-wrapped individual marmalade serving. 'Are you sure this is animal-free?'

'Meaning you've been stung?' asked Video Guy.

'No, no. Not at all. Least, I haven't been stung yet, and I must have done twenty missions since we started the AASS.

233

But like I say, there's only the one suit. I could only get one in my luggage and stay under the weight you people allow on the plane.'

'So, if I've got to film you, I've got to take a chance that when you liberate these bees they won't come for me, they'll just whizz off happily to find this forest without any trees? They get angry, bees, don't they? My insurance doesn't cover that kind of thing.' Video Guy's most lasting impression of bee behaviour came from old sci-fi films, in which maddened swarms usually pursued screaming blondes to a fatal outcome.

'Don't people die from bee stings?' Carole demanded. 'We don't want that kind of negative publicity.'

'Cheers,' said Video Guy, feeling martyred enough to be entitled to take the last slice of toast.

'There have been cases,' Ashok admitted, 'but only if the person who gets stung is allergic or something. Or maybe a baby.' Cautiously, as if sudden death might occur at any moment, he opened the marmalade and spread some on his toast.

'Well, that's all right then,' said Video Guy. 'Unless I am a baby or something.'

'Well, you're certainly acting like one,' Carole said.

She weighed her options. Most important, they needed a video. Which would require a certain level of theatricality. Meaning a man in a freedom suit. But Video Guy was looking more than a little sick at the idea of recording a mass bee liberation without protective clothing. And there was only one suit.

'I think we should do some kind of demo first,' she said. 'We should picket the place, maybe.'

234

'After we've done the liberation,' said Ashok quickly. 'If we piss off the oppressors, they can get real nasty and call in security to guard the hives and then it gets ugly. Free the slaves first, then we can go down the office and raise hell.'

'Fair enough. That's why it's so good to have your expertise, Ashok.'

'But, hang about,' Video Guy implored. 'If you just go down the office and do a demo and there's two men and a dog down there, it doesn't make a very good film. You need a crowd of some kind. You need to get some conflict organised.'

'We can do that,' Ashok assured him. 'Lookey here.' And he produced, from a roll of papers that had been in his backpack, a dog-eared flyer in Château Saxwold colours. 'This place has these wine-tasting events. Doesn't that mean people will be there?'

'By invitation only,' Video Guy read from the flyer.

'I was thinking we should infiltrate in plain clothes then figure out something to do to get their attention. I brought some visual aids just in case.'

'Yeah?' said Video Guy, finally liking the sound of something.

'Banners and stuff. And we've got some bee balloons we can blow up and release. They're really kind of cute. It's sort of a playful way of saying that keeping bees is wrong.'

'And legal,' Carole approved. 'They can't pin an assault charge on us if all we've got are balloons.'

'So, wait a minute,' said Video Guy. Ashok rolled his eyes. 'Is the plan that we go in, turn over the beehives, sneak into this tasting party, blow up a couple of hundred balloons, toss them gaily into the revels, wave a few banners, cause a bit of mayhem, I get it all on the tape, nobody spots us, no cops are called and we are not forcibly ejected but are free to piss off in our own time, handing out leaflets to the grateful peasantry as we go?'

'We've got to think about this,' Carole agreed. 'Why don't we just go up there for a bit of a visit and check the place out?'

'Best idea I've heard all day,' said Video Guy.

'But it is only breakfast time,' said Ashok.

'What shall we do this morning?' Clare asked Miranda as the waiter removed their plates – plates sullied only by some rejected toast crusts. The full English breakfast option had horrified them both. All the same, the appetising smell of sizzling sausages stole up from the kitchen, since Bel could not restrain herself from frying a few for Oliver's benefit. Sausages, computed Miranda's food evaluator: living death.

They sipped their coffee, finding it agreeably assertive. 'What do people do in the country?' Miranda countered.

'You used to like riding,' said Clare.

This was undeniable. For quite a few years, Miranda would have walked on hot coals and given up chocolate for life for the sake of an hour with a pony. But that was back in the Old Mum days.

'Haven't ridden for years,' she said.

'You don't forget, do you?'

'I suppose not.'

'We used to enjoy going for little rides on holiday.'

A real Marbella cowgirl, that's what Dido had said. Miranda had the impression that she'd never done anything that her mother hadn't been better at.

Clare said, 'There might be a riding place near here.' And she sounded hopeful.

'We can ask, I suppose.'

Miranda was getting that absent look. She'd developed it, Clare remembered, at about eight years old. It meant that she was feeling invaded, and most of her being had fled to the jungle and would only be coming out to conduct guerrilla raids against the parental aggressor.

'And we could go for a walk,' Clare went on, thinking that walking when you didn't have anywhere specific to go would be a complete waste of time.

'Where to?' asked Miranda, wondering if she was going to spoil another pair of shoes.

'There must be something to see,' Clare insisted, not really convinced. She cast a glance out of the window. What could there possibly be out there to interest a discriminating urban mind? More of that dreary grass. A mis-shapen tree, obviously half-dead, it really needed to be cut down. An untidy sort of outcrop that was presumably meant to be a wall or a hedge. A few bedraggled flowers in an insipid yellow colour.

Miranda also looked out of the window. The old tree in the garden was a marvellous gnarled shape. It was about to burst into blossom, the buds were swelling on the new twigs, and the trunk was covered with lichen. You never saw lichen in the city. Wasn't it supposed to be something to do with the air quality? And the primroses were out. Maybe she'd find a pencil and do some drawing. Years since she'd enjoyed making little sketches. She had been quite good at it.

'I'll go and ask,' she said, finishing her coffee.

The hall was empty. Following the revolting stench of sausage, she took the stone-flagged corridor to the back of the building and soon found herself in the kitchen, where the owner, tied up in an unflattering apron, was agitating a frying pan on the Aga. The dog, surely a health hazard, was lying at her feet and – aha! – the waiter was taking a break with a mug of coffee. Oliver, his name was Oliver. The sort of stupid name people had in the country.

'Hello,' she said, in best such-a-nice-girl mode. 'We were just thinking of going for a walk. Maybe you could tell us a good way to go?'

'Oh, absolutely,' he said.

'Tell them the way over the fields to Yattenham,' the owner suggested, chasing a couple of sausages onto a plate that was already heavy with bacon, eggs, tomatoes and . . . dear God . . . fried bread. Fried bread: total human catastrophe. The dog watched her every move.

'Ah – yes,' he said, as if he couldn't quite remember the way. 'Good idea. Let me get you a leaflet.'

'What leaflet?' the owner demanded, poised with her loaded plate.

'The leaflets we had done for our guests,' he said. 'With little maps and directions. You know.'

'Oh, yes,' she said, and giggled, though why this should be funny Miranda could not imagine. The dog tried jumping up for the plate, so she held it high above her head, out of his reach. 'Get down, Garrick. Bad dog.'

'And we were wondering . . . is there a riding centre or something near here?'

'Ah . . .' Oliver thought immediately of Lucy and her horses. Could he? Would she? It was going to need work.

'Not exactly,' he said, 'but we can arrange riding for our guests. If you can give me twenty-four hours . . .'

'No problem,' said Miranda. Totally inefficient, but what else could you expect? Had she really fancied this bloke? Or just felt weakened by all that red wine? He was actually going to eat those sausages. Maybe she should be thankful that Mum's all-pervasive public image had saved her from total embarrassment.

Miranda returned to the dining room with a slip of paper bearing printed directions and a map. 'They're going to ask about the riding. And they've got a map of walks. We could do this one, over the fields to the next village, taking in some woodland.'

'Very well organised,' Clare approved. 'I hope it isn't going to be muddy, or anything.'

Suitably protected, in boots, parkas, lip gloss with sunscreen, and warm scarves, the CEO of Agraria and her daughter set forth some twenty minutes later, passing between the two stone dogs and turning right out of the Manor House gates, before climbing with care over the stile in the hedge across the lane and taking the footpath that led along the margin of the field. It was a glorious morning.

'Oliver! Oh my God! Oliver!'

Never in his entire life had he heard his mother sound so shocked. And distressed. She was almost screaming. Oliver leaped from the table and ran out to see what was happening.

The path to the kitchen garden was strewn with feathers which stirred in his slipstream as he passed. There, in the middle of the trampled plants, stood the Wendy house, its blue sides spattered with blood. He nearly fell over the first dead chicken, which lay on the path, a chewed stump of neck sticking from its half-raw shoulders. In the enclosure, an almost complete carcass was jammed head-first under the house, one leg torn away. Another was nothing but a lump of bloody down. The remaining four were surreally unmarked, having dropped dead from fright.

Such a domestic atrocity. Instead of the nursery-rhyme picture of the chicken house, surrounded by its blamelessly foolish inhabitants, pecking about in the dust, here was a massacre in miniature, with bodies halted by death in bizarre attitudes, wings splayed in the struggle to get off the ground and fly to safety. Evidence of the chickens' last panic was everywhere, in the scattered feathers on the ground and clumps of bloodied down stuck to the netting.

His mother was almost as pitiful as her dead poultry, standing by a broken-down rosemary bush, dissolved in tears, dabbing at her running mascara. He put his arms around her.

'I did shut them up last night,' he told her. 'Something must have got in.'

'What could have done it? It can't have been Garrick, I know he was in the kitchen all night. Look, it hasn't even eaten them. They've all been just killed and left. That one isn't even touched. It must have had a heart attack. Poor thing.'

'It's a fox, it must be.'

'But how did it get in? Isn't the wire netting supposed to be fox-proof?'

'Over there.' He pointed to the far side of the run, where a half-tunnel of freshly scraped earth showed that the killer had dug his way in.

'I thought we didn't have foxes round here? Didn't your friend Jimmy say you never got foxes and badgers together and we had a badger somewhere?'

'Yes, that's what he said. Something's changed.'

'I'll never dare have chickens again,' she wailed. 'Such a horrible way to die. I'll never forgive myself.'

'At least we don't have to worry about dinner tonight.'

'Oliver! How could you!'

Something had indeed changed, as Oliver found ten minutes later. Driving back to his cottage to fetch his tools, he slowed down to pass Jimmy on the lane. For a very quiet man, Jimmy was animated. He began the conversation, which Oliver had never known him do before, and the words couldn't wait to get out of his mouth.

'You hear anything last night over your way?'

'I was up late working, I didn't hear anything.'

''Cause I got a fox in my barns. Or maybe more than one. Terrible thing I saw when I come down. I heard 'em immediately but by the time I was down there half of 'em was gone, nearly. And the rest won't be laying. That's my work for the week gone. For the month, maybe. I've got dead ducks all over the show.'

'My mother's lost all hers too. You know, those silly spotty hens she had.'

'Has she? I reckon it was more than one. Must have been. You didn't see nothing yesterday? I'm wondering where the animals come from. Not the usual thing, more than one fox. Not on a rampage like that. They've killed so many, could have been three or four, even. Something's not right. You spoken to Colin? I'm going over there now, see what's happening at his place.'

Colin had heard nothing, but remembered passing a white van on the road on his way back from the pub, and thinking it strange, since there was nothing down the lane except the farms and the Manor, and even tourists never got lost down there.

It seemed logical to go to the pub next, and even more so when a white van which could well have been the same vehicle was found in the car park. The landlord supplied the next clue.

'White van? With three people? I got them here,' he said. 'Came from London last night, got here so late I'd given up hope.'

'What are they doing here?' Oliver asked.

'What d'you mean, what are they doing? Same as anybody else, I suppose, having a bit of a break for Easter.'

'They're sabs or something,' said the girl from Yattenham who came in to help out on weekends. 'When I did their rooms this morning they had all kinds of animal rights stuff in there, leaflets and papers all over the place.'

When it was established that the trio had gone out, Oliver got a torch and shone it through the van's rear windows. Then he examined the front, where the passenger seat was also littered with documents, and flung himself back to the bar in a rage.

'You're not going to believe this,' he told them. 'They've only brought a bunch of foxes up from London and let them loose down our lane. The van's full of cages in the back and there's some report they're writing in the front. And a whole pack of those bee leaflets – remember them? Anti Apian Slavery Society. They're in there too.'

'Bloody hell,' said the landlord, seeing an immediate

conflict between his takings for the weekend and his regular customers.

'Bloody hell,' said Colin, clenching his fists as if getting ready to beat up the first bee-liberator he saw.

'Bloody fools,' said Jimmy.

'Call the police,' said Colin to the landlord, who winced and tried to think of a reason not to, but Colin added, 'No point, is there? Nobody in the station at Yattenham today, won't be anyone till Tuesday. They'd have to send men from Ipswich, and they'll have enough to do.'

'Call out the neighbourhood,' Jimmy advised. 'Only thing to do now, get a shoot organised.'

The telephone was in the custody of the landlord, who, in an event of this nature, occupied the position of Switzerland in World War II, useful to everyone and despised by all. He stood looking uncertainly from one face to another, hoping they would all find it expedient to preserve his neutrality.

'Why don't we call Lucy?' Oliver suggested.

The landlord promptly pulled over his telephone book and looked for the vet's number, but she appeared in the doorway as he was dialling, wearing her riding hat and a stern expression.

'Have you heard anything about foxes?' she asked.

'Have we heard.'

'I'll say we've heard.'

'And seen. Why, what have you heard?'

'I just met these . . .' Ladylike to the fingertips, Lucy's vocabulary wasn't up to the job of describing the kind of person she had met. 'Saboteurs, or animal rights people or whatever they are. They actually came to the surgery to put

243

up that ridiculous leaflet about bees. And then they told me, the woman told me . . .' She struggled for words again.

'About the foxes,' Oliver added.

'Thirty-eight,' she said. *'Thirty-eight.* Can you believe it? They rounded up thirty-eight foxes in London and drove them out here and let them loose.'

'On one of my fields,' Colin said.

'Oh, bloody hell.' She was blinking hard. For an awkward moment, it seemed that the gallant Lucy was going to cry. 'Well,' she said, taking a deep breath to stop the tears, 'you've seen them, have you?'

'No,' said Oliver, 'but they got my mother's chickens. And a lot of Jimmy's ducks. He got the worst of it. My mother just kept them for amusement but Jimmy's birds are his living.'

'The price I'd get for them, that's what we were counting on to cover the feed bill,' Jimmy was moved to a confidence. 'I dunno what I can do now. I was counting on getting at least fifty to market next week.'

'Though your mother must be . . .'

'Pretty distraught,' Oliver confirmed.

'So,' Lucy took another deep breath. 'What to do?'

'Rough shoot,' Jimmy advised. 'That's the best way.'

'I mean, does that stupid woman realise the foxes will just starve? They'll have no territory of their own, no shelter, they'll be seen off by the animals we do have, they won't find food, once we've mended our fences as it were, and they'll just starve to death. Or be killed by the others. Or – you know, she put flea collars on them? Like they were pets. They'll strangle themselves. It's just . . . senseless.'

'Get all the guns together, get everyone out beating . . .'

244

As he spoke, Jimmy realised the flaws in his plan. 'That's what we used to do, when the foxes were out of control. I remember twenty guns, more than twenty. Down in Yattenham Forest. When I was a kid, that was.'

'You won't get twenty today,' Lucy said. 'There's Colin, who can't hit a barn door at ten yards, that brother of Florian's, who couldn't bring down a geriatric grouse, you and your dad, that's about it. We ought to get them as fast as we can, too. Before they do more damage, while we can round them all up, before they get scattered around the whole county. Thirty-eight!'

'My dad's eyes aren't what they were,' Jimmy said.

'What about the hunt?' Colin asked. 'They're still in business, aren't they? With the license and everything?'

'What hunt?' asked Oliver, realising that his mettle was to be tested again. He'd never been quite sure how he felt about hunting.

'Our local would be the Haverham Foxhounds. They're pretty small. And the season's nearly over. They don't come this way usually because of the livestock,' said Lucy. 'But I suppose we could ask the master to bring some hounds over and work the area. That'd flush the foxes out.'

'Maybe they know some guns could help us out,' said Jimmy.

'They're bound to. I've met their vet, I could give him a call. Might have to get a special license for land they don't cover in the normal way. With so many, shooting them's probably the most humane way. Thirty-eight of them! These people must be mad.'

'It won't be like a native animal that knows its own territory,' said Jimmy.

'I'll have a word,' said Lucy. 'Leave it to me.' And since they knew her to be a force in the land, the three men agreed to leave the hunt to her.

'Luce,' said Oliver, following her out of the pub, 'I know you're in a hurry . . .'

'But,' she prompted him.

'I need a favour.'

'If it's anything to do with making life hell for that Agraria woman, I'll be delighted. Whatever it is. Within reason.'

'You've heard.'

'Half the county's heard. We're counting on you, Oliver. If she doesn't go back to London on a stretcher we'll be deeply disappointed.'

'In that case . . .' He took a deep breath and ventured on to the territory that Lucy held most sacred. 'I was wondering about your horses.'

Back in the pub, Colin and Jimmy turned their attention to the landlord.

'You'll be putting them nutters out,' Colin told him.

'They're out already,' the landlord said, wilfully obtuse.

'Then when they come back, you put 'em out,' said Colin. 'They can sleep in their damn van, if they're so keen.'

CHAPTER 9

Enter the Easter Bunny

'The egg,' said Florian, holding up a fine large specimen, 'is the symbol of new life, of the fertility of nature, of light emerging from darkness, of ideas coming to the surface from the depths of consciousness, of the putting into action of the plans made during the winter.'

In developing the offices of Château Saxwold, he had diverted a torrent of public money into the restoration of a mass of semi-derelict farm buildings much larger than Oliver's modest establishment. Another desolate collection of ruins had been transformed into a handsome complex of warm red-brick structures, most of which were called a Centre. The purpose of each building was explained by a plaque, written in gold copperplate on the *domaine* colour of dark blue. The door of each building was flanked by a barrel tub planted with yellow primulas.

The former cow shed was the Education Centre, wired for everything and ready to welcome teams of local schoolchildren learning geography, if they ever had time off from their

247

tests. Florian also organised seminars for other cultivators interested in biodynamic growing. The diary was on the wall. April 30: *How Moist Is Moist?* May 28: *Let Your Humus Decide.* June 25: *The Do's and Don'ts of Mulching.*

The original farmhouse had been designated the Accommodation Centre, a rambling mass of rooms through which Addleworth relations perpetually drifted in search of their spouses, their children, their host, their car keys and their missing Wellington boots.

A great barn had become the Visitor Centre, containing a poster display of wine-making in Suffolk since Roman times, a massive and cobwebbed old wine press imported from France, a cider press of local oak, and a sales desk loaded with corkscrews and vintage charts imprinted with the *domaine* logo, and equipped with the latest devices for parting fools from their money. It was here that Florian sat on Good Friday morning, with his eldest nephew, a paint box and a basket of eggs.

'I think we should have a ritual,' he said, while the child wriggled with boredom. 'I think we should paint eggs to honour the Goddess, and place them on the altar.'

'I think that's stupid,' said his nephew, frowning. 'I hate eggs. They smell. Or if they aren't cooked, they're all runny. They're disgusting.'

'No they aren't,' said Florian. 'They're a miracle. Every one. Every egg contains everything you need to grow a chicken. It's a new-life pack. Just add a cockerel to fertilise it and a mother hen to keep it warm, and there you go.'

'I don't want to paint eggs,' said his nephew firmly. 'I want to watch *Cavegirl.*'

'Your mother says you're not allowed,' said Florian. His

248

nephew pouted, and folded his arms, and leaned back on the back legs of his chair, kicked the table leg, and fell backwards, cracking his head on the flagstones, whereupon he yelled to the limit of his lung capacity.

'You see,' said Florian, choosing a paintbrush. 'You shouldn't diss the Goddess. Flowers appear on the earth where she walks.'

As if he had conjured her, Dido appeared in the doorway, her finger outstretched for the bell, the full sun of a glorious spring morning backlighting her form, so it seemed that they were having a visitation from Rossetti's Beatrice.

Dido had woken late but enthusiastically, and run out into Great Saxwold to embrace the beauty of the day, which enthusiastically embraced her back. She drifted towards the church, wandered around the churchyard reading gravestones and feeling pleasantly sad about the shortness of life, especially for infants born before the discovery of antibiotics.

In a while, Toni buzzed up on her moped, grouching into the wind at having to water the fucking church flowers for her fucking stepmother. Dido, not wishing to embarrass her unlucky opponent of the night before, lurked out of sight behind an ancient yew.

Once the moped had droned away, she went into the church and spent half an hour sitting in an old pew admiring the flowers and accumulating rapture while she tried to think of a good reason to wait until the evening before finding Florian again. Instead, she could only think of reasons why she should proceed directly to Château Saxwold, without passing Go or collecting anything other than a couple of violets from the hedge, which now nestled in the top buttonhole of her blouse.

'Hello,' she said to him, while the rest of the world whirled away into infinite irrelevance. 'You invited me. Do you remember?'

'Yes,' he said, as the radiance of the utter rightness of her being there shone around them. 'Hello.'

'I know it's this evening, your wine-tasting, but I thought I'd come early.'

'How terrific.'

'I could help you get ready, maybe.'

'Yes, you could.'

'I was in the area, you see. I came with some friends.'

'That was lucky.'

'Yes, it was, wasn't it?'

'Oh God,' said his nephew, catching the drift of the conversation immediately, and getting up from the floor. Indignantly, he rubbed his head as he stomped towards the door. 'If you're going to be stupid, I'm going to watch *Cavegirl*.'

'All right,' said Florian. 'Off you go. This lady can help me paint the eggs.'

'All right, then, I will,' the child replied.

A zephyr of concern crossed Dido's face. For a moment, a fault line appeared in the radiant rightness of everything.

'He's only my nephew,' Florian said quickly. 'I'm babysitting while my sister's gone shopping.'

'Oh, good,' she said. 'I love painting.'

He picked up the chair that the child had overturned and she radiated into it.

'I love painting too,' he said, choosing the palest, the smoothest, the most symmetrical egg in the basket specially for her. And together they picked out clean brushes, and tinkled them in water, and thought about colours. Chrome Yellow. Lemon Yellow. Burnt Sienna. Ultramarine. Crimson Lake. Pink. They were all glorious. Impossible to choose.

'What goddess were you talking about?' Dido asked, at last going for Cerulean Blue and thinking of a swirl around the pointy end of her egg.

Florian decided to tiptoe into the issue, in case anything should dim the rightness. 'It's Easter, you see. Which was originally the festival of the spring equinox. There used to be a pagan celebration for it. Welcoming the season of new growth and everything.'

'Pagan festivals,' murmured Dido, bringing her brush towards the egg.

'It was called Eostar, after the goddess Ostara. She was the Saxon goddess of spring and the moon. All about fertility and potential.'

'Before Christianity screwed everything up,' said Dido, feeling a strange tingling somewhere above the top of her jeans. 'What is an equinox? I can't ever remember.'

'When day and night are of equal length. The old religion of England was all based on what people observed about the stars, so it was linked to the moon and the sun and everything. Then Christianity came and sort of overlaid it all. Then science comes along and we just graft that on again. So they borrowed Ostara's name for oestrogen.'

Was that a bit brutal? Florian quivered with anxiety, until Dido made a sound like the chuckle of crystal stream water running over pebbles of pink-and-white quartz. 'That's so clever,' she said. She loved to be lectured, provided it wasn't about getting a life or checking her credit card statements and stupid stuff like that.

'And terribly English, when you think about it. Don't sweep away all the old things, just graft on the new and let the old beliefs kind of grow through them. Organic culture, almost. Or just a fudge, depending how you look on it.'

'Do you sell fudge?' Dido asked, feeling that a little confectionery would go down very well after all this exhausting chat about hormones.

'Actually, we do. I've made a range flavoured with traditional cordials. Cowslip Sack. Sloe Gin. Rowan Malmsey. They're quite good, you must try some.'

'Have you got cowslips?' she asked. Cowslips! Desperately romantic. When they got married, she could carry a posy of them. What colour were they, anyway? 'They are flowers, aren't they?'

'Oh yes. They're endangered, of course. We have got some in the wild, but I had to grow them specially for the fudge. Ostara had a hare's head, and she laid eggs. So there's your Easter bunny.'

'Wow, that is so cool,' said Dido. The paint had dried on her brush while she was listening. Definitely, a tingling like fairy dust all around the upper pelvic area. And she just loved the idea of magic and religion and science all flowing together into a great belief system binding all the ages and all the races of humanity together. It was all so beautiful it made her want to dance.

'In a way,' said Florian, who loved to be listened to more than anything else, 'I like to think we're part of the same process here. Helping to find a new balance between modern science and ancient wisdom. Working within modern agricultural policy to bring the needs of the world into equilibrium with the forces of nature.'

252

'That was in the leaflet you gave me.'

She had read his leaflet! Was it the equinoctial forces that made him feel as if fireworks were going off somewhere under his heart?

'So,' Dido continued hopefully, washing off her paint-brush and thinking about starting with Cerulean Blue again, 'did you really say you were going to have a pagan festival?'

'I was thinking of it. I usually just do private rituals for the equinoxes. Just me and whoever's here who wants to come. But with the tasting and everything, the house is going to be full, so I thought maybe we should celebrate the vernal equinox. I've been reading about meditation to stim-ulate the crops. Imagine how powerful it would be to have a group meditation out in the fields somewhere, under the full moon, harnessing the energy of the stars and planets . . .'

The eggs did get painted, some hours later, by Florian's sister and her younger children, while the seigneur showed Dido around his *domaine* in the hazy afternoon sunshine, and they munched on the cowslip fudge.

'Are you sure this is a path?' Clare was feeling tired. They had been walking for hours. Three hours? Four hours? It was all very pretty, all the green plants and everything, but they didn't seem to be getting anywhere.

'Yes, of course I'm sure,' said Miranda, irritated. Did her mother think she couldn't read a map?

Her navigation, of course, was faultless. The map was something else. Oliver had been way ahead of them. What was the first thing people wanted to do when they got out in the country? Go for a walk. Very well, a walk they should have. He had sat up far into the night, plotting a route that was not merely circular, but snaked around the Manor in a spiral, taking in all the least pleasant aspects of the landscape and dodging in and out of woodland so that there was never a view of anything that might be enough of a landmark to make them realise they were going round in a circle. Nor would they be able to see what hazards were coming up ahead . . .

Clare had had the worst of it, because she started walking in front of her daughter. Years of being trailed by assistants made her feel that one step ahead was her natural place. Miranda walked behind her mother, which made her feel like a five-year-old even before her legs started to ache. All the same, she could see a few of the dangers before falling into them. And she had the map.

The path went uphill quite often, but never seemed to come down, except when it suddenly plunged into what looked like a pretty sort of dell but was actually a complete swamp of bottomless mud that pulled your boots off as you struggled through it. When they had waded through that, the path almost disappeared in a thicket of brambles, treacherously undergrown by stinging nettles which were only six inches high but vicious all the same.

Clare started to complain at that point, but even she had to admit that the map was perfectly clear so they pushed on through, getting scratched severely on the way. For a long while they skirted an enormous field given over to pigs, from which the smell, carried firmly over to them by a prevailing breeze, was revolting.

Now they had reached a stream, very prettily full of yellow irises and green duckweed, over which the way was plainly indicated by a narrow white-painted bridge. The span was a single plank, with handrails on either side that were hardly more than battens nailed to narrow wooden posts.

'Look,' Miranda showed her mother the map, 'we cross here, then turn left and go through this forest bit, and then we're there.'

'It looks very old,' Clare said, stepping onto the bridge with hesitation. 'You don't suppose it could be rotten?'

'It's just weathered,' Miranda assured her. 'It's probably been here twenty years.'

'That's what I mean.'

'It would be fenced off if it wasn't safe.'

'I suppose it would.'

Cautiously, Clare took a few steps. The bridge, overhung with budding alder branches, trembled slightly. Upstream, something plopped into the water.

'Oh!' cried Clare. 'What was that?'

'Probably only a duck,' said Miranda, watching some small creature cruise determinedly away downstream and disappear. Maybe it was a water rat. The idea of saying the word 'rat' to her mother had its appeal, but she didn't want to be wantonly cruel. So she fibbed. It felt curiously pleasant.

Clare was shuffling across the bridge saying, 'I really don't think this is safe,' when the edifice proved her right. There was a crack, a crunch, a noise of rotting wood crumbling, and the plank tipped, the handrail was twisted away, and Clare lost her balance, screamed, and fell into the water. Which was shallow, but horribly muddy, full of sinister twiggy things, and cold. She splashed frantically. Some birds flew out of the tree tops, screeching in alarm.

255

'Don't panic!' Miranda called, seeing a way down the stream bank.

'That is the most irritating thing you could possibly say,' her mother shouted. 'Get me out of here.'

'All right, all right. I'm coming.'

But she was still at the top of the bank when her mother found her feet, realised that when she stood the water hardly came above her knees, felt ridiculous and waded grimly to the edge of the stream. Miranda could at least help her scramble back onto dry ground.

With muddy feet, slimy legs, wet clothes and a green veil of duckweed pretty much all over, Clare was not the picture of elegance.

'Oh no. What are we going to do now?' Miranda said. Dilemmas involving mud were new to both of them. 'Your clothes are all wet.'

'Yes, they are,' Clare agreed, trying not to sound as angry as she felt. 'And I'm freezing cold already. That mud! It was full of . . . things! Horrible!'

With disgusted fingertips, she pulled off one of her boots and tried to wipe off a hank of green algae with a wisp of long grass. Grass! How could she possibly have anything to do with grass? Normally, the only grass with which she would welcome contact was the organic wheatgrass bought in by the juice bar near Agraria's offices: £15 a tray.

'We can't go on, unless we can find another way over that stream thing,' said Miranda. 'But if we turn back . . . we've been out for hours. We'll have to walk miles.'

'Then that's what we'll have to do, won't we? God! These people! No concept of safety or maintenance. How could they leave a bridge in that condition? They could be sued.'

'We're not far from the village. If we could just get over the stream somewhere, I could . . .' Ridiculous Girl Guide situation! Miranda despised Girl Guides. Ludicrous Enid Blyton anachronism, probably just a cover-up for lezzie old schoolteachers who hadn't realised that all that was over and it was cool to be out.

'If it had been anybody except me, their ass would be sued from here to . . . kingdom come.' Her mother wasn't listening. So what else was new?

'I'm sure we could get a taxi in the village,' Miranda insisted.

'Taxi! Are you out of your mind? I'm not having anyone see me in this state.' The words were fired off like a thirty-second burst from an AK47. 'I'm a public figure, Miranda. I have to project an image, convey authority, give people confidence. I can't go splashing around in wet clothes covered in mud.'

'But it's three hours' walk back to the hotel,' Miranda argued, consulting the map again. 'And we are close to the next village now. There must be a taxi somewhere.'

'There is no way in this world I am going into any village like this,' said Clare, tossing her dripping boot aside with a spasm of her muddy hand. She picked accusingly at the top of her sock, trying to convince the garment that it had a duty to strip itself off without any further input from her.

'But I could go, and then I could get a taxi. I can leave you my parka. You can sit somewhere in the sun, and I'll be back in half an hour with some dry clothes.'

They considered this solution. 'That could work,' her mother admitted.

'I think it's the best idea,' Miranda urged. 'Look, there's that tree thing.' She pointed uncertainly at the trunk of an old alder that had long ago fallen by the stream bank and now promised to make an inoffensive seat. As she did not normally meet fallen trees, she wasn't sure what to call it. 'It does look quite dry. You could sit on it, maybe.'

'The weather isn't too bad,' her mother admitted.

'I can't think of anything else. I mean, it's not like a lot of people must come this way.'

'Well, obviously, if people came this way, the bridge would have fallen in before now. That must be why they thought they could get away with it.'

'So you'd be quite safe. Nobody would see you.'

'You're sure it isn't far?'

How bizarre, Miranda thought. I'm feeling a bit protective here. She does look pathetic, all covered in slime and stuff. I'd be hysterical if it was me. Poor old Mum. She'd hate me to say that.

'I'll be back as soon as I can,' she said, unwrapping her scarf and unzipping her parka. 'Here. You can put these on. You've got your mobile, haven't you?'

'Haven't you got yours?'

'You'd better have it then, if it's the only one we've got.'

And that, thought Miranda, as she turned back to investigate the remains of the bridge, is the most family-type conversation we've had for years. I feel quite like giving her a hug. Would she welcome a hug? Don't be silly.

The bridge, she could see now that it was fallen, had been made of old railway sleepers, several used as piles and driven haphazardly into the bank at each side, and one balanced on their ends, making a path across the water. On the far side, one of the upended sleepers had broken away, causing the span to tip and fall. But the nearest end was solid, and over the stream, within easy reach, hung tree branches of promising size, and the collapsed pile itself was partly above water. Surely with a little daring . . .

'Do be careful, darling!' she heard her mother behind her as she stepped up on the fallen bridge. Slither, grab – skip! She was over the other side. Easy-peasy. Me Jane.

'I'll be back soon,' she promised, and set off with a pleasant sense of having mastered a little bit of nature.

Being single by an English hedgerow in spring is a poignant experience. A lot of budding, swelling and unfurling was happening among the vegetation. The shining faces of violets, coy and flirtatious, were half-hidden by their heart-shaped leaves. Shy primroses, so pale and modest, were waiting to be discovered in the long grass by your feet, and above your head, great billows of white blossom showered petal confetti all over you.

Leaves bursting out of their buds, stems uncoiling like whips, growing tips of everything thrusting out everywhere. Everything was urgent, and blatant, and bent on display. Arums flashing open their green outer jackets, waving about a pale, penis-shaped item that was upstanding inside. Hairy young ferns uncurling their new shoots. Merkins of moss, breaking out in russet fuzz. Once your eye had seen and your mind had made the connections, every hedge was a great green orgy.

Nor were you the only one to have noticed. As Miranda swung along the path, she observed that birds were fluttering about in a frenzy. Tiny finches were dipping and twittering side by side on the same twig. Big soft doves cooed passionately in the tree tops. Magpies played kiss-chase from one field to the next. All in pairs, every one. Damn it, she was the only living thing in the landscape that wasn't courting.

Clare, meanwhile, took a seat on the fallen tree. After she had picked every single minute green leaf of duckweed off her coat, she had nothing on her mind. There was nothing she could do, and nowhere she could go, having taken off both her waterlogged boots and both her wet socks and placed them neatly on the bark beside her. She could think about things, and, hating to waste even half an hour of time, she intended to think about things, especially the responsible land use strategy for Agraria, but her mind was unwilling and anyway, her Palm was at the hotel and she hadn't even a pencil to write stuff down, so what was the point?

The sun was in her eyes. A large bee zoomed past, intent on something. Strange that a mere insect could seem so purposeful. Ridiculous, of course. What purpose could an insect have, after all?

Perhaps this accident would have an up-side. Miranda definitely seemed to be a bit more confident, now she had a mission and a role. She'd always needed to have her time structured. Left alone, her whole life would probably have just drifted away . . .

Something was looking at her. She had the definite feeling of being watched. For a moment, Clare was sure it must be a photographer or a journalist or something. Damn! Where were they, whoever they were?

Good heavens, it was an animal. Quite a way off, up at the far end of the field. Some little brown animal was looking at her. She saw it when it moved. Very odd, the way it moved. Irregular, ungainly. Almost like a little kangaroo. Tee-tum, tee-tum. Then it paused, and sort of sat up. It did look very like a kangaroo, but smaller, of course, with longer ears.

Tee-tum, tee-tum, tee-tum. The animal was coming towards her again. Extraordinary, it didn't seem worried. It was completely calm. And brown. Long ears with black tips. Rather beautiful, in a bizarre sort of way. It couldn't possibly be a kangaroo, unless one had escaped from a wildlife park or something. Could it have rabies? Would it bite her? Was it angry?

Good Lord. Another one. Coming up the slope, rather quickly. Not exactly running. Bounding, really. Cutting easily through the long green grass, almost like a boat bobbing over the waves. A funny elliptical movement. Boing-boing-boing! Just as brown, ears just as long. More like a rabbit than a kangaroo, really.

Whatever they were, the two animals had seen each other. Getting closer. The first one stood up on its hind legs. The second one stopped for an instant and twitched its ears. Then it moved forward again.

Why, this was like being in the middle of a wildlife documentary. In her mind's ear, she heard David Attenborough's confidential murmur. 'The two animals approach each other warily through the long grass . . .'

The two of them were face to face now. And jumping about. Trying to bop each other with their forelegs. Extraordinary. You'd have said the two rabbit things were dancing. Or maybe fighting. Leaping all over the field, now, making crazy shapes, tearing off in different directions with that curious lolloping run then they turned – zap! As quick as a whip, a corkscrew turn. So fast you could hardly believe you'd seen them do it. And standing up on their hind legs again and getting into a real boxing match.

As she watched, the shape of the creatures stirred some memories. Those long, long legs, jointed eccentrically; those long, long ears, tipped with black. The gleaming eyes on the side of the small head, the sinuous body, the magical speed of their movements.

Never in her life had Clare seen a hare, nor had she ever consciously noticed a photograph, a film or a sculpture of one. The March Hare who met Alice in Wonderland was not part of her heritage; her parents had felt that they knew their place and avoided all literature, especially that written for children, because it was the province of the upper classes and might damn them as having social pretensions. All the same, from a sludge of unremarked impressions and a long-denied share of the collective unconscious, Clare found the name. A hare. Two hares. Real, true, living, mad March hares, and she was a witness to their lunacy.

She was impressed with herself. For the benefit of no one, a beatific smile spread across her face, smoothing the forehead that had been wrinkled with anxiety for years and soothing the jaw that she habitually held tense and ready for denial. Her time instinct, which normally monitored the progress made on her enterprises in every waking minute, gently failed as she watched the animals leaping over the shining grass.

When eventually the hares cavorted out of her sight, Clare's mind glided into a state not far from a waking dream. She was so seldom aware of the earth and sky that they were now a marvellous surprise. So wide a sky, so much light, so many clouds. And the damp ground, cool under her bare soles, giving off a rustle of tiny lives, of grass blades growing and insects bustling between them. It seemed reasonable to think that the world was full of wonders.

Miranda arrived some time later, with dry clothes and news of a taxi waiting at the end of the field. She found her mother looking surprisingly calm, and in an unprecedentedly good mood.

At the end of the afternoon, Tolvo and Juri transferred one precious sterling note from Tolvo's money belt to his pocket, took their dictionary and set off down the lane, making for Great Saxwold. The village was a disappointment to them. The building which was definitely labelled 'shop' was shut, and had obviously been shut for years. A careful search of all the other buildings did not turn up anything else resembling a place where two very hungry men would be able to buy a chicken. Nor was there evidence of a bus going to anywhere else that might have a shop.

They found a place that seemed to be a restaurant. There was a picture of some kind of bird on its sign. Tolvo tried to decipher what could have been the menu, written on a double-sided blackboard in the yard outside. The names of what might have been dishes were impossible to understand and the prices were enormous, much too much for food, almost enough to buy a car. As there were quite a few cars in the yard, they decided that this was some kind of car exchange, and trudged on.

For a while they stood by the roadside, hoping to hitch a ride from a passing motorist, but nothing came along except a truck driven by a thin small man who shook his head at Tolvo's upraised thumb. In the end they went into the church.

'This really isn't too bad,' said Tolvo, looking around the interior. 'It's obviously a poor village so they don't have much gold, but they're doing their best with these flowers.'

'What are we doing?' said Juri. 'We can't get a chicken here. There isn't even a picture of a chicken in this place. Not even if I was hallucinating. Which I soon will be. Protein! God give me protein, with feathers on it. Please!'

'There aren't any chickens in the Bible. I've never heard that Jesus had anything to do with chickens.'

'Exactly. This place is useless. Marx was absolutely right about religion. Unless you think you can arrange a miracle.'

'At least we can sit down,' Tolvo said. 'They've got a lot of seats.'

'Yes, we could sit down here. If you've got a well-fed arse to sit on all this wood. Can't they afford cushions? What are those stupid things on the floor?' Juri pointed at the line of tapestry kneelers in each pew, lovingly worked at the rate of two a year by the retired postmistress in Yattenham.

'Foot rests? I don't know.'

'I thought you knew everything.' Juri sat down on a pew and found it more welcoming than it looked. After a couple of minutes, he pulled up his feet and lay experimentally along the seat. 'I suppose I can stand this. At least we're not in that fucking caravan for a few hours. OK, I'm going to have a kip. If I can forget how hungry I am long enough to be able to get to sleep. I pray that God will stop me from having another nightmare about potatoes.'

He shut his eyes and immediately managed to slip into a doze. Tolvo, feeling bored with no one to talk to, stretched out on the next pew and soon found that it really was comfortable enough for a half-hour nap.

When he opened his eyes, an angel was leaning over the back of the pew and looking at him. She had the most kissable lips he had ever seen. She had enormous eyes and they were outlined in an extremely degenerate black. She had clouds of golden hair, with streaks of a decadent pink in it. A fallen angel, obviously. The kind he had always hoped to meet.

She spoke to him. He did not understand.

'What are you doing here?' she said, speaking more slowly. And in English. An English angel. Quick, quick, think of some English words.

'Hello,' he said, pulling himself up to a sitting position and then, because it seemed less than manly to sit, standing up before the celestial being.

'Yes, hello?' she answered him. She was trying to sound cynical. In an angelic voice, it sounded absolutely adorable. 'I said, what are you doing here?'

'Hello. Yes. What are we doing. We are doing – nothing.'

'Why?'

'Why?'

'Yes, why? Why are you here doing nothing?'

'Please excuse me because I don't speak very well English.'

'Are you a tourist?'

'No. No tourist. We working.'

'Working where?'

'Farm.'

'What farm? Colin Burton's farm? Big man, red face? Over there?'

The angel raised her heavenly arm, sheathed in fabulously depraved black leather, and gestured in what might have been the direction of their farm, but after wandering around for hours Tolvo was not exactly sure. But her description, once he had translated it to himself, fitted the man with the money.

'Big man, red face. Farm. We work. Yes.'

'You're picking potatoes on his farm?'

'Potatoes. Yes. We work . . . potatoes.'

The dreadful word roused Juri, whose eyelids flickered open. Sensing trouble, he sat up in a hurry, which alarmed the angel, who jumped half out of her skin and uttered a whole banner of heavenly expletives.

'What the fuck?' Juri demanded in his own language. 'Who is this? What is this? Am I dreaming?'

'Who the fuck's this?' the angel demanded, in English.

'We could be dreaming,' Tolvo agreed, trying to calm his friend with a waving hand. 'Just be cool a minute. Don't frighten it.' Then in English, he told the angel, 'This my friend. Juri. His name. My friend.'

'Toni,' she said, extending an angelic hand to be shaken. Juri immediately shook it with a will, saying his name through a blatant grin. 'Pleased to meet you,' said the angel, sounding just like the people on the tapes at the language laboratory. But she was turning radiantly towards Tolvo.

The hand was as light and warm and fragile as a feather from the wing of a cherubim. A naughty cherubim, obviously, since there was a black lace glove involved. Tolvo said his name.

'Volvo?' said the angel Toni, with a peal of golden giggles.

'Tolvo. Finland name. My mother coming from Finland.' Juri got him by the shoulders and hissed in his ear, 'Does she know where we can buy a chicken?'

'Shut up,' said Tolvo.

'Ask her. Go on. She must know.' Juri had big hands and he grabbed you like a bear.

Tolvo winced and said, 'Shut up, you idiot.'

'You're the idiot,' Juri punched him in the arm in a manner that could only just be called friendly. 'Go on, ask her. Since you're getting on so well.'

'What's he saying?' asked the angel Toni.

'He says . . .' Tolvo's mind had got rusty through lack of use. 'He says . . . please, we want to buy a chicken.'

'A chicken?' she repeated.

Tolvo said it again, taking care to pronounce each word correctly. Juri flapped his elbows and made clucking noises, which echoed irreverently from the ancient vaulted ceiling.

'Why?' asked the angel Toni. 'Why do you want a chicken?'

'Why? A chicken? To eating. To buy a chicken to eating. Do you know where . . .'

'Are you hungry?' demanded the angel Toni, miming eating with her black lace hands. A look of divine compassion was coming over her face. She looked more forgiving than ten thousand icons. A miracle could possibly be imminent.

'Yes! Yes!' This was from Juri, now also miming eating, though he managed to give his friend an encouraging shove in the kidney area as well.

'Yes. We have hungry,' Tolvo agreed, with what he hoped was romantic dignity.

'Right. Well. Chicken. That's easy. It's your lucky day. We can definitely sort you out a chicken. Come with me. Today, Chickens R Us. Little do you know that I've just plucked six of the stinking little fuckers. Come on.' And the angel was

267

making for the church door, and beckoning them to follow, flapping her own elbows and clucking, in a paradisically pretty way. She had a small motorbike, and, with truly supernatural agility, she manoeuvred all three of them on to it and buzzed unsteadily away down another lane, in search of poultry.

CHAPTER 10

Free Bees

At the news desk at the television studio in Norwich, the invitation to a wine-tasting at Château Saxwold, scheduled plumb in the middle of the great event vacuum of the Easter weekend, had been viewed as a godsend. The outside broadcast van, crowned with a white satellite dish, arrived early at the *domaine* office and was awarded a prime position in the car park. The reporter with the Betty Boop eyelashes had herself filmed with Florian, who walked earnestly with her along the rows of sprouting vines, delighted to be able to bore for East Anglia on the subject of biodynamic agriculture.

Betty Boop then did a piece to camera, at the end of which she intended to take a swig of the 1999 Pinot and deliver a witty parody of a wine buff's banter about its taste. Lulled by Florian's oratory, she gulped the murky liquid with enthusiasm. When the wine hit her innocent taste buds it induced a violent spit, a convulsive retch and an extended oh-no second, followed by a disgusted 'Fucking hell.'

'It is rather young, still,' Florian advised.

'We're all young,' she spluttered. 'You don't have to be that rude with it. Have you got anything else this colour? I'm not paid enough to drink any more of that. Don't you realise it tastes like cat's piss?'

'I'm a dog person,' said Florian, with dignity.

Betty Boop repaired her makeup and completed the recording with a glass of diluted Lucozade, thoughtfully offered by one of the wine-maker's nieces. Happily, this led to the filming of the whole tribe of moppets dancing on the lawn with Dido, and the dog, a sequence of sure-fire ratings candy that sweetened the atmosphere considerably.

'Now, we just need some shots of the actual tasting itself,' she told Florian. 'And if you're going to make a speech, or something.'

'Sure,' he said, making hasty plans.

The Visitor Centre was reasonably full by 7pm, since the day had turned cloudy in the late afternoon and an icy east wind had got up, making a good two hundred people aware that indoor amusement was the preferred option and the promise of a free drink would be well worth accepting. A locust-like swarm of Addleworth relations flew in to swell the crowd.

Florian watched with doting eyes while Dido organised the moppets to fill glasses and patter prettily around the gathering with bowls of crisps, peanuts and his sister's artistic crostini that dribbled pesto down the eater's wrist in a way that only a member of the Old Posh would endure with gallantry. By 7.30, when the free glasses had either been finished or tipped furtively out into the flower tubs, he judged that it would be wise to say a few words.

'Okay, peeps!' he called out, leaping like Errol Flynn to the centre of the tasting table. 'Just a few words to say welcome and thank you all for . . .'

'Killer!' The word was shouted from the gallery.

'Slave master!'

'Oppressor!'

'Free the bees!'

'What's happening?' Betty Boop demanded.

'Don't ask me.' Florian peered up at the gallery with an expression of benign amazement. When your family has successfully dodged blame since the days of William the Conqueror, you have some useful racial memories.

'It's a demonstration,' said a second man with a camera, who came from nowhere and jumped on a chair to get a view of what he hoped would be chaos and dismay.

'We're working for animal rights,' declared an American voice. Heads turned, and identified its source: a tall man wearing what looked like a giant Babygro, spray-painted in black and yellow bands. On his head, a black bobble hat and spring-mounted glitter balls did not quite hide long brown hair. He clutched a sheaf of leaflets to his chest and was stuffing them into people's hands. Betty Boop snatched one at once.

'AASS Ass. Or is it arse? But isn't it the same, if you're American?'

'We are citizens of the planet,' he intoned.

'Free the bees!' shouted the voice from the gallery.

'Free the bees!' shouted the American, flinging the rest of his leaflets into the crowd.

A net of yellow balloons appeared over the gallery rail. 'Brilliant,' muttered Betty Boop to her cameraman. 'You are getting this, aren't you?'

'You bet!' he assured her, jumping on the nearest window seat for a good angle.

The slogan-shouting faltered as the net was positioned and untied, then suddenly the cascade of yellow balloons, fastened to cardboard wings and marked with black stripes and smiley faces, tumbled down on the crowd. The children were delighted, and ran about the hall trying to catch them and shrieking, 'Free bees! Free bees!'

'Damn!' said the cameraman. 'Damn, damn, damn!'

'What?' his reporter demanded.

'Running out of tape,' he told her.

'No worries!' cried Video Guy 'I'm getting it. We can talk later.'

'Are you with them?' Betty Boop asked, delighted that her schleppy little weekend story was turning into a real news item.

'I'm the official film-maker,' he said. 'Don't worry. I'm getting some great stuff here.'

'Thank Christ for that.'

The balloons were soon captured, and occasional pops around the room suggested that their visual appeal was going to be limited. Betty Boop took Video Guy by the elbow and pointed him in Florian's direction. The wine-maker had climbed down from the table, and was standing nonplussed against the wall, trying to decide whether he should ask his uncles to evict the intruders or welcome the whole thing in the spirit of the hare-eared goddess Ostara and new beginnings in general.

'How do you feel about this!' the reporter shouted at him.

'I don't know, really,' he said.

'Yes you do,' she insisted.

'It's nice for the children,' he said.

'Bugger the children. What about you?'

'I just like people to have a good time,' he said.

The reporter asked herself how Jeremy Paxman would have handled this. 'You don't really mean that!' she yelled at him.

'Yes I do.'

'You must be thick!'

'People have said that,' Florian agreed.

'Look,' said the reporter, turning back to the leaflets on the table. 'They're calling you a slave master and an oppressor and saying you're cruel to animals.'

'I love animals,' said Florian. 'It's not like I've got the bees chained to their honeycombs or anything. If my bees weren't happy, they'd fly away, wouldn't they?'

'Go and look at the beehives,' intoned the American voice.

'Yes,' Florian said in an agreeable tone. 'Why don't we do that?'

While the company in the hall began to break up and climb back into their cars in search of alcoholic drinks that could actually be ingested without toxic shock, Florian set off across the courtyard in the direction of the beehives, his dog at his heels, trailing the reporter, Video Guy and the official cameraman, who had gone to the van to get a spare magazine of tape. Dido ran after them, followed by the three youngest and most infatuated children, waving their bee balloons firmly in their little fists.

The hives had been installed under the wall of the old vegetable garden, where Florian was now growing patches of everything he had found mentioned in his collection of old herbalist literature as a suitable flavour for wines, cordials or sweetmeats. Inside squares of willow hurdles, the red roses were setting their buds, the mounds of lavender were spiky with blue-grey shoots, the cowslips nodded like a patch of sunshine and the newly sown borage was still nothing but lines of green cotyledons, fluttering like butterflies in the evening breeze.

The beehives, which normally stood facing this smorgasbord of historic pollen sources in a neat row, had been tipped over and broken open.

'Oh my God,' Florian said, his slender hands flying up to his temples. His dog quivered against his shins in sympathy. A few bees were hovering disconsolately over their broken homes, trying to settle on the shattered fragments of their honeycombs as if they could hardly believe the evidence of their multiple eyes. 'What's been going on here?'

'We've freed the bees!' declared the American, waving his arms.

'No you haven't,' Florian said, ripping the band off his ponytail in exasperation. 'You absolute idiots. Don't you realise you've totally traumatised them? This is the very worst time of year you could possibly have chosen. You fools, don't you know anything? This is their nesting time. The swarms will be totally disoriented now. Half of them will probably just fly off and die. I'm going to have to call up a specialist and get him to see if he can find any of the queens. Although – where are we going to start?'

To the embarrassment of Video Guy, who had been getting the most satisfactory close shot of his anguished face, Florian suddenly lost control of his finely chiselled features and burst into tears.

As if to avenge him, a black cloud of insects suddenly whirled over the red-brick wall, droning like a distant Spitfire, and flew angrily up over the garden. One of the children screamed.

'They don't look very happy,' said Dido, distraught to see her loved one weeping.

'How would you feel?' he asked, wiping his cheeks with the backs of his hands. 'They've been evicted, haven't they?'

'It's fixable, Florian,' his brother-in-law called from the scene of the carnage. 'There's not too much actual damage. The hives are quite repairable. Give me a few hours.'

Florian sniffed. 'They might choose somewhere else in a few hours.'

'No they won't. They look pretty set on staying right here.' And his sister's husband pointed to the end of the garden, where the black cloud of bees wheeled like a squadron of bombers and began to fly back.

'They really don't look happy now,' said Dido.

'They really aren't happy,' said Florian. 'What do you expect?'

'I've seen this,' the American said. 'This is quite normal. They'll spread out and settle down in the wild. Just give them space . . .'

Video Guy was the first to run, followed by the children, who started the shrieking. Florian took Dido passionately by the hand and swept her along after them. Seeing the bee-keeper himself in flight, the dog, the cameraman, the other representatives of the Addleworth clan and all the rest of the onlookers legged it after him. Betty Boop, whose kitten heels kept sticking in the turf, came in last, just before the door of the Visitor Centre was slammed with relief.

Which left Ashok, the American, in his freedom suit, standing triumphantly in front of the overturned hives.

'There's no need to panic!' he shouted. 'They won't hurt you. It's perfectly natural. They're just swarming . . .'

He disappeared under a blanket of black insects, a gesticulating figure which Florian watched anxiously from the window of the Centre.

'Have they got him?' asked Dido.

'I think so,' said Florian, trying to sound regretful.

'Will they sting him?' she asked, trying to sound concerned.

'Well, a few of them probably will.'

'And how do you feel about that?' demanded Betty Boop, her reporter's instincts reasserting themselves.

'Not deeply moved,' Florian admitted. 'Possibly quite grateful. If you go around evicting thousands of creatures who've just settled into their nice new homes and just want to get on with their lives, you can't really expect too much in the way of public sympathy, can you?'

'So you're saying he deserved it?' said Betty Boop hopefully.

'Oh, do shut up, you silly cow,' said Dido, 'Can't you see he's upset?'

Dinner at what they presumed to be the Saxwold Manor Hotel was everything that Miranda and her mother hoped it would be. They kept their hopes to themselves, being alarmed by the feelings they were having as a result of fresh air and extended exercise. They were hungry, but hardly knew what that feeling was, being used only to feeling anxious in the presence of food.

They were tired, another feeling they could hardly recognise. If they walked, or ran, or climbed, or bicycled in their London lives, it was in a gym, where a digital display would tell them how far, how fast and how many calories they had burned, then finish up with an electronic fanfare and a cheery motivational message, like 'Top of Target – You're a Winner!' Walking around the countryside in a very big circle, then falling into a muddy stream and sitting around watching a couple of hares dancing was an experience of a seriously different quality.

They were also relaxed, something else far outside their normal range of feeling. In fact, if Clare had been asked to remember, she wouldn't have been able to identify ten seconds in the whole of the past thirty-five years when she had felt relaxed. Every moment of consciousness had been taken, first by her children and then by her ambition, and she had never dared to use the rare moments of calm for anything except worrying about the last thing or planning the next thing. And Miranda well, most people, her mother included, thought that Miranda had just been born tense.

Cream of Jerusalem Artichoke Soup. Parfait of Duck's Liver, Red Onion Marmalade. Feuilletée of Three Terrines. Borcht à la Russe with Dumplings. Salade Saxwold. Quiche of Garden Vegetables, Tomato Sorbet. Magret of Suffolk Duckling, Wild Sorrel Sauce. They read the menu with a rising sense of daring. Cream! Dumplings! Quiche! Could they? Just this once? Duck, computed Miranda's built-in nutritional meter: bad, but not a total disaster if you cut off the skin.

The dining room was quiet and softly lit for the evening, with a low fire purring in the grate. Only two other tables were occupied. At one, the Vicar and his wife conscientiously sampled what they had been told was a set-up which Bel was staging for some potential buyers who thought her house was already a restaurant. At the other, Colin and Jimmy munched philosophically through what they knew well were the carcasses of the fox victims, using large doses of whisky to help them play their part in the charade.

Every now and then they sneaked glances in Clare's direction, which she returned with benevolent smiles, feeling immensely flattered that people who were probably actual farmers recognised her when she'd only been in the job a few months. There, she reassured herself, the farmers understand. It's those dumb-ass conservationists who get it all wrong.

Miranda read down the menu: *Marmite of Corn-Fed Chicken, Baby Spring Vegetables. Roast Sausages with Stilton Mash.* Bloody hell. Chicken: OK in small portions.

'Have you any sea bass?' she asked the waiter, trying to go down fighting.

Actually, there was a definite thrill in talking to the waiter, when less than twenty-four hours ago he could have been so much more to her. And he was still pretty fine. But it would have got complicated. Lucky escape, or what?

Snotty cow, thought Oliver, watching the way she read the menu as if she had a PhD in Merde de Taureau Français. I was well out of that.

'We only have fish in season, madam,' he murmured. It was difficult to talk at full volume when, for the sake of impersonating a waiter, you had only just managed to pour yourself into your dinner jacket. Amazing how much his waist had expanded since becoming a farmer.

Pretentious bastard, thought Miranda. It's ludicrous for

some little country place like this to ponce around with a woofed-up menu written in Bullshit French when they're probably going to drag it all out of the freezer and slap it in the microwave. And he looks positively porky in that suit. Goodness, I'm hungry.

'Well,' said Clare, making up her mind. 'This is a special occasion. I'd like the borscht and the duck.'

Miranda blinked in shock. Dumplings? Her mother was having the thing with dumplings? 'I'll have the . . . the . . .' Heavens, was there no low-fat option at all? 'The chicken, please. What is the salad?'

Oliver, whose Bullshit French vocabulary had already been stretched to the limit, struggled for words. 'Ah – a mixture of – ah – green – er – seasonal – um – leaves and – ah . . .' Snotty cow was still looking expectant. Nobody ever asked what was in salad, what was the matter with her? 'I'll go and ask,' he said, feeling lame.

'Don't bother,' said Miranda grandly. 'I'm sure it's fine.'

'You are sure?' OK, that was a wind-up. But only a small one. He really couldn't resist.

'A salad is a salad,' she said. 'I'll have that. How much trouble can I get into with a salad?'

You have no idea, thought Oliver.

Clare was studying his freshly printed wine list, compiled from the labels on what was left of the half-decent cellar he had started in his City days plus the greatest hits from the wine warehouse on the Ipswich bypass. 'This one,' she said, pointing to the most expensive item. 'Lacrime dei Serafimi, Montalcino 1955. What's that like?'

Like lying on warm crimson satin at sunset in Tuscany, thought Oliver, though you will never know. That's my top favourite, there's only one bottle left and you can't have it. He threw his upper body into that strangely deferential swagger which wine waiters master along with their vintage charts. 'If I may suggest,' he began, letting his Biro hover suggestively over a wine warehouse special, 'the Lacrime might be a touch overpriced . . .'

'That's no problem,' she decided. 'We'll have that. After all, this is a special occasion.'

'Right you are,' he muttered, trying not to grit his teeth, and making notes in his pretend order book, which was actually a pink notepad decorated with Hello Kitty faces which some distant relative had sent Toni for her birthday.

Pretentious idiot, thought Miranda, trying to act like some big-time sommelier in a place like this. However, as Oliver strode away to the door, she couldn't fail to notice that the trousers fitted rather well.

Thirty seconds later, Oliver hurtled through the kitchen door shouting, 'Champagne! Where are the glasses! We've got to keep them busy!'

'What are they eating?' Bel demanded, waving her largest wooden spoon.

His mother was pacing about in front of the Aga in a kind of euphoria. She had spent a most enjoyable afternoon playing at being a master chef, beginning by bullying Toni into the garden to dig vegetables and de-feather the foxes' unlucky victims. The dog, scenting disaster, had installed himself in his basket and was watching the proceedings with an expression of pained mistrust. Garrick had no plans to move until the chaos subsided.

In and around the Aga, every pan was hissing and every pot simmering, while in the sink a tap dripped helplessly on a mountain of those utensils which had hissed and simmered earlier. The air was dense with good smells but the floor had been trodden to a treacherous swamp of mud, vegetable peelings and stray feathers.

At the end of the kitchen table sat Tolvo and Juri, who had been welcomed by Bel as ideal tasters for her artistry. Once Toni had extracted an account of their deprivation, Bel's maternal instincts crashed into overdrive and she issued her guests with a serial banquet, fussing around them to make sure they were not too shy to eat it. After a while, she even remembered a few words of Polish, the exhortations which her own mother had used to make her offspring eat.

The two young men were now sitting in stupefied heaps, not really sure that they were not dreaming, morbidly suspicious of their butter-basted, sauce-glazed good luck, their satiated minds half-heartedly alert for the closing of the trap into which they had surely walked while their best instincts suggested that all they had to do now was be grateful. Toni, sitting on a worktop, had meanwhile amused herself carving small turnips into waterlilies.

'Nibbles! Have we got any nibbles?' Oliver rummaged in a cupboard which sometimes contained cheese straws. 'They've gone and ordered one of my wines. We've got to keep them busy while I get over to my place to find it.'

'I'll go,' Toni suggested.

'No you won't. You take them the champagne. Say it's on the house. Talk pretty, for God's sake. You know you can do it.'

'I thought you hated this fat-cat minister bitch, whatever she is.'

'I do, I do. But we need the money. The bigger the bill

the better, remember. Get 'em drunk, then they'll really start spending money.'

'Fair enough,' said Toni. 'Fuck off on my bike then. Leave the shampoo to me.'

'Thanks,' Oliver said, catching the bike's keys as she tossed them at him. She was a brat, of course, but his step-sister could come through when she had to.

'But what are they eating, Ollie? I've got to know!' This was from Bel as he flung open the door.

'Chicken and duck, borscht and salad!' he shouted over his shoulder as he bore down upon the moped.

'Borscht very good!' said Tolvo, hoping he was helping and giving a thumbs-up sign. If these people were running a restaurant, they didn't seem to have a clue how to go about it, but as he and Juri had benefited so superbly from their incompetence, it seemed wise to shut up and encourage them.

'Shampoo, shampoo, what kind of glasses have we got for shampoo?' muttered Toni, taking over the search of the glass cupboard. It seemed to her that champagne, being a luxury type of booze, ought to be served in luxury-sized glasses. Meaning the biggest ones there were. She pulled out a pair of monstrous glass balloons that someone had given her father, way back when she had been too young to appreciate that their capacity was one entire bottle of wine apiece.

Bel wiped her hands on one of the nine tea towels that she had in use and found various items which, when flung together onto a dish and decorated with one of Toni's turnip water lilies, looked passably like creative canapés. A bottle was found, in the fridge, to general relief, and after Toni had dragged out the cork with a short struggle, the entire contents were poured into the glasses and the time-consuming offering assembled.

''Ere you go,' said Toni, swooping down on Clare and Miranda with her loaded tray. 'On the 'ouse.'

'Oh my goodness!' cried Clare. The nice thing about politics, she had already discovered, was that people kept trying to buy you and giving you presents. But the nice thing about this – OK, distinctly amateurish – sweetener was that she had the leisure to enjoy it and her daughter to share it with.

Miranda eyed the turnip and tried not to wince. Vegetable sculpture. Design atrocity. Complete lack of cultural syntax. Still, what else could you expect in the country?

Half a mile away in his own house, Oliver was carefully rolling his last bottle of Lacrime dei Serafimi over the bed of his scanner. He planned to stick the copy of the label on a bottle of Florian's evil Pinot. The plan delighted him so highly that he got careless. Not so careless that he forgot to check on his pigs before jumping back on the moped, but as he left them he slammed shut the gate to their field so exuberantly that it rebounded off the gatepost, and the catch did not catch.

While he was buzzing back to The Manor House, the wind caught the gate. Slowly, invitingly, it swung open. There was just enough light in the sky for the nearest of the pigs, already lolling drowsily on the straw in her shelter, to be able to observe the opening gate.

Miss Piggy, who was nearest to the exit, got back on her feet. Various piglets were still trundling about in the twilight, and a group of three of them trotted over to investigate.

A new field! A new world! What pig could pass up such an opportunity?

Pretty soon, Oliver's seven pigs, and all their fifty-one offspring, had spread out down the lane and were rooting in the hedges.

Colin's pigs found this a most interesting development. A few of them started rooting in the hedges themselves, from their own side. The hedges were still young, and had not grown roots deep enough to resist a double-sided assault. Pretty soon, nearly three hundred pigs were spread out along the lane and A327, the car park of The Pigeon & Pipkin, the churchyard at St Oswin's and several front gardens in Great Saxwold.

The trouble with being offered free champagne, when you have the leisure to enjoy it, is that you are likely to do just that. In the case of Clare and Miranda, they went on to enjoy their dinner, including most of a very interesting bottle of wine, and some outrageous desserts, and a few glasses of an agreeable yellow drink called Cowslip Sack. By 10pm, they had collapsed into their beds.

The trouble with giving people free champagne is that other people may demand equal favour. Which meant that Colin and Jimmy had polished off a bottle of whisky, helped by a final push from Oliver, who felt he damn well deserved it for pulling off a bloody brilliant scam. So far.

'Where's that mother of yours?' Colin demanded, impressed to the point of chivalry by the meal he had eaten. 'You're not leaving her in the kitchen after all this?' So they invited Bel to join them, and persuaded her into a small glass of Baileys. Following the morning's tragedy and the afternoon's hard work, it made her feel quite dizzy. In a nice way. The world was going mad, but it really wasn't too awful.

The two boys who Toni had collected seemed decent enough, and were scrubbing up the saucepans and sweeping the floor, generally trying to be helpful, which meant that Toni was not quite helping them, but joking around the kitchen in a good-hearted sort of way. The boys couldn't understand a word, of course, but they obviously adored her, and a bit of adoration never did a woman any harm. The real Toni, the dear little girl who Bel had always believed was hiding behind the façade of hostility, was finally making an appearance.

Oliver was stamping around looking pleased with himself and giving orders again, just the way he used to do when he was a banker. Bel had seen the way that girl looked at him. And the way he looked at her. And the way they had sneaked out together last night. There was still hope of grandchildren there. And the debt-collector man was going to get his five hundred pounds. And, if she was not much mistaken, this Colin chap had a twinkle in his eye and was aiming it at her in a certain unmistakable way. Counting it all in, things were suddenly looking good.

CHAPTER 11

Pigging Out

Just before 2am, Colin and Jimmy marched out to their vehicles with the determination of men who know they're drunk, know the nearest cop is half the county away and have to get home somehow. They set off down the lane. Fortunately, Jimmy was leading, at a cautious speed, so when the first piglet trotted across his headlights he was well able to pull up and let it pass unhurt.

'What?' yelled Colin, seeing the other man climbing out of his truck.

'Pig!' Jimmy yelled back.

'Shit!' yelled Colin, getting out himself and lurching forward to join him. 'Is it one of mine? Which way did it go?'

'There,' said Jimmy, turning on his flashlight to probe the dark hedge bank to the right.

'It's over there,' said Colin, seeing a pale shape over on the left.

'I got it,' Jimmy insisted. 'It's one of yours.'

'It's over that way,' Colin told him. 'It's one of Oliver's –
I can see the dark back on it.'

Then another pale shape loomed out of the night.

Then a gaggle of spotted piglets appeared from behind
them and scampered frantically off into the darkness to join
their relations. Some squealing was heard in the middle
distance.

'There's a lot of them,' Jimmy confirmed.

'There's his and mine,' said Colin.

Slowly, the various bits of their intelligence emerged from
the fog of whisky and joined up into a scenario.

'If one's out, they're all out,' said Jimmy.

'Bugger,' said Colin.

'Yup,' said Jimmy. 'You best go on and get your men out
to catch 'em.'

'And you best go back and see what Oliver can do,' said
Colin.

They argued a while longer about the best way to achieve
these goals, because the lane was too narrow for Colin to pass
Jimmy, or for Jimmy to turn until the gateway of Oliver's
farm. Furthermore, the lane was totally bestrewn with pigs. In
the end, Jimmy drove cautiously on and turned when he could
at the end of the lane, then headed back to the Manor House.

Colin, whose car was a large and prosperous model that
had begun its life carrying company directors to board meetings, decided to reverse down the lane. This was not a wise
choice for a man in his condition. He ran into a ditch in the
first bend, blocking Jimmy's way to the Manor House.
Finishing the trip on foot at least sobered them up, but not
much.

In another hour, Jimmy was out with Oliver, Toni and the

two Lithuanians, working with a will to catch each pig and piglet and load them into the back of Jimmy's truck. Colin had roused the rest of his illegals, who were working through the runaways from their own side. The stillness of the night was shattered by shouting and squealing, just as the darkness was broken by searchlights, headlamps, torches and the lights outside the house, which Oliver turned on when pigs were discovered in the garden.

Clare woke up first, resenting enormously the loss of the first dreamless sleep she had achieved for weeks. Miranda was awake soon afterwards, feeling cross and thirsty. They sat together on the window seat on the landing, trying to make sense of the chaotic scenes that were occasionally visible in the pool of light outside. A truckful of pigs roared into the hotel car park, turned around briskly and drove away.

'Why are they transporting animals in the middle of the night?' Clare asked. 'How on earth do they expect us to sleep with all this going on?'

'They don't think, we're in the country,' said Miranda. 'Anybody with half a brain got out of the gene pool generations ago. Only the stupid ones stayed behind.'

Clare considered ringing up one of her staff and getting something done. She weighed the mental effort against the likely outcome. She tried to remember where her phone was, and what numbers she had in it. She thought of what would happen if the media got hold of the story.

Very strange, this feeling of impotence. This feeling of *choosing* impotence. Well, choosing to do nothing, anyway. Yes, this is unsatisfactory, and no, I'm not going to sort it out. Quite refreshing really.

Local problem, get local action. While Clare was thinking

about rousing the hotel staff and demanding some peace, a big pink pig cantered across the lawn below their window. After it the waiter came running, hurdling over the ornamental hedges, minus his jacket and tie, the lights picking up his white shirt. It more or less answered her questions.

Miranda, she noticed, was giggling. Was that good? Anyway, the best course of action seemed to be the traditional one: make a cup of tea and try to forget about everything.

One of the things Clare had decided she liked about this hotel was the absence of complimentary guest-sized offerings of anything. In the bathroom, she had found real soap, not a small pat of something that reeked of chemical freesias, and some agreeable bath oil in a decanter, and woman-sized bottles of shampoo. In the bedroom she had found mineral water and some pleasantly brainless magazines, and a delightful absence of the tray crowded with ugly cups, a fiddly kettle, stale tea bags, and sachets of non-dairy creamer and non-coffee coffee. It was all very civilised.

A family-run hotel, she reasoned, would expect guests to behave like family. So she put on slippers, and headed downstairs to the kitchen.

On the highest part of Florian's *domaine* was a place that felt properly spiritual. It was a mound, with steep sides and a flattened top. Only half of it was really his and the boundary hedge ran over it. From the first spring aconite to the last autumn crocus, the mound was always thickly covered with flowers, probably because it had always been too much of a hill to cultivate. Even in the moonlight, they could see the pale splashes of the primroses, set off by the indigo fingers of bugle and the crimson lips of the first field orchids.

A grove of trees had survived on the far side of the hedge, and a large oak now spread its branches just far enough to keep the rain off a couple of vineyard workers if the weather turned nasty. The oak, as Florian enjoyed telling Dido, was the sacred tree of ancient Europe and probably the subject of a druidic cult. So the mound was probably a temple, the site of sacred rituals for thousands of years. The ideal venue for a sacred rite to welcome Ostara.

Since the rest of the resident Addleworths were now exhausted by the strain of calling the police, giving their statements, shepherding the punters from the wine-tasting safely into their vehicles and distracting the bees long enough for Ashok to be carried to an ambulance, Florian found himself leading the midnight meditation for Dido alone.

They sat cross-legged on the grass. Dido gazed at the moon. Florian shut his eyes. The wind sighed thoughtfully in the oak tree. It isn't easy to settle into a meditation when you are alone with the most wonderful being on the planet and sap is rising all around you.

An acorn, which had been hanging on to its twig all winter, suddenly surrendered to its biological destiny and fell earthwards, hitting Dido on the forehead. She took her eyes off the moon and looked at Florian. Had he thrown that? His eyes were perfectly shut. He had the longest eyelashes. They were all dark against his white skin. A tiny, tiny crease between his eyebrows, the merest shadow of a frown. He was so gorgeously serious. Not the sort to chuck an acorn at a moment of spiritual intimacy.

Dido looked at the moon again. Was it full? Was it just a sliver short of full? It was huge, whatever. So beautiful. Like a great big primrose, really, all silvery and luminous. Was that a bat flittering about? Such a pity they sent those astronauts. Better not to know what was up there. Better not to spoil the wonder of gazing at it. Was that an ant or something running across her ankle? Wouldn't it be just perfect if Florian leaned over and kissed her just now? Spiritual intimacy was fine, but the sexy sort was better.

Florian tried a leaf meditation. A leaf. A leaf. A small leaf. A small leaf unfolding. A small leaf unfolding on a winding stem. A small leaf unfolding on a winding stem that was snaking around Dido's warm, pliable waist and pulling her over . . . no. Try again. A leaf. A leaf. A long leaf. A long leaf in the grass, rising above the blades. A long leaf in the grass, rising above the blades, caressing Dido's smooth creamy thigh, ever so gently . . . no, no.

Anyway, it wasn't going to work. Women never did work out with him. He just wasn't one of those men who could get with the Zen of sex. He never knew the unknowable moment, he never made the move when the move should be made, he always ended up with the energy all tangled and the underwear snagged and the whole thing turning into a total farce. Then the woman either laughed or felt sorry for him or both. Most often it had been both. What use was a hare-eared goddess if she couldn't just lollop by and sort this out for him?

A touch. A touch of something warm and smooth. Warm and smooth and definitely flesh. Without opening his eyes, he reached out and touched back. Touched and caressed. Definitely flesh. Beautiful, pliable, creamy-smooth flesh. Flesh without any clothes. It was her. It was happening. Thank you, Ostara. He reached out with a grateful arm.

A snuffle! Delicious, provocative, almost animal sound! Some movement! She was pressing closer. There seemed to be no end to the flesh. And a complete absence of clothes. Sky-clad already! And a presence of hair. Short hair. Hair that really wasn't like her hair at all. Actually . . . bristles.

Florian's eyes snapped open. He saw flesh. It was darkish. He saw his own arm. It was around the middle of a pig.

He leaped to his feet, for the first time in his devotional life achieving a fluid transition from a half-lotus to standing without putting a hand on the ground. A sound burst out from behind his teeth, something between 'crumbs', 'shit', and 'crikey', but expelled too fast to be a word at all. The pig, concerned for a moment, took its snout out of the ground, looked around, flapped its ears, twitched its curly tail and then carried on rooting for acorns.

'What?' said Dido, turning dreamily in his direction. 'Oh goodness,' she said, seeing that a pig had come between them. 'How did he get here?'

She hadn't seen anything. Phew! Florian's heart did a back flip, then shock subsided, embarrassment backed off and relief took over. She was fine. She was being terribly brave. Not one of the feeble urban sort at all. Absolutely made for country life. Now she was getting little-girl curious, holding her hair out of her eyes to look at the pig better. Instinctively, he took a couple of strides around the animal's hindquarters and put his arm around her. For protection, obviously.

'It looks like one of Oliver's,' he said. 'He's a friend of mine, he's got a farm the other side of the village. He's keeping a few of these. Beccles Black Back. Very ancient breed, probably directly descended from the wild pigs domesticated in the Iron Age. Bags of character.'

'He looks really happy.' Dido nestled comfortably into Florian's shoulder, feeling really happy herself.

'They love acorns. Their natural diet. That's probably what attracted him up here.' The pig, Florian could see, was a female but he sensed magic in the offing and chose not to give way to any more pedantry in case it spoiled the moment.

'Should we do anything? Will he be safe?'

'Oh, he'll be fine. Unless he starts rooting up my vines when he's had enough acorns. In which case, he'll be in danger from me. Better go down to the house and phone Oliver, get him over to pick him up. We can shut the gate down there, keep him from wandering off.'

'I thought we'd materialised him, just for a moment,' said Dido. 'People are always telling you that you can create stuff just by meditating.'

'Not pigs, though. Cosmic harmony, world peace, a new Porsche — that sort of thing . . . well, some people do it for a Porsche.'

She laughed. He could feel the joyful little earthquake all the way along his arm and down the outside of his ribs.

Since the night was beautiful and balmy, and the moon was huge, it seemed right to spend a little while watching the pig munching in rapture under the oak tree, then set off back to the house. They went hand in hand, slithering down the steep slope, feeling in a bit of a dream state in which everything happened in slow motion.

So Dido slipped slowly to the ground, her long hair swirling around her face like water weed, her captured hand gently dragging Florian down with her, so they settled together into the soft grass, and their arms and legs drifted into the right places and the last tendril of curls slipped away from Dido's lips and left them perfectly positioned for a kiss. So Florian knew the unknowable moment and made the move when the move should be made, and all the moves after that, so it was quite some time before they at last arrived at the farmhouse and Florian found the right state of consciousness to pick up the phone and call Oliver.

'Oh, no, now what? For heaven's sake!' Deep in the quiet depths of the house, a phone was ringing. And ringing. And ringing, ringing, ringing. A mobile phone, with a silly electronic warble. Oliver's mobile phone. That was his ringing tone, the Nokia tune, the thirteen notes that have driven more sane people crazy than any other melody in history. The most annoying sound detectable by the human ear. Especially at – what was it? – 5am.

Bel, exhausted by excitement and cooking, lulled by the Baileys and Colin Burton's admiration, had slept right through the pig-catching process. If she hadn't hated the Nokia tune more than Satan himself, she would never have woken so early. Her bed was soft and warm but . . . another demanding day of pretending to be a hotel keeper was ahead of her. And she'd forgotten to defrost the croissants. Time to get up.

Oliver's phone was on the hall table, and it rang again just as she got to the bottom of the stairs.

'Hello?' she answered. How the hall echoed! 'Hello?' she said again, lowering her voice.

It was Florian. He tried, poor lamb, but there was no mistaking that patrician voice. Rounded but gentle, cooing

294

like an aristocratic dove. Looking for Oliver.

'He isn't here,' she murmured firmly. 'He's left his phone here. Do you know what time it is, Florian? Is something wrong?'

Something about Oliver's voicemail. Then something about a pig.

'Can't it wait until morning?'

Something about his vines. The poor boy really was obsessed about his vineyard. Just like Oliver and his farm. As bad as each other. What was it with young men now — why couldn't they just think about finding a nice girl and getting on with what really mattered in life?

'Florian, darling, it's five o'clock in the morning. Can't it wait a few hours? I can't go out and find Oliver and wake him up now, when I'll be needing him to do the breakfasts soon anyway.'

The boy was all confused. He didn't understand. Of course he didn't understand. And she couldn't explain. Not there, on that silly little phone, in the middle of the house. Much too risky.

'Florian, darling. Just trust me. Leave him a message on his voicemail thing. He'll get it when he wakes up. It'll only be a couple of hours. I'm sure the pig won't dig up all your vines in that time. I'm going to say goodbye now.'

Was that the right button? She pressed several of them until the phone's screen went blank, then remembered the frozen croissants and set off for the kitchen.

In the house of a woman like Bel Hardcastle, the kitchen feels like the engine room of an ocean liner, perpetually humming with power as the great edifice cruises serenely onwards. Inside the Aga, the unseen heat pulsed on cue, sending the hot water gurgling obediently up the pipes, while the fridge throbbed gently in the corner, the dishwasher cooled at the end of its final cycle and Garrick was snoring in his basket under the table. He opened his eyes as Bel came into the room, and gave her a persecuted look.

Somebody had left a light on. She could see that the room was spotless. It was never spotless when she was in charge of it, and Toni had never been known to clean anything, so those Lithuanian boys must have worked for hours.

'Marvellous boys,' she said to herself aloud. 'Such a good job they've done. Poor young things, they must be quite desperate for money to risk their lives to come over here from their own country and work on that farm for next to nothing, and having to live on potatoes in a horrible old caravan. Outrageous! You'll see, Colin Burton. If you want to get your feet under the table in my house, you'll have to start treating your people properly.'

'Ah . . . they're over there,' said a tactful voice somewhere in the shadows. It was the mother of that girl. Wearing a spotless white waffle robe, and sitting at the table having a mug of tea. 'The boys,' she said, smiling quite pleasantly. 'That is them, isn't it? They're all over there.'

Bel adjusted her eyes to the half light and made out three sleeping forms on the old sofa at the far end of the room. Toni and Volvo, or whatever he was called, propping each other up with their arms around each other, and the other boy sprawling with his head back and snoring. Dead to the world, all of them. No wonder Garrick was looking peeved. He usually slept on the sofa.

'They look so sweet,' said Bel.

'They were out there running about after those pigs for

hours,' said the other woman. A slight edge in her voice.

'What pigs?' asked Bel.

'I don't know what pigs. There were dozens of them.'

'Pink or black?'

'Both, I think. They made a hell of a noise. Lorries, search-lights . . .'

Bel's antennae picked up the transmission. 'Oh dear, did they wake you up?'

'Yes.'

'I am *so* sorry. I had no idea.' Bel tried to decide what a real hotel keeper would say. Nothing that might lead to a demand for a refund, she decided. 'Still, we are in the country. Pigs are apparently quite lively. They do get out of their fields sometimes and of course farmers have to look after their livestock. But I'm sure I don't have to tell you that.'

The other woman looked suitably flattered, but altogether far too alert for the time of day. Had she been nosing around down here? Bel was suspicious.

'Did I hear you say they were from abroad?'

'Oh dear,' said Bel. 'You didn't hear me talking to myself, did you?'

'I couldn't help it. Where *are* they from?'

'Oh, I don't know.' Help! There was a government min-ister sitting here in her kitchen with two illegal immigrants! She was going to get everybody into trouble if she didn't find a way to cover up. 'They're students, obviously. Learning English. From . . . Norwich, I think. It's terrible what the farmers round here pay these young people.'

'The farmers? I thought they were working for you?'

'Oh! Well, they do. Of course they do. They work for me as well. They help out. You know. On the weekends. To make a bit more money. It's so hard for the young nowadays. When they have these tuition fees and what-are-they-called? The top fees or something. Thousands they have to pay for themselves now, don't they?'

Immediately on taking up her new job, Clare had mastered the art of disowning responsibility for any and all fuck-ups perpetrated by any branch of government, including, when necessary, her own. She said, 'Higher education funding is enormously difficult to get right,' and issued a small, unencouraging smile.

Whew! thought Bel. I'm really getting quite good at all this pretending. 'Can I make you some more tea?' she said.

'I do hope you don't mind me having helped myself,' said Clare, willingly handing over her empty mug. 'I couldn't sleep. I just fancied a cup. But there was nothing in the room.'

'Ah – no. Those trays – I don't do that,' said Bel. 'I know I should but I just think they're so vulgar.'

'So do I,' said Clare.

'So here you are in my kitchen and that's fine,' said Bel, making a discreet move towards the deep freeze, which was behind her guest's back, and extracting the croissants. The kettle boiled and she took down the teapot and made a proper brew.

There are people who can make a pot of tea, pour their own cup and take it away from the rest of the company to drink alone, but Bel was not one of them. To her, a pot of tea demanded to be properly shared, with all the appropriate rituals and conversation. Besides, there was business to be done here. She produced sugar and milk, then took a chair opposite her guest and said, 'Tell me about your daughter. Does she have a boyfriend?'

Clare flinched at the question, but only slightly. She was in that soft, pale state of vulnerability that comes with being in a strange place and having had too little sleep, and this woman seemed warm and kind and rather silly, so there was not much downside in confiding in her. Besides, no one had treated her like a mother for years.

'Miranda,' she began. 'I worry about her, you know.'

'Children,' Bel agreed. 'Born to make you crazy. I know.'

'She's doing very well, of course, but she never looks happy.'

'But such a pretty girl. I thought so the moment I saw her. But you want her to settle down, don't you?'

In about ten minutes, Clare confided feelings she'd never known she had. Tea and sympathy, coming on top of exertion, fresh air, mad March hares and a good dinner, managed to open up a heart that had been slammed shut since its teenage years. It made her feel almost dizzy. And vaguely grateful, to this silly, fluffy woman, with her warm kitchen and her pretty little business. If it was a business. Clare was beginning to wonder if there wasn't some other agenda. A woman doesn't acquire the title of Former City Superwoman without a nose for the truth. Nothing you could put your finger on, nothing you could call evidence, just the faintest smell of something not right.

'So tell me about your son,' Clare said.

'Oliver! Well, you've seen him, haven't you?'

'A very nice young man.'

'Well, though I say it as shouldn't, he is a very nice young man. Girls have always been mad about him. But does he take any notice . . . ?'

In about twenty minutes, Bel had covered what she

considered to be the core agenda. Oliver was a nice young man. He thoroughly merited a nice young woman, who was guaranteed to live in a state of exalted bliss as his wife and have beautiful, healthy children of which any grandparent could be proud. But he'd given up a marvellous career and a huge salary to buy himself a farm in the country and he never met any women at all. All the young were mad and it was the fault of feminists and the media. Especially the media. Therefore all parents of the young had a moral responsibility to get them wed by any means whatever as soon as possible.

'I rather thought,' Bel ventured finally, 'that he liked your daughter. You know, when you arrived, I thought they were friends already and he'd invited you for the weekend.'

That explains a few things, Clare thought. Aloud, she said, 'Did you say he had a farm as well?'

'Just down the road. All organic, you know. At least, it will be, when he's finished making the soil good again. It was all full of pesticides when he bought the place so he has to spend years waiting for an organic certificate. Lucky he made pots of money when he was working for that bank.'

Only a tiny white lie, she reassured herself. Another of Bel's talents was thinking while prattling. This was, after all, a government minister. Naturally, no hint of financial crisis would be allowed to escape her lips. But would a minister consider a humble hotel keeper the ideal parent of the ideal son-in-law?

Suddenly, she realised why Clare's face was so familiar. No, not from the television. No, not from the newspapers. From long, long ago. From the fast-track London girls' school where Bel had struggled to get more than a C for anything, and Clare, the young Clare, had been the queen of the shiny girls, a prefect with a sense-of-humour bypass, the bookies' favourite for head girl and nothing but a blur of speed on prize-giving days.

They had had one single conversation. In all their years of sitting in the same classrooms and suffering under the same PE teachers, the shiny young Clare had deigned to talk to her only once. A perfectly innocent conversation about what they were going to do when they left school. Bel had never understood what she had said that was so wrong, but the queen of the shiny girls had suddenly frozen her out and walked away. Bel had burst into tears and rushed to the locker rooms. And here that shiny girl was, all these years later, in her dressing gown, in Bel's kitchen.

Revenge was not Bel's style. She had never liked pain, and plotting revenge made you remember your pain. Better to forget whatever had hurt you and move on. Besides, the price of being shiny seemed to be that you were heartless, hypocritical and hated by everybody. Bel found that she was glad she had never gone to Cambridge or become a millionaire or done any of the things that shiny girls did. She felt stronger for feeling that. Deciding to say nothing made her feel stronger still.

'Your son must be quite bright,' Clare was saying.

'Oh yes,' Bel agreed, fighting sudden smugness. 'He was always the top of the class at school. And he got a very good degree, though we didn't notice that he did so much work.'

'He didn't seem like an ordinary waiter.'

'Well . . .' This was the moment. Yes, she had the strength! Mentally, Bel crossed herself and said a prayer. 'This isn't an ordinary hotel, you know.'

'I was beginning to wonder.'

'It's really my home. I just . . . you know, when you arrived . . . everything seemed so perfect . . .' She flapped her hands to signal helplessness. Helplessness in the path of fate.

'Oh my goodness!' Suddenly Clare felt cold. Deadly cold. Had she been tricked? Was this some kind of set-up? She looked at the other woman, who seemed particularly helpless but not guilty in the way a party to a political conspiracy would look guilty. 'You mean . . . this is your home?' Clare suggested it in a gentle voice. 'Have we made some terrible mistake?'

Bell nodded, then put her head on one side and smiled. 'I suppose. Just a little one.'

No hint of guile here. No, this was not more than an honest misunderstanding. It shouldn't be difficult to square. Put on a show of humanity, that would do the trick. 'A little mistake! But you poor woman . . . you mean, we've walked into your own home?'

'Well, yes, but that's OK. It was so obvious they liked each other, I just thought, why not go along with it?'

If this gets into the media – no, no, this must NEVER get into the media. Clare had rapidly considered all the angles and saw that the only possible thing to do in this absurd situation was play along with it. If this woman was obsessed with getting her son married . . . well, there was the answer.

'But the inconvenience we must have caused you! That dinner, last night. A very good dinner, by the way. Quite sensational. But how . . . ?'

'Well, they were our own chickens. And the ducks from the farm next door. I always have people over on Saturday evening. I think they quite enjoyed a bit of play-acting, even the Vicar. It was all good fun, really. It's so quiet here in the country, people like a little diversion. And you were perfect guests of course.'

'But all the same . . . I'm so embarrassed.' A total lie, naturally; a Former City Superwoman was almost incapable of feeling embarrassed. 'Of course, we must pack our things and leave you in peace immediately.'

'I refuse to allow it! You're settled now, and this is a precious weekend for you, to spend some time with your daughter. You can't possibly waste half a day driving all over the countryside looking for a hotel. Stay! Don't think of moving! Just be our guests and make yourselves at home. And, who knows? If we leave the young people alone to manage things their own way . . .' Bel reached over and gave Clare's arm a conspiratorial squeeze. 'Who knows what will happen, eh?'

'Do you know, I was thinking the exact same thing?'

'There you are then. You accept. We keep up the whole pretence. I won't tell my son, you don't tell your daughter.'

'But you've put yourself out so much for us and we're total strangers – I insist you let me give you some money.'

Bel issued a flurry of flimsy objections then allowed herself to be persuaded.

They shook hands over the teapot.

'There,' said Bel, feeling highly satisfied with her management of the situation. 'Now you go on back up to bed. You've got at least an hour to relax before breakfast.'

Under the table, Garrick turned around in his basket and settled down to sleep again. On the sofa, Juri continued to snore quietly. Tolvo was half-awake, and he had an idea that the angel Toni was awake too. His instinct was right; Toni had been awake for some time, and listening with fascination to the whole conversation.

CHAPTER 12

Tally Who?

Carole had curled her long body uncomfortably across the front seats of the rental van in the car park of the Sports Hall in Yattenham St Mary. She was stiff and cold. In fact, her nose was so cold the tip was nothing but a button of pain. When her mobile phone rang and she tried to sit up, she banged the side of her kneecap on the steering wheel and sent a nasty twinge up her thigh. The device was in her handbag in the passenger's footwell.

'Yes?' she answered, rubbing her leg through her jeans.

'Animal Rights Ipswich,' said a woman's voice. 'Was it you I spoke to yesterday?'

'About the bees?'

'Yes.'

'Yes. What happened? We had a demonstration but you never showed up.'

'Saturday's a big sabbing day for us. Specially yesterday, for the end of the season. Can't let the scum knock off for the summer without giving them something to think about. How did it go?'

'Pretty good, I think.'

'Any arrests? Don't expect so – police round here, they're all in the pockets of the abusers.'

'Well, they called the police, obviously. We had to give names and addresses. The—' she paused for words, realising she had a new language to learn, 'the abusers didn't want to press charges.'

'They're clever, they don't like the publicity, don't want people to know their filthy business. Anybody hurt? These people, they're barbarians, they'll stop at nothing. Somebody pushed me in the chest yesterday.'

'We've got one person in hospital,' said Carole. 'They said it was the bee stings but you don't know, do you?'

'They come out with baseball bats, fence posts, iron bars, everything. They're sick people. Sounds interesting, your bee campaign. All power to you. Give us a bit more notice next time, eh?'

'Right. Right.' Carole sat up properly and opened the vehicle's door. Now she was fully awake, the smell of the fox mess in the back of the van was making her feel ill.

'So, where are you? Are you still in the area?'

'Yeah. The bastards threw us out of the pub so we're sleeping in our van. We're in somewhere called Yattering . . . Yattenham, is it?'

'Yeah, well, the publicans, they're just as bad. Don't want to lose their regular business, do they? You'll be in Yattenham St Mary. Perfect. Fancy a bit of sabbing, by any chance? We got word the scum are coming your way today. Trying to outwit us as usual. They think we're thick, you see. Think we don't know what filthy plans they're making. But we got a watch on their kennels. Using our technology.

They've got some plan to come over to Great Saxwold. And we think there's a good chance they ain't got no licence. Not their usual killing fields, you see. Trying their filthy tricks on us. The police will just stand by and watch 'em get away with it, if we don't do nothing. The law, the courts, they all side with the scum. This ain't London, as I expect you found out yesterday.'

'You've got a lot on your plate out here,' Carole agreed.

'Did you say you had somebody filming you?'

'Yes, we brought a cameraman with us. A historic event, we wanted a proper record.'

'Could be a good day for him. Specially if it's a really bad kill, entrails and everything. Lot of money goes for film of that kind of thing. So you gonna come with us?'

Carole shivered. The obsessive voice on the phone was talking without stopping. She had the distinct impression that she was out of her depth and dealing with people who did not fit the accepted definition of sane.

'Of course,' the voice was saying, 'you coming from London, it'll be a bit much for you, what we have to deal with out here. People can't usually stand it . . .'

'You can count us in,' said Carole, feeling challenged. 'Where's it all happening?'

'We're meeting up in the car park of some pub. The Pigeon & Pipkin?'

'I know it. That's the bastard who threw us out. What time?'

'Seven, seven-thirty. I'll see you there.'

Carole cut the connection and went to wake up Video Guy, who had said he couldn't stand the smell in the van and had gone to sleep in the shelter of the Sports Hall doorway.

The morning proceeded with the weary sense of ritual that settles over any occasion in which a matter of great importance can only be enacted after a great deal of standing patiently about waiting for every individual concerned to play his or her tiny part in the drama. In England, only shooting a feature film and re-enacting a historical event in full costume are carried off with the same combination of boredom, concentration and punctilious correctness.

The sun was nothing but a red blush behind the thick quilts of white mist that lay over the fields when two mini-vans full of policemen parked outside The Pigeon & Pipkin. The officers got out and formed into groups. One group stayed with the vehicles while the rest set off at a brisk walk along Saxwold Farm Lane.

The mist had hardly thinned when a number of cars turned in by the pub, and Carole decided to leave her van outside the Old Post Office in case the landlord turned hostile again. 'And leave a window open,' said Video Guy. 'Get rid of that smell before we have to drive back to London.'

About twenty saboteurs were soon gathered, one in a home-made fox suit, the rest with banners reading 'Death 2 Hunt Scum' and 'Honk If You Hate Hunting.' Most of them also made for Saxwold Farm Lane. The police and the saboteurs who stayed behind in the car park eyed each other with reciprocal disgust.

'This stinks, this does,' said Carole's contact among the sabs. 'The scum don't get out of bed Sundays, as a rule. Creatures of habit, same day same place every year. They don't venture down these parts, either. I tell you, there's a real stink about this.'

Just before 8am, when the sun was a full red orb above the

hedges and the mist had shrunk down into the dells, a short procession of vehicles drove slowly through the village and turned down the lane. First came an old brown lorry, then a slightly younger Range Rover towing a much newer double horsebox, then the khaki-green carcass of an ancient Land Rover, towing a box of the same vintage, then a long estate car and two small saloons, all with small and newish horse transporters attached.

As this caravan passed them, the saboteurs roused themselves to a fury, brandished their placards and chanted, 'Scum, scum, scum.' The police, standing between them and the road, shifted nervously and looked up and down the line of protesters.

The procession turned through the gate into Jimmy's farm and halted when the man in the fox costume tried to throw himself on the bonnet of the Land Rover. Two officers stepped forward to pull him off, and the vehicles drove forward and parked where Jimmy's father directed them. When the engines were all turned off, the eager yelping of the hounds could be heard from the lorry.

Two huntsmen in red coats appeared, one carrying a clipboard with the permit for the day's hunting attached to it. The senior police officer approached them and a short conversation took place while he read the paper through and noted down its reference number and signatory in his book. People, mostly young women, were moving about in silence, opening the horseboxes. The horses were led out and held while their rugs were folded back and their saddles heaved into place and fastened.

Another engine was heard, and the shiny blue Range Rover with the Château Saxwold logo skidded to a stop at the gate. Surprised, some of the saboteurs turned around and banged on its doors with their fists.

'Guns!' somebody called out. 'They're bringing guns!'

With the help of six policemen who held back the protesters, the vehicle inched into the yard and Jimmy closed the farm gate behind it. The driver, Florian's brother-in-law, got out, with two other men, old shooting friends who had been persuaded to add their guns to the field.

'They haven't got a permit!' shouted the man in the fox suit, with Video Guy at his elbow.

The police, following orders, remained silent.

'They haven't got a permit! It's illegal!' shouted Carole's contact. 'What's going on here? This wasn't on their website. They can't get away with this! We demand to speak to somebody about it!'

The senior police officer nodded and handed back the clipboard. He surveyed the protesters for a moment, then walked over towards them.

'Who's in charge?' he asked, an energetic, greying man who looked as if he would have preferred to be taking his sons off for football training, which indeed he would.

'It's me,' said Carole's contact. 'What's happening here? Why are there guns come up? Why wasn't this on their website?'

'I don't know about their website,' said the officer. 'I can tell you that this isn't a meet, as such.'

'Then why have they got the hounds here?'

'If you'll let me speak. This is a special operation that the farmer's asked for. He lost over a hundred ducks a few days ago. And everyone else with poultry around here, it's the same story. The suspicion is, there's been some fox-dumping.

Urban foxes released on farmland. Our information is there could have been nearly forty of them. So the master's agreed to bring a few hounds over the area and see what they can find. If they do find, the hounds will be withdrawn and there'll be a rough shoot.'

Carole felt as if someone had poured ice water down her throat. There was a deep chill somewhere at her centre. Instinctively, she hunched her shoulders inside her several sweaters and, with trembling fingers, pulled a strand of hair down over her face.

'They can't do that. That's illegal,' her contact was saying.

'They can, madam, and it is legal. The permit was issued yesterday, I've just seen it and it is in order. I would caution you, for your own safety, to obey the marshals if the shoot takes place. Most of this land is private, there is no public right of way except on the marked footpaths. You want to blame somebody, blame whoever brought forty foxes up here and let them loose.'

'That's not against the law,' said the woman, defiantly. 'At least they cared about the animals, whoever did it, instead of torturing them.'

'Some bunch of bloody idiots, up from London,' said another voice. 'Haven't they heard of fox sanctuaries?'

Seeing a good chance to avoid any more argument, the officer stepped back, and focused his eyes somewhere above the protesters' heads. Carole stepped back also, trying to lose herself behind the other sabs, suddenly afraid that she would be recognised and called to account for the day's brutality. The plan didn't work.

'Don't you be intimidated,' her contact said, dragging her back into the front line. 'You stand your ground. We're

310

not accepting this. We're here to stop the scum from killing and that's what we'll be doing. They can't threaten us with guns. They think they've got so much filthy money they can do what they like.'

'They don't look like millionaires to me,' said Video Guy, taking his eye away from his viewfinder to make sure of what he was seeing. 'Is this it, then? There's hardly ten people. I was expecting hundreds. Loads of toffs knocking back the old cherry brandy, all done up in top hats and all that gear. This lot look as if they're out for a day at Ikea.'

The riders had mounted. While their horses had been groomed until their spring coats gleamed like the bonnet of a new Rolls-Royce, the riders let them down. True, the huntsmen wore red coats, but they were faded and much-repaired. One other adult male was wearing old jeans and a fleece jacket. The remaining three riders were girls of about fourteen, neat but scarcely elegant in pigtails and gilets, their ample hard hats overhanging their delicate teenage noses. Set against the architecture of Jimmy's farmyard, which was heavy on concrete blocks, concrete posts, and concrete in general, the tableau had a definite lack of romance.

Finally, the back doors of the lorry were opened and the hounds scampered out, a handful of dogs whose white coats were marked with caramel blotches. They made a more satisfying picture as they frolicked around the huntsmen and lifted legs on the car tyres, though they seemed to think they were in a dog food commercial, not a small-scale cull of rural vermin, or an exercise in mass murder, depending on your viewpoint.

'Is that it?' said Video Guy again. 'That's six dogs, that is.

You count them. I was expecting a whole great pack of them, all baying for blood and stuff.'

Oliver, bleary-eyed after two hours of sleep, woke himself up with a shower and went over to Jimmy's, as an act of friendship, to see the huntsmen arrive. 'Is it always like this?' he asked, as the crowd of protesters mobbed the contingent from the Château.

'Nutters,' Jimmy replied.

'What we hope,' said the master, 'is that they haven't had time to go out spraying. They spray the land to spoil the dogs' scent. Of course, they don't know where to spray, so it's usually ineffective. But if they've done that here, it may throw the dogs completely. This is a new one on me. I've heard of these lunatics dumping foxes, but we've never had it round here before. You're new round here, aren't you?' This was to Oliver alone.

'I'm afraid I am,' he said.

'You're the one going organic?'

'Trying to.'

'Yeah, I know what you mean.'

I'm still trying to pass, thought Oliver. It's been nearly three years, and I'm still trying to look like I know what I'm doing, when everyone knows I haven't a fucking clue what I'm doing. Who am I trying to kid?

Still, he stayed to watch the riders set off, and remarked their quietness, and their competence, and also a certain anxiety about this task. They did not complain, nor talk themselves up as they set off. They were people setting about an emergency job on a Sunday morning, and it was nothing either to whine or boast about. Most of his life, he had worked with people whose local dialect was egotistical blag and whose religion was pushing their own advantage. My God, he thought, as he hurried over to the Manor, no wonder this species is endangered.

'Who am I, again?' Lucy Vinny came to the kitchen of the Manor for a cup of coffee before assuming the role into which Oliver had persuaded her.

'You're the riding stables,' he said.

'Do I have a name?'

'If you like. Up to you.'

'I'll be Hoofprints, then. Bit twee, but there was a place round here called that, until it went bust. And what about money?'

'Charge what you like. Make 'em pay cash. You've got to get something out of this, after all.'

'Are you sure? Haven't they tumbled it yet?'

'They haven't a clue,' said Oliver.

'Not a clue,' said Bel. 'Trust me. Why should they suspect anything?'

'I can't believe they're so stupid. And that woman's minister for farming or something? Ruling class, total farce. If you ask me.' This was from Toni, who had relapsed into her usual sulk as soon as Tolvo and Juri left to go back to their caravan.

'And we're talking about a one-hour hack, down the bridle path over your bottom field. Where're the hounds?'

'Over Jimmy's.'

'Fine. And you?'

'I'm going to the Château. Florian's caught one of my pigs over there. I've got to fetch him back.'

'My horses aren't crazy about pigs. Where are the rest of yours?'

313

'Top field. By the cottage. Shouldn't give you any problem.'

'Not if we stay well away from them. And you said they could ride, these women?'

'They said they could ride.'

Lucy sniffed. 'They always say they can ride. We'll see, shall we?'

She had hitched the horses side by side to the five-barred gate to the garden. Tulip, Samson and Smithie. Tulip she was riding herself, her current pride and joy, an elegant four-year-old with a russet coat and a flowing Arab tail that nearly touched the ground. Samson was also her own horse, bought off a farmer when he was too old to be hunted, to live usefully as a steady paddock companion for the others. His ancestors included shire horses, for he was big and mostly black, with a white face and shaggy white feet. Nobody was quite sure how old he was but on his good days he was still game for a gallop.

Smithie was all black and another one who could fairly be called bomb-proof, having started his working life as a city police horse. His owner, a weekend wallet from whom Lucy had called in a favour, had bought him as a starter horse for his long-legged daughter, who always called Smithie a perfect gentleman. So, Lucy reasoned to herself, the horses know their job and no matter how useless these women are, we should be OK here.

'They look awfully big,' said Clare to her daughter, as they came around the corner of the Manor House, kitted out in jeans and sweaters, and saw their mounts for the first time.

'Big can be good,' Miranda reassured her. 'At least they won't have been messed around by children. The one with

314

the white feet looks pretty old. Not a lot of excitement there.'

'Why don't I have that one?' Clare suggested at once. 'You can have the good-looking one.'

'Thanks, Mum,' said Miranda. Sometimes it was useful to be able to project the confidence you didn't feel. So strange, to see her mother looking hesitant for once. 'Don't worry. We'll be fine. Thank you.' This was to Lucy, who was holding out a hard hat with a blue velvet cover. Miranda boldly snapped it on, took hold of Smithie's reins, put her foot in the proper stirrup and stepped up into the saddle, refusing to feel bad about their joint surrender to the full English breakfast less than an hour ago.

Inside the house, Oliver watched the proceedings on the drive, keeping out of sight behind his mother's ample curtains and waiting until the riders had turned a corner before setting off for the Château. How awkward the two of them looked, perched up there on the horses! How ridiculous that the woman charged with planning the death of an entire culture should have absolutely no idea what that culture was or why it might deserve a fair deal. Or any conception that it might be the very foundation of all society, the provider of their nourishment and their stake in the natural world.

Still, the girl didn't look too bad. A bit stiff. Nervous, probably. Nice legs. Well, who cared? Stuck-up metro-totty. Serve her right if she falls off. No, delete that. I need them back in shape to pay their bill tomorrow. He had the bill running up in the computer. With the full English breakfasts added in, it was nearly up to £900 already.

Cynicism had always been difficult for Oliver. His heart

was too big and too susceptible to wonder. One of the things he had hated about urban life was the constant requirement for sneering and negativity. Now, after nearly three years in the country, and on what turned out to be a shining morning full of birdsong, he found his lust for revenge faltering, undermined by all kinds of inconveniently decent feelings.

There was guilt. Just a few twinges, but they niggled. And an undeniable sense of absurdity. He'd enjoyed the whole deception so much it was almost wicked. All the emotions that had built up over the past months, the rage over his squandered savings and the grief over the dead lambs, all the feelings he'd refused to acknowledge and tried to drown at the pub, he'd poured them all into this ridiculous scam as if he could erase all his past mistakes by making an even bigger one.

His next task was to retrieve the pig that had strayed into Florian's *domaine*. A quick roll call of the animals now safe at home revealed that Miss Piggy was the truant. Oliver tried to argue with himself as he negotiated the winding lanes leading towards Château Saxwold. No, it's not a mistake, exactly. It would only be a mistake if it went wrong, and it wasn't going to go wrong. It's just a lark. Anyone would see that.

OK, so technically he was committing fraud. Obtaining pecuniary advantage by deception, that's the legal definition. But he was helping his mother out of a tight spot. What could be more noble than that?

The alleged victims were hardly suffering. They were looking pretty damn content, actually. All shiny and relaxed. Not to mention well fed and rested, which was more than he could say of himself. In fact, he was the one suffering. The suckers had had a pretty pleasant weekend out of it, so far. So where was the harm, really?

Although there was the question of Miranda. He had a very clear memory of that hour or so they had spent together when things had gone right. In fact, when he thought about it, things had never gone so right with any woman anywhere at any time as they had with Miranda in that sweet-as-a-nut interlude at the Yattenham Arms. Maybe he was missing something good there. Something really good. On the other hand, maybe his memory was playing tricks. Nothing could be that good. Not in real life. Could it?

When he arrived at Florian's house, there was no sign of human life. The door to the farmhouse kitchen was open and a couple of chickens were wandering in and out. Inside, Florian's dog paced disconsolately up and down the room, pausing every now and then to gaze soulfully at the door to the rest of the house. This door was shut and firmly latched. On the table, a puddle of milk and several abandoned cereal bowls suggested that children had recently breakfasted.

'Anybody home?' called Oliver. 'Hello? Florian?'

The dog suddenly lifted its muzzle and let out a howl. Not a loud sound, but desperately mournful.

'Florian?' Oliver called again, having a sense that the man wasn't far away.

A few minutes later, the sound of bare feet on oak staircase came from the far side of the door, the latch was raised and Florian appeared in the doorway. The lower half of his milk-white body was wrapped in an ancient bath towel. The dog immediately leaped up and tried to lick his master's face.

317

'Oh, Oliver. Hi,' said Florian. He was looking vague. 'What's up?'

'I said I'd be over for the pig,' Oliver reminded him.

'Of course you did. Sorry. Only just woken up. What time is it?'

'Late. Ten. Eleven almost.'

'Crikey.' He looked around the deserted kitchen as if he hadn't seen it for many years. 'I suppose my sister's taken her lot to church. Give me five minutes. I'll be right with you.'

This was not the normal Florian. He was showing no anxiety at all about what the pig might have done to the vines. He was moving like a sleepwalker. He was ignoring the dog. A soft confusion had replaced his keynote aristocratic poise. As he turned to slip out of the door again, Oliver noticed a couple of dead oak leaves caught in his hair and some pink weals on his back, just below waist level. Exactly as if somebody had taken a handful of him. It was all a bit odd.

After much more than five minutes, Florian reappeared in clothes and led Oliver out to the area near the oak tree, where there were tracks in the soft ground but no sign of the animal itself. Florian remained distracted. He seemed to be almost smiling to himself.

'There she is,' said Oliver at last, spotting Miss Piggy lying flat out on the grass in a sunny spot. At the sound of her master's voice, she flapped an ear. Since Florian continued to act as spaced as a visitor from a distant galaxy, it took a while to chivvy her onto her trotters, over to the car park and up a ramp into the back of Oliver's pick-up.

'At least she didn't get near the vines,' said Oliver.

'Yes. No. No she didn't, did she? Quite lucky, really.' Florian was gazing into the middle distance.

318

'Are you OK?' Oliver asked him.

'I'm brilliant,' he said, sounding slightly surprised. 'Why?'

'You seem a bit – I don't know – *zoned,* maybe?'

'Sorry. Didn't get much sleep. Time for a coffee before you go?'

They returned to the farmhouse kitchen. Florian's dog was standing in the middle of the floor, its head lowered and its eyes, which protruded like half-spheres of obsidian from the side of its head, fixed resentfully upon a person who was sitting at the end of the table. This person was holding a scrap of buttered toast towards the dog and saying, 'It's no good you looking at me like that.'

A person with masses of hair, who smelled nice. A female person. She saw Florian and something that could only be described as a glow appeared on her face.

Florian said, 'Hello, darling.'

'Hello, sweet thing,' said the person, putting the toast back on her plate and wafting to her feet. She wore a sweatshirt of Florian's, and probably some knickers.

Florian and the person seemed to be drawn together by some atomic force. They collided affectionately in front of the Aga. Something that was somewhere between a kiss and a nestle took place. Then the pair withdrew a few inches, seeming embarrassed, and turned as one being towards Oliver.

'This is Dido,' said Florian graciously. 'This is Oliver. His farm is the other side of the village. He came over to pick up the pig.'

They said hello simultaneously. Then the person said, 'Did you find it OK?'

'Oh yes. No trouble at all.' Then Oliver found himself saying, 'Oh well. Must be getting back.'

On the way out of the car park, he slowed down to pass Florian's sister, who was driving her children back from the morning service at St Oswin's. She wound down her window as she drew level with him.

'Is she still there?' she asked in a conspiratorial shout. 'The girlfriend?'

'There is some woman there,' he confirmed.

'Does it look OK?' she called anxiously, while her children on the back seat giggled and kicked each other.

'Well, the dog's pretty upset.'

'So far so good, then. He met her in London, you know. Well, he was never going to meet anyone suitable hanging around down the pub with you lot, was he? She must be dotty about him. But he'll screw it up, he always does.' And she let in the clutch and shot the car forward in a shower of gravel, before slamming on the brakes when the vehicle was at a crazy angle about six inches from the kitchen door.

As he drove back through the village, a black cloud settled on Oliver's morning. Damn Florian. Damn woman. And what was wrong with The Pigeon & Pipkin, anyway?

The tone used by Florian's sister offended him. Why, she'd talked about him and Colin and Jimmy, not to mention her own brother, as if they were all desperate Bridget-Jones-style spinsters whose gonads were shrivelling from lack of use. Quite unnecessary. Absolutely outrageous. A man had no need to 'meet somebody suitable'. A man, in Oliver's mind, was always knee-deep in suitable somebodies, and if the mood took him and he did want to get married, why, all that he had to do was to choose one of them.

Even Colin had managed to find somebody. OK, Colin had found the last Mrs Burton on the Internet, and the one before her through some Russian marriage bureau. This was not the sort of arrangement Oliver had in mind for himself, of course. He intended to fall in love. One day.

One day, as he had always planned should happen, he would meet this woman and he would know that she was the one. He would adore her utterly and she would worship him totally – but in a spirited sort of way. It would all be simple and inevitable and absolutely glorious. That was the plan. A perfectly normal plan and bound to work out. One day.

He couldn't help remembering that, in his City days, people who said that their plans were simple and inevitable and bound to work out one day were always complete time-wasters. In fact, most of them were certifiably insane. But that was finance. Falling in love was something completely different.

Clare and Miranda, accompanied by Lucy, set off down the lane on their horses. The last wisps of mist had gone, leaving the new leaves glistening and dew drops sparkling on the budding twigs. Tulip, asked by Lucy to lead at a sedate walk, found this responsibility overpoweringly thrilling, and started to dance sideways and toss her head; she was at an age to be excited about everything and, if there was nothing to get excited about, to imagine a rattlesnake in every gateway just to make life a bit more interesting.

Samson and Smithie clopped along peacefully side by side, requiring no input from their riders, who slowly remembered how it felt to balance on a bald, slippery saddle and bend their legs around their horses' ribs, while keeping their feet contorted correctly in their stirrups and the reins threaded through their fingers, and at the same time sitting up gracefully and looking cheerful. The sun was up now, warm on their backs and as yellow as the dandelions twinkling in the young grass.

Just occasionally, when Samson's ears picked up the far-off cry of the hounds, the sound reminded him of his hunting days and he too tossed his head but, as Clare told herself, taking a severe tone, it was *nothing* to worry about. How pleasant this was. That young woman in charge looked remarkably intelligent. And Miranda – how confident she was, all of a sudden, managing that huge animal. Already, she looked quite different from the scurrying, frowning young executive she appeared in London. There was a sort of bloom on her cheeks and a sparkle in her eye. But how in the world to get her and that young man together?

It was, she admitted to herself, oddly satisfying to be conspiring to find her daughter a husband. Why, it was like . . . the time she baked a cake, or tied Miranda's tie on the first day of school. She had forgotten how these arcane rituals of traditional parenting created an illusion of comfort. She almost felt that she was making up, somehow, for being a non-traditional mother. As if there was anything to make up. Miranda was born modern, she would never have wanted an old-style mum. All the same, there was a sense of rightness about the idea. All because of that woman – what was her name? Bel. Quite an operator, in her way. Something about her niggled at Clare's memory. The way she flapped her hands, maybe.

Their hour passed in a dream of perfection, woman and horse in harmony, a few fluffy clouds scudding across the broad blue sky. They walked, they trotted. Samson stood obediently still beside the restless Tulip while Miranda persuaded Smithie into a sedate canter. For most of its length the bridle path was a broad grassy track running between high hedges, not an environment which offered a horse much scope for ambition.

Coming back, they cut across one side of Oliver's land and came out in Saxwold Farm Lane, just after Oliver himself had turned into it from the village road in his rattling pick-up. He stopped to let the riders pass, but, being distracted by his thoughts, he forgot Lucy's warning about pigs. Lucy, congratulating herself on bringing off the morning without any mishaps, also forgot that a pig had a role in Oliver's morning mission.

The sight of Miss Piggy in the back of the truck was exactly the outrage that Tulip had been looking for all morning. The moment she saw the pig, she shied like a scalded cat and threw Lucy into the hedge. Then she bolted down the lane.

Samson, who seemed to have been nursing a sense of grievance over the canter he had been denied, tried to jump in the air with all four feet at once, causing Clare to shriek, which alarmed Smithie, and, in a chaos of hoofbeats and a flurry of mud, the two senior horses heaved into action and followed their companion. All three shot through the first open gateway, which led into one of Jimmy's fields.

'Pull them up!' shouted Lucy, struggling back on her feet in time to see thousands of pounds' worth of horse heading for the horizon at a wild canter. 'Pull them up! Pull on your reins!'

'What's she saying?' cried Clare to Miranda.

'Dunno!' shouted Miranda. Once he got into his stride, Smithie had a fine, smooth action that was really not difficult to get into. Stuff was coming back to her, the long-forgotten exhortations of her childhood riding instructors. She was coping. She could do this. Actually, it was fun.

'I can't stop him!' Clare had dragged on her reins with all her strength, but better women than she had tried and failed to stop Samson when his mind was made up for a gallop. He had long ago learned to tuck in his nose and drop his head, causing a novice rider, such as Clare, to find an alarming nothingness in front of her, shriek again, drop all pretences and grab his mane for dear life.

Smithie, meanwhile, had decided that if this was a race, he was damn well not going to let that stupid mare win it. And Tulip had an instinct that there were other horses about, the rest of her herd just over there in the distance somewhere. So all three horses swept up the field and over the brow of the hill together. Smithie won by a nose when Tulip suddenly lost her confidence and slowed down at the summit.

'Damn!' said Lucy. 'Now how are we going to catch them?'

'We'll drive after them in this,' Oliver proposed. 'Just let me get rid of the pig.'

'You and your stupid pig.'

'I'm sorry, I forgot.'

'No, my fault. I should have remembered.'

Off-centre to the top of the hill was a small copse of hazel trees, where Carole, Video Guy and some of the less fit among the saboteurs had found a sheltered place for a smoke and a moan. When three bolting horses passed near them, Carole's contact among the sabs leapt to her feet.

'There!' she shouted. 'There they are! Told you. It is an illegal hunt. The scum are trying to con us all! There's the rest of them. The bastards! Look, there's a loose horse with them – they've been riding all over the county while we've been sitting here. Come on.' She grabbed Video Guy by the arm and pulled him up beside her. 'Come on, you've got to get this. This'll be evidence. Come on. For God's sake, run!'

A few hundred yards further on, to the immense relief of Clare and Miranda, the horses suddenly slowed to a walk. With awkward fingers, the two women gathered up their reins and created an illusion of being in control again. The ground was grassy here, and sloped down again to a small stream, hardly more than a cleft in the meadow. On the far side of it the land rose steeply, overgrown with bushes and gorse breaking into crests of golden blossom. While they watched, a couple of hounds ran into view.

'That's why they've stopped,' said Miranda, getting back her breath. 'They don't want to go through the gorse.'

'I don't care why they've stopped, I just don't want them to take off again. What's going on over there?' said Clare, daring to sit upright and fish for a lost stirrup with her toes. An incautious touch of her foot, however, sent Samson forward another few steps. Then he decided that the grass in front of him looked too good to pass on and dropped his nose for a snack, almost pulling the reins out of Clare's inexpert hands.

'It looks like people hunting,' said Miranda, daring to stand in her stirrups for a better view. 'I can see a couple of other horses. And there are hounds, look.'

All six hounds were working the bank side now, running in and out of the cover, piling on top of each other and yelping with excitement, watched by one of the huntsmen and a girl on a pony.

'What are they doing?' asked Clare. 'Why are they just standing and watching?'

'I don't know what they're doing,' said Miranda. Together, they took in the intent attitudes of the riders and sensed the accord between the people and their animals, built up over the winter of working together.

Clare felt an unexpected flutter of respect and was about to try putting this unusual feeling into words when the huntsman's horn caught the sun and a few notes rang out over the field. This was enough to remind Samson of his glory days. He took his nose out of the grass and lurched downhill.

'Oh God!' cried Clare, now finding that she had useless yards of rein in her hands. 'I can't stop him.'

The next happenings were only established afterwards. The hounds at first obeyed the master's call and gathered around him. The rest of the hunt, trailed by the main body of the saboteurs, appeared above them on the far side of the stream. Seeing what she took to be the rest of her herd, Tulip let out a passionate neigh and flew down to join them, followed instantly by Smithie. The two younger horses hardly broke stride as they nipped smoothly over the stream at its narrowest point, but Samson hesitated on the bank, then heaved himself over in a clumsy cat jump that left Clare once more clinging on to his neck.

'Who is that woman?' panted Video Guy as he scrambled in pursuit. 'I know I know her.'

There was shouting, and confusion, and questions, and brandished placards, and sheer terror on Clare's part, and considerable fear from Miranda, and much milling and stamping from the horses. All accelerated to pandemonium when a fox streaked from under a gorse bush and ran in the direction of the lane. This was too much for the hounds, who gave chase, and for the saboteurs, who let out howls of fury and ran forward in an attempt to head off the riders.

'I know I know her face,' said Video Guy, staggering out of the melee with his camera held above his head. 'I know she's . . . fuck me, she's the Minister. Did we know this about her?'

'All we knew was she's supposed to be the Treasury's choice for helping them meet their housing targets and bury the countryside in concrete,' gasped Carole, who was not accustomed to physical activity, nor to paying attention to rural politics.

'Fucking brilliant then, isn't it?' Video Guy checked to be sure he had plenty of tape left and leaped back into the melee.

As the whole posse of horses and people set off after the hounds, Clare's luck ran out. Samson dithered again on the stream bank, giving one of the saboteurs the opportunity to wave a placard under his nose. It was a great shot for the camera. The venerable animal reared up on his hind legs for the first time in at least twelve years, and pitched Clare squarely into two feet of muddy water.

'Hang about. I've got to get this!' shouted Video Guy, bounding forward in delight. The Minister! Hunting! And falling off her horse! Unbeatable!

A blinding pain shot up Clare's left arm, which was much

later discovered to be attached to a broken collarbone. While she floundered to her feet, slipping in the mud, Video Guy staggered around her, trying to get close-ups of her anguished face and her mud-spattered body. Soon one of the huntsmen saw her plight and dismounted to help her to her feet. Video Guy got a solid thirty-second shot of his red coat before the huntsman's elbow caught him in the face. In the general confusion, he scrambled away and rushed back to the safety of the copse. There he lost no time in connecting his technology to that of his favourite news agency.

The fox, meanwhile, fled down the lane and into the pub car park. There he saw something familiar. And safe. And a way into it.

At the end of the morning, when Carole returned to the van, she found the fox jammed under the driving seat. She got a warm, furry feeling and decided the whole weekend had been well spent. 'Look at you! Is that my little Sweeney? Who's a clever boy then? You coming back to London with us then? You don't want to live in the nasty countryside at all, do you?'

CHAPTER 13

Back to Reality

A few hours later, Clare was wheeled into a small ward in the nearest hospital and helped onto a bed. Her arm was braced in a plastic splint. Miranda had stripped off her muddy clothes and a nurse had given her a hospital gown. She felt exhausted and woozy with analgesics, despite which her whole body was a throbbing collage of pain.

'Take my advice and run away now,' advised the man on the other bed. He had long hair and an American accent. 'This place is just awful. Why do you people live like this? No wonder Madonna's come home to California. Get out as soon as you can. You don't want to stay here.'

'You don't want to stay here,' said the doctor, switching off the light behind Clare's X-rays. 'We haven't got the facilities to treat this properly. Have you got health insurance?'

'Well, yes,' said Clare. The pain was blinding, but she sat bolt upright on the bed, determined not to be disempowered by the patient process. 'I am insured. But it's only a broken bone, isn't it? Why is it such a problem?'

'This is just a little rural hospital. We can do minor injuries and respite care for the chronic sick. We can't do operations. This is a messy fracture near a major artery and it needs to be set under a general anaesthetic. And you need to stay in hospital overnight, or ideally for a couple of days until the swelling has reduced. Most of the major hospitals I could send you to round here won't have a bed. I couldn't transfer you until Tuesday and we haven't got an ambulance anyway. So if you have health insurance, you'd better make the call.'

'Why can't she go home?' asked Miranda.

'Twenty-four hours' observation in hospital is standard practice. There's a risk of blood clots and we need to keep the injury as still as possible.'

'Can I get some more of that morphine or whatever?' interrupted the American.

'You can treat *him*,' Miranda pointed out.

'Oh, I only have bee stings,' the American said. 'And shock. But that was yesterday. They're going to let me out tonight.'

Rapidly, Clare computed the options. Neither the doctor nor the patient had any idea who she was. Which meant she was safe for the moment, although they did not appreciate the political sensitivities of a minister in a nominally Left Wing government in Britain making use of her health insurance. Nearly as damaging as sending your child to a fee-paying school. Not to mention the danger that somebody would get hold of this hotel escapade. And on top of the negative impact of her speech . . . heavens, she'd almost forgotten that! No, no, no. Low profile, low profile, low profile, that was the way to go here. And besides, there was the question of Miranda and that young man. There could be an up-side to this, of a sort.

'I'll be fine here,' she said to the doctor, hoping she sounded confident. 'I don't want to lose my no-claims bonus, do I?'

'It's up to you, of course. This is all we've got,' he said, indicating the hard couch protected by a paper sheet and the flimsy curtain for privacy. The room was small, and bare, apart from a stack of surplus supplies in cardboard boxes at the far end and some antiquated pieces of equipment draped in dust sheets.

'But Mum . . .' Miranda began.

'I said, I'll be fine,' Clare repeated firmly.

'Whoa,' said the American. 'Scary lady.'

'OK. OK. If that's what you want.'

'It's the best thing,' Clare said. 'I've thought about it. Trust me.'

'I said OK.' And then, feeling guilty about feeling hostile, Miranda gave her mother half a hug on her uninjured side, which was still agony. 'Shall I bring over your things?'

'A change of clothes would be a good idea,' said Clare, trying not to look disdainful as she picked at the utilitarian, much-laundered hospital gown. 'Why are these things always green? It would make you look ill even if you weren't.'

Out in the car park, Oliver waited beside his car, in the first phase of a personal epiphany, in which the sufferer blames everybody else. He was a simmering brew of anxiety, remorse and annoyance. The ingredients were added in this order: what if she's seriously hurt? What if she sues somebody? What if she figures out what's going on here? This would never have happened if I hadn't started this lunatic scam. This would never have happened if my mother wasn't a financial no-brain. This would never have happened if the stupid bitch hadn't said she could ride. This would never have happened if that evil woman had a scrap of respect for rural life, or rural values, or rural reality of any kind.

At the door of the hospital, Miranda appeared. She was walking briskly on stiff legs like a referee about to hand out a red card. Obviously, she was angry about something. Now what?

'Can we go back to the hotel, please?'

Cliché, of course, but she did look rather beautiful, especially when her eyes flashed.

'Sure.'

They got into the car and set off. Be polite, thought Oliver. Be soothing. She's upset. See if you can defuse this. Whatever it is. You've done negotiation training. And you don't want any trouble until that bill is paid.

'How is she?'

'How is my mother? Don't ask. Don't ask because I don't know. I've never known how my mother is, or why my mother is, or what to do about it.'

'I meant, what sort of injury is it?'

'Don't worry, it's not serious. Well, it could be, but it isn't. She's got a broken collarbone.'

'She was in a lot of pain.'

'She deserves to be in a lot of pain. And she's determined to stay in there until Tuesday. She doesn't have to. She pays a fortune in health insurance, she could be in a private ward in a London hospital with marble floors and orchids, if she wanted.'

'So why . . . ?'

'Don't ask me. I don't know. She said she wanted the experience. Have you got a cigarette?'

'I don't smoke.'

'I don't smoke either. Sometimes I wish I did.'

Women! Especially London women. Couldn't they at least try to make sense? Oliver drove on in silence.

Men! Stupid men! Stupid country, full of stupid men and their stupid animals. Miranda looked out of the window. It was still a glorious day.

While she was in the bathroom of the Rose Room, collecting together the contents of her mother's wash bag, she heard her phone ring. Who could be calling? The office? Oh, please no. Some friend from London? But nobody she knew stayed in London over a long weekend. Everyone she knew went to Cuba, or Venice or Barcelona. The call register told her it was Dido.

'Well hello, stranger!'

'Stranger yourself!'

'Can you talk?'

'That's why I'm calling. He's out fixing the beehives. Oh, M . . . he's so fabulous.'

'Good.'

'It's such an amazing scene here.'

'Good. Good.'

'You must come over. You must meet him properly.'

'Great. Love to. But . . .'

'M, darling, I need a favour. They've taken his car off to this fox thing . . .'

'And you need a ride somewhere?'

'I need my clothes! They're all at the pub still.'

'No problem, but I've got to go to the hospital first.'

'What hospital? Who's in hospital?'

'It's a long story,' Miranda said. 'But I'll make it short.'

Her mother, when Miranda arrived back at the hospital with her suitcase, must have been feeling better because she was back to her old demanding, main-chancing self. 'We've got to pay the hotel in cash,' she announced, snapping four different bank cards out of her wallet.

'They'll take a cheque, won't they?' Miranda asked.

'I don't want a paper trail, it's just something else for the media to start twisting. Trust me, Miranda, this is the best way. I'm sorry, but you'll have to find a machine somewhere and take out as much as you can.'

The nearest cash point was in a town half an hour away, so it was some hours later that Miranda collected Dido at the Château and drove her down to The Pigeon & Pipkin to get her stuff. Her friend was looking more than ever like a wide-eyed child, which was pretty normal for day one of a consummated passion. She put a few items in her bag, then sat on the end of the bed and talked nonstop for an hour, entirely on the subject of Florian.

'Look,' said Miranda eventually, 'when we go to that place, why don't you invite me in and I can meet him, like you say? I'm not going to sit in that hotel having dinner by myself, that's for sure.'

'Why? I thought you said it was a really great place?'

'It would be awkward, that's all.'

'Miranda . . . what have you done? I know that tone of voice.'

'Nothing, nothing.'

'Yes, you have. It was that waiter. Don't say it all turned to custard.'

'Yeah, well. I'm not lucky that way, am I?'

'You said he was gorgeous.'

'I must have been drunk. He's just another dickhead, only the rural variety, which is even worse.'

'He found out who your mother is?'

'Yes.'

'And he cared, obviously. Oh, rats.'

'Well, it was only going to be a bit of fun.'

'You sounded really . . . quite keen on him.'

'Well, I was probably just keen on getting away with something under the mother's nose. I just thought she was trying to manipulate me and I just wanted to subvert that, I suppose. If you think about it, I should be beyond all that now. And beyond boys, and bits of fun. It's all just . . . silly. Isn't it?'

With difficulty, Dido focused on her friend. Subtly, she was not looking quite like the old Miranda. Sad, slightly, but also brighter, sharper, clearer. 'You're changing,' she said.

'I feel different,' said Miranda. 'It's been good, being here. You know, I was really enjoying this morning. Until the stupid hunt business, of course. But it was kind of beautiful to watch, until those mad people turned up and Mum fell off her horse. It just made sense, somehow.'

Dido sniffed doubtfully. Florian had explained to her, very gently, that whoever had dumped thirty-eight urban foxes in a field near Great Saxwold had done a very bad thing, and that the animals were going to die whichever way you sliced it, and that the shoot was a more humane end for them than being allowed to starve to death, but she still found the whole idea horrible. 'I think it's very tough, all the same,' she said. 'People in the country have to do such beastly things. You don't really want to know about what goes on out here, do you?'

'Maybe that's why what I do in London doesn't make sense. It's all just so far away from reality. A mass delusion. Millions of people preferring not to know how they're keeping alive.'

Dido wriggled. 'You used to think cities were beautiful.'

'Well, maybe I've changed. Cities have to go on and people have to live in them but it's all about money, really. And people's egos. Tomorrow in the office, I'm going to have to write a press release about *the new paradigm of metropolitan aesthetics* and I just think it's all mad. I can see why people like Oliver hate people like my mother. You might as well be a little plastic man on an architect's model, for all your life counts with them.'

'Miranda! You've never said that much about any man in all the time I've known you!'

'Will you shut up about men? This isn't about him. It's about me. About my life and what I want to do with it.'

'Sorry,' said Dido, who could sense the right time to back off, particularly when it was specifically announced to her. 'Sorry. Well – what do you want to do with your life?'

'How do I know? Why is everybody asking me all these questions? Will you just get your things together so we can get out of here?'

'OK, OK. I'm getting. I'm getting.' And Dido scraped some garments off the floor and some jewellery off the windowsill, and said, 'I'm ready. Let's go.'

Florian had prepared dinner. It was something he did very rarely, but the overwhelming need to impress Dido was driving him to do crazy things. Amazingly for one so slender, he was a good cook, in the English tradition of eccentric upper-class countrymen. He was not a tidy cook, nor a design-led cook, nor in the least the sort of man who proudly assembles little piles of food with balsamic vinegar dribbled around them. Florian was the sort of man who used butter by the handful and liked to make a pie in a dish as big as a bucket, its inside bubbling with fabulous fragrant stuff and the top covered in a thick, lopsided blanket of pastry.

When it was ready, he took a big spoon, hacked the pie into wads, dolloped onto plates and passed down the table until his lover, her friend, his sister, her husband, her husband's friends and his five nephews and nieces were all content and so was his lurcher. The dog was far too well bred to come around begging at the table, but when given his own plate he finally felt reassured that his master was still devoted to him, and withdrew after eating to an old leather-covered armchair in the far corner of the dining room.

'And since this is a special occasion,' Florian said, nodding at Miranda, 'we shall open the first bottle of the 2003 Pinot.'

The red liquid was poured into seven glasses and they sipped. And sipped again. And again. Florian held the glass to the light of the guttering silver candelabra in the centre of the table, suddenly looking like one of Caravaggio's most ecstatic boy angels.

'Excellent!' said one of his brother-in-law's shooting friends, flourishing his glass. 'Congratulate the wine-maker.'

'It's very good,' said Miranda, making a successful effort not to sound surprised.

'It *is* very good,' said Florian, claiming his right to sound roundly astonished. 'Bloody hell.'

'You've got rid of that cat's pee taste,' said his sister, claiming her right to sibling honesty.

'Can I try it?' asked the eldest nephew.

'Have you got much of this?' his brother-in-law asked.

'Have I got much of it? 2003 was a heavily-aspected Jupiter year. Amazing summer. Weather held right through to September. Convinced a lot of people about global warming. We couldn't pick the grapes fast enough. I've got about seven hundred bottles.' Florian drained his glass, wondering if life could possibly get any better.

'In that case,' said the other one of the brother-in-law's friends, 'I'd better open a couple more, hadn't I?'

Manners never desert a man of Florian's breeding for long, even when he has viticultural medals of honour dancing before his eyes, so he soon turned to Miranda and asked, 'So tell me, where were you and your mother staying?'

'The Saxwold Manor Hotel,' she said.

'Over in Lower Saxwold,' Florian prompted her.

'Um – this is Great Saxwold, isn't it? I get so confused.'

'What, this village? Yes, this is Great. The Manor Hotel is over in Lower.'

'Lower Saxwold is ten miles north of here,' his sister put in, hoping to be helpful.

'But our hotel is definitely in this village.'

'I didn't know we had a hotel here. I thought the Saxwold Manor Hotel was up in Lower. They've taken a few bottles of my Cowslip Sack.'

'I think I had that last night. But our hotel really is in this village.'

'Run by two gay blokes with a pair of Dalmatians?'

'No, run by this nice woman called Bel something, with a mad Labrador. And her son who helps out on the weekends, and some girl with a lot of black eyeliner.'

'That isn't a hotel,' said the sister, before anyone could stop her. 'That's Bel Hardcastle's house. Two stone dogs outside. Lots of chintz.'

'That sounds right. It must be our hotel. We're staying there.'

A semi-curdled silence took place. The sister, in all innocence, took a second helping of carrots, while her husband tried to kick her under the table. The children, sensing adult misbehaviour, sat with widening eyes. The friends, mostly interested in the wine, refilled their glasses. Miranda felt uneasy. Dido gazed adoringly at Florian, wondering what he was thinking. Florian thought: yikes! Mercury quincunx Pluto in here somewhere. The truth will out.

'How can you be staying there?' the sister pressed on, rubbing her shin and wondering why her husband had to be so clumsy all the time. 'It's just a house.'

'Well . . . we are. I mean . . . there's breakfast. And room service. And a dining room. And a waiter.'

'Is Oliver up to something?' the sister demanded, suddenly feeling pieces of a puzzle falling into place. 'Florian? Are you men doing some stupid wind-up?'

'He said his name was Oliver,' said Miranda, feeling slightly dizzy.

Florian was congenitally inclined to telling the truth and doing good, and now, being in love as well, felt infused with the desire to make everyone else as happy as he was. 'It wasn't his idea,' he said. 'It was his sister started it. The one with the black eyes? The Goth? It was her idea.'

'She told us where to find it. When we went into the pub to ask the way,' said Miranda. 'We didn't realise she worked there.'

'And she told you the way to her mother's house. Really, her stepmother. Who she's annoyed with, because she doesn't like living here. They moved out of London a couple of years ago because she was getting into trouble.'

'So now she's getting into trouble here,' said the sister, who seemed to find this oddly satisfying.

'But – nobody said anything.'

'Well,' said Florian, putting his elbows on the table and running his fingers through his hair while he tried to think of the best spin to put on things. 'This is all so difficult . . .'

'He did say his name was Oliver,' Miranda repeated.

'He did mention you,' Florian admitted, suddenly seeing a way to turn this sticky situation around. 'You see . . . oh dear, I don't want to embarrass anybody.'

'Please,' said Miranda. 'Just tell me what I should know.'

'Well, you see, Toni sent you off to the Manor thinking it would be a laugh. And then Oliver thought you were friends of his mother, people she'd asked to stay the weekend. And well – like I mentioned, he was pretty pleased. And then his *mother* thought that you were friends of his. So they'd sort of got in over their heads before they realised what was going on.'

'Well, that is a bit embarrassing. But surely, they must have figured out they'd made a mistake at some point?' Something about the explanation didn't work, but Miranda couldn't decide what it was.

340

'Well, yes. At least, Oliver did. But you see – oh dear, I'm going to get into trouble.'

'Why?' said Miranda, now in a fever of curiosity. 'Why should you get into trouble?'

'Well, I don't know I should say.'

'You've got to say, you can't leave me up in the air like this.' Her curiosity was now so hot it made Miranda feel as if she was about to burst into flames. 'What is it, Florian, what's been happening? You've got to tell me.'

'Yes,' put in Dido, who, like the rest of the table, had been hanging on every faltering word. 'You've got to tell her, Florian. Whatever it is. She's got to know.'

At the word of his beloved, Florian felt it appropriate to give in. 'Oh dear, I suppose that's right. Yes, of course it's right. Well you see . . . no, I can't. I really shouldn't, it's too personal.'

The table erupted in a storm of exclamation.

'Yes you can!' shouted Florian's sister.

'For God's sake!' cried her husband.

'Get it over with!' exhorted his friends.

'Tell her! Tell her!' chanted the children.

'Sweet thing,' murmured Dido, 'you've got to 'fess up.'

'But . . .' Florian's face was crumpled in agony and he looked as if he was going to pull his own hair out by the roots. His dog slunk off its chair and curled protectively around his feet.

'TELL HER!' everyone shouted together.

'Oh, all right. You see, Miranda, the thing is, I mean, what it is, it's this, really, you see . . .'

'TELL HER!' they shouted again.

'OK. OK. I'm going to tell you. The thing is, Miranda –

he sort of rather as it were . . . well, he fell for you. I mean, he really liked you. Actually, he thought you were just absolutely what the Americans would call some kind of wonderful. So of course, when he realised that you thought you'd arrived at a hotel and there'd been a ridiculous mistake, he – well – he decided to persuade his mother to go along with it all. Because, really, he simply couldn't bear to straighten everything out because then he'd probably never see you again.'

'Aaaaaaaaaah,' said the children. And Dido.

'Oh,' said Miranda. No, I will not blush. I will not. I never blush. But it was hot in the dining room and the 2003 Pinot had been at work. Perhaps she was looking a bit flushed anyway. 'But I thought . . . I thought he did quite like me. But when he found out who my mother was, it all went Pete Tong, somehow.'

'Do forgive me,' said Florian. 'I know I should know but of course we haven't actually met. Your mother is . . .'

'Well, she's called herself the CEO of Agraria. It's Minister for Agriculture, really.'

'Is she? Minister for Agriculture. That's pretty impressive.'

'Oh for God's sake,' said his sister. 'Nobody's impressed round here. Half the county's ready to burn her in effigy. I mean, I know she's your mother, but she hasn't had much respect for farmers, has she?'

'She's definitely upset some people,' Miranda admitted. 'I don't think she should have let them give her a job in politics, really. And she does tend to intimidate people.'

'But not Oliver, surely?' said Florian's sister. 'Not with his background.'

'Did you know that Oliver's our local downshifter?' asked Florian. 'Did he mention that he has a secret past?'

'No-o,' said Miranda, getting a vague, disturbing but pleasant sense of what was to come. Florian outlined Oliver's first career to her, in as much as he had grasped the exact nature of it.

'So he made his fortune, then sold up everything and came down here,' he finished.

'And lost it all on that farm of his,' added his sister.

'That's not fair,' snapped Florian. 'He invested. The return will come. That's all. I mean, look at this place. It just takes time.'

'Oh God,' said Miranda, now seeing what she assumed was the full picture. 'You mean they played along with the hotel thing all weekend just because . . .'

'He really was taken with you,' Florian said, seeing with relief that Miranda's face was registering all kinds of emotions, but not disbelief. 'You're not offended, are you?'

'I feel so bad,' she said. 'If anyone should be offended, it ought to be him. I've been – well, I thought he was the waiter. So I suppose I wasn't very nice.'

'Why should you be nice?' demanded Florian's sister. 'He tricked you. I'd feel pretty cross, if it was me.'

'Children,' Florian announced, determined to divert the conversation before his good work was undone. 'I've made Uncle Florian's Famous Brown Bread Ice Cream. It's in the freezer and if you're very, very, very good and clear all the plates nicely, your mum will get you some.'

Grudgingly, his sister rose among her cheering brood and marched off to the nearest barn, where the domestic deep freeze purred quietly alongside the industrial models preserving the aromatic herbs and flowers from the previous year.

'Don't feel bad,' Florian said to Miranda. 'It really was done for the best.' Dido reached over and squeezed her hand. 'I've got to know Oliver pretty well, the last couple of years,' Florian continued. 'He's had a lot of stress with the farm, it was a pretty steep learning curve. And – ah – never had a girlfriend since he's been here, that I know of. I was gob-smacked when I heard what had been going on at the Manor. Not that he told me. It was our vet – Lucy. Who took you riding, by the way. She thought I knew, so there was a bit of a misunderstanding.'

Oh. My. God, said Miranda's inner schoolteacher. Oh. My. God. This is not a boy, it's a grown-up guy. You came on to him. You practically pinched his bum. Your behaviour has been nothing short of utterly pathetic.

A certain sensation tried to assert itself. Flat. Insig-nificant. Lowly. Wet. That old invertebrate feeling. Oh no, she said to it. Not this. I haven't felt this for . . . oh, a couple of days. Good heavens, a couple of days! Forty-eight hours of feeling reasonably OK. And I'm used to it. And I like it. I will not feel like a worm. I will not. Yes, this is embarrass-ing. Yes, I've been pathetic. No, I do not feel like a worm. Simple. Now slither along, please. I'm OK and I'm a grown-up and I'm going to deal with this.

With his laptop, working at his desk by the kitchen window of the cottage, Oliver toiled reluctantly to finish his most elaborate creation, the bill. Yesterday, he had been proud of it. A letterhead, the sort of letterhead country house hotels always had, a line drawing of the building wreathed in roses, printed on the flash printer. Purchases and prices, which needed to look convincingly blurry, all itemised in a tiny font and printed on an old inkjet. The Rose Suite. The Wisteria Suite. Room Service. Continental Breakfast. Dinner. Full English Breakfast.

Yesterday, the whole deal had seemed basically sweet. Cash-flow crisis sorted and a good laugh on top. A fun way to hit back at the people who'd fucked up his life. Putting them in hospital, well, that was too extreme. That had not been part of the plan. And – well, the girl. Maybe that was where it had all started to lose its shine. He felt bad about Miranda, a large sort of bad, probably with several different areas, shapeless but oppressive all the same. Knock off the last breakfast, maybe. Gesture of goodwill. The bad feeling persisted.

It was the courage, that was the problem. They'd been so bloody brave. Who'd have thought that some Islington princess would even get on a horse, let alone fall off it, break half her bones and then get up all covered with mud and walk away telling everyone she was quite OK and not to make a fuss? When anyone else would have expected her to pull rank, threaten to sue and call for her personal helicopter. And the daughter. Not a scream, not a tear, not a tantrum. Difficult for her, obviously. Distressing, perhaps, if these people actually felt distress, which he doubted. Oh, damn it – why the hell did Miranda have to be the daughter of the Wicked Witch of London NW1?

Oliver was approaching the second stage of a personal epiphany, in which the subject thinks, just for a second, that his own actions may possibly have had some bearing on the situation, then violently rejects the idea. Their own bloody fault, of course. Miranda had never said who she was. She'd just sat there being sweet and let him find out. Why, her behaviour had been just as dodgy as his! All he'd done was exactly what they'd asked. Still, grace under pressure. Unexpected. Worth a free breakfast. But no more.

He set off for the Manor to deliver his masterpiece.

Miranda. Miranda. She'd been running through his mind all night. Hadn't he always intended to meet someone like Miranda, one day? Someone with that amazing combination of confidence and fragility. Someone who gave him a strange, magical, tender sort of feeling that he'd never had before. Someone who it would be pretty great to be adored by, in a spirited sort of way. Why, the whole affair had that sense of inevitability about it that he'd been expecting to feel one day – but not now.

It really wasn't fair. He hadn't had any warning. How was a man supposed to know, when the doorbell rings in his mother's house on a miserable wet night, and he goes to answer it, that the woman on the doorstep is going to be the one? His life was temporarily looking like a complete mess, and so she turns up now. It really wasn't fair.

He came into the Manor through the back door. The kitchen was quiet, and smelled strange. Irritatingly, the only person in the room was his stepsister, who was sitting on the sofa, lacing up her boots.

'Is that the bill? How much is it?' said Toni. The strange smell, he realised, was some scent she was wearing.

'You smell terrible,' he said, fraternally.

'Since you gave me this muck for Christmas, you should know,' she said, with sisterly logic. 'Go on, how much is it?'

'There,' he answered, showing her the total. 'Nine hundred and fifty-six pounds and forty pence.'

'No VAT?'

'I thought about it. But it might be committing fraud, you know. Charging VAT when we aren't actually registered.'

'We aren't actually a hotel, bro. Haven't we been committing fraud all weekend?'

'Well . . .'

'Making money by deception, or something? Course we have. I dunno what you and Bel are doing this for, anyway.'

'We're doing it because we need the money, if you must know. What did you think that bailiff was here for? My mother's in real trouble and I'm trying to help her. Not that I'd expect you to care.'

'Well, if she's so stuffed for money, why's she blown the whole scam, then?'

Oliver immediately had the feeling of bright mauve nausea that was uniquely associated with his mother. 'What do you mean, blown the whole scam?'

'She told her. That Minister woman. She told her what the whole game was. Last night. Well, this morning, really. In here. Right after we'd all been out chasing your pigs.'

And Toni gave him the edited highlights of the conversation between her stepmother and Clare Marlow, which she had overheard on waking up that morning.

'So they know everything,' Oliver said, the nausea giving way to deep dark chills.

'Yeah. And they decided they'd play along and hope you'll get together with wossername.'

'That's just . . .' He had an instant attack of emotional thermostat disorder. On top of the chills came the anger, hot and strong. And the embarrassment, like burning lava. And the freezing consciousness of absolute, utter, complete, all-round total disaster, riding in like the iceberg in front of the *Titanic*. 'My bloody mother.'

'What is she like, eh?'

'Interfering . . .'

'Telling everybody what to do. Now you know what I've had to put up with.'

'Thinks she can dictate your life.'

'Should have married Saddam Hussein. They'd have got along just fine.'

'That is a bit strong. Oh hell, no it isn't. God, what a fucking mess.'

'You do like her, though. Wossername.'

'Don't be stupid.'

'You do. Go on, you've got to admit it. You come over all unnecessary when she's around.'

'I do not.'

'Yes you do, I've seen you.'

'Rubbish. Toni, I'm not getting into another of your stupid conversations. You don't know what you're talking about. I'm going to find my mother and sort this out.'

He discovered Bel in the sitting room, peacefully watching television while Garrick lay zonked on the rug in front of the fire. The conversation began stridently, got ugly quickly, proceeded with a lot of shouting, reduced Bel to tears and ended when Oliver stormed out of the house, slammed the front door so hard that the carved walnut pediment above it fell down, and drove off down the lane to his own home, swearing all the way.

Bel got up and walked around the room, dabbing her eyes dry. After a while, she heard a distant car engine. Car

348

coming down the lane. Not stopping at Oliver's. Not stopping at Colin's. Not stopping at Jimmy's. It was that girl, and she was coming back.

She darted across the room for the light switch. When the house was dark, except for the hall and stairs, she went back to the sitting room, sat by the window and waited. This was not over. She was not defeated. She had one last card to play, one final move to make.

Later that night, Tolvo sat with his angel on the garden wall, and named the stars for her. 'Alpha Orion,' he said, pointing up at the heavens. 'Big and red. Easy to see. And with him is Beta, his name is also Rigel. More big. Blue star, very big. Most bright in Orion.'

'Where's Orion?' said Toni. Nobody had shown her stars before. Come to think of it, you never saw stars in London. Too many fucking streetlights and office blocks and shop signs and car headlights.

'Orion is man. Is hunter. I learn this word today. Hunter. With two dogs. Big dog and little dog.'

'Cool,' said Toni, meaning the singer, as well as the song.

'You have cold?' He put his arm around the angel's shoulders. Of course she was cold, she wore these thin clothes. Nobody in England had proper clothes, he had noticed.

'No,' said Toni.

Politely, Tolvo removed his arm. Politely, Toni took hold of it by the hand and put it back around her shoulders.

'Do you understand girlfriend?' she asked him.

'Girlfriend?'

'Yes. Do you understand what it is? Girlfriend?'

'Girlfriend? Of course.'

'Well, I can be your girlfriend. If you like.'

Tolvo ran this through the program of his English syntax. Girlfriend. Can be, is possible. Yours. Mine. My girlfriend, is possible. Is possible? Nasty, slippery stuff, language. Nothing solid about it, you could never trust it. Not pure and constant and beautiful like mathematics. Language was just a mess. He ran the words through the program again. Same answer.

'Yes?' he suggested.

'Cool,' said Toni. 'Good. Cool means good, OK?'

CHAPTER 14

Settling Up

As if the clear skies had done their job and gone home, Monday dawned dark and rainy. The rain fell in earnest, a torrent from the almost-black sky. Miranda heard it before she opened her eyes, hammering brutally on the roof. A buzzing like a wasp. No, that was somebody on a moped or something.

Miranda got up and went to the window. It looked as if it had been raining since the beginning of recorded time and would keep on raining until the end of eternity, because any other weather apart from total rain was just a tiny geophysical blip in a water-based climate. Or possibly even just a hallucination, and never really real at all.

Just as this was not a real hotel. She had come back full of the intention to sort out this hideous misunderstanding immediately, but found the house dark and deserted. And it had been late. Late for the country, anyway. She could hardly have woken people up to tell them – whatever she had to tell them. Difficult to call. I know you're pretending. No, please, you don't have to pretend, I know. I've behaved badly and I apologise. You've behaved badly and you really should apologise too. This is all too silly and ridiculous.

The silliest and most ridiculous part of it was the idea that Oliver had created this massive deception because he fancied her. Florian must have been wrong about that. Miranda's experience of life so far told her that she was a woman who definitely lacked the Cleopatra factor. Nobody was ever going to throw away an empire or launch a thousand ships for her sake. Maybe it wasn't all her fault, perhaps modern males had lost the faculty of romantic madness anyway. Normally, she reckoned she was doing well if she could inspire a man to change a light bulb for her.

So it was quite impossible that a man like Oliver – who, now she knew more about him, was really quite impressive as well as undeniably fit – would have been ready to make a complete fool of himself for a whole weekend just to keep her around. There had to be another explanation. Given that he was a farmer, it was probably some revenge plot against her mother.

As she dressed and packed her things, the idea of slipping away and saying nothing and forgetting the whole business as fast as possible seemed highly attractive. No, she told herself. The old Miranda might have done that. Back in the worm era, slithering away was an option. The new Miranda will not do this. And besides . . .

Her phone rang. Her mother.

'I'll be over in an hour or so,' Miranda said.

'Don't forget to pay the bill. You've got the cash on you, haven't you?'

Miranda opened her mouth to break the news, then

hesitated. Did her mother need to know? Wouldn't it just get even more complicated if she knew? And suppose she took it badly, wigged out and went on one of her rampages? Horrible thought.

'Don't worry, Mum,' she said. 'It's all under control.'

'Promise me.' Her mother sounded rather weak. Almost pathetic, in fact.

'Of course I promise. How are you, anyway? How did you sleep?'

'They gave me a pill in the end. That American man — remember him? He said he was some kind of animal rights activist but I think he's got some mental disorder. He talked for hours about saving bees from people making honey. Then when his people came and took him away, there was a person with Alzheimer's from the main ward wandering about talking all the time. They've only got one nurse on at nights here. She couldn't possibly cope. Rural health care. I had no idea.'

'But that's what your health insurance is for, so you don't have to suffer like that.'

'But ordinary people have to suffer like that.'

Clare's main concern about ordinary people had always been not to be one of them. Miranda decided her mother must be reacting to her painkillers. Especially when she said, 'Don't be late for breakfast, darling,' before she hung up.

The house seemed extraordinarily quiet, but those smells of coffee and bacon were drifting up from the kitchen. Miranda took a deep breath and went in search of somebody. Mrs Hardcastle and her son. Either would do, but she had a preference for Mrs Hardcastle, since the conversation with Oliver was going to be even more difficult.

Mrs Hardcastle was planted in front of the Aga, shaking pans.

'Good morning,' Miranda began.

'It's a terrible morning! The sky is crying because you have to leave us.'

'Look, this is really – well, I don't know what to say here.'

'Don't say anything. Just tell me what you'd like for breakfast. Our waiter isn't here yet, I don't know why.'

'He isn't really a waiter. This isn't really a hotel. I mean, is it?'

Bel made a last attempt to override reality. 'What are you saying? Of course . . .'

'No, please. I know what's been going on. One of your neighbours, the one who makes wine? He told me last night. And can I say – I'm really embarrassed about the way I must have behaved.'

'You know everything about it?' Bel tried, for the last, last time. 'That boy, what's his name, Florian, with the vineyard, he told you everything about our little play-acting here? Oh well. Oh dear. Why do people have to do all this telling?'

'He didn't mean anything bad. It was all sort of accidental.'

'Oh, but you're not angry at us? Or with Oliver? It was all an accident with us, you see. He thought you were friends of mine and I thought you were friends of his, and by the time we really talked about it, you were here and you had your rooms and it seemed that the best thing we could do was just go along with everything and hope for the best.'

'No of course I'm not angry. I suppose it's quite flattering really. Not angry at all. I mean, our rooms were just beautiful. This is such a beautiful house. I just feel really silly.'

Miranda was enveloped in a firm, bacon-scented hug.

'What for, my dear! If anyone should feel silly, it's us. But you know what these men are, when the heart is involved, they just can't think properly. You're really not angry?'

'How could I be?' Ignore that heart stuff. Trust a mother to get it all wrong. 'You've been so thoughtful and we've had a lovely weekend. Really heavenly, until the accident.'

'Ah, the accident. And your mother, the poor woman. How is she?'

'I've just spoken to her, she's not too bad. Oh, she doesn't know. I'm not going to tell her. She's in politics, you know. Things can get complicated. It's best she doesn't find out. She wanted to pay our bill in cash, for some reason so – here it is.' Miranda held out the money, the notes just visible over the lip of the open envelope.

'No, no, no,' said Bel at once, waving away the money with her non-stick cookware. 'Don't be so silly. We can't possibly take money, after playing this silly trick on you.'

'But you must. Please. You've been to so much trouble . . .'

In this game, Miranda was definitely the weaker player. Bel remonstrated, protested, waved the frying pan, flapped a tea towel and refused in a dozen different forms of words.

'My mother absolutely insists,' said Miranda, her final throw

Bel played confidently for the match point. 'And I absolutely refuse. If you don't want your mother to know, you can buy a new dress. Two new dresses. And some shoes, probably. Now you're not going to make me get angry here, are you?'

So Miranda conceded. She allowed herself to be seated at the table and given a large cooked breakfast, with second helpings. Bel commanded her to eat this. It gave her the opportunity to deliver an entertaining, if not very subtle, lecture on the merits of her son. Which gave Miranda even more cause to believe that this brilliant, wonderful and utterly desirable man couldn't possibly have liked her. No, she decided as she sliced into her second sausage, he must have just been playing along in his role as a sexually harassed waiter. Florian had it all wrong. Men had no idea about love, anyway. Nor did mothers.

'Goodbye, dear. No, no, I mean – au revoir. You're not embarrassed, are you? We should be embarrassed! I don't know how we managed to make such fools of ourselves. But if you like weekends in the country – why don't you come again. You're always welcome. No, I mean that . . .'

Miranda extricated herself as politely as she could and got into her car. Slowly, slowly – well, it was pouring with rain still – she drove away down the lane. And past the cottage. His cottage. Where he was. Probably. Definitely, since there were three vehicles outside, the car, the pick-up and the tractor. So he was there. Such a pity that he didn't really fancy her. But that would make things easier. Although it was going to be a bloody tricky conversation, all the same. After all, she fancied him. Still. Actually, more.

She could still drive on. A worm would drive on. A woman would go in and say what she had to say. Miranda turned the steering wheel and felt the car slither around on the muddy road and slide into the farmyard.

'Oh,' he said, when he opened the front door and saw her there. He looked like a man who had recently had a really bad night and was now following it with a really bad hangover. Or a man in the third stage of a personal epiphany, in which the sufferer recognises that it's all his fault, accepts a wholly excessive amount of blame, decides that he has definitively screwed things up with the only woman he could possibly fall in love with ever, and consumes a proportionately excessive amount of alcohol.

'Yes, it's me,' she said. 'I'm just leaving but I think we should talk.'

'We don't have to,' he said. 'I know I've been a complete prat and I apologise without reservation.'

'It is raining out here.' She felt water trickling down her neck. 'I'd much rather come in.'

'If you have to, I suppose you have to,' he said, leading the way through the hall to the room that was called the living room although no living whatever was done in it and most of its capacity was taken up with books on shelves, a large sofa devoid of cushions and the fireplace, in which some logs were burning briskly. 'I'm sorry, that was rude.'

'So you know I know,' Miranda began, sitting on a hard chair next to a table, which was piled high with leaflets and the official forms to which they related. Some of the forms, she noticed, were half-completed, but all of them were dusty and yellowed. Evidence of paperwork-phobia. A touching weakness, really, in someone said to be brilliant, wonderful and utterly desirable.

'And now I know that you know that I know,' he said. Click. Sweet as a nut. Amazing that stuff was working again.

'And I'm really embarrassed about how I behaved,' she said.

'*You're* embarrassed,' he said.

'I made all kinds of assumptions. I was bang out of order.'

'*You* were out of order.' This was getting ridiculous. He demanded better from his compromised mental powers. 'It was all entirely my fault. Truly, Miranda, you've got nothing to apologise for. It started out as a misunderstanding between my mother and me but then it just got totally out of control and there's nobody really to blame but me.'

They said a few more things of the same kind, after which a silence threatened, because most of the skills that they would normally have employed in a conversation, the hearing, the seeing, the empathy, the subtexting and the body language, had wilfully deployed themselves on another mission.

Oliver started leaning against the doorframe, and watching Miranda as if she was the most fascinating creature on the planet, which, to him, at that moment, she was. And Miranda, who found she had to comb her damp hair out of her eyes with her fingertips, felt his interest like rays of sunlight warming her skin. But no, she told herself, she must be mistaken. And anyway, it was too late to save the situation now.

'So,' she said, the autopilot being unable to change the flight plan. 'I'd better be off.'

'Of course,' he said. He wanted desperately to say something to stop her, but his brain seemed to have turned to polenta and there was nothing witty or compelling or even coherent in it.

'No hard feelings.' She offered a handshake. 'We'll probably laugh about this one day.'

'No hard feelings,' he said, accepting the offer. 'I'm sure we will. Laugh about it.'

Twenty seconds later, he was standing in the pouring rain, shutting her car door. She started the engine, he stepped away. He waved to her to turn, wondering if she could see him in the downpour. She put the car in gear and set off to reverse exactly as suggested.

The car balked and slithered disobediently off at a tangent. Oliver saw that the tyre nearest to him was no longer fully circular. He let out a yell and she wound down her window.

'You've got a flat,' he said, pointing to the back of the car, where he could see clearly now that the tyre was nothing but a crust of deflated rubber. 'Jump out, go inside. I'll change it for you.'

No normal man enjoys the opportunity to change a tyre in a muddy farmyard in the pouring rain. At this point, Oliver, as he even admitted to himself, was not a normal man. His blood was running through his veins in a trail of stardust and his heart was doing the macarena. He found himself grinning at the wheel nuts as he bashed them into motion and chuckling at the spare tyre as he heaved it into place. At least another fifteen minutes with this wonderful, adorable woman. A last chance! Why, anything could happen now.

Then, as he picked up the deflated tyre, a Pete Tong element in the situation became clear. The cause of the puncture was obvious. It was a nail. A nail he knew. A nail he had bought himself, and used, not six months ago, to fix the carved walnut pediment above his mother's front door. A nail that told him more than he wanted to know.

Miranda was sitting on the sofa in the living room, aware that her pulse was racing. She'd never had this feeling before, but there was no mistaking it. Nor was there any mistaking the way Oliver had been looking at her. Florian was perhaps not completely wrong about everything. Amazingly, this terrific man seemed to like her. In spite of everything. And now they had been mysteriously bonded for another ten minutes or so by a freak accident. She looked out of the window, and saw him twizzling a bit of metal with the macho grace of a great matador flourishing his cape. Never in her life before had Miranda formed a relationship with a man who could and would change a car tyre. She was dazzled by the sight.

Besides, she felt the hand of destiny stirring things up. They had failed to seize the day, and the day was giving them a second chance. Dido would have considered this as proof positive that a happening of huge importance had been preordained.

Soon Oliver shouldered through his front door, soaked to the skin and in a peculiar mood. She noticed only the first of these phenomena.

'Do you realise,' he began from the kitchen, where he picked up a towel to scrub his head dry, 'do you realise what that was about?'

'My flat tyre?' How could a flat tyre be about anything? She was mystified.

'My bloody mother,' he said, appearing in the doorway of the living room. 'That's what this is about.'

'*Your* bloody mother?' said Miranda. 'I thought we had enough problems with my bloody mother.'

'Well exactly. They're an absolute pair. Let me see if I can explain,' he went on. It seemed acceptable to sit beside her on the sofa. 'OK, the hotel stunt was my idea. But do you realise that my mother actually told your mother what was going on yesterday, and then the two of them, having decided that you and I were going to be some kind of dream couple, then decided to keep the whole thing going?'

'You're not serious. *My* mother did that?'

'Well, I'm sure my mother talked her into it, but yes, she did. They had this whole conspiracy thing going. But then my sister told me what was up, and you obviously found out anyway, and we thought that was going to be the end of it. But then my mother, once the game was over, went out and put this nail,' he produced the guilty hardware from the pocket of his wet shirt, 'under the tyre of your car, so that all this would happen and you wouldn't be able to escape until . . . well, until all this.'

'Your mother did that?'

'Yes. My mother does stuff like that all the time. Complete power-freak.'

'Snap,' said Miranda, with feeling. Feeling of many kinds.

There took place a free and frank exchange of mother stories which, since both the mothers in question had committed many crimes of both maternal and non-maternal natures in their children's lives, lasted a long time and caused them to laugh a great deal. This in turn engendered a feeling neither of them had ever had before. It was warm, and soft, and so connected they felt almost blended, as if they had swapped pieces of their souls.

The room was suddenly quiet. The noise of the logs smouldering was enormous. They felt something pulling them towards each other, something they couldn't find any reason to resist. His face was cold from the rain. Her face was warm from the fire. The kiss seemed to last about two hundred years.

When they separated, Oliver spent about half a lifetime looking at Miranda's eyelashes, which he found were uniquely long, and glossy, and magnificent. Through the arm that was most around her, he could feel her heart beating. It made him feel reckless. 'Look,' he said, picking what seemed to be the simplest part of the issue. 'Do you really have to go back to London today?'

'No,' said Miranda. 'Not tonight, anyway.' And maybe not ever, said the look in her eyes. Except for shopping, now and then.

'Could we . . . I mean, would you . . . maybe we could see each other? I mean, just because our mothers thought it was a great idea, that doesn't mean they were totally off-beam, does it? We shouldn't let them run our lives, should we? I don't know how . . .'

'We can work something out,' said Miranda, for once grateful that she had the gift of sounding certain about things when she really had no idea what was happening. 'You're right, we can't let this go, can we?'

Then it seemed the most natural thing in the world to lean into the warm mass of his chest and get started on another kiss.

Outside the cottage it was still raining. On the crest of the hill, on the edge of the copse, a doe hare was sitting motionless under a gorse bush, her coat the colour of the damp earth. Sensing these words, and the actions which followed them, she flicked her ears and decided that at last it was safe to go home. Some mortals were a whole lot easier to enchant than others, especially in these choice-rich times, but, being a goddess and sure of her divine powers, she had never really been worried there.

'Have you heard anything?' Bel paced in front of her sitting-room window, every five seconds pausing to peer out into the blinding rain and look for a car, while calling Clare on her mobile.

'Nothing,' said Clare. 'She was supposed to be here hours ago.'

'She hasn't rung?'

'No. What's going on?'

'She drove off but she can't have got far. Her car broke down. She had a puncture. She hasn't rung?'

'No. I haven't heard anything. How do you know she had a puncture?'

'I know. Trust me. Well, in the normal way, she would call you, wouldn't she? So, she's with him. She must be. I don't count my chickens – what am I saying, I haven't got any chickens, poor things. But to me, it looks good. I'll say goodbye. Keep me posted.'

She rang off and looked around for something to do to take her mind off the situation. Anything. It was raining, she couldn't do any gardening. It was a bank holiday, she couldn't do any shopping. There was nothing on the TV except sport. *The Archers* wouldn't be on the radio until the evening. What she really wanted to do was plan the wedding. But of course, the girl would have her own ideas. Especially being the way she was, so determined. And with a lot of style about her. But it couldn't hurt to dream a little. Otherwise she was going to die of anxiety.

Toni's moped droned to a crescendo outside, then was silent. The kitchen door crashed open. The noise of boots was heard on the kitchen floor.

'Don't go one step further in those wet things,' ordered Bel as she rushed to the kitchen.

'All right, all right,' her stepdaughter shouted. 'Give me a break here, will you.'

Toni was standing in the middle of the room, pulling off

her rain cape and her sodden leather jacket. Her jeans, where the cape had not covered them, were almost black with water. Her helmet was already on the table, raindrops still running off it.

'What on earth did you want to go out in weather like this for?' Bel demanded, bustling to the utility room for a dry towel.

'Money,' Toni answered.

'What money?' said Bel, handing over the towel in exchange for the dripping cape.

'My money,' said Toni. 'Which you are going to give to that bailiff geezer tomorrow. Because, let's face it, nobody paid a hotel bill here this morning, did they?'

'Well, of course they didn't. That's all over now. What money, Toni? What have you been doing?'

'This money.' From one of the pockets of her jeans, Toni extracted a damp roll of notes. She took her stepmother's hand and folded the fingers firmly around the notes. 'And I seem to have plenty more. So you can tell the court to sod off now, can't you?'

'Toni . . .'

'Of course, technically, today is my birthday. I am eighteen today. I forgive you for forgetting, with all that's been going on. So I am now officially a trustafarian. I am an heiress. Actually, I am totally, definitely, no-problems, no-questions, no-argument – rich. The solicitors wrote me months ago. They paid out last week, because of the bank holiday. Sweet, eh?'

'Toni . . .' Bel's face scrambled. Her eyes ached. Her breath wouldn't behave. She was going to cry. But this was all a disaster. She'd forgotten the birthday. The big birthday. And Toni was going to get into trouble.

'Don't cry, Mum.' With more emotion than practice, Toni gave her a hug. Bel burst into tears. 'Don't worry. I'm not going to do anything. I'm happy here now. I like it. It's cool. I'm going to stay here and finish at college and then go to art school or something. I might have to get married, of course.'

This was too much. Bel let out a howl that brought Garrick into the room at a wobbling canter.

'I don't mean like, *have to get married*. You're so old-fashioned, people haven't done that for a hundred years. Honestly, it's like living in a bloody Jane Austen novel round here.'

'Well, what do you mean?' demanded Bel, wondering what would be so wrong with living in a Jane Austen novel.

'I mean, I might get married.'

'To that boy. Volvo, whatever his name is. You're much too young.'

'Tolvo. I don't mean big-deal married. Just for a first marriage, sort of thing. If he gets into any hassle with the Immigration. By the way, do you mind if he stays here? Just until he gets a job and can get his own place?'

By all the laws of nature, such as nature was understood in London at the dawn of the twenty-first century, it was inevitable that one day Clare Marlow would be lunched by a television producer. Since that magic Monday when film of her falling off a horse on the hunting field had swept the evening news bulletins and started a political firestorm, she had never been out of the headlines.

She had managed the row over her resignation superbly,

grabbing every opportunity to denounce the government's policy on so-called responsible land use as nothing but a shamefully corrupt exercise in letting the rich get richer while the poor got shafted.

There really had been something of the Joan of Arc about her, sitting in one TV studio after another with her broken shoulder in a cast, eviscerating the opposition, debunking the jargon, waxing passionate about the degradation of rural culture and the disenfranchisement of the rural population. People were talking openly about the post-democratic age now, all thanks to Clare Marlow.

She seemed to have the political Midas touch, the ability to make events over which she had no logical control start working out in her favour. As if God, or something, was on her side, another big scandal blew up around genetically modified potatoes, which, when fried in oil from genetically modified maize, turned out to give lab rats a whole new kind of cancer. Never in the history of parliamentary debate had anyone ever said 'I told you so' with as much style as Clare Marlow.

So now, she was something of a national heroine, posing for fashion spreads celebrating her famously windswept elegance, inviting the readers of celebrity magazines into the country kitchen of her lovely home and, of course, working on her first novel. The next step in her public life really was inevitable.

'I don't know if you've ever watched *I'm A Celebrity*,' the producer began. Softly, softly.

'As in – *Get Me Out Of Here*? But of course. It was ground-breaking reality TV, in its day, of course.'

'Absolutely. That's why we're going to bring it back. After we fix a few of the problems with the old format, of course.'

'Problems?'

'The main thing was recognition. They couldn't get real celebrities. It was down to the Z-list by the second series. We think the key is to stick to the A-list. Which means managing the programme rather differently.'

'How do you mean?'

'Take the mud, for example. It had a tendency just to look dirty. We want a different sort of mud that looks really – *muddy*.'

'People had to eat maggots and things, didn't they?'

'Oh, you mean the bush tucker challenge? That was actually very popular. With the viewers. We're keeping that. They'll be more like grubs than actual maggots, really. Nothing that in the bush lifestyle of the Native Australian would not be considered a normal part of the diet. So what we're going to do is give every group of celebrities a native guide to teach them what are the wholesome bugs to eat and how to prepare them. But I think the bush tucker thing will only be something that's voted in for the unpopular contestants. The viewers have to dislike someone enough to make them do that. It wouldn't be a problem for you. Not at all.'

Clare twirled her glass of water. He was lying, of course, but that was natural. As for mud – well, she could do mud. 1) money, 2) politics, 3) television. It was all working out according to plan.

367

MISTER FABULOUS AND FRIENDS

Celia Brayfield

Andy Forrest — a man with broad shoulders and a safe pair of hands, a man whose hormones are raising hell in the Last Chance Saloon. Life, love and masculinity are about to catch up with Andy and his old friends Sam, Rhys, Mickey and George: a lawyer, a doctor, an award-winning commercials director and a professional failurist.

Five part-time pop idols who get together now and then to play a bit of rock and roll and keep themselves from going crazy. Five men each with their fair share of baggage — wives, children, lovers and a goddess. Five men who've reached a dangerous age. It's time to move on, but where to? Start a new life? Fix the old one? Divorce? Sex? Prison? Or just go out in a blaze of glory? Decisions, decisions . . .

Funny, moving, wry — *Mister Fabulous and Friends* is the second Westwick novel from Celia Brayfield, a companion to *Getting Home*.

'Cunningly plotted, extremely well written
and compulsively readable'
Beryl Bainbridge

'I couldn't be wrested away from it though they tried'
Fay Weldon

HEARTSWAP

Celia Brayfield

Flora drinks herbal tea, meditates and believes in the abundance of the universe. Georgie drinks black coffee, drives a car called Flat Eric and believes in hard work. But they agree about a lot of things. They're getting married, they know all men are victims of their own biology, but they're not choosing Hillary Clinton for a role model. Which means they've got the whole biology thing sorted. So when their old boss bets them they can't seduce each other's fiancés, they're up for it.

Will it all go horribly wrong? Are men really all the same? Biology is destiny – true or false? To get the answers, read Celia Brayfield's delightful comedy, set in millennial London and inspired by Mozart's opera *Così fan tutte*.

'Delicious . . . the perfect antidote to most of
its genre. A laugh-out-loud book'
Ireland Evening Herald

'Most authors would give their eye-teeth to write this well'
The Times

SUNSET

Celia Brayfield

Tropical sun, cheap booze and more natural beauty than you could shake David Attenborough at, Kim came to Los Alcazares for the same reasons as all the other people who are stuck out here. She had to get away.

Los Alcazares is a holiday paradise. It's also a place of fantastic dreams and incredible secrets, an island in the ocean where ley lines cross and tectonic plates crash, a geological hot spot where you can't trust anything – not even the earth itself.

Kim trusts Matthew, her lover. She trusts Stella, her friend. But she may have been wrong. A man has been killed on Los Alcazares and both of them were there when he died. That's what they're saying anyway; but the island is full of talk. At the beach bar where there is no beach, Kim waits for Matthew to find out finally what she can believe.

'Celia Brayfield's style is as exhuberant as it is poetic'
Express

'Brayfield is a fine prose stylist; her characterisation is good, as is the sense of place'
Sunday Times

GETTING HOME

Celia Brayfield

Westwick, the ultimate suburb. Nothing ever happens in Westwick; that's why people live there. Nice people, like Stephanie Sands. Loving husband, adorable son, dream job and a beautiful garden – life is just about perfect for Stephanie until the day her husband is kidnapped.

Big mistake, losing your husband in the suburbs. The neighbours turn nasty. The TV totty sees Stephanie as a media victim and the totty's husband sees Stephanie as 'lonely' – codeword for desperate. Stephanie discovers that she isn't the kind of woman to take this lying down. Suddenly it's a jungle out there – adultery, blackmail, sleaze in high places and lust on the lawns, until Westwick scrambles the helicopters and takes to the streets with an army of eco-warriors in the hilarious live-TV climax.

Getting Home has outraged upholders of Volvo culture everywhere. It's the funniest and wickedest novel yet from one of our most gifted modern storytellers.

'Deliciously comic – lightning flashes of wit and scalpel-sharp observation.'
Daily Mail

'With a sharp wit and snappy dialogue Brayfield has produced a very funny, cleverly plotted novel that displays Fay Weldon's understanding of the pleasure to be derived from seeing the bad get their just desserts'
Daily Telegraph

HARVEST

Celia Brayfield

The lover, Grace, clever and passionate, ran away to find new happiness, but can't escape her guilt. The wife, Jane, loves her children, her brilliant career and her French farmhouse, but wakes up crying and alone. The daughter, Imogen, beautiful and talented, but also a wild child hungry for revenge.

Three women who all made the same mistake loving Michael Knight; a TV star, a public figure but also, in private, a serial adulterer driven to destroy the women whose love he craves.

Now, as friends and family gather to celebrate his birthday, Michael reaps what he has sown.

'A great black comedy'
Daily Express

'The fierceness with which she manipulates her characters and plot and traces the psychology of revenge and female dependence grabs the attention'
Sunday Times

'A cool thriller, cleverly overlaid with issues of power and deception as it heads to its shattering conclusion'
Woman's Journal

PEARLS

Celia Brayfield

London, the eighties: greed is good and Cathy Bourton breaks into the boy's clubs of the City, armed with such beauty men never see anything else – until it's too late . . .

London, the sixties: love is all you need – but it's only rock 'n' roll to Monty, whose voice is her fortune, whose passion is her fate . . .

Paris, city of lovers, where Princess Ayesha rules the night-club underworld, hiding her chilling secret, waiting for her moment of revenge . . .

Three women, and James Bourton, the man who loved all of them, the hero with everything to hide – and Malaysia in World War II, where the greatest betrayal of all forged their future . . .

'Readers will devour it'
Anthony Burgess, *Independent*

Other bestselling Time Warner Paperback titles available by mail:

☐	Mister Fabulous and Friends	Celia Brayfield	£6.99
☐	Heartswap	Celia Brayfield	£5.99
☐	Sunset	Celia Brayfield	£5.99
☐	Getting Home	Celia Brayfield	£5.99
☐	Harvest	Celia Brayfield	£5.99
☐	Pearls	Celia Brayfield	£5.99

The prices shown above are correct at time of going to press. However, the publishers reserve the right to increase prices on covers from those previously advertised, without further notice.

——————————————— **timewarner** ———————————————
paperbacks

TIME WARNER PAPERBACKS
PO Box 121, Kettering, Northants NN14 4ZQ
Tel: 01832 737525, Fax: 01832 733076
Email: aspenhouse@FSBDial.co.uk

POST AND PACKING:
Payments can be made as follows: cheque, postal order (payable to Time Warner Books) or by credit cards. Do not send cash or currency.
All UK Orders   **FREE OF CHARGE**
EC & Overseas   25% of order value

Name (BLOCK LETTERS) . . . .

Address . . . .

. . . .

Post/zip code: . . . .

☐ Please keep me in touch with future Time Warner publications

☐ I enclose my remittance £ . . . .

☐ I wish to pay by Visa/Access/Mastercard/Eurocard

Card Expiry Date ☐☐☐☐